Contents

WHEN ALL ELSE FAILS,
PLAY THE WITCH CARD

"You could file a complaint of witchcraft against him," the man in the gray hood suggested. "It's much more likely to attract public attention than simple collaboration with the enemy."

"Against the *abbot*?" Hoheneck said.

"Isn't the abbot the only person we were talking about?" someone behind Hoheneck muttered under his breath.

"But the abbot . . . who's going to investigate the charge?" Hoheneck asked. "And how, since the up-timers have abolished witchcraft as a crime?"

"Why, the bishop of Würzburg, I presume," the man in the gray hood said smoothly. "Fulda does fall within his ecclesiastical jurisdiction, after all. Or so he contends, at least." He looked directly at Hatzfeld, who was, after all, the bishop of Würzburg. "The Holy Father has never ruled definitively in the matter."

"Sufficient unto the day . . ." the voice behind Hoheneck muttered, just loudly enough to be heard.

"And it remains a crime under imperial law," Hatzfeld continued, "so when the ursurping Swede is expelled . . ."

"I have been quite consistent in my refusal to deal with the up-timers," the bishop of Würzburg said.

"So you will handle it—the investigation into the witchcraft allegations—from here?" The question came from the clerk who was taking the minutes.

"If we aren't all running away from the Swede by the time the investigation is ripe," the same unidentifiable under-the-breath muttering came again.

1635
The Tangled Web

VIRGINIA DeMARCE

1635: THE TANGLED WEB

Copyright © 2009 by Virginia DeMarce

"Prince and Abbot" was previously published in slightly different form in *The Grantville Gazette*, June 2006, copyright © 2006 by Virginia DeMarce; "Mail Stop" was previously published in slightly different form in *The Grantville Gazette*, January 2007, copyright © 2007 by Virginia DeMarce.

A Baen Books Original

Baen Publishing Enterprises
P.O. Box 1403
Riverdale, NY 10471
www.baen.com

ISBN: 978-1-4391-3454-2

Cover art by Tom Kidd

First Baen paperback printing, July 2011

Library of Congress Control Number: 2009037540

Distributed by Simon & Schuster
1230 Avenue of the Americas
New York, NY 10020

Pages by Joy Freeman (www.pagesbyjoy.com)
Printed in the United States of America

Preface by Eric Flint

1635: The Tangled Web is set in the 1632 universe, also known as the Ring of Fire universe. I created that alternate history universe with the novel *1632*, published in 2000. Many novels, anthologies and magazine stories, and articles have followed since. Most of those novels have been collaborations between myself and several different authors. With the exception of David Weber, those authors emerged within the 1632 universe itself, as writers who were first published in the *Ring of Fire* anthology and the electronic magazine devoted to the 1632 series, the *Grantville Gazette*.

Virginia DeMarce has been one of those authors. She was first published in the *Ring of Fire* anthology with the story "Biting Time." She took the character of Veronica, the grandmother of Gretchen Richter and a minor figure in the novel *1632*, and developed her considerably. That development would continue in Virginia's first collaborative novel with me, *1634: The Bavarian Crisis*, in which Veronica is a major character.

Before co-authoring that novel, Virginia produced

many other stories which were published in the *Grantville Gazette,* and she continues to do so. She also co-authored the recent novel *1635: The Dreeson Incident* with me, and was (along with me) the major author in the anthology *1634: The Ram Rebellion.* That anthology consists of related stories by a number of different authors which follow a common story arch, and culminates in the short novel *The Ram Rebellion,* which Virginia and I wrote together.

In short, she is a central author in the unfolding and by now very extensive 1632 series—which it would probably be more accurate to call a literary complex rather than a series. As regular readers of the series are well aware, once you get past *1632, 1633* and the first *Ring of Fire* anthology, the various novels and anthologies in the series do not follow the linear Book 1-2-3 sequence which is typical of most series. Some of the novels and all of the anthologies overlap each other, often with stories that take place simultaneously but in different areas and involving different characters.

(See the afterword for my recommendations concerning the reading order of the series, along with a sketch of the various upcoming volumes.)

With this volume, we're trying a new experiment. I say "a" new experiment because the 1632 series has been experimenting almost since the beginning. The first anthology, *Ring of Fire,* had a number of stories by well-established authors like David Weber and Mercedes Lackey. This is the typical pattern for shared universe anthologies. But I also set aside half the book for stories by new authors, which I organized by using the 1632 conference in Baen Books' online discussion area, Baen's Bar. (If you've never been there, go to www.baen.com and select "Baen's Bar" from the far right side of the top menu.)

Several of the authors who have since become prominent in the 1632 series got started in that anthology. In particular, in addition to Virginia herself, Andrew Dennis got started there with his story "Between the Armies." Since then, Andrew has collaborated with me on the novels *1634: The Galileo Affair* and *1635: The Cannon Law* and will be doing the same with several more volumes to come.

Following the success of that experiment, we launched the online magazine *Grantville Gazette*, with stories and articles by many different authors. (Over sixty authors, the last time I counted.) That magazine has now come out with twenty-six issues in electronic form, along with five editions in paper format. And there are more coming.

But there's been one thing that all of these volumes have had in common, leaving aside the purely electronic editions. They've all had at least one story by me in them. With this volume, we're expanding that format and, for the first time since the inception of the 1632 series, producing a volume which consists of stories written entirely by another author.

The author, in this case, is Virginia DeMarce—and this volume consists of four inter-related stories (one of them a short novel) which intersect with, and in some places overlap, the stories contained in the novel *1635: The Dreeson Incident* and in the forthcoming anthology *1635: The Wars on the Rhine*. I say "in this case," because if this experiment is successful—which means "sells enough copies," to put it crudely—then we will be able to repeat it with later volumes. Virginia is by no means the only author working in the 1632 series who could produce volumes of their own which would be well worth publishing.

But that's for the future. For the moment, enjoy this volume by Virginia DeMarce—and rest assured that the courier Martin Wackernagel and the deeds of the three young dukes of Württemberg will continue to appear and resonate throughout the series. For the title of this book could just as easily be applied to the 1632 series as a whole.

A tangled web, indeed.

Prince and Abbot

This Troublesome Monk

Fulda, December 1632

"Maybe they should have held the battle of Lützen last month after all," Wes Jenkins said. "Just have kept Gustavus Adolphus out of it. Up-time, it seems to have cleared a whole batch of people off the playing board that we could just as well have done without."

"Pappenheim?" Harlan Stull asked. He was sitting far back in his chair, so his burly chest didn't bump into the table. Before the Ring of Fire, he had been a miner and was the UMWA contact man for the New United States' administrative team in Fulda. He was also a nephew of Dennis Stull, who was running the procurement office that the New United States had set up in Erfurt, where Gustavus Adolphus also had his main supply depot in Thuringia. All the rest of them figured that was something which would turn out to be real handy in the long run.

"Johann Bernhard Schenk von Schweinsberg. The

only thing that I love about him is his name. 'Barkeep from Pig Hill.' What a beautifully aristocratic name, once you translate that 'von' bit, no matter how many centuries the pigs have been sitting on top of their hill." Wes grinned. "Up-time, he was running around the battlefield, blessing the soldiers and calling for them to fight for the Catholic faith, when he ran into a squadron that wasn't friendly. They shot him neatly. Pistol to the head. So he was killed at Lützen, just like Pappenheim. Their bodies were carried into the Pleissenburg together to be embalmed, which would be a great thing for them to be, if you ask me, and good riddance to the two of them."

Wes got up and looked out the window. Grantville hadn't had much information for the administrative staff of the New United States to prepare them for the job they faced in Fulda. Encyclopedia articles and a few tourist brochures from Len Tanner. That was about it. The tourist brochures hadn't been of much use. Up-time, practically the whole town had been redeveloped between 1632 and the twentieth century, it seemed.

The building where they were sitting right now didn't have a picture in any of them. It would have been torn down in the eighteenth century and replaced. The big tan sandstone cathedral with its two tall curvy-topped towers wasn't here yet, either. Now, maybe, it never would be built. Instead, there was a church called the basilica. One of the monks had told him that it was eight hundred years old. That was now, 1632, not in the year 2000.

Wes was willing to believe it—that the basilica was eight hundred years old. There was another one too, one that had survived until the twentieth century. That one had a photo in the brochures. St. Michael's it was called. The oldness of St. Michael's church had practically seemed to press down on his shoulders when he went through it. It was a burial church. Eight hundred years of dead monks. Already, in 1632, eight hundred years of dead monks.

"What's the prince-abbot of Fulda done to you?" Andrea Hill looked at her boss with some worry. His thin face was dominated by a long nose. Wes had always been wiry, but since the Ring of Fire, he had gone down to skin and bones. He would just be annoyed if she acted like a substitute mom, though, so she was careful not to fuss at him about it. "He's been gone since before the king told us to take charge of Fulda."

"Where's he been?" Fred Pence, Andrea's son-in-law, had just arrived the week before, with the second group sent from Grantville.

"He ran off to the Habsburgs when Gustavus Adolphus and the Hessians came through and took 'Priests' Alley' here and along the Rhine River in the fall of 1631. Fulda gave up without a single shot. We haven't seen hide nor hair of him."

Wes came back from the window. "At least, with the abbot and chapter monks gone, most of the people seem to prefer us to the Hessians as an occupation force. Even the monks who are still around, at least since we promised to try to get their library back from our noble ally the landgrave of Hesse, who swiped it."

"Don't get their hopes up. When these brigands swipe stuff, it stays swiped. Our side just as much as their side." Roy Copenhaver, the economic liaison, was already thoroughly disillusioned by how little, between them, Bernhard of Saxe-Weimar for Gustavus Adolphus and the Hessian commander Albrecht Thilo von Uslar had left in Fulda in the way of resources for the Grantvillers to work with. Although, he had to admit, the monks who escaped to Cologne had supposedly taken most of the abbey's treasury with them, so he couldn't blame their own new captain general or his Hessian allies for that.

Andrea stuck her pencil through her graying hair. "Not to mention that they stole their archives themselves. That is, the monks who ran off to Cologne took the records with them and aren't about to send them back. Anita in Würzburg and Janie in Bamberg at least have something to work with when they get these disputes about who has a right to what laid in front of them. I'm having to start from scratch."

Wes sat down again, looking at the letter in front of him. "We have a Christmas present. The abbot's coming back, Ed Piazza says. In all his full glory, waving the banner of the Counter-Reformation and claiming that he has the right to do his thing under 'freedom of religion' and the constitution of the New United States."

"From Cologne?" Andrea asked hopefully. "With archives?"

"No, from Prague. He attached himself to Tilly and ran in a different direction, taking what little he had in the way of an army with him. He's been hanging around with Wallenstein since then. He must be fairly tough, though—he's been living like a common soldier. Duke John George of Saxony gave him a safe-conduct through Saxony to come back and an escort to the border of the New United States. They handed him over down by Halle." Wes sighed. "Good old Duke John George. With friends like that, we *really* don't need enemies."

"Is he bringing imperial troops disguised as his personal staff?" Harlan asked.

"God, I hope not. The landgrave of Hesse would be only too happy to send a batch of his troops back into Fulda in the guise of 'protecting' the king of Sweden's new allies, given how few of our own people Frank Jackson has been able to spare for us here." Derek Utt, the military administrator, spent as much of his time keeping a wary eye out for raiding "friendly" troops as he did for raiding "enemy" troops.

"How many military, exactly, do we have now?" Wes asked him.

"Besides me? A half-dozen up-timers. Seven, if you count Gus Szymanski, who's the emergency medical technician and nearly sixty years old. Aside from Gus, the most senior person is Mark Early, who's nearly thirty. He's doing most of my administrative stuff. Procurement, quarters, payroll. The next is Johnny Furbee, who is twenty-seven. I'm basically using him to help me train some military police from local town and village militias. The other four are kids. Good kids, and at least they all have high school diplomas, which Johnny doesn't, but they're still kids trying to teach what little they know about modern military procedures to a couple hundred of those ex-mercenary combat veterans that Gretchen picked out from the prisoners. The training that Johnny is giving the militias is *ad hoc* since he was never an MP himself and neither was I, but it's something, and at least they have a vested interest in keeping the ex-mercenaries from

raping their wives and daughters. The kids and the
new MPs do good to keep *our* people from relaps-
ing into looting the locals, to tell the truth. That's it.
I don't know whether to hope Frank sends us more
down-timers or be glad that we don't have too many
to control."

Wes looked at him, thinking that Derek himself
had just turned thirty. But he was not only older in
years than the younger men he called "kids." He was
a lot older in experience. Derek was a Gulf War vet.
He'd been a member of the active reserves; married,
with a kid, just a baby. They were left up-time. Wes
understood. His wife Lena had been left up-time too,
although his two daughters were in Grantville, Chandra
with two kids and Lenore finally going to get married
next month, which he would have to miss. Not that
he would have chosen Bryant Holloway for her if he
had been doing the picking.

Derek had lived in Fairmont. He had just come
over to Grantville the afternoon of the Ring of Fire
to go to the sport shop with his sister Lisa's husband.
He had volunteered for the army the afternoon that
Mike Stearns called for people. Once Mike and Frank
Jackson had gotten past their first stage of relying so
heavily on the United Mine Workers, he had moved
up fast in the army of the New United States.

Wes nodded his head. "If he tries to bring in
troops disguised as staff, stop them at the border,
but I really don't think that Ed and Frank would
let him get that far with them. He's free to come
back as an abbot. He can walk right in carrying
his staff. Hell, he can even ride in, if he wants to.
We'll even provide him with an escort from the

Thuringian border to the gates of the abbey. But he's not a prince of the Holy Roman Empire any more and he might as well learn it right there as anywhere else. What route is he taking?"

The meeting got down to the nitty gritty.

Grantville, December 1632

"Because you are offering a salary."

Ed Piazza looked at the down-time woman who was sitting in a straight chair across from his desk. He knew that the chair was hard and remarkably uncomfortable. In his first job, a wise old teacher showed him that by sawing a quarter of an inch off the front legs of a chair and sanding them, front and back, so they sat flush on the floor, it wasn't enough to notice but anyone using it was constantly sliding toward the front, in the direction of the floor, requiring him to brace his legs. It was remarkably useful for keeping parent-teacher conferences within their assigned time limits and Ed had taken his pair of wooden chairs with him from job to job, defying the advance of metal folding chairs. Even now, the people he motioned toward them rarely stayed in his office any longer than was absolutely necessary.

"How did you hear about the job?"

"Miss Susan Beattie told Mrs. Kortney Pence who told Mrs." She paused. "Schandra? Sandra? Tsandra? Prickett."

"Chandra," Ed said.

"Mrs. Prickett. Who told me, all at a meeting of the League of Women Voters. Miss Beattie thought of me because her father knows Mr. Birdie Newhouse who knows my brother Dietrich."

Ed sorted it out in his mind. From Orville Beattie's daughter to Andrea Hill's daughter who was married to Fred Pence to Wes Jenkins's daughter. All adult children of members of the NUS administration in Fulda. Grantville had been a pretty small town, after all, before the Ring of Fire.

"'Because you are offering a salary.' That is the most forthright reply I have had from anyone applying for this job. When I asked why he wanted it, I mean. Or she. Would you care to explain, Mrs. Stade?"

"My husband went bankrupt. Nobody can blame the Ring of Fire for that. He went bankrupt before it. He died in April 1631. Because of the bankruptcy, he didn't leave me any money to live on. He didn't leave a business for me to fight with the guilds about over whether or not a woman can run it. All of this was in Arnstadt, though he was born in Stadtilm. His father was born in Badenburg, which is how I came to meet him and marry him. I am from Badenburg. I married and went away from my family. Now I am a widow, childless, and do not want to go back and live on the charity of my brothers and sisters. I have used up my dowry. I want work, my own income."

She nodded emphatically. "I also consider myself qualified. My husband was a councilman before he failed in his business; my father is a councilman. I presume that one of my brothers will succeed him on the council. I know politics—more widely than most, since I have ties in three cities, and through my brother Dietrich and the problems with Herr Newhouse's land, have come to know a fourth, your own. I can also help the administration figure out where the disputes are between the Fulda city council and the abbey, I think. There are bound to be a lot of old grudges."

She paused and smiled, reaching through the slit in the side of her skirt for her pocket. "And I carry the constitution of the New United States with me, everywhere I go. I have learned it by heart. As well as anyone, I can tell your administrators in Fulda what the abbot can and cannot do, under the down-time law. I will be very happy to tell the abbot of Fulda what he can and cannot do under this constitution."

Ed got up, walked to the side of the room, and moved an upholstered office chair from its place near the wall. "Have a more comfortable seat," he suggested.

Johann Bernhard Schenk von Schweinsberg was not happy. He was nearly fifty years old and had never before heard of such a thing. He glared at Ed Piazza.

"It's 'take it or leave it,'" Ed said. "The condition of our permitting you to go back to Fulda is that you take along our appointee to serve as a liaison between you and the NUS administration there."

"It is wholly inappropriate," the abbot of Fulda said. "Utterly inappropriate."

"My name is Clara Bachmeierin," the woman said. "Widowed Stade. I am from Badenburg. I am Lutheran. We have dealt with the up-timers since they first arrived. You have not. You have been away, among the imperials. We have learned to understand their politics. You have not. Stop making a sour face at me. I have reached an age at which no one will consider my presence scandalous or shocking. I am thirty-six, no girl. I will share the quarters of Mrs. Hill. She has an apartment upstairs.

Her son-in-law, Mr. Pence, has an apartment downstairs in the same building, which he shares with two other men. He thinks it is safer for Mrs. Hill to be upstairs."

"You are a Protestant."

"That's what I just said," she answered.

"A Protestant and a female. Not a suitable advisor for a Catholic ruler. Not a suitable advisor for an abbot."

"Listen, Schweinsberg," Ed Piazza interrupted them, "at least half of your former subjects were Protestant, when you became abbot in 1623 and began a stronger enforcement of the Counter-Reformation. That is, half of them were still Protestant *after* the last three or four abbots had been using their authority over the past half-century to try to coerce them into becoming Catholic again, using differential tax rates, forbidding Protestants to hold public office, giving them the option of conversion or exile."

"It is our duty to bring people back into the fold of the church," Schweinsberg said. "It was our guilt that the Protestant revolt occurred in the first place, damning so many souls to hell. Since you are supposedly Catholic yourself, Herr Piazza, you should be doing the same."

Ed leaned forward. "You're going to be learning a lot of new lessons. The first one is about separation of church and state. If you want the people of Fulda to be Catholic, you will have to entice them. Persuade them of the rightness of your doctrines. Feed them barbecue at revival meetings, I don't care. But you may not force them to convert. You may not compel them to hear your missionaries. All carrots, no sticks."

Schweinsberg scowled.

"Remember. They are not your subjects." Ed paused

between each of those words for emphasis. "You no longer exercise legal jurisdiction over them. You are the church; the NUS is the state. I am quite sure that Mrs. Stade will be happy to explain it to you. The two of you will have plenty of time for conversation between here and the border, so she can tell you how the system works."

Clara Bachmeierin, otherwise known as Mrs. Stade, smiled blandly.

Ed Piazza continued. "There are ways that you can take advantage of our system, no doubt, but only if you work within it. If you try to go around it or subvert it, somebody in authority is going to think about the appropriate penalties for collaborating with the enemy. When you leave here, you're going to be carrying a written notification to that effect, signed by President Stearns."

Game Board

Fulda, January 1633

"Why can't they all at least be happy Catholics together?" Harlan Stull asked plaintively. He was looking at a complaint from the Franciscan Order that some sixty years before, a former abbot of Fulda had given one of their buildings, which they had abandoned and were no longer using, to the Jesuits, who still had it and were using it for a school. The Franciscans wanted it back now. The Jesuits thought that possession was nine points of the law.

"*Why*," Wes Jenkins said, "is not up to us Methodist good old boys to figure out. 'Ours not to reason why.' Though I sort of wish that they had sent us a couple of Catholics from Grantville to help us understand it, instead of shipping them all down into Würzburg and Bamberg. But I don't think that this is a religious problem. They're all Catholics. I hereby declare officially that it's a land title problem. Put it into Andrea's in-box and let's move on to something else."

"But," Harlan was practically wailing. "Why does it make any difference to them that the abbot and these guys who are supposed to be monks here, the chapter, are Benedictines but they squabble with these other monks who are Franciscans and who say they aren't monks but friars and both of them are jealous of the Jesuits? Aren't they all in the same bathtub together?"

"They weren't up-time," Wes pointed out. "Ed Piazza and Tino Nobili were practically in a boxing match half the time about stuff that went on at St. Vincent's, with Father Mazzare refereeing. Or trying to."

Andrea tried to think of something that would be helpful. "Think of the Middle Ages. Before the Reformation. They were all Catholics then—well, except for the Jews and Saracens—and they fought each other all the time. Remember what Melissa Mailey said about the Norman Conquest?"

"I think it's this way," Fred Pence said. "The Yankees and the Dodgers and all those other teams all played baseball, but that didn't mean that they weren't in competition with one another. For one thing, baseball was the way they made their living, so they were competing for the same pot of dough and the same fans. Like these guys. They're all playing the same game, but that doesn't mean that they're all on the same team. Sometimes they hate each other more than they do the people who play football or basketball. That's how I'm laying it out, for voter registration. The Catholics are football; the Lutherans are baseball; the Calvinists up on the border by Hesse are basketball, and the occasional oddballs are soccer and ice hockey."

Harlan stared at him.

"Well, it works," Fred protested. "Hey, guys, I'm a Nondenominational Evangelical. Or I was, when there was a church for me to go to. We don't have one in Grantville, even. I've been having to make do with the Baptists. This is even weirder for me than it is for you Methodists. But I think that I'm starting to understand it."

"How?" Wes asked hopefully.

"I got the pewterer downtown to make some molds and pour me baseball and other players, like little Monopoly markers. Then I've got a big map of Fulda and all its little outliers that are mixed up with Isenburg and Hanau and imperial knights like the von Hutten family and whatever. Not a decent topo map. The places are just little six-sided pieces of paper, like a game board. And I got some paint for the players. So a Lutheran is a baseball player and if he's an independent imperial knight, he's got a blue bat instead of a green one. A Jesuit is a yellow football player; a Franciscan is a red one, and if she's a nun, she's pink. The Benedictines here at the abbey are orange. Stuff like that. And I've got them set down on the spots where they belong. It's all on a table in my office. You should come by and look at it some time. By the time we get around to holding elections,

I should know which precinct is what and where the trouble spots will probably be. Andrea's putting her land title markers on it, too."

Andrea cleared her throat. "Speaking of land titles . . ."

"Yes?"

"I've made one great discovery. The monks took the archives, but most of the local district administrators and provosts of the abbey's estates kept duplicate copies on the local level, because it would take all day for someone to run over to Fulda and look something up. So if the budget has money for me to hire some clerks, we can reconstitute a working administrative archive. Not the historical papal bulls that were five hundred years old and stuff like that, but land documents and surveys from the last half century or so."

"The budget," Harlan said, "is very tight."

"Consider it an investment." Andrea reached up and pulled out the pencil she had stuck in her hair earlier in the meeting. "If we don't figure out who owes us how much in the way of taxes and rents and dues, there won't be a budget at all."

"Anything else?" Wes asked.

"We have a petition from a convent of Franciscan nuns here in the town of Fulda itself, phrased in such a way that it appears to be presented on behalf of the women of the town in general, on the subject of women's property rights. It's rather interesting." She picked up a piece of paper and started to read. "A laywoman who was a member of their Third Order . . ." She looked up. "That's sort of like a lodge auxiliary, by the way. Or it would be, if they were Disciples of Christ, like me." She went back to reading, ". . . made during her lifetime a contingent donation to them that was to take effect after her death. She has since died and her stepson, who does not deny that she had a right to make a gift while living, challenges her right to make a post mortem donation on the grounds that it is equivalent to a bequest . . ."

Harlan Stull's eyes started to glaze over. His definition of "interesting" rarely involved probate law.

"Andrea," Wes said. "Hire a lawyer. A local lawyer. Full time. That's an order."

Variant Visions

Grantville, January 1633

"We ought to give him some kind of a send-off," Linda Bartolli said, looking at the rest of Grantville's *quondam* St. Vincent's and current St. Mary's worship committee. "After all, he *is* an abbot and Fulda is really historical. I looked it up in the encyclopedia."

"It should be your call. You're the organist, so most of the extra work would fall on you," Denise Adducci said.

"Well, on Brian, too," Linda said. "And the choir."

"How's it going for Brian now? Is Tino still making trouble?" Noelle Murphy asked.

Linda sighed. When her brother agreed to take on directing the St. Mary's choir after the Ring of Fire, its former director having been left up-time, Tino Nobili had made a great big fuss. Brian's wife Debra was Methodist, which in Tino's view disqualified him for exercising anything that might be considered a public office in the church. What with Tino's wife Vivian being the parish secretary and her and Brian's parents now being full-time parish volunteers, things could get a bit touchy now and then.

"Tino seems to have settled down some. It helped that the only other person who volunteered to be choir director was Danielle Kowach. He likes the Kowaches and Mahons even less than he likes us, and having Danielle would have meant that both the organist and director would have been women."

Johann Bernhard Schenk von Schweinsberg assured himself that he supported the endeavors of the Jesuit Order and favored all its efforts in spreading the faith. The Jesuits were so—what was the English word?— dynamic. Not to mention incredibly numerous. They and the Capuchins—those two orders multiplied like rabbits, these days.

Nonetheless, he still found it somewhat disconcerting that the Jesuits seemed to have thrown themselves so very enthusiastically into the Grantville parish. Plus, of course . . . von Spee came from a respectable family, but . . . Athanasius Kircher was certainly an intelligent man—some people said that he was an outright genius—but by no means was his family upper class. Schweinsberg knew this perfectly well, since Kircher's father had been a minor civil bureaucrat from Geisa who worked for the abbots of Fulda and tried to support a large family on a small salary. Of course, the father had earned a doctorate, but the family's more distant ancestry consisted entirely of commoners. Quite ordinary ones.

"I would point out," Kircher was saying with some humor, "that it is also something of a stretch for men born into families of ordinary imperial knights to sit in the diet as princes of the empire. You and your predecessors have been there by virtue of your election as abbots, not by right of birth. The church provides this 'social mobility' for you, too."

"But the statutes of Fulda provide that none but men of noble birth may be accepted as members of the chapter."

"The statutes of Fulda," Kircher answered gently. "Not the statutes of Saint Benedict, if you would bother to read them, nor even the statutes as established by your founders. Not Saint Boniface; not Saint Sturmius; not Saint Lullus. That provision developed during later history, and can be changed. If you do not want to ossify and have Fulda cease to exist for a lack of recruits, it even *should* be changed. Even now, it is the *conventus* of commoners among your monks that serves the parishes of the *Stift*, not the noble chapter monks. How many parishes are there? Fifty?"

"About that many. Parishes, that is. But no one would dare to challenge the statutes. Why, that might lead to a commoner being elected abbot some day."

"Banz did. That abbey also had these requirements from the middle ages that only nobles could be accepted in the chapter. When so much of Franconia became Protestant, there were no longer enough surplus sons of Catholic nobles to fill the slots. More than half a century ago, they obtained an exemption from the bishop of Würzburg that they could accept commoners, both as members of the chapter and students at the school."

"The bishops of Würzburg—" the abbot began.

"Yes, I am entirely aware of the conflict," Kircher said patiently. "After all, my father was working for Abbot Balthasar von Dernbach when Bishop Echter conspired with the knights and nobles of the *Stift* to expel him because of his efforts to impose Catholic reform. The commitment of Bishop Echter to Catholic reform was unquestionably genuine. However, if by getting rid of a reforming abbot, he might extend the authority of Würzburg over the abbey and its territories . . . with the full intent of reforming them himself, of course . . . Well, bishops are not angels. Echter was a great man, but he is not likely ever to be sainted, I suppose."

"I will never compromise Fulda's independence by asking the bishop of Würzburg to authorize a change in our statutes. Even if I could, as a practical matter, since Hatzfeld has opted to remain under the protection of the archbishop of Cologne rather than to return to his see and come to terms with these allies of the Swede."

"You could always just ask the pope himself," Kircher suggested. "That would not affect the legal independence of Fulda from Würzburg in any way. Presuming, of course, that you are willing to defy your fellow nobles and their desire to drop extra sons into sinecures with guaranteed incomes."

Brian Grady had given a fair amount of consideration to the music for the special service, had beaten the bushes for people who were willing to sing *just this once* and scheduled four extra rehearsals. They were using the good choir robes, too. And he had a right to do something Irish, he thought.

A couple of years before, he had gotten a copy of *How the Irish Saved Civilization* with a medieval-looking dust jacket for Christmas. He suspected that his sister had gotten it out of a discount bin at the grocery warehouse in Fairmont, but, hey, in a family the size of the Gradys, the motto had to be, "Affordable Christmas presents are where you find them." He'd read it. He agreed with every single word, so he had given it to the new national library. Other people ought to read it, too, and understand the importance of being Irish.

Besides, he didn't intend to read it again. It was sort of out of his field. When he wasn't directing the choir, he taught physical education.

"Be thou my vision, O Lord of my heart,
"Naught be all else to me, save that thou art;
"Thou my best thought, by day or by night,
"Waking or sleeping, thy presence my light."

Basically, he was using the version that appeared in most hymnals, set to the "Slane" melody, which he loved.

"Be thou my wisdom and thou my true word,
"I ever with thee and thou with me, Lord;
"Be thou my great Father, and I thy true son;
"Be thou in me dwelling, and I with thee one."

He had thought that the abbot might like it, since he came from a family of knights and knights went around fighting in armor. Tournaments and jousts and stuff like that. He'd heard the story, of course, that the only reason that the guy was here in Grantville now, getting a special service, was that he hadn't been killed in the same battle when the king of Sweden was killed, up-time.

> "Be thou my breastplate, my sword for the fight;
> "Be thou my whole armor, be thou my true might;
> "Be thou my soul's shelter, be thou my strong
>   tower:
> "O raise thou me heavenward, great Power of
>   my power."

So take that, Martin Luther, you blasted German, Brian thought. A good Catholic Irishman wrote a fine Irish Catholic version of "A Mighty Fortress" seven centuries before you were even born.

> "Riches I heed not, nor man's empty praise:
> "Be thou mine inheritance now and always;
> "Thou and thou only the first in my heart;
> "O Sovereign of heaven, my treasure thou art."

So far, so good. The choir was on key. Brian threw a smile to his sister Linda at the organ, who pulled a few stops. Then for the final verse he broke the choir out into the other arrangement he had, not in the hymnal—John Leavitt's, the one set to "Thaxted" from the Jupiter movement of Gustav Holst's "The Planets."

> "Great God of heaven, my victory won,
> "May I reach heaven's joys, O bright heaven's
>   Sun!

"Heart of my own heart, whatever befall,
"Still be my vision, O Ruler of all.
"Great God of heaven, my victory won,
"May I reach heaven's joys, O bright heaven's
*   Sun!*
"Amen!"

"Outrageous, of course," Tino Nobili said to Schweinsberg after mass. "I'm sure that you agree with me. A woman as organist and women in the choir! Irish folk music and modern composers rather than plainsong. Trust me, sir, this is not the direction the entire church had gone, not even in the up-time world. I was a member of the Pope Pius X Society. I have their mailings. I will give you some of them to take with you, to read."

The abbot thanked him gravely. Personally, he had enjoyed the music and no one expected a parish in a small city to follow all of the liturgical prescriptions for the choir of the Sistine Chapel, of course. Or even those for the choir of the Abbey of Fulda.

Fulda, February 1633

"Do you prefer to be called Mrs. Stade or Miss Bachmeier?" Wes Jenkins asked.

Clara thought a moment. "I am a widow, so I am certainly not Mrs. Stade, even though Herr Piazza calls me that. Caspar has been dead for almost two years. How about Ms. Bachmeierin? I understand that Ms. covers every marital status for your people. And I do prefer the feminine form of my family name. I am a woman, after all—not a man. Being called Bachmeier sounds very odd to me."

"That'll do fine," Wes said, leaning an elbow on the mantel.

They were all standing up. The cleaning crew had taken the table and chairs out of the conference room so they could mop and wax the floor.

She was leaning against the window sill. The administration building had windows with sills. The immediately past abbot, a guy named von Schwalbach, had torn down some medieval monstrosity about twenty years ago and built a nice little renaissance-style palace with corridors and paved floors and big windows with clear glass panes.

The afternoon sun came in at an angle, making a bright narrow stripe across her hair and face. And body, above the waist. He found himself thinking that whatever she called herself, she was definitely a woman. A fine-looking woman. He hoped that the late Caspar had appreciated his good luck. Then he realized that he hadn't cared what a woman looked like since Lena was left up-time.

"If you don't mind," Andrea Hill said, "since we will be sharing an apartment, I will call you Clara. And call me Andrea, please."

She looked at Wes watching the German woman and thought, *chaperone time?* Lenore, Wes's older girl, wasn't much younger than her own daughter Kortney. She'd have to ask Kortney, next time she wrote, if Lenore and Chandra had their fingers in whatever pie led up to shipping Ms. Bachmeierin over to Fulda. She knew they had been worried about having their dad walking around like one of the living dead for so long.

Well, she couldn't blame Wes. She'd felt that way herself for quite a while after her husband Harry died back in 1997, but gradually the world had turned itself back right side up. She had felt it worse when her first husband left her in 1965. Harry, at least, had not wanted to go. But if Bob hadn't left, she wouldn't have gone back to school and gotten the A.A. degree that led her to this job, or married Harry, or had her two girls, so . . .

"When's the abbot due?" Harlan Stull asked.

"In about a half an hour. Maybe I should have asked you first, but I thought it was reasonable to agree when he wanted to go to the monastery first, before he came over to meet all of you. He's supposed to be in charge of it, after all," Clara answered.

"Supposed to be?"

"I'm not sure how much support he has. Neither is he, really. That's one thing he wants to find out."

"Brief me," Wes said, thinking he might as well find out sooner than later what caliber of person Ed had picked.

"Well, he was elected abbot in 1623. Three years later, he brought in some reformed Benedictines from someplace in Switzerland to help him reorganize the abbey. The year after that, that was in 1627, after he got their report, he talked the pope into sending the nuncio—that was Pietro Luigi Caraffa back then—as a papal visitor, a kind of inspector to conduct a visitation of the abbey. Caraffa issued a whole batch of reform decrees that pointed out that according to the rule of Saint Benedict, authority belonged to the abbot. They were pretty critical of the way the noble-born monks in the Fulda chapter had encroached on it.

After Caraffa left—he couldn't very well stay here permanently—the provosts, the monks who administered the abbey's property, got up a rebellion against the changes."

She paused for breath.

"I can see," Fred Pence said, "that I'm going to end up with stripes and checks and spots on my orange helmets."

Clara looked at him, then ignored him. "The monks who are in Cologne now mostly belonged to the opposition party. The pope confirmed the changes, but it didn't make much impression on them. The chapter seemed to be absolutely dead set on keeping the privilege of only admitting nobles. I didn't get a very clear view from the abbot as to whether they object to praying in the same room as ordinary people or if they just object to sharing the abbey's income with them. If the latter, the New United States has probably solved one problem for him."

"From what I hear," Orville Beattie said, "the party of his monks that headed off to Cologne probably won't be too enthusiastic about the fact that he's reappeared. The leader of them, a guy named Johann Adolf von Hoheneck, would have been elected as abbot by now if Schweinsberg had gotten himself shot on schedule, so to speak. Hoheneck is feeling a bit deprived, they say. Just gossip, you understand."

Orville had been sent up from Würzburg by Johnnie F.—Johnnie Haun, that was—to run Steve Salatto's brainchild of a "Hearts and Minds" program in Fulda. Up-time, Orville had worked for the state and farmed part time, but he was in the military down-time. "Hearts and Minds" was a military program. Having another up-time military person in Fulda made Derek Utt feel better, even though Orville spent most of his time out of town. Although Orville was Presbyterian, which made the liaison guy from the landgrave of Hesse, Urban von Boyneburg, feel better about things too, he seemed to be finding his feet pretty fast in dealing with Catholics and Lutherans.

"Okay, Hoheneck in Cologne. Probably one of the bad guys." Harlan Stull made a note.

"That's where they took the archives," Andrea said. "Can Schweinsberg get them back?"

"I don't know," Clara answered honestly. "We can ask him to try. But Hoheneck is on very good terms with Ferdinand of Bavaria, who is the archbishop and elector of Cologne. Through him, of course, he can get support from Duke Maximilian of Bavaria and the Leaguists and the Imperials. That probably means that he isn't going to pay much attention to long-distance instructions from Schweinsberg here in Fulda, vow of obedience or no vow of obedience."

"You know," Orville was saying, down at the other end of the room where a different conversation had broken out, "one thing that we really ought to do, when we get a chance, is ask von Boyneburg to come in and give us a briefing about dealing with the imperial knights. Apparently, here in Fulda, they have a legal status that's different from the knights in Hesse. More like the ones in Franconia."

Harlan Stull sighed. "I'll try to fit it into the agenda one of these days."

"Well, if your supporters followed you when you went off with Tilly's army, and Hoheneck's bunch ran off to Cologne with him, carrying the archives, who were the monks we found at Fulda when we got here?" Wes Jenkins thought this was a reasonable question.

"The Saint Gall monks," the abbot answered. "In the abbey. The monks who belong to the *conventus* of commoners don't reside here permanently. They are parish pastors and only come to the abbey for meetings and special events. And, then, some lay brothers, who do things like caring for the gardens, are still here."

"That means what? Who are these Saint Gall monks?" Wes wondered if Schweinsberg missed having the administration building as a palace. He was living over in the abbey dormitory these days.

"In 1626, I asked the Benedictine Abbey at Saint Gall, that's in Switzerland, to lend us some of their monks to reform us here at Fulda. That is, to show us how to conform more closely to the rule of Saint Benedict. They kindly sent us several, to serve as models for chanting the offices and following the church year, things like that. When the rest of us left for fear of the Swedes and Hessians, they stayed."

"Reform you?"

"Introduce the Tridentine reforms. The prescriptions of the Council of Trent. That was about, oh, seventy years ago. It went on for years. The council, I mean. The abbots have been trying to bring Fulda into conformity ever since, without a lot of luck. The noble families are thoroughly entrenched in the chapter. The younger sons they send us are usually fairly hard-working when it comes to doing things like administering the abbey's estates. That's what nobles do, after all. But they rarely have much enthusiasm about performing specifically monastic duties."

"What's the problem?" Wes was genuinely curious.

"We've tried, goodness knows. The Jesuit school. The seminar for future priests. And we've made some progress. Getting rid of the concubines, for example."

"Concubines?"

"Wives, really. Instead of living in little monastic cells, seventy-five years ago the chapter monks mostly lived in their own houses in town with their wives and children. Not that it was legal for them to have wives, of course, which is why they were called concubines by the reformers."

"Didn't Catholics get a bit uptight about married monks?"

"The laity? No more than they did about married priests in general, really. Not as long as they did the rest of their work okay. It's the hierarchy that disapproves of clerical matrimony, mainly, not the people. At the time of Trent, even the dukes of Bavaria tried hard to get the pope and cardinals to accept married priests."

Wes shook his head.

"The part that is properly in Franconia is called the 'Rhön and Werra' canton of the imperial knights." Urban von Boyneburg looked at the up-timers and pointed to the wall map.

Derek Utt had made a blown-up map on a dozen pieces of paper taped together, from a little one in a down-time atlas. Ortelius, it was called. Ed Piazza had ordered a dozen copies of the atlas and distributed them around. It wasn't a very good map and the original had been made fifty years ago, so it was out of date, but it was better than any other map of Fulda that they had.

"That's basically over here. You do know what an imperial knight is? And where the Werra River runs?"

Wes Jenkins nodded.

Boyneburg continued. "Most of the Franconian imperial knights are Protestant—Lutheran, in fact. Their families accepted that confession almost a century ago and they have been able to maintain it in spite of pressure from the bishops. So are the ones here in the Fulda region, in what we called the Buchenland or, in Latin, *Buchonia*. Most of the abbot's own family is Protestant, for that matter."

"What's a *'Buchen'*?" Fred Pence asked.

Boyneburg looked blank. He could point to a *Buchen* if they asked him to, but . . .

"A beech tree," Orville said in English. "This region is heavily wooded with beech trees."

Boyneburg resumed the lecture. "In October 1631, right after the battle of Breitenfeld, the imperial knights of the Fulda region had a meeting right here in the city and decided that they would like to join with the Franconian knights as the 'Buchen Quarter.' Since then, they have negotiated with the king of Sweden. He has been willing to recognize them as immediate, with no territorial lord standing between them and him, as long as they pay him tribute. Which is plenty, by the way. The Ebersburgs are expected to come up with twenty imperial *Thaler* monthly, the von Schlitz have to pay forty *Thaler* a month. Even the Buchenau family, which isn't very prominent or prosperous, is being assessed thirteen *Thaler* monthly by the Swedes, to support the Protestant cause."

"Where does Hesse-Kassel stand on this?" Derek Utt asked.

"Well, you must know that Hesse does not have any imperial knights within its lands. The lower nobility of Hesse, its *Ritterschaft*, is subject to the landgrave. Not *reichsfrei*. They are *landsässig*, vassals of the landgrave rather than of the emperor. Or of the king of Sweden, since he has now put himself in the emperor's place, for all practical purposes."

Wes Jenkins nodded.

Boyneburg went on. "I'm afraid that my lord the landgrave rather alienated the imperial knights of the Buchen Quarter last year, by moving to make them *landsässig* in Fulda. That was before your town's arrival of course, when he hoped to be able to attach Fulda as one of his permanent possessions. Of course, the abbot of Fulda would also like to make the knights within his territory his vassals. Any territorial ruler would, naturally. It's just that Hesse and Württemberg have been more successful at mediatizing them—well, at mediatizing us, since I am a member of the Hessian nobility—than most other principalities."

He paused. "The imperial knights of Buchen, ah, resist the idea of giving up their freedom and liberties to become the subjects of a territorial ruler very strongly."

"So, at the moment, they are still classified as free knights, but they are paying through the nose for the privilege. A lot more than their taxes would be if they were subjects of the abbot," Wes Jenkins summed up.

Boyneburg nodded his agreement.

"Clara, since the NUS is sitting in the former chair of the abbot as Fulda's head of state or civil government, where do you think we stand as far as our relations with these guys are concerned?"

"These knights in the Buchen are in a little different position than those in Hesse. They do, most of them, have some lands that are allods. That is, lands that they own in their own right and for which they do not owe any feudal dues. Just taxes to the emperor. Or, now, to King Gustavus Adolphus. But most of them also hold other lands as fiefs from Fulda. So the New United States is, I think, their feudal lord, their *Lehensherr*, for those lands, as well as being their *Landesherr*."

"We don't want to be anybody's f . . . never mind, feudal lord," Harlan Stull exploded.

"Well, it doesn't matter what we want," Andrea Hill said, "until the New United States gets around to changing the land system, we *are*. Not as individuals, but the administration is. So we are, collectively, as representatives of the government. That's pretty clear from the land title stuff that I've collected."

Fulda, February 1633

"I'm it, I think," Mark Early said. "The whole Special Commission on the Establishment of Freedom of Religion in the Franconian Prince-Bishoprics and the Prince-Abbey of Fulda. At least as far as Fulda is concerned. That's what my orders say. It's what my wife Susan says, too, and since she's working directly for Mike Stearns, I guess it's for real."

"How do you intend to do it, on top of all the rest of your work?"

"If you want me to do it, Wes, Derek's just going to have to make someone else bookkeeper and paymaster. Either pull one of the kids into the job or use a down-timer."

"Derek, do you see any options to that?"

"No, to tell the truth. They say that they'll send Joel Matowski out to help Mark, but he can't be freed up until late summer or early fall, probably. And when he does get here, he'll have a steep learning curve."

"That's the down side. Is there an up side?"

"Fulda's a lot smaller than Würzburg or Bamberg, so maybe one guy can do it," Andrea offered.

"I don't think so," Wes said. "Even if we free up Mark, he's going to need help and it obviously isn't going to be an up-timer. Do we have any down-time staff who could lend a hand, at least with scheduling the hearings and taking the minutes? Filing the records. Stuff like that."

Harlan Stull shook his head.

"What about Clara?" Derek asked.

"Clara?"

"Well, it looks to me like a lot of what this Special Commission is going to be doing is trying to get the Lutheran imperial knights and the Catholic abbot and chapter at the monastery to coexist and leave the ordinary people who belong to each other's religion alone. She's already been working with the abbot, so she should have a head start, so to speak. Then if we can get someone local . . . Andrea, did you ever hire a lawyer full time?"

"I did. But the Special Commission can't have him.

I'm not just paying him full time. I'm using him full time. Maybe he can recommend someone else."

"Oh, sure, they always can," Harlan said. "A younger brother or a nephew or their cousin's brother-in-law."

Roy Copenhaver shook his head. "Aren't we supposed to avoid nepotism?"

"Hey, until we get an actual civil service, it works as well as any other hiring system. The trick is to make sure that we fire the incompetents who don't work out, and even with a civil service they didn't manage that, up-time. Neither West Virginia nor the feds."

"Are you a cynic?"

"I'm a realist. Okay, I'll ask Clara about it; see if she'd be willing to," Harlan said. In addition to his other duties, he was personnel manager.

"How about Herr von Boyneburg?" Clara asked.

"But he doesn't even work for us," Mark Early protested. "He works for the landgrave of Hesse-Kassel."

"But it would be a good idea for someone who works for the landgrave of Hesse-Kassel to learn about separation of church and state. Wouldn't it?"

"Yeah, I guess so. When you put it that way," Harlan answered. "Seems weird, though."

"They have their own problems," Clara said. "People in the border villages along the Werra who even now walk over into neighboring Lutheran territories to take communion, after all these years and in spite of the fact that they've made it illegal. Maybe they could just learn to let them do it in peace. Plus there's an occasional Calvinist imperial knight with lands well inside Fulda territory, so they could learn to make it a trade-off. The abbot stops hassling the Calvinists and Lutherans.

The Calvinists stop hassling the Lutherans. Then the Lutherans could stop hassling the Calvinists, too, maybe. Or at least stop calling one another crypto-Calvinists."

She smiled. "Are you sending an observer to the Rudolstadt Colloquy?" she asked.

"H . . . that is, heck no!" Harlan answered.

"Do we need a pilgrimage church up on *top* of a hill?" Andrea asked.

Roy Copenhaver winced. "You know, sometimes I ask myself if this place is worth all the grief that it's causing us. There can't be more than fifty thousand people in the *Stift* and town of Fulda, combined. Total. If that many. Maybe forty thousand if you count out all the subjects of somebody else who are just living here."

"We did get Fulda as sort of an appendage to Würzburg and Bamberg, I think. An afterthought. It's nowhere near as big. Nowhere near as exciting. But if Mike hadn't taken it on, it would have gone to Hesse-Kassel, like Paderborn and Corvey did. And the landgrave would have done the same sort of stuff to the folks here as he's doing to the folks there, so maybe it's worthwhile," Andrea answered.

"What's he doing?"

"The longer he manages to hang on to them, the tighter he's squeezing the Catholics. He started out in 1631 just swiping valuable stuff, but being pretty generous about letting the ordinary people keep their religion. But as time goes on, first one church and then another gets handed over to the Protestants; first one and then another Catholic priest gets exiled, till there's just one little church in each town where he allows Catholic services. He fires the Catholic schoolteachers.

Then the Jesuits have to go; then the Franciscans and Benedictines and the other religious orders. Then he introduces a religious test for holding public office. So far, he hasn't made it illegal to be Catholic, but it's definitely creeping Calvinism, now that he sees some prospect that Gustavus Adolphus will grant them to him as permanent possessions. SOP, pretty much, for seventeenth-century Germany when a ruler who has one religion takes over a territory that has another."

"What about this pilgrimage church Andrea was talking about?" Fred Pence asked.

"According to Steve Salatto," Wes said, "the purpose of this exercise is to keep resources out of the hands of the CPE's opponents. So they can't use them to oppose the Confederated Principalities of Europe. Are the pilgrimages compulsory?"

"Not by law, no," Andrea answered. "I suppose that if a priest sticks someone with a pilgrimage as a penance, it's sort of morally compulsory. But the constable or bailiff isn't going to make the guy go."

"Does it have income?"

"Just what the pilgrims donate. It doesn't have farms or estates or anything attached that support it with dues."

"I don't think we need it," Wes said. "If it's going to cost him money to keep it up, pay the priests and so on, give it back to the abbot, land title and all. Make that a rule. If it's going to cost the abbot money, give it back to him. Parochial schools, the seminary for boys who are studying to be priests, and stuff like that. If it's going to generate income, keep it."

He leaned back and yawned. "Solomon had nothing on me when it came to snap decisions."

Ways and Means

Fulda, April 1633

"Your administration has abolished the tithes," the abbot said.

"Yep." Roy Copenhaver took a drag on his clay pipe. He still missed cigarettes, but the region right around here was about the largest manufacturer of clay pipes in Europe, from cheapos to deluxe.

"Not just the tithes that the church actually collected itself, but the ones that other investors had bought up as well."

"So they can sue us. They probably will. It doesn't make any difference in the long run. Everybody's busy. Congress didn't get around to making a law. Mike Stearns didn't get around to issuing an executive order. Steve Salatto didn't get around to sending us any general edict. We had to do something. Whatever Wes decided to do about it, somebody would have sued us, so we just wiped the things out as far as Fulda is concerned. We're building legal fees into the budget request for the next fiscal year."

"As the secular government, you are now collecting the taxes."

"That's true, too."

"And you have confiscated the abbey's estates that produce income in the form of rents and dues."

"*Ummn-hmmn*. That's what you get for running off with Tilly and hanging out with Wallenstein, pardon my French."

"So how do you expect me to support all the things that you have so *generously* returned to the church? How do I pay for roofs for the schools and matrons for the orphanages and priests for the churches?"

"Pass the plate. That's how we did it up-time. If they really want the stuff, they'll cough up the money. Nobody says you can't lay a guilt trip on them, even. Try sermons. My wife Jen and I were Pentecostals, up-time. That's how our preachers did it."

"Were?"

"Are. But our church was outside the Ring of Fire. There's an old retired preacher, Reverend Chalker, who was caught in it. Must be eighty years old. He was visiting Lana Soper at the assisted living center when it hit, and he's been holding tent services. We should manage to get a temporary building up fairly soon, but there aren't very many of us."

Roy looked at the abbot. "Stop feeling sorry for yourself. You're in a lot better shape here in Fulda than we are back in Grantville. You saw St. Mary's. Nice church building, right downtown. Bet you never got out into the Five Hollows to take a look at our little arrangement."

"I suppose there's something to be said for poverty," the abbot said. "Beyond the fact that it's in the Rule of Saint Benedict. Which got more than a little stretched over the centuries, as you can tell."

"What?"

"Without the income attached to the prebends, the only monks who are likely to come back to the abbey are the ones who are willing to live like monks. Which is what I've been trying to get them to do for a decade."

✧   ✧   ✧

"I think that it might be a good idea for you to send them to Rome," Johann Bernhard Schenk von Schweinsberg said, tapping the pile of pamphlets. "That's why I brought them over."

The rector of Fulda's Jesuit *collegium* ran his fingers thoughtfully through his beard.

"I rather liked Father Mazzare, you understand. And Kircher has a lot of respect for him. But if the holy father is to come to an informed decision, then he should know that the views of the up-time Catholics were no more monolithic than ours are. I, ah, feel rather sure that Herr Agostino Nobili of Grantville would be happy to share all the rest of his piles of pamphlets with the *magisterium*."

"I will send them," the rector countered, "to Father-General Vitelleschi."

"Understood."

"There is no sense in encouraging the more reactionary elements in the College of Cardinals."

"I suspect," the abbot said, "that they are perfectly capable of sending researchers to Grantville to look up the Modernist controversy in the encyclopedias for themselves. The Grantvillers will make no move to stop them. The up-timers are strange that way. Most of their leaders appear to be strongly committed to the belief that ideas should flow freely, even when they disagree with them."

"What did you make of Herr Piazza?" the rector asked. "In some ways, he may be more important for the church than Stearns himself, since he is Catholic and can be expected to understand our problems more clearly. Does he share that belief?"

"Almost certainly, since he is a strong supporter of the priest. It is as if they drink it in with their mother's milk. Father Mazzare played a piece of music for me on his 'phonograph.' Oddly, it contained German lines. *'Die Gedanken sind frei.'* He said that it was folk music. I was not able to determine why they think that folk music and popular music are two different genres. After all, *'Volk'* and *'populus'* basically designate the same concept."

The conversation meandered on throughout dinner, adding the mystery of "country" as a designation for music. Why would "country" differ from "folk" or "popular," since certainly the great majority of the people lived in rural areas?

Fulda, May 1633

"It could have been a disaster," Derek Utt said, "but it wasn't. Figure that once more we've managed to squeak through by the skin of our teeth. No religious vigilante of any existing persuasion even shot at Willard Thornton, much less hit him."

"I must say," Wes answered, "that the last thing we needed at this juncture was an LDS missionary."

"So you sicced him on Würzburg and Bamberg? So Steve Salatto needs him? So Vince Marcantonio needs him?" Andrea Hill asked.

"They have more resources to deal with it. At least, Steve does. I'm not so sure about Vince. Bamberg is worse understaffed than we are."

"Hey," Roy Copenhaver interrupted, "Willard's not a bad guy. He's worked at the Home Center for years.

I thought you said that people were just interested in his bicycle."

"I had the pewterer pour a new mold," Fred Pence said, "just in case. I'll be running out of sports pretty soon, but LDS is golf. I've still got tennis in reserve in case somebody wanders in making converts to something else."

"I haven't heard that he caused any problems," Orville Beattie added. "I don't think that he made any converts here in town, but he left a lot of pamphlets and flyers behind, so I'll keep an eye out."

"Here in town?"

Orville sighed. Derek Utt was getting pretty quick on the uptake.

"On his way out, pushing that bicycle, he stopped at Barracktown. Over there where you've planted the wives and not-exactly-wives of the down-time soldiers. Plus their kids and the usual crop of peddlers who sell them stuff that we won't issue. I haven't managed to get rid of those sutlers; throw one out and two more sprout up, it seems like. I think he made more of an impression there than he did in Fulda. Now maybe the women just wanted to wallpaper their cabins to keep out the drafts, but he must have left several pounds of printed paper behind him."

"What on earth about the Mormons would appeal to the wives of a bunch of mercenaries?" Harlan Stull asked.

"They seemed to find the emphasis that husbands should be sober, orderly, hard-working heads of their households and spend their free time going to church meetings . . . umm, an improvement on the *status quo* if they could get it."

"I thought that Gretchen had vouched for these guys as okay," Harlan protested.

"Okay by the standards of seventeenth-century mercenaries, which leaves quite a bit of leeway, so to speak. Once you get to know them," Derek answered.

"It's not as if any of the existing churches spend much time trying to improve conditions for those poor women and children," Andrea said. "There's sort of a vacuum there."

"And nature abhors one. Thanks, Orville. I guess. At least for letting me know," Derek said.

"By the way," Andrea asked, "what have we done about getting a grade school set up out there?"

They all looked at her.

"Well," she pointed out, "the people in Fulda won't let those kids go to the town schools."

"Prejudice," Derek said.

Everybody started to talk at once.

"Not in the district limits. There were rules about that up-time, too. We've made a little settlement where there wasn't one before."

"Can we make the town take them?"

"Not if we're serious about self-government."

"We're not in the school business."

"What about Ronnie Dreeson?"

"Maybe the abbot could set one up."

"Using what for money? We've swiped all his revenues. It would have to be a charity school of some kind."

"It's a peculiar religious mix out there at Barracktown," Derek said. "People who are supposed to be Catholic and a bunch of different kinds of Protestants, all tossed in together. Plus one Turk that I know of who has a Portuguese wife. And an Armenian."

"If we'd quartered the soldiers out in the villages, the kids could have gone to the village schools."

"We're not quartering soldiers on civilians, remember. That's why we have the barracks. And Barracktown."

"Anyway, the village schools around here are all Catholic and the Protestants wouldn't want to send their kids. There's no such thing as an irreligious school. Non-religious school. Nondenominational school. Whatever."

"Maybe Clara can think of something."

"H . . . I mean heck, Andrea. Why'd you have to bring up those kids?" Harlan stood up, gathering his papers together. "As if we didn't have enough on our plates."

This Troublesome Monk

Bonn, Archdiocese of Cologne, May 1633

"You could file a complaint of witchcraft against him," the man in the gray hood suggested. "It's much more likely to attract public attention than simple collaboration with the enemy."

"Against the *abbot*?"

Johann Adolf von Hoheneck would prefer to be abbot of Fulda himself, rather than just the ex-provost of the ecclesiastical estate of Petersberg, which had been confiscated by the New United States in any case, which made him just a chapter monk of Fulda now, much to his chagrin. Still, Schweinsberg was the abbot and he found the idea of bringing him down a little distasteful. Particularly in the way of setting precedents. A person had to think long-term.

"Isn't the abbot the only person we were talking about?" someone muttered under his breath.

Hoheneck looked at the Capuchin, shaking his head. "We don't have anyone on the ground there to file it, even if the rest of us agreed. The only monks who stayed were the ones from Saint Gall, who surely won't. Perhaps a few of Schweinsberg's supporters have come back, but not in any numbers, as far as I have heard. They wouldn't either, in any case."

"Maybe if we made it worth someone's while, one of them would." The archbishop's confessor was a tenacious man.

"Not in the chapter, then," Franz von Hatzfeld said. "But, surely, there must be someone in the town of Fulda? Someone among the city councilors and guildsmen?"

"Why not file the accusation against one of the up-timers?" Hoheneck was uneasy at the prospect of trying to bring down the abbot. The more he thought about it, the uneasier he got. The bishop of Würzburg wasn't the only high ecclesiastical official with a desire to expand his jurisdiction. He did not consider Cologne to be exempt from it—especially not when the archbishop was a Bavarian duke. How would it be to his advantage to bring down the abbot if the archbishop mediatized the abbey in the process?

"I don't think that is prudent right now," Hatzfeld said. "But you could include the down-time woman they sent to advise him in the accusation. That always allows for all sorts of sexual innuendoes."

"But the abbot . . , who's going to investigate the charge?" Hoheneck asked. "And how, since the up-timers have abolished witchcraft as a crime?"

"Why, the bishop of Würzburg, I presume," the man in the gray hood said smoothly. "Fulda does fall within his ecclesiastical jurisdiction, after all. Or so he contends, at least." He looked directly at Hatzfeld, who was, after all, the bishop of Würzburg. "The Holy Father has never ruled definitively in the matter."

"Sufficient unto the day . . ." someone muttered, just loudly enough to be heard.

"And it remains a crime under imperial law," Hatzfeld continued, "so when the ursurping Swede is expelled . . ."

"The bishop of Würzburg," Hoheneck bowed to Hatzfeld, "isn't there. Just his suffragan. The bishop of Würzburg is here, in Bonn."

He frowned. Hatzfeld was here in Bonn—under the archbishop's thumb. Hatzfeld's family was supporting him, so he wasn't living on the archbishop's charity the way most of the rest of the refugee Rheinland clerics were, but he still didn't like the way it looked.

"Why, I should think that is all to the good," the archbishop's confessor said, also bowing to Hatzfeld. "No problems stemming from delayed correspondence. No interceptions by the Jew Nasi and his agents. It should be possible for us to make our wishes clear to him directly. And he should be willing. Unless he is, like Schweinsberg, falling prey to the temptation to save whatever he can save."

"I have been quite consistent in my refusal to deal with the up-timers," the bishop of Würzburg said.

"So you will handle it—the investigation into the witchcraft allegations—from here?" The question came from the clerk who was taking the minutes.

"If we aren't all running away from the Swede by the time the investigation is ripe." That was the same unidentifiable under-the-breath muttering. Hoheneck wished that the men who had not been invited to the table were sitting across from him rather than behind him. He couldn't tell who it was.

"Hatzfeld can't very well go down to Fulda and hold hearings right under the up-timers' noses, much less use judicial torture while they are occupying the *Stift* lands," he said. "Who's going to take the depositions and keep the protocols?"

"Could we possibly get Hesse to file the complaint?" a Jesuit sitting next to Hatzfeld asked.

"Hesse? He's one of Gustavus Adolphus's strongest allies," the Capuchin said.

"Sure, but if he thought that he could bring the abbot down . . . not realizing that we have a candidate waiting in the wings to take his place." The Jesuit tapped his index finger on the table. "It wouldn't have to be Hesse himself. He's bound to have agents in Fulda."

"He has a regular liaison with the up-timers," Hatzfeld said. "One of the Boyneburgs."

"Too close. Too public," Hoheneck protested.

"Could we talk Neuhoff into going back?" the Jesuit asked. "Pretending to be reconciled to Schweinsberg? Then a couple of months later, horrified at what he has seen since his return, devastated with shock, appalled . . . you know the script . . . he files the allegations."

"It might work," Hoheneck answered. "Hermann has a pretty good reputation. And he's scholarly. He corresponds with Grotius, you know."

"Every literate person in Europe corresponds with Grotius, I think."

Hoheneck resisted turning his head to see where the *sotto voce* comments were coming from.

"That's no special distinction," whoever it was continued.

"Schweinsberg could hit back by accusing Neuhoff of Arminian sympathies," the Jesuit said. "That's why Grotius had to get out of the Netherlands. That would turn off the landgrave of Hesse pretty fast."

"Arminianism is a Calvinist fight—not a Catholic one." The Capuchin pushed back his hood.

"Hesse-Kassel is a Calvinist," Hoheneck pointed out.

"What difference does that make? If a slur works, use it."

Hoheneck shook his head with annoyance. It was the voice from behind him again.

"Where do we start?" That was Hatzfeld.

"Let's hire somebody to write a pamphlet," Hoheneck suggested. "Just to test the waters."

"Obscene illustrations?" the muttering voice behind him asked in a hopeful tone.

Hoheneck turned around and glared at the group of men. "If you pay for the woodcuts," he said. "Whoever you are."

"Lovely," the voice continued. It came from a little man wearing a flat hat. "The serpent's long, long tongue extending and . . ." He smiled.

"This is," the Capuchin said, "the archbishop's palace. Control your imagination, Gruyard."

"Hoheneck's getting cold feet," Archbishop Ferdinand's confessor said.

"They've never been warm," the archbishop answered. "He's a cold fish, overall. Your putting Gruyard to mutter behind him today got more of a rise out of him than I've ever seen before."

"How much practical assistance can we expect from your brothers?"

"Very little, this summer. As you know, Maximilian and Albrecht have more immediate concerns. The recent events in Bohemia have been very worrisome. Austria needs Bavaria's support."

He frowned at the Capuchin. "For that matter, we have more immediate concerns than Fulda, too. One of Gustavus Adolphus's generals with twenty-five thousand men looking at my eastern border is one of those thoughts that make worries about the status of Fulda seem comparatively insignificant."

"Great oaks from little acorns grow," his confessor said piously. "Moreover, I doubt that there are more than ten thousand men looking at your eastern border. And those are mostly Hessians under von Uslar rather than Swedes."

The archbishop frowned his displeasure.

"Think of Fulda as the first domino in bringing down the CPE and unraveling? Something?"

"As a grand conspirator," the archbishop said, "you . . . never mind. And get Gruyard out of my palace. I don't care where you put him, except not in any other building that belongs to the archdiocese, but get him out. He makes my flesh crawl."

"He's good at what he does."

"That's the problem."

Where Are We and What Are We Doing Here?

Stift Fulda, June 1633

"Where are we?" Mark Early asked.

"This is Neuenberg," the abbot answered. "I served as provost here before I was elected abbot. Among several other places where I was provost. That's why I came along today, to introduce you to the people here."

"What does a provost do?"

The abbot started a long explanation.

"Middle management." Clara Bachmeierin inserted the English term into the conversation.

Mark nodded.

The breeze picked up. Clara grabbed for her files. She was acting as clerk today. Boyneburg's horse boy picked up a couple of rocks and gave them to her for paperweights.

"Why are we sitting under a tree instead of inside?" Mark asked.

"It's a linden tree," Boyneburg said.

"Why are we sitting under a linden tree?"

"People around here conduct important business under the village linden tree. Always have, as far as I know. Well, maybe not in the dead of winter or a pouring rain, but generally that's where the village council meets and anything else important gets done."

Mark sighed. "When in Rome." He put on his sunglasses.

"I'd take those off if I were you," Clara recommended. "There will be better times to introduce the peasants of Neuenberg to modern technology."

He put them back in his breast pocket and squinted into the sun. A bunch of people were coming out of the chapel.

"Bailiff," Mark said, "announce that the session of the Special Commission on the Establishment of Freedom of Religion in the Franconian Prince-Bishoprics and the Prince-Abbey of Fulda will come to order."

An elderly farmer looked at him. "The bailiff's sick. Something he ate, probably. You don't want him here."

"Do you have an under-bailiff?"

"Nein."

"A constable?"

"He's the bailiff."

"Somebody," Mark said, "announce that the session of the Special Commission on the Establishment of Freedom of Religion in the Franconian Prince-Bishoprics and the Prince-Abbey of Fulda will come to order."

None of the villagers moved.

Urban von Boyneburg got up and announced it.

"Pardon, Your Honor," the elderly farmer said, "but we would like to bring to Your Honor's attention that it's a good day for making hay, and we would just as soon be done with this business by the time the dew goes off."

Fulda, June 1633

"It's gross," Andrea Hill said. She was holding the pamphlet by one corner, between her thumb and her index finger, as far away from her body as she could get it. "And the town is plastered with them."

"Come on, Andrea," Wes Jenkins said placidly. "Whatever it is, it can't be that bad."

"Oh yes it can." She threw it onto the table in front of him. "Poor Clara. They put her name in the thing, in the caption to that hideous picture. And all of our soldiers I saw out on the street were looking at the placards that go with it and going 'har, har, har!' So *you*"—she stopped and pointed at Derek Utt—"can just get up and go out there and make them stop it."

Derek reached over and pulled the pamphlet out from in front of Wes. Thumbed through it once. Got up.

Orville Beattie came into the conference room, carrying another copy. Wes grabbed the first one from where Derek had dropped it. As he looked through it, his face went white and pinched.

"Clara I understand," Fred Pence said as he came in, "but who's Salome? The one in the Bible?"

Andrea glared at him. He realized that it was one of those mornings when it was just generally a bad thing to be a male human being, and a worse one to be a son-in-law.

"The prioress," Andrea said. "At the Benedictine convent here in town. You've surely walked past it. Ascension of Mary, it's called. There's a plaque by the door. She's been here since 1630. She and three others came from the abbey of Kühbach in the diocese of Augsburg to start it up. They've been through hard times, what with the Hessians and everything. And us, considering that we confiscated the estates that the abbot had assigned to support them. They're dirt poor. There are days when they're going hungry, until Clara or I take the rest of our supper over to them. This is just so . . . unfair. Her name is Salome. Salome von Pflaumern."

Harlan Stull raised an eyebrow. "Does that explain why your per diem has gone up, you and Clara? You're feeding six rather than two? Or ten rather than two? How many are there?"

"Well, we felt bad about it. If we hadn't taken away all of the abbot's income-producing property, the provosts on the abbey's farms would be sending them something to eat, at least. And they could fix the roof. It's leaking into the chapel."

"Why the hell do they name girls Salome, anyhow?" Orville Beattie asked. "It seems like a bad omen from the start."

"Not that one," Andrea said. "Not the one with the seven veils and John the Baptist's head. There's another one, who stood next to Mary at the cross. She's a saint. Girls get named for her."

"More than enough room for confusion, if you ask me," Fred said. He was clearly going to be on Andrea's shit list today no matter what he did, so he figured he might as well earn it.

"Where did Mark and the rest of the Special Commission go today?" Wes Jenkins asked.

Andrea looked at his face and shivered.

"Neuenberg," Orville Beattie answered. "That's not far."

"Go get them. Bring them back. Take a dozen guards with you, at least. God, this is sick!"

Orville moved fast.

"Andrea," Wes spit out. "Get your tame lawyer in here this minute. And the mayor and the whole city council."

❖   ❖   ❖

"We've let you keep your gate guards. Did somebody bring this smut in through one of the gates. If so, which one, and when?" Wes Jenkins glared.

The captain of Fulda's militia shook his head. "There has been no large shipment of printed matter for several weeks, sir. Not to the best of our knowledge. I do have confidence in my men."

"Are you interested in the other option, then?"

"Which other option?" Adam Landau asked rather hesitantly. He was the mayor. It was his job to speak for the others, no matter how dangerous an activity that currently appeared to be.

"That some sick creep brought a manuscript and the woodcuts into Fulda in his private baggage and it was printed here?"

The council members looked at one another. Then at the militia captain. Then back at one another. This possibility was even less pleasant.

The head of the clothmakers' guild cleared his throat. "Ah. Freedom of the press, sir?" Esaias Geyder said tentatively.

Wes blew up. "There are a few little things for you to think about. First, this is a military occupation force, when you come right down to it. Fulda has not adopted the constitution of the New United States. It hasn't even voted on whether or not to adopt it. And if your friendly local collection of imperial knights doesn't manage to get its act together, it's not likely that there will be a vote any time soon, because we won't be able to organize an election. Not that things here are any worse than they are in the rest of Franconia, but that's neither here nor there.

"Second." He looked at the head of the clothmakers' guild. "There are some things that I am simply not having happen in the name of freedom of the press. Andrea's lawyer here can write back to Grantville. He'll have somebody send the information, if you want to footnote me, but there really are court decisions about this stuff. Freedom of speech doesn't extend to yelling 'fire' in a crowded theater. 'Your right to swing your fist ends where it collides with someone else's nose.' That sort of stuff."

"What aren't you going to have happen here?" the militia captain asked.

"Witch hunts, first and foremost. How old are you, Captain Wiegand? Old enough to remember them?" Wes waved at the group. "You have to be old enough, Kaus. You're at least sixty, and they were only thirty years ago. What about you, Rabich? I've never heard that you suffer from memory loss when it comes to your property rights. You're here at city hall hassling Andrea every other day. Has 'burning alive' slipped your mind? Not a few cases, precisely. Somewhere between two hundred fifty and three hundred, from what we've been able to find out."

Otto Kaus swallowed nervously. Eberhard Rabich took a half-step back.

Wiegand stepped forward. "They're old enough, sir. So am I, for that matter. I was ten at the last burning, but for three years, Judge Nuss took the school to watch."

"Took the *school*," Andrea Hill gasped.

"It was a regular sort of thing, ma'am." He turned back to Wes Jenkins. "Herr Kaus is a bit nervous. Some of his relatives were burned. Some of Frau Rabich's relatives, too. It's hard for families to get away from the taint, somehow."

"Well, and shouldn't it be?" Lorenz Mangold, new head of the butchers' guild, pushed himself to the front. "Think about it. Anna Hahn, old Hans's widow, got away. And then had the gall to come back and live here after Judge Nuss was arrested and put in prison. But there's bound to have been some truth to the accusations, or the bishop of Bamberg wouldn't have burned her son as a witch a few years ago, would he? Not when he had risen as far as chancellor of the diocese. I say that where there's smoke, there's fire."

The other members of the Fulda city council appeared to have forgotten about the up-timers. They had all turned and were staring at Mangold.

Captain Wiegand backed inconspicuously out of the room. Derek Utt got up from the table and followed him. By mutual, unspoken, consent, Wiegand ran to summon his elite guard unit; Derek headed for the corridor where the MP office was.

The situation in the city hall conference room was deteriorating rapidly. Rabich pointed at Mangold, yelling that he was related to Judge Nuss's second wife. Mangold retorted that Mayor Landau was married to a cousin of the Kaus woman who, like Hans Hahn's wife, had escaped. Mangold raised accusations of witch-friendliness against the late Landgrave Moritz of Hesse-Kassel. Someone pointed out that the prince of Isenburg-Buedingen had also sheltered accused witches who escaped. This led to rancorous comments by Mangold about the role of the imperial cameral court, which had denied that Fulda could exercise jurisdiction over non-resident accused witches.

Derek Utt came back with two soldiers per council member. This crowded the room, but quieted things down quite a bit.

Wes Jenkins wasn't exactly happy, but he was feeling rather vindicated in his decision to push hard. It looked like, this sort of thing was still a lot closer to the surface than anyone in the NUS administration had realized before.

With Lorenz Mangold, at least. The rest of them were looking at the man very unhappily, with sort of *Return of the Creature from the Black Lagoon* expressions on their faces, Wes thought.

Wiegand came back.

"Mangold has had a man staying with him for several days," he reported. "He left first thing this morning. I've sent the guard company to try to track him."

"Description?" Derek Utt asked. "Do you have a sketch?"

"He was wearing a brown doublet with leather buttons."

"Half the men in *Stift* Fulda are wearing a brown doublet with leather buttons."

"Some people prefer bone buttons," Esaias Geyder said. He was wearing a brown doublet with bone buttons himself.

"How many people here have seen Mangold's guest?" Captain Wiegand asked.

Nobody admitted to having seen the man.

"How did you find out about him?" Derek Utt asked.

"Mangold's cook. She's been having to serve up an extra plate each night, but he didn't give her any extra market money."

"Is there anyone around you can take to her to and get a sketch from her description?"

"There's the painter who lives in the St. Severi church," Rabich suggested nervously. "He's been there for four years, now, through imperials and Hessians, and the New United States. Sleeps in the sacristy and paints murals on the wall. They're not bad. The sexton brings food in for him and empties his slops. That's all he's asked the vestry board for—food and his paints."

"Go get him," Wes said to Captain Wiegand.

"Don't frighten him," Andrea added. "Tell him that he's not in trouble before you haul him over to the city hall. Even better, just take him to Herr Mangold's kitchen."

Wiegand shook his head. "I have the cook here."

"Then take her to the church."

"No, this has to be official. I'll bring him here. Nicely, ma'am."

"He really, really, did not want to come with me," Captain Wiegand said. "But it's just as well I brought him. Otherwise, he wouldn't have seen the placards."

"Are those still nailed up all over town?" Wes exploded.

"Nobody said to take them down."

"Well, get somebody out to *take* them, then. Before Ms. Bachmeierin and the abbot get back. I'm not going to have Clara see that filth."

Derek Utt gestured. Two soldiers per council member became one soldier per council member.

"Why is it important that he saw the placards?" he asked.

"He says that he knows the artist," Wiegand said. "Recognizes him from his style. He says that it's as plain to an artist as a signature, if two men have ever worked in the same studio. Last time he heard of this woodcut maker, he was working in Cologne, in Bonn, really, since that is where the archbishop resides, for a Lorrainer named Felix Gruyard."

"Does that name ring a bell with anyone?"

Head shakes all around. Negative.

"Who's the printmaker?"

The artist himself answered. "Alain van Beekx. A Netherlander."

Head shakes again.

Wes looked at the artist. "This van Beekx. What does he do for a living?"

"He makes filthy pictures, sir."

"Well," Wes said, "I'm happy to meet you. One man today who tells the truth, the whole truth, and nothing but the truth."

"That isn't the whole truth, sir," the artist said.

Wes waited.

Waited some more.

"He forges documents. That's how he makes most of his money. If someone needs 'evidence' and doesn't have any, van Beekx will come up with it. There's a lot of 'evidence' against me on file in Cologne. It looks very real. Any court would convict me on it. If he's involved in this, with Gruyard, there's probably a lot of 'evidence' against you tucked away somewhere, just waiting until some court asks for it. If you don't mind, I'd just as soon go back to the church, sir. It's been a very peaceful place for me these last few years."

"As soon as you make a deposition and sign it."

The artist's shoulders drooped. Andrea's lawyer, whose name Wes could never seem to remember, led him out.

Wes dismissed the city council. They left the conference room but kept milling around in the vestibule. Captain Wiegand closed the door from the outside.

"Okay," Andrea said, "tell me something." She picked up the pamphlet with which the morning had started, again between thumb and forefinger.

"What?"

"Who from here went up to Cologne and described Clara to this van Beekx creep? The 'Salome' doesn't look a thing like the prioress. It's just a sort of generic nun, and not even wearing the same kind of habit that the Benedictines do. But the 'Clara,' even if there wasn't a name to the picture, you could almost recognize."

Orville Beattie looked at it. "The abbot, too. Even when he's a snake."

"It's this van Beekx who's the snake," Wes spit out.

"Yeah," Fred Pence said. "Pretty good caricaturist, though."

"Or maybe someone sent them sketches. If that artist ever came out of the church and took a look at us, who would notice? He didn't look very happy about making a deposition. I've got an appointment, guys." Dropping that happy thought on the table, Orville left.

They delegated the delicate task of acquainting Clara with the existence of the placards, all of which had been pulled down before the Special Commission returned from Neuenberg, and the pamphlet, to Andrea.

"My goodness," Clara said. "How . . . unusual . . . to see my own face on a depiction of the Whore of Babylon. Because I speak with you foreigners, I suppose. The tower of Babel and all that. And the prioress is the Whore of Rome because she's a nun, I suppose."

She giggled. "But the idea of depicting the abbot as a snake with a forked tongue is really rather ingenious. Considering what he is doing with it."

"Aren't . . ." Andrea's voice quavered. "Aren't you even a little bit shocked?"

"Well, I don't like the witchcraft accusation," Clara said pragmatically. "Those can be dangerous, over here in Franconia. But I've seen woodcuts like that all my life. With this kind of iconography."

"Where?"

Clara looked at her with surprise. "Illustrating Lutheran pamphlets about the nature of the pope as the anti-Christ, of course. We read some of them in confirmation class."

Andrea started to make strangling noises.

"Fourteen-year-olds have a rather crude sense of humor, of course. Our favorite was one of the pope. You could tell it was the pope because he was wearing a triple tiara, but he had breasts that drooped down to here"—Clara gestured expressively—"and a big swollen belly covered with fish scales and was giving birth to the Leviathan, that's the great beast from Revelations, while the devil stood behind him and . . ."

"Stop," Andrea said. "I think I get the idea."

Clara thought a moment. "I expect that they, the Catholics, make that kind of picture about us, too. But I wonder why Catholic propagandists in Cologne, if you say that's where this came from, used the Whore of Rome image? That's ours, not theirs."

After she had thought for a couple of minutes, Andrea began to wonder about that herself.

"Mark," Andrea said the next morning. "I think there's something we need to talk about. About the Special Commission. There's something that came up when I was talking to Clara that made me think that, maybe, the road to getting seventeenth-century Europeans to get to the point of religious live-and-let-live is several thousand miles longer than any of us ever dreamed."

"Maybe," Mark said after he had heard her out. "Maybe. But you're forgetting something."

"What?"

"She *is* working with us on the Commission. And so is the abbot. Captain Wiegand is really pretty decent. No matter how much of this conditioning they got as kids."

July seemed to go by in a blur. Sitting in Würzburg, Steve Salatto got the latest mailbag from Fulda and wished that he had better communications. In Grantville, Ed Piazza pointed out to Arnold Bellamy that the folks in the field were pretty exposed and that he was planning to continue letting them function on a fairly long leash. No, he said. He really did not think that Wes went overboard. Under the circumstances. Maybe a little ballistic, but not overboard.

In Fulda, the news arrived that the CPE delegations were off to Paris and London to conduct negotiations. Everyone figured that getting ready for that must be why they hadn't been getting much in the way of instructions from the Department of International Affairs lately. The Special Commission held a bunch more sessions.

And ever since the affair of the placards, Wes kept hovering around Clara in a very overprotective manner, fretting every time the Special Commission went out of town until it was back safely. The rest of them thought it was funny, but he didn't even seem to realize that he was doing it.

Mark Early reported that they would finish up Fulda proper by the end of the month and start on the imperial knights the beginning of August. One at a time, he groaned. The imperial knights of Buchen Quarter were so jealous of their individual prerogatives that they hadn't been able to agree on a common time and place to hold even an introductory meeting so he could explain what the Special Commission's assignment was.

"Like hell they'll get away with that," Wes exploded.

The imperial knights of the Buchen Quarter were obviously not happy to be meeting in Fulda. Well, in a mown hay field outside Fulda. However, the combined visitation of the military administrator's regiment and the Fulda militia to each of their territories, individually, had been enough to persuade them of the prudence of agreeing.

Actually, Derek Utt thought, looking around the field, his soldiers weren't looking too bad these days. They had decent uniforms, finally. He wouldn't have chosen sickly orange himself—that was the best way he could describe the color—being more used to camouflage. But nobody expected them to be fighting in the field, so Frank Jackson hadn't sent them greeny-brown combat uniforms from Erfurt or Magdeburg. He hadn't sent them blue dress uniforms styled more or less after those used during the American Civil War, either—these being a product of what Melissa Mailey, in one of her more acerbic moments, called "reenactors' nostalgia" combined with the relative cheapness of cloth dyed with Erfurt woad. Dennis Stull, the civilian head of procurement, had just sent Derek a bank draft and a recommendation to do his best.

His best, when delegated to Harlan Stull's fiscal frugality, had turned out to be sickly orange. Good quality English fabric, Harlan said, but a bad dye lot. Or at least some Frankfurt merchant's bad guess as to whether or not the color would be popular. They'd paid the wives to make the uniforms up, which kept the money in the family as much as possible, so to speak.

They were even developing some *esprit de corps*. They were calling themselves the Fulda Barracks Regiment, these days. One of the sutlers had found them a set of regimental colors. Derek suspected that the banner had started life as some rich lady's party dress, but it had white and orange satin, so they were happy. And a logo. He couldn't make out what the logo was supposed to be—it looked to him like a lopsided blob—but it had one, and they had chipped in to pay for the flag themselves. Their weapons weren't as fancy as the ones carried by the imperial knights, but then his guys weren't planning on riding around in tournaments. They just planned on riding around looking mean. So far, he had been able to get horses for about half of them to ride at a time and was dual-training them as dragoons.

Out in the boondocks like this, Derek had decided, flexibility came in ahead of doctrine any day. He didn't care what the army's organizational table called them. He just had a job to do. Horses were a convenience, frequently very handy in a pinch, even if your label said "infantry."

Of course, the horses had to be taken care of, but he was paying some of the older kids from Barracktown to do that.

Which reminded him that Andrea was still nagging about a school out there.

Plus, the regiment wanted an anthem.

He had learned that the Swedish custom was to sing Psalm 46—that was *"Ein feste Burg"*—and then start Psalm 67, starting to advance before the singing finished. That would not work for the Fulda Barracks Regiment. Too many of the men had been on the receiving end of those advances, so to speak. He'd have to think about an anthem. The first requirement was that it had to be something that neither the Catholics nor the Lutherans could claim. The second requirement was that it had to be something he was willing to hear them sing every day. And an anthem ought to be uplifting. Martial, militant, but not some dirty marching song.

Derek's eyes jerked back to the center of the field when Wes Jenkins yelled again.

One of the knights was waving around a copy of that obscene pamphlet with Clara Bachmeierin's name in it. Refusing to receive the Whore of Babylon as an envoy from the Special Commission.

Wes went on yelling. For a Methodist, he had picked up a colorful vocabulary.

The guy with the pamphlet was backing down.

"I don't see what you're screaming about," another one of them—Karl von Schlitz—was saying to Wes. "You had them all torn down before one person in ten saw them. And it cost enough to get van Beekx to . . ." His voice trailed off. "Add in the Whore of Rome, too."

Wes had stopped yelling. He was smiling. "Just how, Herr von Schlitz," he asked, "do you happen to know how much it cost to do that?"

Derek moved his men in to form a double line, closer to the knights. Wiegand brought the city militia to replace them around the edges of the field.

This contributed a lot to the continuation of rational discussion. By the end of the afternoon, all of the imperial knights of the Fulda region were willing to swear upon their Bibles that Clara Bachmeierin was a desirable member of the Special Commission.

A couple of them even expressed the view that the Special Commission was desirable.

Not von Schlitz. Over some protest by his colleagues, he was "voluntarily" remaining in Fulda for meaningful discussions with the NUS administration about alleged treasonous contacts with the archbishop of Cologne.

Fulda, August 1633

August was a pretty good month. The NUS administration got news of the first flight of the *Las Vegas Belle*. Wes dipped into his own pockets and held a party for the whole town of Fulda. Barbequed mutton. As he said, his pay had mostly just been accumulating, since there really wasn't a lot in Fulda that a person could spend it on.

Harlan Stull wasn't sure how many of the guests

really believed in airplanes, but the government wasn't paying for it, so it wasn't his problem.

Then the news of the second Battle of White Mountain arrived. The abbot asked Roy Copenhaver if he was pardoned for having been hanging out with Wallenstein. If he was, he suggested, it would be really nice to have some of that income-producing property back, because otherwise the clergy of *Stift* Fulda were going to have a pretty hungry winter. Most of the population hadn't really gotten into the swing of voluntary church contributions.

"Herr Piazza," he said, "says that if I am to save souls, I must use carrots rather than sticks."

"Sounds like Ed."

"So." The abbot smiled. He was missing more than a few teeth. "I need a supply of carrots. Please."

Roy didn't give him any property back, but the administration did agree to turn over the wine from two formerly monastic vineyards for him to sell. Mostly because Harlan didn't want to get into wine marketing, which seemed to involve international cartels and a lot of other really complicated stuff, but Schweinsberg seemed a lot happier after he had sold it.

And Johnny Furbee married his German girlfriend. She was from Barracktown, though, so it didn't gain them any brownie points with the citizens of Fulda.

Fulda, September 1633

What with the news of the Dutch defeat at Dunkirk, September was a downer. People started to ask questions like, "Are they *ever* going to remember to rotate us out

of here?" About all that could be said for September
was that the Special Commission wound up the hearings and hired a wagon to take the accumulated paper
to Grantville. Joel Matowski turned up, too late to do
the Special Commission any good, really, but by having
him there, Derek Utt would be able to send his other
up-timers, in rotation, for some R&R in Grantville.

Since the wagonload of paper was going anyway,
Wes sent along Karl von Schlitz under guard. Mostly
to counter the rumors that he had been torturing the
man. Let the Nice Nellies see for themselves. Anyway,
Derek and Wiegand hadn't managed to get much out
of him. Mangold was Catholic, so it was easy enough
to see why he might have linked himself up with the
monks who had gone into exile in Cologne. But von
Schlitz was Lutheran. It didn't seem to add up.

Well, it hadn't, until Andrea's drab little lawyer
pointed out that a lot of Lutherans hated Calvinists
even more than they did Catholics and von Schlitz
was one of them. Combine that with the landgrave of
Hesse's efforts to make the knights his vassals before
the NUS showed up, and figure that the NUS was
allied with the king of Sweden who was allied with
the Hessians, who were Calvinists . . .

It made sense, in a warped sort of way. But now
Ed Piazza could worry about it. And maybe Francisco
Nasi could get more out of the guy.

Wes wrote a memo to Ed Piazza on the topic of
needed legal reforms, with a courtesy copy to Steve
Salatto. In the course of it, he mentioned that the
administration in Fulda had made several arrests in
connection with an outbreak of scurrilous pamphlets,
commented that he had refused to authorize the

use of judicial torture in the case, and added that, by the way, the pamphlets had been produced on a very ingenious down-time designed and manufactured duplicating machine marketed by a Herr Vignelli from Bozen. He sent this memo off in the same mail bag as his memo on the topic of needed improvements in the postal system, which was appended to his memo on rural transportation which accompanied his urgent memo in regard to cost overruns in the land titles department.

Fulda, October, 1633

As Harlan Stull said to Fred Pence, being in Fulda was sort of like being the little ball out on the far end of a stick that was just barely plugged in to some kid's Tinker Toy construction. What with the abysmal radio reception, if it hadn't had a post office on the mail route from Frankfurt to Eisenach, it could have been on the Moon. They didn't learn about Wismar until two weeks after it had happened. They didn't learn that the CPE had turned into the United States of Europe with Mike Stearns as prime minister for a couple of weeks after that.

One thing they learned from a private courier who rode the route from Erfurt to Frankfurt regularly, two weeks before the letter from Grantville showed up, was that the guard on von Schlitz hadn't been heavy enough. A batch of riders, presumably from his personal guards and presumably led by his two oldest sons, had run down the wagon on a pretty deserted stretch of road, shot the two guards and the teamster, and taken him off it. He had disappeared. Gone to ground somewhere. He had kin all over the place.

The Fulda Barracks Regiment put up two memorial plaques. It had not occurred to the men to commemorate their fallen, but Derek had suggested it.

Nobody except their relatives told them anything about what was going on in Magdeburg. They had to read it in the newspaper. That was even how Wes found out that the landgrave of Hesse-Kassel had signed on to some grand railroad project. In the future tense, of course, but at some point people would be coming through to survey a railway route running through Hersfeld and then through Butzbach, down to Frankfurt am Main and then through to Mainz.

"Has Hesse-Darmstadt signed on?" Clara asked. "Butzbach belongs to an uncle of the landgrave of Hesse-Darmstadt, not to Kassel. They'll have to go through quite a bit of Hesse-Homburg before they even get to Butzbach. That belongs to another uncle of the landgrave of Hesse-Darmstadt."

Wes didn't know. The paper hadn't said anything.

"The line is supposed to run twenty miles north and then twenty miles west of here, more or less," Harlan Stull grunted. "It shouldn't affect us at all."

"Once they actually build the thing," Roy Copenhaver pointed out, "it will open up new markets. Even for farmers this far away."

"Yeah, but that will be years. Why didn't they bring it down this way, and then to Frankfurt along the Kinzig River valley?"

"To do that, they would have to go through Schlitz and the *Reichsritter* wouldn't cooperate. He's Lutheran, so Oxenstierna didn't want to piss him off."

"I remember that stuff. Schlitz beer. One thing about up-time that no one will miss. Horse's piss."

In Grantville, during the first week in October, Ed Piazza, while digging through the latest stack of usually worthwhile memoranda churned out by Wes Jenkins, found the three paragraphs that specifically addressed the production of scurrilous propaganda pamphlets by means of inexpensive down-time manufactured duplicating machines, yanked the page to the top, and radioed the essential data to Francisco Nasi in Magdeburg.

Fulda, November 1633

"So," Wes Jenkins announced, "it is now official. We are the United States of Europe—the USE—rather than the CPE. Mike Stearns is prime minister of the new nation—it's going to have a British-style parliamentary system rather than being modeled on the up-time USA. Ed Piazza's the president of the NUS now, but it's only a state—province, rather—in the new country."

It took the rest of the staff meeting to digest this information.

"Hey, Orville," Wes said on the way out, "who the hell is Brillo?"

"You know, the cartoons. The stories. Contrary down-time ram. Some of them were published in the *Grantville Times*. Why?"

"Steve Salatto wants to know how he connects to the peasant revolt."

Fred Pence frowned. "What peasant revolt? I'm out in the precincts every week and I haven't heard anything about a peasant revolt."

"It hasn't happened yet," Orville said. "It may happen in Würzburg and Bamberg."

"I'll tell Steve that I never heard of the stupid ram." Wes paused. "Why are they having a peasant revolt?"

"I dunno."

Roy Copenhaver wandered into the "Hearts and Minds" office. "Orville?"

"Yeah?"

"Who's actually running these estates that the NUS confiscated from the Abbey of Fulda?"

"They aren't like plantations with overseers and things. Mostly, after we abolished the stuff connected with serfdom, we've just let the farmers get on with it. I guess the village councils are running them."

"Who's collecting the rents and taxes and stuff?"

"We're collecting the taxes, using the district administrators, the *Amtmaenner*. As for the rents and dues, the real estate stuff, ask Harlan or Andrea. That's their department. All I can tell you is that we haven't had any major complaints from the granges on my watch."

"Andrea, who's doing the actual collection of revenues from the estates the government holds?"

Roy looked around. Andrea's little domain was buzzing, with a half dozen clerks clustered around ledgers and box files. Harlan had complained a lot about the cost of reconstituting the records. It was way over budget. She had looked at him and answered, "Well, if the original estimates were realistic, nobody would ever authorize starting *any* project at all. You have to break it to them gradually."

The clerks were jabbering away in the standard means of communication, which was German with a bunch of English terms thrown in. Terms like "paper trail" and all sorts of acronyms. The up-timers did the same thing when they spoke English. There might have been English words for technical terms like *landsässig* and *Stift* that von Boyneburg had taught them, but it was certain that not a single one of the Grantvillers in Fulda knew what they were. Anyway, mostly, except when the Grantvillers were by themselves, they all spoke German. Or Gerglish. Or Amideutsch.

Andrea was wearing the down-time full skirts that went right to the floor. She said they were warmer. The one she had on today was a sort of dull gold color, like the shade that used to be in the crayon boxes. She was also wearing a gray knit sweat shirt with a hood and a wool up-time ladies' suit jacket. It was pink. Because she spent her days with pens, pencils, and dusty ledgers, she had added, in this world without dry cleaning, a set of down-time removable linen cuffs to keep the pink wool clean at the wrists. Roy couldn't have described this ensemble to his wife Jen in any detail if she had asked. He could and did stand there hoping, inarticulately but profoundly, that the ensemble did not represent the wave of the future as far as fashion was concerned.

Andrea shook her head. "Ask Harlan. We do the titles, not the collections. This office just figures out *who* owes us and sometimes how much. Not to mention how far the payments are in arrears."

❖   ❖   ❖

"You don't mean it," Roy said.

"Well, it's not as if I have a budget for a property management staff," Harlan protested. "It was the only thing I could think of that made sense. So I contracted it out."

"The abbot's collecting them?"

"Straight percentage."

"Is he scamming? Skimming? Doing any of the other stuff with which West Virginia state employees are so familiar?"

"I don't think so, but how the h . . . heck should I know. It's not as if I have a staff of auditors at my disposal."

"Wes is going to have a cow."

A Bunch of Damned Anarchists

Fulda, December 1633

"I tell you," Wes proclaimed, "these imperial knights are a bunch of damned anarchists. I've never seen anything like it. Each and every one of them thinks that he's a little universe all to himself and not bound by anything that anyone else decides. Certainly not by a majority vote. Not even by a majority vote of their own organization that they set up themselves and voluntarily joined."

"That is," Clara said, "their definition of liberty, after all. That no one else can tell you what to do. Or, for the *Reichsritter*, liberties. Not to be subject to someone else. To determine one's own destiny freely."

"What have they done now to set you off?" Fred asked.

"I was over at the Buchen Quarter meeting. They're still trying to decide what they want to do about the election next spring. Some of them, like Ilten, are willing to take part in it. He was actually radical enough to say that he would accept a majority vote. Some of them, von der Tann right at the head of them, don't want anything to do with it. The Till von Berlepsch guy got up and talked for a good hour about how they defied the abbot back in 1576 and his ancestor was involved. Riedesel, over on the western border—he has lands at Eisenbach and Lauterbach—won't have a thing to do with anything that might put him under Fulda. His family has been fighting the abbots for centuries, it sounds like. Fighting as in armies and such. When his ancestor introduced the Reformation, it just gave them one more thing to fight about."

"It's not as if they ought to be worried that the NUS administration is going to try to make them Catholic again, just because we're working with the abbot on some stuff. Haven't we managed to make that clear?" Fred's frustration was plain in his voice.

Urban von Boyneburg, who was still in Fulda keeping an eye out for any possible advantages that might accrue to the landgrave of Hesse-Kassel, started another mini-lecture. "It's clear to them that *you* won't. And that for as long as you are around, Schweinsberg won't. But even though they're anteing up a lot of money to Gustavus Adolphus, they're trying to hedge their bets in case he doesn't win the war—keeping a weather eye out on what the imperials and the Leaguists are doing and the possibility that this abbot could be tossed out and replaced. It's not as if there's no precedent, since they tossed one out themselves, back in grandpa's day. There are several of them who think that if there's another tilt and the emperor comes out on top, they could plead 'coercion' for making the tribute payments to Gustavus Adolphus and get off lightly, but not for formally voting themselves into the USE and State of Thuringia. Or even for letting themselves be voted in."

"So what did they do, finally?" Fred asked Wes.

"Tabled it and adjourned until after New Year's."

Fulda, January 1634

"Great party," Fred said. "Post-Christmas, pre-New-Year, whatever you want to call it. I'm really glad that Kortney and Jared could come over to Fulda for the holidays. It was nice of the nursing school to let her take a whole month off from her classes."

"Well, they're calling it an internship and they got an exchange," Andrea answered. "She's substituting here for Gus Szymanski so he and Theresa could go home and spend Christmas with his sister Garnet. She's had a lonely life. Gus will be talking to the EMT students about his experiences during a year of actual field practice."

"True. Kortney was up before I was this morning, heading out to the barracks to check on people."

"Where's Jared?"

"Clara took him with her over to the abbey. One of the novices is going to show him around, and he'll write a report for having done a field trip, since he's missing a couple of weeks of school."

"Did you watch Wes dancing with Clara?"

Fred grinned. "Cheek and cheek and all that, for all that they are still officially on 'last name' terms. They had so much trouble prying their hands apart that I suspected Jeffie Garand of daubing their palms with super glue at first. Do you suppose Wes thinks that nobody has noticed that he is the only one of us who *doesn't* call her by her first name. We ribbed him about it. He says that he's 'way too old' for her to be interested in him."

"Well," Andrea said. "*I* had fun at the party. Wes danced with Clara. Johnny danced with Antonia. Jeffie danced with Gertrud. You danced with Kortney. And *I* got to dance with all the other guys. I was the belle of the ball. Too bad it didn't happen forty years ago, when it would have been more exciting."

"Yeah." Fred got up. "Better get to work, I guess. It's too bad that Eden and Jen couldn't come for the holidays too, but at least Harlan and Roy get to go over to Grantville occasionally to deal with the budget people."

"That fruit candy was good. Nice change from the usual stuff," Harlan said.

"Where did it come from?"

"Andrea's lawyer ordered it from Frankfurt. He knows someone down there who imports it. The fruit is called currants."

"Wes didn't eat much."

"He was too busy dancing with Clara."

"Would you call that dancing?"

"Wes is like me." Harlan grinned. "Methodists of the generation who still suspect that dancing is sinful, but think that God won't really be offended if you just get out on the floor and walk around, without actually performing a dance step. And ignore the music. If you have no rhythm at all, you're practically not dancing."

"Clara looked good at the party," Roy said. "She dresses a lot sharper than Andrea."

Fred grinned. "According to Kortney, her mom doesn't have any fashion sense at all."

"That," Roy said, "is really a relief to hear."

"How long do you suppose it has been since Wes asked a girl for a date?" Derek asked.

"He started going steady with Lena in high school," Harlan answered. "And he's what? Fifty, maybe? Fifty-two? Enough older than me that we were never in school together."

"Do you think," Andrea asked, "that Wes would be 'way too old for you' to marry?"

Clara looked at her. "If Caspar were still alive, he would be several years older than Mr. Jenkins. Plus, he would be much sicker."

Andrea raised her eyebrows.

Clara shrugged. "Caspar was always having a physician in to bleed him or going to the apothecary for a dose of medicine. If a disease existed that was not fatal, Caspar had it. At least, he thought that he had it. After thirteen years of that, I was really rather surprised when he actually died. It was his mother's fault, I think. He was her only child who lived and she was always afraid that he would die." Her eyes twinkled. "I am pretty sure that Mr. Jenkins is feeling quite healthy. He never takes time off work to be sick."

Her face became more serious. "I wish, though,

that he was not always so angry. Not at people. To us, who work for him, he is kind. For all of the people in Fulda, he is anxious. Concerned. But angry at the world. At the things that happen."

"Wes didn't want this job. Ed Piazza twisted his arm to get him to take it. Grantville doesn't have that many people with degrees in public administration. I sat in on some of their arguments, before we came over here. Wes pointed out that he didn't handle this kind of thing. He was a manager, but he was deputy director of the Marion County parks department. The worst threats he faced on the average day were cracks in the asphalt on tennis courts or vandalism to the catchers' cages on the baseball diamonds. Anything worse than that, he called the sheriff's department and let them take care of it. He had a staff that worried about scheduling conflicts when more than one family reunion wanted to use the same shelter on a Sunday afternoon."

"But he does it wonderfully. This job. I admire him so very much."

"But he thinks that he's a fake, Clara. Every morning he gets up thinking that this will be the day that some Leaguist with a lot more regiments than he has figures out that he's just blowing smoke and moves into the spot on the map that he's responsible for, slaughtering and raping his way across it. That's why he's so uptight about everything. Because it's his duty to protect it now, and he's not at all sure that he can."

"Perhaps he can't. But he tries his best, every single day." Clara crossed her arms across her chest, shivering a little, as if she were cold. "That's one of the reasons that I certainly would not object . . . But he should not marry me, you know, because I am barren. He has daughters, but if he marries again, he should choose a woman who can give him sons."

"What's the other reason you would not object?" Andrea was genuinely curious.

"Oh, there are many. He has a good job, his social position is suitable, my family would not protest, all of those. But the main one . . ." Clara winked. "When I dance with him, I do not think that he is 'way too old' at all."

Andrea looked down at her daughter from her perch on the desk. "Why do you suppose?"

Kortney shrugged. "It doesn't make sense. It just is. Line up a couple of hundred men and let a woman take a look at them. In front of a hundred ninety-nine, every internal organ from her eardrums to her kidneys will get together and announce, 'I would rather kiss a toad.' Perfectly nice, reasonably good-looking, reasonably sober, reasonably hard-working guys, a lot of them. Not losers. No obvious way to tell them apart. Then there's the one for whom the same organs all stand up and shout 'Boing.'"

"Maybe it's an anti-promiscuity gene," Andrea said. "But I know what you mean. It's probably the reason that the ladies who eat lunch at Cora's back in Grantville repeat the sentence 'I just can't tell what she sees in him' as often as they do. Bunch of gossips."

"Well, that's true. Because if you take the hundred ninety-nine leftovers and let another gal look them over, she'll react to one that the first one ignored completely. Some girls miss out on it, of course. They're mostly the ones that we keep seeing at the clinic, over and over."

"Clara's never said a word against her husband. But you pick up things, rooming together as long as we have now. To use your word, I have a suspicion that he was a platter of deep-fried toad, served up by her family, and she just made the best of it. So she hasn't had much experience with these kinds of feelings. And, of course, she's handicapped by wanting what she thinks is best for Wes instead of just wanting what she wants."

"Which is Wes." Kortney giggled.

"And even though he was obviously going 'wow' the first time he saw Clara, somewhere deep in his heart, Wes thinks that he's still married to Lena. And he's *such* an upright citizen."

"And you say the ladies at Cora's are gossips, Mom. We aren't?"

"Well, not malicious. Just trying to figure out a way to dig them out of this impasse."

Kortney frowned. "Did Clara ever have a gyne exam? That is, did the doctors or midwives or whatever have any idea why she never got pregnant?"

"You could ask her, I guess." Andrea folded her arms and stuck her chilly fingers up her sleeves. "That is, if you have the nerve."

"That's one thing you learn in nursing school, Mom. Not to be afraid to ask embarrassing questions. They really ought to make it a prerequisite for being admitted."

"Well, I don't think that she will be embarrassed. That's one thing that I've been learning this year. I guess I just assumed that since back in Victorian times, people were more prudish than we are, then a couple hundred years before, they would be even more prudish. It doesn't work that way. People in the seventeenth century haven't gotten to Victorianism at all yet. Honest to God, some of the things that Clara says just make me blush."

"Well," Kortney said, washing her hands, "I can't tell on the basis of a regular gyne exam that there's any reason at all why you didn't have children. All your organs are there, in the right place, healthy, no polyps, no obvious endometriosis, none of the stuff that we look for first. Maybe it was your husband's problem."

She launched into the next set of embarrassing questions.

"You've got to be kidding. On the *average*?" Kortney snorted her coffee. "Every three *months*?"

"Well, the first five years that we were married." Clara said. "After that, less often. You understand that Caspar was afraid that spilling his seed too often would weaken his vital humors and they were not strong to begin with. I know that one physician did tell him that it would improve his likelihood of begetting heirs if he increased the frequency to what was recommended in the Old Testament, but he changed doctors."

"I didn't even know that the Old Testament recommended anything."

"Twice a week, except during a woman's courses. At least, that was what the physician told us. Although he added that he himself, on the basis of experience, thought three times in the week was preferable for couples who desired offspring. Perhaps in these latter days men's vital forces are weaker than they were in biblical times. After all," she said seriously, "the Old Testament patriarchs lived much longer, too. It was not until much later that things became worse, so that today 'our years are seventy, or eighty if we have the strength.'"

Buchen Quarter, January 1634

"It's an interesting concept," Ruprecht von Ilten looked at the other imperial knights of the Fulda region. Unfortunately, the questions that they had tabled before Christmas could not remain tabled indefinitely, so they were having another meeting.

"Why do we all have copies of the constitution of the New United States?" Johann von der Tann was stomping around the room.

"Because Herr Wesley Jenkins sent them to us, to read before he makes his presentation."

"Are you trying to be deliberately naive, von Ilten?"

"Apparently, in the spring of 1632, when its representatives met with the king of Sweden, the ambassadress, the Abrabanel woman, made this point." Claus von Berlepsch was representing his brother.

"Which point?" Eberhard von Buchenau asked.

"That the purpose of the constitution was not to take away rights, but to establish them."

"Her name is Rebecca, the Abrabanel woman. Rebecca the deceiver, who misled Isaac into granting the blessing to the wrong son. They can't expect us to believe this," von der Tann protested.

"It's an interesting idea. If, of course, it is true." Von Ilten rather hoped that it was true.

"I'm not ready to commit myself to anything," von der Tann said.

Von Buchenau echoed him. "None of us are."

❖   ❖   ❖

"This is quite true," Wes Jenkins said. "Under the constitution of the New United States, there are no 'subjects.' Only 'citizens.' Because we know that you have been seriously concerned that your status under the law might be diminished by such developments as the landgrave of Hesse's efforts to reduce you to the status of *Landsassen* within *Stift* Fulda, several members of the administration have cooperated to produce this special presentation. I assure you that we are sincerely grateful that the imperial knights of the Buchen Quarter are devoting so much of their valuable time to considering our modest efforts."

Wes continued his introductory remarks, thinking to himself, "drone on, Mr. Jenkins, drone on" to Woody Guthrie's tune. He loathed these apparently endless speeches, but had resigned himself to the fact that he now lived in a world in which brevity was equated to rudeness on formal occasions. At least he didn't have to write them. Andrea's lawyer, upon request, had dredged up a nephew who was willing to write his speeches, among such other duties as might from time to time be assigned.

"How could it possibly work? That we would be incorporated within this new state—the State of Thuringia—if this election decides that Franconia will join it, but not be mediatized?"

"The idea is really strange. But it seems to be true. I certainly was able to buy copies of the constitution of the original 'United States'—the one they came from—with no problem at all. Just ordered them from Frankfurt, the way I would any other book," von Ilten said.

"How did it work?" Von Buchenau looked at his colleague. Von Ilten had a suspiciously scholarly bent, but on the other hand, it saved his friends a lot of work, because he read the books and explained things to the rest of them.

"Well, the national government was made up of a group of 'states' just as the Holy Roman Empire is constituted from the different states of the Germanies. And Bohemia, of course. But for the 'citizens' within each state—and they are very oddly named, I must say, I cannot pronounce some of these at all—the 'state' did not stand between them and the 'country.' They were directly citizens of the 'country' as well and had a vote in choosing delegates to the 'senate' and 'house of representatives' just as the members of the Bench of Imperial Knights chooses who will exercise their vote in the *Reichstag*. At least, if I understand it properly."

"This means that if we agreed to be incorporated into this State of Thuringia, we would still vote directly for our representative in the USE parliament, rather than being mediatized under the president of the state?"

"Yes, as I understand it. And, of course, we would also have a vote in choosing the president of the state of Thuringia as well."

"How does that work?"

"Hmm," Wes Jenkins said. "Around here, when someone says, 'A man's home is his castle,' I guess he really means it. This hall looks bigger every time I see it." He was standing with his back to the fireplace. Wearing an overcoat.

"It wasn't that hard to design the presentation," Clara said. Her breath made little patterns of steam in the air. She was wrapped up in three shawls.

The rest of the delegation now appreciated her insistence on bringing along three folding screens to this meeting. When they were set up in a semi-circle around the fireplace, they not only cut down significantly on the drafts but also to some extent reflected the heat from the fire back on the group. Otherwise, it would have dissipated into the cavernous hall.

Andrea shivered. "Do you suppose that reasonable nobles like Count Ludwig Guenther deliberately build themselves modern houses? Or is it living in freezing *Burgs* like this one that makes the unreasonable nobles the way they are?"

After their first three days as guests of von Buchenau, they had all come to appreciate that one of the main advances in modern architecture—seventeenth-century modern German architecture—was the ceiling. In this old fashioned great hall, what little warmth the fireplaces produced just floated up and up and up until it went out an unglazed window. When they got back to Fulda, they would have to say something nice to the abbey's one-time construction foreman, now the NUS administration's construction foreman, about the ceilings in the administration building.

"Actually, I thought it went pretty well, this time," Wes said. "Some of them don't buy into it at all, of course. Von Schlitz is still in hiding somewhere and I'm sure that several of the others share his opinions. And some of the ones who were considering it at the meeting will relapse into their old ways of thinking before the election."

Clara got up and moved over toward the fireplace. "Of course, I left something out."

"Left something out?"

"As we have presented it to the knights, it is very strong in showing that they will become direct citizens of the United States of Europe if they accept the constitution of the New United States. Well, now, the State of Thuringia. It will be the same constitution, with just a few name changes."

"So?"

"Ah. Haven't you noticed? I left out entirely that all of the people who are now *their* subjects will also become direct citizens of the United States of Europe, in all ways equal to them, and will have just as much right to vote for their representatives in congress and parliament and the president of the State of Thuringia as they do."

Wes stared at her. Now that he thought about it . . .

"Really, I just thought it was prudent to omit it." She looked at the rest of the delegation with an innocent expression on her face. "In some ways, it is very convenient that this is such an isolated backwater that the more extreme propaganda of the Committees of Correspondence has been slow to reach it. Possibly even von Ilten does not realize that if the election succeeds and Franconia becomes part of the State of Thuringia, all the little local legal jurisdictions will be abolished. It is in a subordinate clause, after all, in a subparagraph."

"Clara," Fred Pence started.

"If they aren't bright enough to figure out for

themselves that although they will not be mediatized, neither will they any longer mediatize their tenants, was it our duty to stir up trouble by mentioning the matter?"

Fulda, February 1634

"It's a pretty complicated ballot," Fred pointed out. "It has a lot of 'if, then' items on it."

"What do you mean?" Roy asked.

"'If' the person votes in favor of incorporation into the State of Thuringia-Franconia, 'then' there's a question about whether it will all be one county, Fulda and all the imperial knights together, or whether each little imperial knighthood will be its own county. Or county-equivalent, depending on what they decide to call it. Then a question for choosing the name. Of course, someone who votes against incorporation can still vote about the name, but it's hard to see why he'd want to. Or she. I've tried to make it as clear as possible. Do you think we ought to offer some kind of voter assistance, Orville?"

"We can't very well put someone in every single precinct to answer the voters' questions. We just don't have enough people."

"I've trained as many volunteers as I can, working from the voter registration lists. Picking a couple of people out of each precinct. It's been sort of trickle-down, but I've done it. It's not going to be perfect. Nothing is. But I've sent stuff with the directions out to the provosts and the *Amtmaenner* and the village mayors. They've been, or most of them have been, holding meetings to explain it to everyone. At least, I hope they have. In most cases, it's probably a bunch of guys sitting around in the village tavern and having a beer. If that. And the League of Women Voters has helped."

"What League of Women Voters? Since when do we have a League of Women Voters?" Wes Jenkins was frowning.

"The one in Barracktown," Derek answered. "The LDS in Grantville has kept sending them stuff, ever since Willard Thornton went through, way back when. You know Liz Carstairs, Wes—Howard's wife, works for Mike Stearns?"

"Sure."

"Well, she's one of them, you know. Willard's sister. She sent a lot of League of Women Voters stuff along with the LDS Ladies Relief Society stuff. So they organized one. That was, oh, months ago. I'm not sure it's real clear in their minds about which is which, but they have one."

Andrea clapped her hands. "That's great. What about poll watchers, Fred?"

"Derek is splitting up the soldiers from Fulda Barracks into small groups and sending a detachment to watch the polls in each of the *Reichsritterschaften*."

"Intimidation?" Harlan asked. "We don't want that."

"Anti-intimidation," Fred answered. "If they're not there, several of the knights will be standing around with their own guards 'guiding' the voters."

"What about the *Stift* territories proper?"

"We'll just have to spread ourselves pretty thin. Derek has arranged with Captain Wiegand for the members of the Fulda city militia to vote first thing in the morning and then be available to ride circuit with us, from one polling place to another."

"That reminds me," Andrea said. "Derek, did you ever get a school started out at Barracktown this winter?"

"Uh, yeah. Well, we don't have a building, but we have a teacher."

"Who?"

"Um, your lawyer's sister-in-law's nephew who needed to find a job to tide him over after the University of Tuebingen closed down because Horn and Bernhard have been marching all over the place down there in Swabia. He's only nineteen, but he works cheap, which is lucky. I wasn't authorized to hire a teacher, so I recruited him as a private, with a promise that I'd discharge him when the university opens up again. In writing. Notarized. He has a copy. His name's Biehr."

"Beer?"

"Yes, Biehr. The sister-in-law's sister married a German."

"Andrea, isn't your lawyer German?" Roy Copenhaver asked. "If not, why not? I never can remember his name."

"If there's no building . . ." Andrea persisted.

"In the loft of Sergeant Hartke's house. His wife fixed it up, and we're paying them some rent."

Harlan frowned. "I don't remember that item in the budget."

"That's because the budget didn't have an item for renting space for a base school."

"Where's it coming from?"

"Umm."

"Textbooks? Supplies?" Harlan was adding up sums on his notepad.

"We didn't have any to start with. But Howard Carstairs shipped over a whole set of German translations of LDS Sunday School materials."

"Err, Derek . . ." Roy frowned. "Separation of church and state, remember."

"It was those books or no books. Which choice do you like better? They're perfectly all right for learning ah, bay, tsay, day, ay, eff, gay." Derek whistled the German alphabet to the tune of "Twinkle, Twinkle, Little Star." "Remember the budget and keep it holy. Anyway, Mary Kat says that she thinks it will get by."

Everybody grinned. Two weeks before, last man on the military rotation he had set up after Joel Matowski arrived, Derek had sneaked back to Grantville and, after a long courtship conducted almost entirely by letter, married Mary Kathryn Riddle. Since she was the daughter of the chief justice, first of the NUS and then of the newly-born State of Thuringia, not to mention a legal eagle herself, it probably would get by. This time.

"Any chance of more leave coming up?" Derek asked hopefully.

"For you?" Wes put a doleful expression on his face and shook his head.

"Well, Dave Frost married Mackenzie Ellis when he was back home in January, too. Lawson got married last November. Devoted new husbands and all that, you know." Dave and Lawson were two of Derek's four "kids," all of whom had done a lot of growing up. "Maybe if the others got back a little more often, they could get married, too."

"Isn't Jeffie going to marry Gertrud Hartke?"

Derek frowned. "He'd better."

"Where *is* the rent coming from?" Harlan was not easily diverted.

"The lawyer's relative is from Tuebingen?" Wes asked, thinking back to several sentences earlier. "That's Württemberg. I thought that I told you to hire a local lawyer, Andrea."

"Maybe the boy was just going to the university there. Etienne was living in Frankfurt as a refugee when we hired him. That's pretty close. And he was low bidder."

"Bidder?"

"There's no authorized FTE for a lawyer in my department. I had Harlan put out a RFP for a contractor."

"Life is so full of interesting surprises."

"Etienne says that he needs either another lawyer or two more clerks to handle the work load. Or another lawyer and two more clerks."

Harlan was still adding sums. "Derek, where are you getting the rent for the school loft?"

"Ah. When we built the barracks, some dope put in an item for landscaping. It seemed sort of a pity to let it go to waste. And we've put some potted plants in the school room. Didn't spend any money on them—the moms just cobbled together some pots from scrap wood, filled them with dirt, and dug up a few bushes. I'm hoping it's enough to get us in under the wire if auditors show up."

"Are we ready to certify the results?"

"Yes," Fred Pence said.

"First, in regard to the question of incorporation into the State of Thuringia."

The statistics were tedious, but the question passed.

Eleven of the territories of imperial knights voted to join both the State of Thuringia and the new consolidated subordinate administrative polity (aka SAP, which made Arnold Bellamy very unhappy). Seven voted to join the State of Thuringia but be subordinate administrative polities of their own and keep calling themselves *Reichsritterschaften*. Schlitz voted "the hell with it and a pox on you and both your political parties." Each of the seven separate *Reichsritterschaften* only had a few hundred residents apiece, but that was the will of the people.

Even the dissenting vote in Schlitz was technically the will of the people, though Fred Pence suspected that Karl von Schlitz's two oldest sons had made it fairly plain to the people what their will had better be. That pair would have done well in Chicago under Capone, except that the Mafia probably didn't take Lutherans.

The citizens of the new consolidated SAP voted to distinguish their secular government from that of the Abbey of Fulda. The name of the new polity would be Buchenland (Latin version Buchonia). This gesture on the part of the majority, residents of the former *Stift*, to the minority, residents of Buchen Quarter, was widely recognized as generous.

In a subsidiary question, the citizens of the new polity voted to establish an *Ausschuss* or *Conventus* whose duty would be to design an emblem and coat of arms for the new county.

Applause followed the formal certification.

So did a petition from several imperial knights of the Buchen Quarter, led by Friedrich von der Tann, who alleged that the soldiers of the Fulda Barracks Regiment had, in the course of carrying out their electoral duties, committed attacks, plundering, unjustified arrests, libels and slanders upon the honor of citizens, persecutions, demeaning statements, alienation of assets, and a variety of other crimes and delicts.

Wes told him to give it to the lawyers.

The following day, Derek Utt broke the news that he would now be conducting military musters throughout Buchenland, to establish a county-wide militia.

The imperial knights whose *Ritterschaften* had voted themselves into it discovered that they would no longer have their own private militias.

The rest of the imperial knights said, "I told you so. Don't say that I didn't warn you. Big government. Mediatization."

Captain Wiegand said that the Fulda city militia would be happy to provide training to the new local units.

Von Buchenau refused to allow the muster on his estates, saying that the ballot had not contained any provisions about military musters. Derek, with Wes's backing, arrested him.

His lawyer sent a petition to parliament and the emperor of the United States of Europe, pointing out that he had been paying a tax of thirteen *Thaler* per month to support the Protestant cause, contingent upon the agreement of the envoys of the king of Sweden that they would recognize the immediacy of his territory. He protested that one aspect of being independent was that a ruler could have his own army.

The effort that the von Buchenau militia made to spring him out of jail made it pretty clear that the knightly troops really could use the training that Captain Wiegand had offered, not to mention demonstrating that their equipment was more than a little obsolete.

Wes let the von Buchenau militia out on parole, since they were, when not being militia, the farmers who leased land from the knight and spring planting season was coming up.

After von Buchenau agreed to sign an *Urfehde*, Wes let him out on parole, too.

Schweinsberg told him that this was a really bad idea, and would be interpreted as a sign of weakness rather than as a sign of a generous spirit.

Wes said that the guy was just a nuisance.

Clara Bachmeierin agreed with the abbot.

Salmuenster, Buchenland, March 1634

Joel Matowski looked at the residents of Salmuenster. Thirty-four families. According to the duplicate records that the local administrator had kept, there had been a couple of hundred houses in the town before the war started. He was here to take their oaths of allegiance to the new constitution and run a military muster while he was about it. Salmuenster was about as far from Fulda as you could get and still be a part of the *Stift*—well, part of Buchenland.

The man raising all the objections was named Hans von Hutten.

He was, he said, an imperial knight.

He was, he said, a Franconian imperial knight

proper and was not and had never been a member of the Buchen Quarter, so owed no obligation to any decisions that it might have taken.

"If you aren't," Joel asked, "then why are you here today?"

The answer, delivered by a lawyer carrying several boxes full of paper, involved a series of transactions by which the abbey of Fulda had pawned its outlying possessions in the Kinzig river valley to the von Hutten family, redeemed them, pawned them again, split them, redeemed them, and the like, for the past two and a half centuries.

Von Hutten's position was that he held a currently valid *Pfandschaft* arrangement with the Abbey of Fulda. If the New United States, and then the State of Thuringia-Franconia, had possession of the abbey's former estates, then by extension he held a currently valid *Pfandschaft* arrangement with it. The terms were that until such time as the governing entity, whoever it might be, paid him back the capital sum that his great-grandfather had advanced to the abbot and chapter of Fulda, these lands were damned well his and these people were damned well his and the administration in Fulda had no authority to have conducted an election here by which they illegally voted themselves into Buchenland.

Von Hutten added that he, personally, as a resident of the former prince-diocese of Würzburg, had voted against incorporation, and that even though the majority of the people in Würzburg voted in favor of it, he did not accept that a majority vote was binding upon him. In his view, nothing to which he personally did not agree was binding upon him, because if he accepted the decisions of others it would restrict his liberty.

"Look, man," Joel protested, as he experienced a political epiphany vaguely related to his half-forgotten memories of Ms. Mailey's explanation of how representative government worked, "that's no way to run a railroad."

Von Hutten announced that he was appealing the election results to the emperor, to the imperial cameral court, to the other emperor, to the imperial supreme court, and to anyone else he could think of. He proposed to demand an imperial commission to investigate.

When Joel got back to Fulda, he reported that just because the election went well, this whole thing was not yet a done deal, by any means.

Andrea's lawyer pointed out that all those appeals would be very expensive, so that unless von Hutten had more money than he appeared to, or was calling on outside resources, his complaints would make haste very slowly.

The rest of the meeting was devoted to speculation on possible sources of outside funding.

Wes told Joel to write up a report. They would send it down to Steve Salatto. First to let Steve know that von Hutten was making a nuisance of himself, since he properly belonged to Würzburg. Second to ask for money to buy the pawned districts back from von Hutten, so they could go ahead and incorporate them into the administrative system they were setting up for Buchenland.

Not that Steve would be able to come up with that much money before the next fiscal year, at the earliest.

Who Will Rid Me?

Bonn, Archdiocese of Cologne, March 1634

Walter Butler was leaving it to his associates to work out the details. Overall, he thought, he was in a pretty good position for a Catholic Irishman and professional military enterpriser. Or, if one wished to be crude, a colonel of a mercenary regiment. At least, compared to the position he would have been in if Wallenstein had caught him, once the bastard found out that Butler had been one of the point men for Ferdinand II's generals in organizing his assassination in that other world.

Butler had left Bohemia a year before, hightailing it through Tyrol and the Habsburg lands in Swabia, bringing Dennis MacDonald, Robert Geraldin, and Walter Deveroux with him. While passing through that heavily Leaguist territory, with a decent subsidy that Maximilian of Bavaria had arranged, they had recruited. With four regiments of dragoons, staffed almost to paper strength and well equipped, they had managed to negotiate an advantageous arrangement with the archbishop of Cologne.

Whose confessor was now sitting in the room with them. Along with Franz von Hatzfeldt, the bishop of Würzburg who had been driven from his lands by the Swedes. And von Hoheneck, one of the provosts of the abbey of Fulda. Both Würzburg and Fulda were now run by the "up-timers." That was, Butler presumed, why the others wanted to talk to them.

Since the others had initiated the contact, that meant that Butler and his colleagues had something they needed. Or, at least, that they wanted. Which meant that his negotiating position was good.

At the moment, Deveroux was telling the archbishop's confessor that he was out of his mind. Not a prudent thing to say, but true. Given the layout of the military map right now, there was no way they could take troops into Fulda. Not through Hesse. Not through Mainz and Frankfurt. Not through Württemberg and Franconia. Not. It was too far inside the borders of the USE. Unless the coming summer's campaign changed the way that the Swede's troops were deployed, a raiding party could only figure on being chewed up. No profit. No plunder. Where was the gain in that?

Surprisingly, the bishop of Würzburg was backing Deveroux up. "He's right, you know. It's not that easy to infiltrate any sizable group of men deep into Franconia. Dingolshausen was a disaster. Melchior's men got in, but not a dozen of the original two hundred got out again. Not to mention that it's caused a public relations problem."

Hoheneck interrupted. "They don't have to take men in."

What did he mean by that?

"If they go in themselves," Hoheneck waved in the direction of the four Irishmen, "there can be troops waiting for them. I have full assurances that not all of the imperial knights of the Buchen Quarter were satisfied with the outcome of last month's election. Particularly not now that they realize that although they have not lost their immediacy legally, every damned peasant on their estates has gained the same rights. There hasn't been time for the up-timers to complete the reorganization. The four of them can go in. It's easy for four men. Get a couple of companies together from von Berlepsch, from von der Tann. Von Schlitz will do the organization. I know where he's gone into hiding. Note that he has maintained sufficient influence over his subjects that they voted not to join the State of Thuringia. He'll have them ready for you when you get there."

Butler had intended to keep quiet, but he couldn't.

"What happens to our regiments while we're gone?"

The Capuchin cleared his throat. "If you leave them here, under the command of your lieutenant colonels, the archbishop is willing to continue paying you at the current rate. Plus the additional compensation for the work in Fulda, of course."

"Is there any hope that the imperial knights might let you take their men with you on the way out? It would be really nice," Hatzfeldt said wistfully, "to wreak a little destruction on the Hessians."

"Not a bit. If they strip themselves, the SoTF will just come in with troops from Thuringia and wipe them out."

"Even if they keep their couple hundred troops, the SoTF will just come in with troops from Thuringia and wipe them out."

"Not the same kind of situation as Jena or Badenburg or the Crapper. Not even the same as the Wartburg. A batch of different opponents, up in hilly country, who know the terrain. Even with just a couple of hundred men . . ."

"A couple of hundred men if they were decently equipped. But without . . ."

The archbishop's confessor got up from his chair. "Let me know what you decide." He left the room.

The professionals reverted to shop talk.

"The main objective, then, is to abduct the abbot." Archbishop Ferdinand's confessor nodded his head firmly.

"Yes," Hatzfeldt said. "That has to be the first goal. Get hold of Schweinsberg and get him to Bonn." He waved at the four Irishmen. "Any one of you can do that. We don't care which one. Decide it among yourselves."

"Why us? In particular?" Deveroux asked.

Butler had wondered about that, too.

"Because you speak English," Hatzfeldt said. "Schweinsberg is not the only target. We wish to interview the NUS administrators, which will better be done there. Take Felix Gruyard with you—he's good at what he does. Smuggling out one man is a different matter from smuggling out a half-dozen. These up-timers have learned German, of course. The administrators in Fulda, I mean. But still, it is not their first language. If we want to get the maximum amount of information from them, in a short period of time, it will be much better to have interrogators who can question them in their own language. So split up. One of you to each of the targets. Then, while you are doing that, we hope very much that by holding them the imperial knights will disrupt the administrative system of all of Franconia. The others, in Würzburg and Bamberg, will send their forces toward Fulda. Then, if Melchoir—my brother—can send a force through Saxony and Bayreuth . . ."

"Will send their forces to Fulda?" Butler asked. "Or do you just *hope* that they will send them?"

"It's hard to understand the up-timers. But from all we can learn about them, they are very protective of their own people. It's a calculated risk, of course. But, then, life is a calculated risk."

"Meanwhile, what will you be doing with the abbot?"

"Once he is here, the archbishop and I can persuade him to stop cooperating with these abominable up-timers. Persuade him to stop collaborating with the Protestant Swede. Or, if it comes to that, depose him. The emperor and pope would have to agree to that to make it permanent, but if we keep him in prison here while the haggling is going on, it will have the same effect. The archbishop can appoint me as interim administrator."

Hoheneck cleared his throat.

"You were thinking of some other candidate for administrator?" the archbishop's confessor asked.

"I was just going to point out that any administrator should be appointed by the archbishop of Mainz rather than the archbishop of Cologne," Hoheneck said.

"Casimir Wambold von Umstaedt is a refugee in Cologne also," the Capuchin answered. "He will allow himself to be guided by Archbishop Ferdinand's wisdom, I am sure."

Hoheneck was not so sure of that. After all, the archbishop of Mainz was close to Friedrich von Spee, who had been in Grantville and was now in Magdeburg. Overall, the archbishop of Mainz was closer to the Jesuits than to the Capuchins.

As, in fact, were the abbots of Fulda.

While it appeared that Hatzfeldt might have quite

a lot in common with Echter. If the bishop of Würzburg was going to try to use this to pull Fulda under his authority and come out of it, once the imperials eventually won this war, with an expanded sphere of influence and Fulda nothing more than one mediatized monastery . . . what would be the point in becoming abbot of Fulda?

Privately, he was quite certain that Hatzfeldt was the wrong candidate for administrator.

Fulda, Buchenland, April 1634

"The 'Ram Rebellion' or 'Brillo Movement' does not appear to have spread significantly from Würzburg into Buchenland."

Wes finished up his monthly report.

He was profoundly glad that he had been able to write that last sentence.

Maybe there were some advantages to being in a spot that was such an economic backwater and political boondocks that nobody else cared about it. Not even revolutionaries.

Fulda, Buchenland, May 1634

"It's the surveyors," Orville Beattie said.

Roy Copenhaver turned a page in his notebook. "What surveyors?"

"The ones planning for pushing the railroad network out farther. It's a long way off, considering what a struggle it was to find supplies just for

Halle-Stassfurt-Magdeburg. Iron by itself . . . But they're doing more surveys this summer. Gustavus Adolphus wants to see a line head out from Erfurt-Eisenach to Frankfurt am Main and Mainz. Tie his administration together. So they're laying out a route along the Fulda Gap. The landgrave of Hesse-Kassel signed onto the project and approved having it come through his lands way last fall. Howard Carstairs had some old topo maps he had squirreled away—he served with Third Armored—so they're making pretty good time, in spite of the changes."

"Why does this lead to a peasant revolt?" Wes Jenkins frowned. Surveyors in the north didn't seem to connect with the stuff he had been getting from Steve Salatto to the south.

"The landgrave doesn't seem to have explained it all very well," Orville said. "Not surprising, since he's been out in the field managing armies for Gustavus Adolphus, his wife has been in Magdeburg politicking, he got his brother appointed Secretary of State so he's in Magdeburg too, and they seem to have left a vacuum into which the rumors could come flying. The district administrators can't explain anything to the farmers and village councils because they don't know anything much themselves."

"Anything specific about the rumors?" Roy asked.

Orville wrinkled his nose. "This is what I've gotten from the granges. The leaseholders, the people who actually farm the land, have gotten the impression that they're going to be thrown off with no compensation. Apparently a few of the surveyors made some rather loose statements about using the power of eminent domain to take the right-of-way if owners didn't sell voluntarily. 'Owners' brought to mind landlords. The farmers got the impression that any payments that come out of this will be going to businessmen, or charitable institutions, or nobles, who hold the *Lehen*. Not to the guys on the spot, who will be left holding the short end of the stick and trying to get the value of the broken leases back from the owners. Who most likely won't be interested in making payouts."

"So?" Andrea pulled her pencil out of her hair and started twirling it around with her fingers, like a cheerleader's baton.

"So they're having a peasant revolt. Meetings, gatherings, marches, protests, broadsides, poems, pamphlets, guns pointed at local administrators." Orville put a bright and cheerful expression on his face. "All the regular amenities, as I understand how these things go."

"Brillo?" Wes asked with some trepidation.

"Not in Hesse. His fame does not yet seem to have reached such exciting spots on the map as Friedlos and Schrecksbach. I sort of hate to tell you, though . . ."

"What, Orville?"

"We're seeing more and more of the ram stuff here in Fulda. In Buchenland, that is. Especially to the south where it borders on Würzburg. The 'Hearts and Minds' people are circulating through the whole area, trying to talk things down. The best argument we have right now is that the railroad isn't coming through Fulda anyway."

"Economically," Roy Copenhaver pointed out, "it would be a good thing if it did. Open up markets and the like. If they're running it through Hersfeld, that's still twenty miles of bad road from most of the farms in Buchenland."

"What do you need from us?" Wes asked.

"If all of you, at least as many as can be spared off other jobs, could start spending more time in the field, backing up our efforts, it would be a real help." This time the bright expression on Orville's face was more genuine.

Buchenland, June 1634

"Damn it, Derek!" Wes Jenkins was yelling again. "Your cursed Fulda Barracks Regiment is more trouble than it's worth."

"They are just trying to demonstrate their loyalty to the government."

"Threatening to defect to Hans von Hutten on the grounds that he will let them shoot peasants is not a really outstanding declaration of loyalty. In fact it sounds more like mutiny to me."

"They feel that by not suppressing the revolt, they are failing in their duty."

"They are just itching because they haven't shot or plundered anybody for a year and a half. Especially plundered."

"Garrison duty is always difficult."

"Well, make it plain to them that they can't shoot any of the farmers or citizens of Buchenland unless I give them permission. Peasant revolt or no peasant revolt. And tell them that there is no way that I'm going to turn them over to von Hutten so *he* can shoot our citizens. Or Würzburg's citizens, for that matter. Lock them in the barracks, if you have to."

"Set their wives to guard them," Clara Bachmeierin suggested.

Wes stared at her.

"They have houses now, in Barracktown. Cabins with wood floors, a lot of them. Some even have fireplaces with stone chimneys and hearths. Windows with shutters and oiled paper. Doors with latches. A school for their children. Sergeant Hartke's oldest boy turned out to be so smart that Andrea's lawyer gave him money to go to the Latin school that the Jesuits run here in town. He would rather send the boy to a Calvinist school, but there isn't any. Hardly any of them want to go back to tramping around after a regiment on the march."

Wes looked at Derek, raising his eyebrows.

"I can try it. I really don't want to use Wiegand's Fulda militia to guard them, unless I absolutely have to. If this blows over, they'll need to work together again."

"You really mean that?" Deveroux looked at Karl von Schlitz with disbelief. "They are not holed up behind Fulda's walls, huddling together in the administration building?"

The imperial knight was looking a little pale, having spent quite a lot of time recently living in a rather small pantry off the main kitchen of his great-uncle's long-ago mistress's miniature castle.

"My sons assure me that it is true. Because of the unrest, the administrators, almost all of them, and the abbot as well, are riding the length and breadth of this newly invented Buchenland, trying to make the peasants happy."

"Why should peasants be happy?" Robert Geraldin asked with honest bewilderment.

Dennis MacDonald glared at him. "They shouldn't,

of course. Their suffering in this life will be compensated in the next, like the beggar outside of the rich man's house."

"That," Deveroux said, "is beside the point. Do you have any way of getting their itineraries?"

"Yes. Fritz and Oswald can get them for you."

"Well, glory and hallelujah!"

"Not to mention," one of the von Schlitz sons said, "that they are very lightly guarded, if at all, only by members of the Fulda city militia, because their regiment tried to mutiny."

Deveroux jerked his head up.

"You mean this?"

The son—Friedrich, it was, Fritz von Schlitz—howled with laughter. "Because they won't let the soldiers shoot the peasants, would you believe it? So you will have a peasant revolt to blame any 'accidents' on and the Thuringian troops who pour into Fulda to avenge their administrators after you are long gone will be shooting their own innocent 'citizens.'"

Felix Gruyard smirked.

Walter Butler shook his head. It was enough to make a man believe in divine providence.

Bonn, Archdiocese of Cologne, July 1634

"The archbishop is not receiving callers this morning."

"But," the reporter said cheerfully, "I would like to obtain his comments upon the news that the pope has elevated the priest from Grantville to the dignity of cardinal of the Holy Roman Church and appointed him as cardinal-protector of the United States of Europe."

"Trust me," the doorman said, "you don't want to hear his comments."

"Oh," the reporter said, "but I do. Not to mention that I have a duty to my readers. What are the archbishop's comments?"

"No comment." The servant slammed the door.

Franz von Hatzfeldt looked rather anxiously at Johann Adolf von Hoheneck. "Is this appointment of a cardinal-protector for the USE something we should be taking into consideration in regard to Fulda?"

"There's nothing that we can do about it. It's too late to call the Irishmen and Gruyard back. We don't know exactly where they are. We have no way to communicate with them. And, in any case, we aren't paying them."

Schlitz, July 1634

"So I went into the town to get some news," Gruyard muttered. "I got it, didn't I? We can't sit walled up on top of this stupid hill forever. It isn't as if there's anyone in Fulda who might recognize me."

"It just goes to show," Karl von Schlitz orated, "that the demonic up-timers are in league with the Roman anti-Christ."

"Come down off it," Geraldin said. "Who do you think that you linked up with when you sent those feelers out to Hoheneck? Martin Luther?"

The two sons howled with laughter.

Gruyard smiled.

Walter Butler didn't think it was that funny.

Fulda, July 1634

"What do you suppose this means?" Johann Bernhard von Schweinsberg asked. "Will Gustavus Adolphus allow the archbishop of Mainz to come back to his see? How does it affect the status of the Mainz possessions around Erfurt that voted themselves into the State of Thuringia-Franconia? Will there be a new appointment to the see of Bamberg? How will it change the status of the bishop of Würzburg? Does it mean that Thuringia-Franconia will be granted its own bishop? If so . . . that would be wonderful."

"Why?" Harlan Stull asked.

"Well, there would be someone who could ordain priests. And confirm children. None of that has been done in the *Stift* for three years. Unless the suffragan down in Würzburg has done confirmations in some of the southern parishes that the diocese claims are under its jurisdiction."

"Why don't you ask him?"

"If I asked him, he could interpret it that I was asking him for favors. He could perhaps even interpret it to mean that I was tacitly acknowledging that the abbey of Fulda is under the ecclesiastical jurisdiction of Würzburg."

"Look," Harlan said. "You don't have the property any more. All you've got are a bunch of parishes with people in them. How about cutting out the turf wars?"

Schweinsberg looked at him wearily.

"Herr Stull, I have come to like and respect all of you. But in the course of the history of the church,

Grantville has been a factor for only a short, a very short, time. The abbey of Fulda has been here for eight hundred years. I hope that it will still be here in another eight hundred years, if the last judgment does not intervene. I cannot and will not unilaterally renounce its rights."

"The truth is, Schweinsberg," Wes Jenkins said, "that I quite honestly don't have the vaguest idea what this will really mean. I'll write to Ed Piazza. And I'll set up an appointment for you to meet with Henry Dreeson before he goes home. Once he gets here, that is."

"I took a bunch of newspapers out to the barracks," Derek Utt said. "It should give them something to talk about besides peasant revolts. Distract their minds, sort of. I'm having them practice their new anthem, too. Mary Kat's grandma picked it out. The kid teaching school in Sergeant Hartke's loft translated it into German poetry for me and he is assigning the parts. Biehr, his name is."

Dubious Saints

Fulda, August 1634

Andrea was feeling increasingly frazzled. She was the senior civilian administrator in Fulda. Someone else should have been back a couple of days ago. They couldn't all have been delayed. Or if they were, at least one of them should have sent in a message.

Pushing her bangs out of her face, she started out into the hall.

The land claims lawyer was just coming in, followed by his relatives, the school teacher and the speech writer. And by the little artist who lived in St. Severi church and painted murals.

Andrea stopped and looked. They had an amazing resemblance to one another when they were lined up like that. All four of them, Etienne Baril, his nephew, the teacher, and the artist. No one could ever seem to remember their names. Maybe it was deliberate. *Last night I met upon the stair, a little man who wasn't there*, she thought to herself. These Calvinist refugees survived as a kind of professional migrant labor force, from France to Antwerp to Frankfurt, from Lucca to Geneva to Hamburg, from Scotland to Nuernburg to Hungary, making themselves inconspicuous as they worked away to make the bottom line come out even in the cracks and crannies of administrative back rooms all over the continent. Survival by invisibility.

"What is it?" she asked.

The lawyer nodded to the end of the line. "Paul says . . ."

The little artist spoke up. "Felix Gruyard is in town. Or was. I saw him. He came to services at Saint Severi. I don't go out in the congregation, of course. I watch from the sacristy, so he did not see me."

"Who is Felix Gruyard?" Andrea frowned. Something, right on the edge of her memory. Something to do with that obscene pamphlet. A Lorrainer.

The little artist lifted up his loose tunic. The school teacher pointed to his legs.

"He is the archbishop of Cologne's torturer," the speech writer said. "He is very good at what he does."

The artist dropped his tunic. He held out his hands and arms, unscarred. "He is very careful in his work. The archbishop still wanted me to be able to paint, you see. Even though I am a Calvinist."

Buchenland, August 1634

"That went pretty smoothly," Geraldin said. They had the abbot of Fulda neatly trussed up and loaded on a small hay cart. Pretty fair hay, too.

"What about the other one?" MacDonald asked.

"Leave him down there. He's not going to be moving. Get back to where you were supposed to meet the boss. Shots attract attention and you don't want blood all over your clothes if you pass other people between here and there. I'm on my way."

MacDonald shrugged and headed back to meet Butler and Deveroux at von Berlepsch's.

Wes Jenkins had finally dealt with the way he couldn't help worrying about Clara Bachmeierin whenever she was out in the field by assigning her to ride with him while they tried to pacify the farmers. That way, he figured, he would only have to worry about her when it was absolutely necessary. That would help him keep his mind on other things, such as the importance of believing that railroad surveyors are your friends.

Most of the farmers had a lot of trouble grasping even the basics of that idea. So did Wes, for that matter. He'd read a book once about some of those early railroad barons, back in American history. He expected that his spiel wasn't as convincing as it might have been.

There were getting to be a lot of Brillo pamphlets and poems and songs around. Clara thought they were funny. Wes didn't think they were particularly funny. Oh, a couple of them were cute enough, but not anything that you could compare to Peanuts. Peanuts had always been his favorite comic strip. Once, Reverend Jones, Mary Ellen, that was, had taken the adult Sunday school class through a book called *The Gospel According to Peanuts*. That had been pretty good. He wondered if Clara would like it.

About that time, someone jumped into the pony cart and hit him from behind, rather hard. The horse reared. Men started yelling. They pulled him out of the cart. Three of them were on him, tying up various pieces of his body to other pieces.

"Leave his legs free," someone said. "We have to move them." Two men sat on him, one on each leg.

Clara was yelling, too, until someone shoved a rag in her mouth.

A man behind him was trying to get a blindfold on his eyes. He kept tossing his head up and down. He kept thinking that von Schlitz's sons had tried to blame the attack on the wagon going to Grantville on bandits. If so, it had been the only batch of bandits on that road in the last year and a half. Like this one. This was a perfectly safe road. He wiggled his head away from the blindfold again. That *was* von Schlitz's son. The older one. Fritz.

"Hold still," someone said. "Hold still or I cut her." Wes looked up. A couple of men were holding

Clara's arms. Another man was holding a wicked-looking knife right against her cheek, smiling sweetly.

He let them put the blindfold on.

It was hard to tell how long it took to get where they were going. The path, if he could trust the feel of the horse under him, had more curves than the climb to Pike's Peak.

He'd gone to Pike's Peak with Lena and the girls, once. They had tried to hit all of the important national parks on family vacations. He wondered what Lena was doing now. *Whatever it is, Lena, God bless you.* He said goodbye to his wife.

Nobody was talking except the man who had smiled as he held the knife against Clara's cheek. He seemed to find it entertaining to describe the things he planned to do to them if they did not answer the questions they would be asked.

The sound behind them was probably a door closing. Wes thought that it made a depressingly solid sound. A well-built door, probably. Reinforced panels and a good latch. Where was planned obsolescence when you really needed it?

"They pulled out my gag," Clara was saying, "If you come over here and sit on the floor so that your head is about the height of my hands, I will try to untie your blindfold. That is the best place to start, I think. He put on yours before he put on mine. It is just rough hempcloth, so the knot can't be too tight. He didn't bother to dampen it."

Wes felt his way across toward Clara's voice and slid down.

"I'm really sorry about this, Ms. Bachmeierin," he

started out. "I would have given anything to avoid exposing you to this mishandling."

"I'm sure," Clara mumbled under her breath as her fingers fished around for the ends of the knot. "There, it's coming," she said aloud. She kept pulling.

"It's called the *terratio verborum*," she said suddenly. "Terrorizing with words. That's what he was doing. Describing each instrument and its effect. It's the first stage of judicial torture. He's probably a professional, not having fun, just saving some time by talking while we rode."

Wes stood up and blinked his eyes clear. "It's not a dungeon," he said. "Stone floor and walls, but the window is at the regular height. It's after dark, but it's lighter out than it is in here and I can see the outline. It's barred."

"Untie my blindfold, would you?" Clara asked. "Then we can admire the scenery together."

"Oh," Wes said. "Sorry." She sat down on the floor. He untied it. She stood up again and he started picking at the knots fastening her hands. That was just a length of rag, too, not a rope. It came loose pretty easily. Somebody hadn't belonged to the Boy Scouts. Either the soldiers who tied them up weren't taking this very seriously or they intended to be back pretty soon. He preferred the first thought.

"It's a pantry. See the shelves, over there in back. Somebody's been living in here, I think," Clara commented after her eyes had adjusted.

"Why?"

"Because," Clara said, "there is a table. With a pitcher on it. She walked over and stuck her finger in it. Half full of water. She took a drink and handed it to Wes.

"A chair. And a bed. A cot, but a real, live, genuine, bed with ticking and a stuffed straw mattress."

"Fleas and bedbugs?"

"Probably those too." She stood there, looking at the bed. "After this kind of a day, I'll risk it."

"I'll sleep on the floor by the door, in case someone should—"

Clara had had enough.

"No," she said. "You won't."

She started to take her clothes off.

"I am getting ready to finally get into that bed with you. Before that nasty little man cuts me up in all the pieces he spent the afternoon telling us about so meticulously. So there. Even if it is too dark for you to see my body before it gets sliced and diced, at least you can feel it. And I can feel yours while it is still all there, since he is threatening to pull your fingernails out, too. And other things."

"Ms. Bachmeierin . . ."

"The name," she said, "is Clara. And you are Wesley. Now . . ." She pulled him down to sit next to her on the bed.

"Clara," he said faintly. "We aren't married."

She sighed with exasperation.

"Here," she said. "Your left hand in my left hand. My right hand in your right hand. Now you say, in the present tense, 'I take you for my wedded wife.'"

He complied.

"Now. I take you for my wedded husband. That makes us married. Do you have anything that we can divide and share for a token. A coin or something. That makes it stronger."

"I'm not the kind of strongman who goes around

bending coins with his bare hands." Wes felt around in his pocket. "Would two links from my watch chain do?"

"Superb."

He pulled them off. They solemnly exchanged them.

"Now," Clara said. "We are fully and completely married, to the entire satisfaction of ninety-five percent of the population of Europe." She kissed him again and kicked off her last petticoat. It was midsummer, after all, so she was only wearing three. All of them linen. And a pair of blue jeans under them, of course, since when she rode she now kilted her skirts and petticoats up around her waist.

Wes started to unlace his shoes.

"Ah, who are the other five percent of the population of Europe?"

"Lawyers and bureaucrats!" Clara exploded. Then. "Wesley, if you stop unlacing those shoes, I am going to be very, very, annoyed."

Joel Matowski started to wiggle his way out of the ditch and up onto the path, thinking that if he got out of this, he might just make a visit to the pilgrimage church up on top of a hill that Wes had handed back to the abbot. He hadn't always thought it was wonderful to have a mother who was a ballet teacher. If he got back to Grantville, he would apologize to his mom, ten times over, for all the occasions when he had been cranky about going to lessons or practicing. There were times in life when a lot of ballet training came in really useful. It turned a guy into something of a contortionist, not to mention developing stamina. Wiggle, hump, stretch. He fell back to the bottom twice, but kept pushing. The second night, it rained. He lay there on his back, his mouth open. Over three days after those guys had taken the abbot, by the time he had his legs onto the path and was making pretty good progress pushing the rest of himself upwards with his shoulders and elbows, a good Samaritan came along. Who happened to be a tenant of Ruprecht von Ilten.

"Berlepsch, I think. Tann, Schlitz, and Buchenau for sure. The ones who let the Irishmen use their soldiers. So those castles should be where you will find your various officials. Of course, some of them have more than one castle, and they might use storage barns or other buildings." Von Ilten was looking very anxious.

"None of the others?" the little lawyer asked.

"Not as far as I have been able to determine."

"Damn it, I'm not an invalid," Joel Matowski said. "Just a bit bunged up there and there. I'm riding out with the rest of them."

"How about," Gus Szymanski suggested, "that before you ride out you make a little tour giving speeches to the different groups. First Fulda Barracks. Then the 'Hearts and Minds' team. Then the militia. They'll fan out and cover the villages."

Joel gave a pretty dramatic speech. Ballet didn't require words, but it was really heavy on interpretive gestures.

Shortly after Joel finished the third repeat, he fainted. The Barracktown school teacher held him on his horse, took him to St. Severi's and put him in the sacristy for the little artist to look after. It was either that or the nuns, since the up-timers' "EMT" was going to accompany the other soldiers, and Biehr didn't think that nuns would be a good idea. Not that he had ever met one, but Calvinists had their doubts about nuns just on general principles.

Then Biehr hurried back to the barracks. The regiment would be marching out and he needed to be there to direct the anthem. When the men rode or marched, they would just sing the melody, but for when they were in barracks, he had set it up as a chorale and divided them into tenors, baritones, and basses.

Sergeant Hartke had not gone along with Biehr's suggestion that he should reassign the men to the different companies on the basis of which part they sang, although it would make scheduling rehearsals easier. In fact, Sergeant Hartke's answer had been unreasonably brusque. Biehr thought with frustration that sometimes he just needed to work with them on one part. He saw no obvious reason that all the tenors should not be musketeers and all the baritones pikemen.

He was vaguely dissatisfied, but he had done his best with the translation. Major Utt, of course, had as usual been overly busy. The only guidance he had given was, "Leave out the line about 'we feebly struggle; they in glory shine.' It projects the wrong image."

Butler, Deveroux, and MacDonald interviewed Fred Pence and Johnny Furbee at Berlepsch's. They had planned to put the next three days to good use, riding from one castle to another and interviewing the captives the other parties had picked up. All of a sudden, though, every country road and cow path in Fulda was crawling with people. Soldiers, militiamen, farmers, kids, and a terrifying squadron of women. People who were, clearly, looking for other people.

By mutual consent, they picked up Gruyard from Schlitz's and headed back toward Bonn. They were, after all, practical men, in this for money rather than glory.

Fulda, August 1634

"No, I am not too proud to ask for help. I am also not too stupid to ask for help. I do not care whether some galloping Rambo thinks I am a wimp because I ask for help. Somebody go down to Würzburg with this letter and get us some help. Now."

Andrea had been on her feet for almost twenty-four hours for the second time in three days. Her hair, which usually got a half-hour of attention every morning before she let it appear in public, had gone limp. She had tried to pull it back into a pony tail. It was too short. Exasperated, she had parted it and put it into two pigtails, one behind each ear, tied with pink ribbons. There were three pencils and a pen stuck into various parts of it.

Wes's speech-writer-*cum*-gofer looked at her. The hairdo's effect was remarkable. The closest classical analogy that came to his mind was Medusa.

"I will take it myself," he said. "I don't know anybody else who knows the road and is still in town. They're all out looking for the others."

Würzburg, August 1634

Steve Salatto frowned. "Has Andrea gone off her rocker?"

He meant it as a rhetorical question.

Louis Baril, which was the speech-writer's name if anyone had ever been able to remember it, took it as serious. "It is quite true," he said. "All of it. At least, to the best of our knowledge in Fulda."

"If I send a half dozen people up to Fulda, who's going to be available to help Anita in Bamberg?"

Louis realized that the second question was rhetorical. He shrugged.

"By the time I can get anyone up there, they will probably have already straightened things out. But I guess that the onus is on my shoulders."

He looked at the man. Not much more than a boy, really. "The day's half gone. Are you prepared to start back this evening, or do you need to wait for morning?"

"This evening. The daylight is still long."

"Fine," Steve said. "Weckherlin, find him something to eat and drink and a place to sleep, while I pull together a team to send."

Fulda, September 1634

"Who do you have back?" Saunders Wendell asked. He was Würzburg's UMWA man. Steve had sent him up as head of the emergency assistance team. "Or is that supposed to be 'whom do you have back?'"

"Who cares? About who and whom, I mean. We have Harlan and Roy. They were a team. Von Ilten and his men found them walking back from von Buchenau's. It sounds like when the interviewer didn't show up, von Buchenau started to get cold feet. You tell them." Andrea waved at a down-timer.

He introduced himself. "I'm Ruprecht von Ilten. Buchenau was expecting an Irishman to do the interviewing. When no one had shown up two days after someone was supposed to, Buchenau fed them and let them loose. We gave them mounts and an escort back to Fulda. By the time we got up to the castle, Buchenau was gone."

Wendell shuffled through his notes. "Any idea where?"

"Not according to his wife."

"Any recommendations?"

"She's a second wife. The first one was childless. About seven months gone with her first child. Set her father in to manage the place, I would say."

Andrea pulled herself up straight again. "Only if all of you guarantee to back the kid's succession if it's a girl against more distant claims in the male line."

Von Ilten blinked first.

Wendell looked back at Andrea. "Go on."

"Fred and Johnny. They were a team, too. Our friends here had to buckle a bit more swash to get them out of Berlepsch's hands. Dramatic armed confrontations and all that. Gus Szymanski has the casualty list. Johnny's quite a bit the worse for wear. According to Fred, he put up a good fight. Gus has splinted, salved, set bones, and the like. He should be okay, but he's not going to be on his feet for quite a while. Once it won't hurt him too much to ride in a wagon,

I want to send him back to Grantville to recover. He married Antonia Kruger from Barracktown and their first baby was born and died earlier this year. I expect he'd like to take her to see his folks. His parents were left up-time, but he has a sister. Simon Jones is his uncle. Just get away from Fulda for a while."

"I don't see any problems with that," Wendell concurred.

"Joel you know about. He was with the abbot."

"Yeah. You haven't found the abbot?"

"No. But Joel says that the men who grabbed him were speaking English to one another. Three of them, speaking English with an Irish accent. How many Irishmen can there be on the loose in Fulda? I've been here for close to two years now and there's never been one here before. Not that I know of. And we haven't found Orville and Mark." Andrea caught a sob. "Or Wes and Clara. I'm sorry."

"Who's out hunting now?"

"Mostly the Fulda Barracks Regiment. They've apologized for you know what."

Wendell frowned. "No, I don't know what."

"Derek can explain it to you when they get back. It's just too complicated, and I'm too tired. He has Lawson and Denver with him. Dave Frost is with Captain Wiegand and the Fulda militia. They've combined and split up. Does that make sense? Some of each group are beating their way systematically through every nook and cranny of the von Schlitz properties. Jeffie Garand is with Ruprecht von Ilten's people, heading for Tann. They're all still looking. Everybody's been out. The granges. Even the League of Women Voters."

Wendell rolled his eyes heavenward. "We have one

of those down our way, too. With a sheep named Ewegenia as a logo. She's a caricature of Veleda Riddle."

Andrea stared at him. "Please don't tell Sergeant Hartke's wife."

Last Visions

Bonn, Archdiocese of Cologne, September 1634

"Where is everybody?"

The servant at the boarding house where Walter Butler kept rooms looked at the roaring man as if he were a ghost.

"Fighting, if they are fighting men. Fled, if they had someplace to go. Waiting, if they are the rest of us."

"Do I have any messages? And get me something to eat."

Deveroux came in. "There's no place safe. Looters are out in the town, already. I left MacDonald watching the horses."

Butler turned to the servant. "Pack up all the food that isn't perishable for us." Back to Deveroux. "I'll read these while we're riding."

"Damn," Butler said. "Triple damn."

"What?"

"The archbishop of Mainz went back. The up-timer who is now supposed to be the cardinal-protector of the USE got the Swede to give him a *salva guardia*."

"No way would Gustavus Adolphus give him a safe conduct."

"According to Hatzfeldt, he did." Butler handed the paper to Deveroux. "We may have to reconsider our options."

"We need to catch up with our regiments. Or whatever may be left of them by now. What good is a colonel without a regiment?"

"Hatzfeldt didn't write what he was going to do himself. That's sort of odd."

"Maybe he didn't know himself," MacDonald said. "Maybe he was waiting for something to happen when he had the time to leave you the note."

"Anything else interesting?"

"No. The rest was just bills."

The three of them had their first good laugh of the day.

Gruyard smiled, but did not laugh. He never laughed.

They caught up with the retreating army.

Geraldin had left Fulda before the other three Irishmen and Gruyard. Because of the donkey and the hay cart, he approached Bonn after them.

In some ways, a single man driving a hay cart could get more answers than riders who clearly fell into the category of "armed and dangerous." He didn't even try to go into the city. There wasn't any point. Swinging around it, he headed west, hoping that he was in front of von Uslar's Hessians rather than behind them.

He was, so he kept going. Once he caught up with the army, he turned over the prisoner to the custody of the archbishop's confessor and went on to catch up with Butler and the others. There was a war on and he needed to join his regiment.

Field Headquarters of the Archbishop of Cologne, September 1634

Johann Bernhard Schenk von Schweinsberg thought that this was the fifth interview since he had arrived. Possibly the sixth. He was losing track.

The first two had been fairly polite. The next one had been rather intense. Since then . . .

The interviewer had a copy of the pamphlet. The one with the witchcraft allegations. Clara and Salome.

He would have laughed, if moving his mouth had not been so painful. He was going to miss his teeth, if he lived through this. He had been rather fond of his remaining teeth. They were so useful for chewing things. Especially when he had been eating the hard bread of a common soldier with Wallenstein's army.

Or carrots. He laughed a little anyway.

The clerk who was keeping the protocol of the interview scowled.

Who was here? Schweinsberg took stock of his eyes. The left one hurt less. He opened it.

"Where's Hatzfeldt?" he managed to enunciate.

"Gone to Mainz," a voice answered.

"Shut up, Hoheneck," someone said. "You're here to witness, not to chat."

The interviewer posed the next question.

Schweinsberg opened his mouth carefully. He had to answer. Get as much of the answer out as possible as if it were a reply to the question. Then the end of it, before Gruyard cut his lips again.

"Someone," he said. "Someone is going to have to go to Fulda to . . ." He gasped.

"To take the nuns into custody for the abominable crime of witchcraft?" The questioner offered him an answer.

"To take up the care of the abbey."

His mind drifted back to the abbey church and the plainsong of the reformed monks he had brought from St. Gall. Then to St. Mary's in Grantville.

Heart of my own heart, whatever befall,
Still be my vision, O Ruler of all.
Great God of heaven, my victory won,
May I reach heaven's joys, O bright heaven's Sun!

He sagged down.

Gruyard looked at him consideringly.

A man in black robes, who had been standing inconspicuously in the rear of the room, started forward, the oils in his hand.

"Too late," Gruyard said.

"Is he faking?" the interviewer asked.

"No. He wasn't in very good shape when Geraldin brought him in, I'm afraid. I've done the best I can."

"Too bad," the interviewer said. "He never did confess. A trial would have been very useful. Pamphlets just don't have the same effect. Not in the long run." He turned to the priest. "There's nothing for you to do here. He died an unrepentant, unconfessed sinner, incapable of receiving the last rites."

Someone knocked on the door. "You're going to have to finish up in there. The camp is moving."

The interviewer nodded, then realized that he could not be seen through the door. "We'll be right out."

Hoheneck lingered behind the others. There was

nothing he could do for the abbot, but . . . He noticed that the priest was also still in the room. "Administer the rites," he directed. "Mark the burial site, if you possibly can. At the very least, make a record of it."

The priest nodded.

Johann Adolf von Hoheneck was glad for the bustle of the breaking camp. Saddling his horse, he moved out. He wasn't going with the army. Neuhoff was still in Cologne. He would try to protect the archives and treasury from plunderers. He had to go to Mainz, himself. Get a *salva guardia.* Then to Fulda. To take care of the abbey. He assessed himself without illusions. He might not be much of a monk, he might be an ambitious noble, an unwilling and ungrateful Benedictine, but insofar as God had chosen to make him a monk, he was a monk of Fulda and he would defend its interests. As prince and abbot.

Anthem

Buchenland, September 1634

"Through here," the young man said.

"This is quite a track." The hunting parties had recombined and divided once more. Captain Wiegand looked down rather than ahead, careful where he was placing his feet. A half dozen picked men were following him. The rest of the group was heading for Tann openly and frontally.

"Well, as my grandfather said, it's not as if we don't owe him."

"Owe?"

"The man from the Special Commission. The one you're looking for. Irli his name is, I think. He kept the meeting short and snappy when Grandpa reminded him about the hay. They got in the whole winter's supply at Neuenberg that day, before that thunderstorm and hail hit in the night. It would all have been ruined if he'd held them up."

He stopped a minute, then slid between two rocks. Wiegand suddenly understood why his picked men were all very thin men.

"Down this way. They took them out of the castle and into the cave two days ago."

"How did you ever find this?"

"I, ah, I've got a girlfriend who grew up here. On the von der Tann estate."

Orville Beattie and Mark Early were fine. A bit shopworn after two weeks as von der Tann's "guests," but fine.

Actually, they told Andrea after they got back to Fulda, the man had been pretty considerate.

She decided to hand this one off to Saunders Wendell. He could buck it up the chain to Steve Salatto to decide what to do about it. Especially since the rest of the men had seemed a bit uneasy about this call. She wished Gus would let Harlan out of the infirmary. He was Wes's deputy. She wasn't. But Gus was fussing about Harlan's blood pressure.

✣　　✣　　✣

"Where do you suppose he went?" Clara asked.

"Who?"

"The man who was going to torture us."

"I don't know. But I really prefer not to make a closer acquaintance with him, so to speak," Wes said. "If I have the choice."

"Do you think we're going to get out of here? There hasn't been anybody around. No one at all."

"We'll get out if we ever manage to pry the hinges off this door. Presuming that we manage it before we starve."

"We won't starve for a while yet," Clara said cheerfully. "Consider our good fortune. They locked us in a pantry. Even though we're out of water, we still have a half keg of beer. It even has a slop jar. And a window to throw the slops through, so we don't have to live with them."

Wes put down the garden spade that he was using as a crowbar, sat on the bed, and laughed.

Karl von Schlitz was protesting bitterly against his rearrest. His lawyer had tried to argue double jeopardy. Andrea's lawyer had rebutted.

Von Schlitz's lawyer protested even more strongly in regard to the arrest of the two sons. There was nothing but suspicion against them, he insisted. At the very least, the government should allow them to sign *Urfehden*. The administration had no reason not to release them on bond.

"The hell of it," Derek Utt said to Saunders Wendell, "is that we really don't have anything on them except suspicion. And I swear that we have looked through every building on their estates from cellar to attic, more than once. Being sure to make plenty of noise, so that if Wes and Clara were in some kind of priest's hole, they would hear us and yell. If they can, of course."

Wendell looked grim. "I can't stay much longer. We've got to get back to Steve. They're running a crisis over in Bamberg, too."

"Let's put out placards," Andrea said. "All over Fulda. Not asking about Wes and Clara. Asking if anybody knows anything about some other building that von Schlitz has. List the ones we've looked at. Offer a reward for information about any others. Von Schlitz has to have been hiding *somewhere* between when they took him off the wagon and when he surfaced again."

"All right," her lawyer said. "I'll take care of it. Give me the list and I'll take it to the printer."

"I have it here," Captain Wiegand said. "You can make a copy off this one."

The lawyer took it. Looked down it. Shook his head. "It's not complete."

"Yes it is."

"No." The lawyer turned to Andrea. "Have Louis bring in those duplicate *Urbare* that we had from the provost over that way."

She frowned. Who was Louis? Oh, the gofer. She sent him.

The duplicate ledger landed on the table with a thunk. The lawyer started leafing through it.

"Here, this page. They've omitted everything on it. It has to do with a small estate that the current owner's great-uncle purchased for the use of his mistress."

⋄   ⋄   ⋄

"Someone's coming," Clara said. She listened for a while. "A lot of someones, with horses."

"We'd better get back as far as possible, until we figure out who it is. Why don't you get onto that pantry shelf that we've emptied."

"While you peek out the window? No way!"

"Clara!"

"Either both in the back of the pantry or both peeking out the window. Andrea has told me all about equal rights for women. That's in the constitution, too."

"It doesn't mean," Wes said with some frustration, "that a man can't take care of his own wife."

"It means he can't keep her from having any of the fun. Anyway, I can hear the Fulda Barracks Regiment anthem. No one else sings it." She came up to the window. "Look, I can see the banner too. Orange and white. They've finally figured out where we are."

"Well," Wes said, "that's more than I've managed to do. I was wondering, all the while we were working on those hinges, how we would find our way back. It's nice to have the cavalry come to the rescue. Or the mounted infantry, I suppose, if you want to be technical about it."

"You were their rock, their fortress and their might,
"You, Lord, their captain in the well-fought fight."

Wes frowned. "Derek really shouldn't have let Veleda Riddle pick out an anthem for the regiment, even if she is Mary Kat's grandmother. Why did the only kamikaze Episcopalian in the United States of America have to live in Grantville? They're usually pretty sedate and uptight, but if Veleda has her way, Fred will have to use his reserved tennis figurines for Episcopalians on his map."

Clara leaned her head against his shoulder. "Once we tell them that we married each other, we will have to fill out a lot of paper work, you know."

He cleared his throat. "Maybe we should just tell them that we're going to get married when we have a chance and then do it properly."

"If you think that I am going to move back in with Andrea while her little lawyer spends six weeks or three months drawing up a proper betrothal agreement and marriage contract, you are crazy, Wesley. There isn't even a Lutheran church in Fulda to read the banns."

"But . . . Clara, I'm the administrator. I should be setting a good example, and all that. And I don't want anyone to think that I am treating you with less than complete respect."

"You think they will consider it to be more respectable that I have been in this pantry with you for so many days and we *don't* tell them that we have married each other?" She turned around.

After the way she kissed him, he agreed that he would be a crazy idea to even suggest such a thing as having her move back in with Andrea. But.

"Oh may your soldiers, faithful, true, and bold,
"Fight as the saints who boldly fought of old.
"And win with them the victor's crown of gold."

The horses disappeared behind a hill on the curving road. The singing faded. Pretty soon, the lead horses were in view again.

"Maybe we could have a church ceremony later? I'd really feel a lot better if we had a marriage license from Grantville and Reverend Jones said the words. Even after the fact."

That much, she conceded, could happen. Whenever they went back to Grantville. It would make the lawyers and bureaucrats happier. The main reason they hated do-it-yourself marriage was that it did not leave a record and caused all sorts of subsequent arguments if it turned out that one partner was already married to someone else, or if one or the other party tried to back out. "Not that either of us ever would."

She was still facing him, her arms around his neck. She kissed him again. He agreed it seemed unlikely that either of them would ever try to undo their marriage.

They listened.

"And when the fight is fierce, the warfare long,
"Steals on the ear the distant triumph song,
"And hearts are brave again and arms are strong."

The strains of Ralph Vaughan Williams's "*Sine nomine*" rang through the *Reichsritterschaft* of Schlitz.

"The golden evening brightens in the west.
"Soon, soon to faithful warriors comes their rest."

Wes picked up the garden spade. As soon as they got close enough, if the Fulda Barracks Regiment ever stopped howling out their anthem long enough that they could hear him, he would start banging on the bars to save them time in figuring out where he and Clara were in the building.

He shook his head. That blasted song really stayed with a person. He'd heard it before, he was sure, but couldn't remember what the name was. He'd have to ask what it was called.

"I've had enough."

Wes told the whole staff at once, at the regular morning meeting. "Now that Harlan has agreed to cover Andrea's cost overruns in the land titles department, which I fully agree turned out to be worth it in the long run, I've asked Ed Piazza to relieve me, and he's agreed. I'm going back to Grantville to take over the consular service. Our people still manage to get in enough trouble that the State of Thuringia-Franconia needs its own consular service. With Clara, since her job as liaison has sort of been ended by circumstances."

"You're looking pretty happy," Andrea said. "Aren't you going to miss dear old Fulda?"

"Not the town. And Mel Springer will do fine here in the interim, until we get an elected board of commissioners in the spring and can transfer authority. I have full confidence that all of you will back him up."

The strains of the Fulda Barracks Regiment singing its anthem came up from the square in front of the administration building. Wes got up and walked to the window, looking down, then over at St. Michael's church.

"But. I never thought I'd say it, when he first showed up. But honest to goodness, I'm going to sort of miss Schweinsberg."

He looked up, toward the *Vogelsberg*, out over the hills that surrounded the town. "The guy was more of a politician than a monk, I guess, but still, I'm sorry that the search parties never found him. There are a lot of places he could be, out there. If we had found his body, at least, we could have brought it back so the abbey could give him a decent burial with all the others. He was the abbot. He belongs there."

The Fulda Barracks Regiment down below redoubled its efforts.

Wes glanced back at the table. "Derek, what *is* that song called in English?"

Derek Utt looked at him. "For All the Saints."

Mail Stop

Home, Sweet Home

Frankfurt am Main, March 1633

Martin Wackernagel drew up his horse, first looking back at the route he had just completed and then forward toward the walls of Frankfurt am Main.

Via regia. Die Reichsstraße. There would never be anything to equal the Imperial Road. Sure, if you wanted to be prosaic, it was just one more trade route, a commercial connection between the great cities of Frankfurt and Leipzig and their fairs. It had been for centuries.

But it was more than that. He hoped that it always would be. Merchants, teamsters, journeymen looking for a new place to demonstrate their existing skills and acquire new ones. Crowned heads, princes of the church, pilgrims on their way to the great shrine of St. James of Compostella, Santiago, in Spain. Victorious soldiers who had triumphed and beaten soldiers in retreat. Unemployed soldiers looking for work, entertainers looking for audiences, peddlers, and beggars. Sometimes it was hard to tell them apart, but they all used the road.

Martin loved the road. He had been riding it as a private messenger for fifteen years, ever since he finished the apprenticeship that his father had forced on him and refused to go ahead and become a journeyman in the trade. Not that he had anything against Uncle Reichard. He had been a good master, but he was a belt-maker. Belts were necessary, of course, but not very interesting.

So, then and now, he carried messages from Frankfurt to Erfurt via Hanau, Langenselbold, Gelnhausen, Wächtersbach, Soden and Salmünster, Steinau an der Straße, Schlüchtern, Neuhof, Fulda, Hünfeld, Vacha, Eisenach, and Gotha to Erfurt; then back again. Sometimes he had covered the further stretch to Weimar, Naumburg and Leipzig if there was no one available in Erfurt to pick up the rest of the run, but Frankfurt to Erfurt was his regular route. Or had been, until he started adding the leg that took him to the new city of Grantville, which sent out a truly amazing amount of correspondence.

He knew that all of this caused his mother a lot of distress. She recited with some frequency—every time he got back to Frankfurt, in fact—a lament that she was beginning to wonder if he would ever settle down and get married.

It wasn't as if, being a widow, she needed him to marry and make a home for her. She lived very comfortably with his older sister Merga and her husband Crispin Neumann. She just wanted him to settle down and marry. No special need for it—just a want.

She just could not understand why he loved the road so much.

Good Lord, Mutti, he thought. *Do you suppose you could let it go just this once?*

Mechanical Ingenuity

Bonn, Archdiocese of Cologne, March 1633

Arno Vignelli had something to sell. Of course. He was an Italian engineer. Most engineers were Italian. They made incredibly ingenious machines in Italy. Italians produced clever devices and then crudely set out to make their fortunes by selling them to that portion of Europe's population that lived north of the Alps.

Evrard Holmann's job, at the moment, included investment in new technology on behalf of Duke Ferdinand of Bavaria, Archbishop of Cologne. He shuffled through the papers on his desk. The man now standing in his office was the student of someone famous. Holman shuffled again. He had the information here somewhere, he was sure. He moved the pile in front of him to the side and snagged another one which should have the letter of introduction. Vignelli had also been to Grantville. He had built this particular device on the basis of something he had observed there.

Vignelli ignored Holman's paper shuffling and went on running through his spiel. "Then, at this 'museum,' I saw the machines which lie at the basis of my new invention."

"Museum?" Holmann raised his eyebrows at the unfamiliar term.

"It is, ah, like a cabinet of curiosities, but the size of a building. It is devoted to the history of the region where this Grantville came from. And since it was a region where people used many various and different technical devices, it is full of them. That is where I saw the 'mimeograph.'"

"They let you come and examine this freely, with no restrictions?"

"Well, not freely. There is a charge to visit the 'museum,' but it is really a quite small one. I could afford to return for several days in a row. They had a placard posted that indicated the costs. The fee is reduced for visits by groups of school children. Otherwise, as to 'with no restrictions,' yes. There were guards, but to prevent damage and theft. Not to prevent visitors from examining the exhibits closely."

"Very well. Go on."

"I saw this 'mimeograph.' It is not a press. It works on a very different basis, using 'stencils.' I thought that I could make one. With enough time and money and workmen. It would be difficult and very expensive to make, with much hand-fitting of metal parts, especially teeth, and the need for several springs, but it could be done."

"Expensive?"

"If I had tried to copy the 'mimeograph.' There was a lever to partly open the 'drum' so that it could grasp the 'stencil' for example. If the grasping foot did not come together precisely, the stencil would be torn loose and ruined. Many other complications. But I did not copy it. There was another machine, a 'hectograph' it was called. Much simpler, but calling for more complicated inks. I thought—if there were some way to combine these. That was when I saw the 'washing machine.' More precisely, when I saw the 'wringer' attached to the washing machine." Vignelli smiled.

"Wringer?"

"Two wooden rollers, fastened together and cranked by gears. The laundress feeds the wet clothing through them. The movement of the turning rollers moves the cloth through them; the pressure of the two rollers forces the water out of the cloth much more effectively than it can be wrung out by hand."

Holmann nodded. He could visualize how that worked.

"So," Vignelli beamed. "I thought. Take a tray, like the 'hectograph.' Run it through two rollers, one above and one below, as if feeding the cloth. But how to ink it? One more day, two more days, I came back and looked at them again and again. Then, on the third day, when I came in, I looked at the counter where the girl who took the fee I paid was standing. She gave me a receipt. She 'stamped' the date on it, with a mechanical device. It is quite delightful, and simple. I will have to make one some time."

"You are wandering from the point."

"Not really. To get the ink on the stamp, which transferred it to the receipt, she had a little tray, with a pad in it. Not something alchemical. Just a cloth pad inside the little metal tray, soaked with ordinary printer's ink. Boiled linseed oil and carbon black. She had that in a bottle. There was a hinged lid, so the pad could be closed at night so the ink did not dry out. When I asked her, she showed me how to ink the pad, just using a swab and letting it sink in. And then I knew. The hectograph tray, the inked pad—a thin silk covering is best, but fine linen such as is woven for ladies' handkerchiefs and collars will do—the stencil, the piece of paper on top of the stencil, another waxed sheet to protect the rollers from becoming inky, the whole thing moving back and forth between the two rollers of the 'wringer' until the paper is inked. Simple. Cheap. Anyone could make one—any decent craftsman, at least. It was like a divine revelation."

"Show me," Holmann said. "Archbishop Ferdinand invests in results, not concepts."

"See," Vignelli said after he had finished the first demonstration. "The operator can release or tighten the tension on the rollers. He can make a second pass if the ink is getting dry and the paper does not become dark enough the first time."

"I don't think that I believed you," Holmann said. "But it is clear. How many of these machines do you have available?"

"I have already completed ten. At least, my shop had completed ten at the time I began this journey and that was several weeks ago. I have five more almost finished and my assistants are in the workshop even as I talk to you here. I sold two—well, received orders for two—in Frankfurt on my way to Cologne. The eight available, I can deliver as fast as the parts can be transported, unless, of course, my head assistant, who left for Vienna the same day that I started north, has received orders there."

"Tell me about the 'stencils.'"

"They are not durable. You cannot print a large

number of copies from a single stencil. The best ones that I have made, waxed silk, allow a hundred pages, perhaps. With good fortune, if the stencil does not wrinkle. Waxed paper will not make more than twenty-five copies, usually, before it begins to deteriorate."

"That doesn't sound good," Holmann complained.

Vignelli suspected that a skilled operator could get many more copies from a stencil—perhaps as many as a hundred from a paper stencil and a thousand from a silk one. But not all operators were skilled and presenting inflated claims to the dukes of Bavaria tended to have permanently fatal consequences for the businessman who presented them. The archbishop was a younger brother of Duke Maximilian. Much better that he should perhaps receive a happy surprise rather than an unhappy one.

"But think. They are simple, even if not durable. Once a traditional print shop somewhere—such as in Cologne—has created the form for cutting the stencil, it can make as many stencils as may be needed. If the shop producing the pamphlet or placard will need to make five hundred copies, then make five stencils. Make a couple to spare. They aren't that expensive. If you want the item copied in ten different towns, if it should be the case that the archbishop has bought ten of these copying devices, then make ten stencils. They are lightweight and easy to distribute. Why, they can even be sent through the mail, properly protected and packed."

"Better, but . . ."

"At need, it is even possible to make a stencil without a print shop. Just to copy words from a manuscript."

"How?"

"It is best done for large placards, but this way." Vignelli opened a box and tumbled a batch of multicolored letters on the table. "The up-timers use the Latin letter forms as we prefer them in Italy, not the German *Fraktur*. These, I understand, were for children in their earliest years, so they are large. Such a treasure, but possibly not surprising. I was highly gratified to discover how many Italians reside in this Grantville. The letters had magnets in the back and could be arranged and rearranged on a magnetic board. I have removed the magnets, of course, for safe-keeping. They are in my shop."

"Which is where?"

"I have established myself in Bolzano. Bozen, you may call it, in the Tirol. The duchess has created a very favorable business climate."

"No wonder. The regent, Duke Leopold's widow, is a Medici," Holmann griped. "Damned family of Italian pawnbrokers, even if they have clawed their way up to Grand Dukes of Tuscany and given two queens to France."

"Not to mention a couple of popes," Vignelli answered mildly. "Let me show you how to use these letters to make a stencil. Of course, any craftsman can make such letters from thin wood. There is no need for them to be of this up-time material."

"You just carry them around to impress potential customers, then?"

"Of course. Now. First draw around them on the piece of paper you intend for your stencil. Then cut them out with a razor blade, quite carefully. Only then wax the paper. Otherwise, no matter how careful a craftsman may be, the wax cracks and the ink seeps through. If the wax does not coat the stencil completely, the paper remains permeable to the ink. We are experimenting with hand-stenciling smaller letters by pricking the paper with a needle, but . . ."

Holmann had made up his mind. "Hold that for my workman," he said. "You can explain the rest of it to him. The archbishop will take four of your machines. Is it possible to deliver them, ah, inconspicuously?"

"Certainly," Vignelli said. "They are easy to assemble and I have prepared a sheet of directions. When they are disassembled, no guard at a town gate will give them a second glance. If there were a need for easier passage through tolls and customs or other inspections, the parts can even be shipped separately."

"A need?"

"If, for example, there were some need for the archbishop to ensure the preparation of literature in such a city as Magdeburg, or if a partisan of the emperor who is residing in Nuernberg might need discreet access to a way to provide information to the people. I call it," Vignelli said proudly, "a 'duplicating machine.'"

News of the Day

Frankfurt am Main, March 1633

Martin delivered the bags he was carrying, saw to the stabling of his horse, and picked up the latest newspaper, fresh off the presses. Originally it had appeared weekly, but it came out twice a week now. You could buy it in every post office in Europe, of course, even those outside the CPE, but you got it first in Frankfurt, since that was where it was printed.

He stood there, looking absentmindedly at the sales rack.

There were a lot of other newspapers, of course. You could buy those at the Frankfurt post office, too. Nuernberg, Augsburg, and Leipzig. Berlin, even. Since the beginning, since the day a baby *avisa* grew up to be a regularly circulated commercial newsletter, post offices and newspapers had gone together. Before the war, there had been four or five real newspapers— not just occasional broadsides—in the Germanies, all weeklies. Five years ago, there were a dozen. Before the war, all of them together had printed perhaps five hundred copies per week. Five years ago, perhaps five thousand copies per week. Now, since the Ring of Fire—especially since the main theater of war with its plundering and marauding armies had moved away from the central cities of the Germanies—there were probably two dozen weekly papers and a half dozen that appeared more than once a week. Twelve thousand issues per week, perhaps.

The rumor was that the new paper in Magdeburg might try to publish daily. He had picked up that gossip, as well as a newspaper, in Erfurt. Gossip was still usually a bit ahead of the printed news, especially when it came to things that might affect your job, so he dropped it into his conversation with Max Leim-bacher who ran the newspaper concession. Someday, Max would return the favor. Then he headed for home.

Martin tossed the local paper on the table in his brother-in-law's print shop. "Saved you a trip," he said to the general direction of the back room and sang out a vendor's call. "All the latest news, guaranteed fresh. Notice, relation, and timely information concerning what has happened and occurred in Germany, France, Spain, the Netherlands, England, France, Hungary, Austria, Sweden, Poland, and Silesia, with items from Rome, Venice, and Vienna. Antwerp, Amsterdam, Cologne, Frankfort, Prague, and Linz, *et cetera.*" He tossed the Erfurt paper, and any others he had collected on his route, onto the table after it. The men sitting around picked them up. That was the way it went with newspapers. They went to city councils, to monasteries, to subscription clubs in small towns, and even to village taverns. Well, occasionally to village pastors who tempted their parishioners to more diligent attendance at the weekly sermon by the bribe of getting to read the newspaper afterwards, but more often to village taverns. And, of course, to schools and libraries. Most Latin schools expected their students to keep up with the current news.

One of the men started to read the items in the Frankfurt paper aloud. Not that the others couldn't read, of course, but if someone read aloud, everyone else could join in the discussion.

The Frankfurt paper, as was now usual in the CPE, had the Roman god Mercury in the woodcut in the header. Personally, Martin preferred it to the Thurn and Taxis logo, which showed a regular courier from the imperial postal system, wearing an armband, riding a well-fed horse which he could change at each post-house, blowing a horn and overhauling a hang-dog private messenger on a worn-out nag.

Martin thought defensively that he was not hang-dog

and he took good care of his horse. One of the up-timers in Fulda, the young soldier named Garand whom he had met at Barracktown while turning over some things to Sergeant Hartke's formidable wife, the Dane named Dagmar, had explained a joke to him, caused by a person saying, "I resemble that statement" rather than "I resent that statement." Martin felt strongly that he did not resemble the Thurn and Taxis statement about private couriers.

Merga, who doubled as the saleslady, came thumping forward from behind the counter to hug him. Merga was not only settled down but settling down. Much of the settling was landing on her thighs, which, as she laughed, were safely hidden under her skirts and petticoats, but some of it was also arriving in the vicinity of her chin and waistline. Crispin was a good provider and she was starting to show it.

"Go upstairs and talk to Mutti," she said as she let loose of him. "Her rheumatism has been bad. She hasn't been down in the shop for a week."

Martin groaned. If Mutti had been sitting upstairs by herself for a week, thinking, rather than down in the shop working, where things happened that distracted her, he was going to get the whole drama, from prologue to epilogue.

No use putting it off.

After a few days home in Frankfurt, Martin started to realize that he might be forced to settle down whether he wanted to or not. Now wouldn't *that* make Mutti happy. The minute he did, she would start on the marriage end of the theme.

"I never wanted to be a mail carrier for the imperial

postal system," he said to Crispin. As if Crispin didn't already know, but sometimes it was a comfort to be able to complain. "I don't want to be a courier for the Swedes. Or for the CPE, the way things are developing."

"Why don't you just keep riding on your own, then?"

"I'm not sure that I can. It will be one thing if they let the private messenger system die out naturally. It will be a lot different if the reformed CPE post offices attack the private couriers, physically, by force, the way they attacked the municipal messengers who worked for the city of Cologne, back when the Thurn and Taxis post office was set up there."

"Yes," Crispin agreed. "If the new CPE post office system turns out to be anything like the way the Thurn and Taxis run the imperial post, it won't appreciate competition. A monopoly is a monopoly, after all."

"If I have to work for the postmaster, being nothing but one little cog on a huge set of gears grinding away to move the mail all over the CPE, what kind of a job is that? What would be the joy in that?" Martin lamented to Crispin. "Riding back and forth, at top speed, over the same stretch of road, day in and day out? Never seeing anything but the inside of the postal station. If that happens, I might as well have stayed in Frankfurt and made belts for Uncle Reichard."

"You don't have to ride a short route. Frankfurt is certainly one of the largest *officia* in the Germanies, if it isn't the biggest of all by now. It's not just a station for changing horses; it receives the mail, re-sorts it, distributes it out to a half-dozen different routes. If you could get on here, in central . . . ?"

"I don't want to, Crispin. I just don't. I want to be

on the road. A man might as well be stuck in Frankfurt making belts as stuck in Frankfurt sorting mail."

That evening Martin sat on his bed. No use wasting the candle; he blew it out.

Thinking. Reminding himself of all the reasons why he didn't want to do what Crispin so clearly thought was the sensible thing.

For a century, already, the imperial postal system had emphasized speed and efficiency. "Public, regular, reliable, and rapid" as the advertisements read. Most post routes ran once a week—a few of the busier ones twice. The ideal span from one post stop to the next—from the perspective of a horse, at least—was from eight to ten miles (a mile being, of course, a quite variable concept from place to place). In the real world, where budgets were a factor, the routes of the imperial post, governed by the terms of a 1597 imperial proclamation, had post houses every fifteen miles or so where the rider handed the bags over to a new messenger and fresh horse. The rider stayed there overnight, picked up a set of bags that came in from somewhere else, and went back where he came from.

This distance was so set that people referred to it as "*una posta.*" The main route from Rome to Brussels had ninety-six post stations; the one from Antwerp to Nürnberg not quite so many. Customers could buy printed schedules and maps of the routes, as well as fee schedules, at any post office. They were posted on placards in the offices, as well.

The point was that the businessmen in any town could rely on the regular arrival of the postal courier, blowing his horn to announce that he was there. It was scheduled. "Mail day" structured the life of the towns that had post offices. Learned men, merchants, bureaucrats, clergy, and ordinary people had all become accustomed to being able to send out their correspondence on time, carried by someone whose actual job was to get it where it was supposed to go.

The imperial post and the Swedish field post were built on the assumption that horses and riders could maintain the desired speed for only a limited distance without damaging their future usefulness. Wearing out a horse was fine for emergencies, when speed was of the essence. The military field post that van den Birghden ran out of Frankfurt for the Swedes now could get a message from Frankfurt to Hamburg in five days. Reliably. On the Imperial Road as far as Eisenach. Five days for two hundred fifty miles; twenty post stops where the letter was passed off from one horse and rider pair to the next. And a lot of tenacious negotiation between the postmaster and the rulers of all the various territories along the way to get the routes established and the stations set up, but now the mail left each city regularly, twice a week, in addition to the special letters that were carried by Swedish dragoons. *Der Postschwede*, people called those men. The "mail Swede."

That was an amazing achievement. Martin could see why a Swedish general might want to get a message from Frankfurt to Hamburg fast. Once it got to Hamburg, after all, it could go out to Stockholm by boat. Although now, with the famous up-timer radio, maybe they could transmit the essence of the matter that way and let the post riders proceed at a more reasonable pace. But a lot of urgent things still had to be on paper—documents with signatures and seals, bank drafts, commissions for military officers.

If there wasn't any emergency, however, it was a bad idea to wear out a good horse. Martin admitted that changing horses at a postal station was all right. A fresh horse was a good thing for any courier. But changing riders did not appeal to him. He wanted to keep going.

"Oh well," he said to Crispin over breakfast, "I'm riding out again this morning, so I won't have to worry about it for a couple of weeks."

"Do I need to smile nicely at your future bride while you're gone?" Merga asked.

Martin shook his head. "I'm escaping free and clear one more time. Mutti had a little list, but I managed to avoid meeting any of her candidates."

He jogged off toward the livery stable. Merga shook her head as she watched him go. Marty was nearly thirty-five, after all. It was time for him to think of settling down.

On the Road Again

Gelnhausen, late March 1633

Martin Wackernagel's mother had often predicted that the boy's curiosity would be the death of him. She had predicted it regularly, frequently, all the years that he was growing up. She still predicted it.

So far, it hadn't been. It was still with him, though. It caused him to try to learn everything he could find out about the towns and cities through which he rode along the Imperial Road.

Coming up from the valley of the Main River, through Hanau and Isenburg territory, he reached Gelnhausen. According to the histories, in another world—a world in which Gustavus Adolphus had been killed in November 1632—Gelnhausen, in the summer of 1634, had been so devastated and destroyed by raiding Croats sent by the imperials, that it became uninhabitable and uninhabited for a time.

In this spring of 1633, with the king of Sweden alive, the town sat here, safely tucked within the well-defended borders of the Confederated Principalities of Europe—the CPE. Martin's mouth quirked. *Ambitious name, that—Confederated Medium and Small Principalities of North and Central Germany would be more accurate.* Nonetheless, the trial Croat raid sent toward the miraculously arrived city of Grantville the previous fall had been so effectively turned back by the king of Sweden that it now seemed unlikely that the emperor's commanders would try any such large-scale *razzia* into the valleys of the Werra, the Main, and the Kinzig, even if they could place their light cavalry in a position to begin one. Martin wondered if any of Gelnhausen's city fathers had studied the up-timers' records and realized their good fortune.

In that other world, there had been a boy of eleven or twelve years old whose name was Johann Jakob Christoffel Grimmelshausen. He had grown up to write a novel, perhaps the most famous one written about these wars. Martin had asked, unobtrusively. Yes, the boy was here. What would he write now, if not the *Adventures of Simplicius Simplicissimus*? Would he write anything? It was as if all the foundations of the world were melting under him, Martin thought sometimes, and he could not predict the shape they would take when they became solid again.

One thing that he could still rely on in Gelnhausen was that David Kronberg would be hanging around the post office. David had been hanging around the post office for the past ten years—maybe a bit more. Whenever the mail came in, no matter what frantic efforts his parents made to keep him away, he managed to elude them. David did not care if it was a Thurn and Taxis imperial post rider or a Swedish dragoon or a private courier such as Martin himself. He loved the post office. He wanted to know what was in the news; he wanted to know the gossip.

Kronberg. Or Kronenberger, depending upon the mood of the clerk recording the event in question. Or David ben Abraham. He was a son of parents who were prominent members of the Jewish community in this small imperial city. It wasn't a ghetto, really— not a separate miniature town within a town such as existed in Frankfurt. A neighborhood. Distinctive, but a neighborhood.

Martin, curious as always, had asked questions. There had been a Jewish synagogue in Gelnhausen for at least three hundred years. The current building was fairly new, built only thirty or so years ago. David's uncle, a man named Meier, had worked on it. He was now a builder in Frankfurt. Curious, Martin had looked him up; had even gotten to know him, in a way. It was easier for him than it would be for most Gentiles. His brother-in-law Crispin's grandfather had been a convert. Convert, as the Lutherans saw it; apostate, as the Jews saw it. But Crispin still knew people in Frankfurt's ghetto—he had been able to direct Martin to Meier Kronberg, Meir zum Schwan.

Unlike Meier, David's parents had not left Gelnhausen for the big city of Frankfurt. They would not leave Gelnhausen; would not think about having their son leave Gelnhausen. They definitely did not want to think about their son becoming a postal courier. Even in the atmosphere of the new CPE, Aberlin Kronberg, otherwise known as Aberlin ben Naphtali and Aberlin zur Lilie, and his wife Bessle Zons were having a lot of trouble thinking new thoughts about employment opportunities for their son.

Martin had offered to talk to them; to tell them about the wonderful world of the Imperial Road and all of its possibilities. David had said rather glumly that he did not think it would do much good for a Gentile to talk to them. It might even make things worse.

Today, David was even more melancholy than usual. He was being fenced in, he protested. His parents were arranging for him to marry. They were friendly with the bride's parents. Samuel Wohl—Samuel ben Aron, Samuel zur Leuchte—and Hindle Kalman had contributed a lot of money for the beautiful interior furnishings of the synagogue, the splendid, modern, baroque cabinet in which the Torah was kept. They had contributed, like the Kronbergs, to the purchase of the land where the community had its cemetery.

They were, unfortunately, just exactly the kind of people whom David's parents hoped that his parents-in-law would be. And the Wohls would never, never,

never accept his wish to become a postal courier. They would never even understand it.

"I'm doomed," David said.

"Married?" Martin Wackernagel asked. "You aren't old enough to get married. You can't even be twenty yet."

"For us," David said, "that's old enough. Old enough for our parents to bind us so tightly that we will never get away."

Up and Down

The Imperial Road, early April 1633

After going past the Fulda enclave of Salmuenster, Martin had stopped in Steinau for a couple of days. He usually did. Then, past Schluechtern, he looked up at the Drasenberg, which was one of the main causes of what the Grantvillers called "traffic jams" on the Imperial Road. A rider could climb it easily enough, although, if he was considerate, he would get off his horse and walk. Freight wagons, though, had to pause and let the local teamsters attach a *Vorspann*, an additional team of horses, to the vehicle. Single teams could not master the steep rise.

The first thing that travelers coming from Frankfurt learned about Fulda was that the abbey's teamsters, who provided the extra horses and collected the "escort fees," had a very crude vocabulary. So did the Hanau teamsters who often accompanied commercial wagons this far. The counts of Hanau thought that their employees had a right to bring the wagons across as far as Flieden, or at the very least up as far as the *Landwehr*, a border fortress that was protected by ditches, a wall, and impassable thorn hedges. Fulda's teamsters, at least when there were enough of them on the spot at the foot of the Drasenberg, disputed that. The constant arguments about just who had a right to pull freight wagons up this steep spot in the road were pretty typical of what went on at any territorial crossing in the Germanies. The Grantvillers planned to get rid of this in the CPE, someone had told him. He wished them luck. No matter how many lawyers tried to negotiate complicated treaties, in daily practice the issue was decided by the number of heads, the boldness of the local men, and their bodily strength. Even in the presence of high-born lords, teamsters rarely hesitated to enter into physical contests.

Oh, well. Up the hill, finally. Across some cattle meadows and into the forest. Past the dark ravine called the "murder ditch"—Martin wasn't sure why. He had asked, but had only gotten legends. Top of the hill at the thorn field. Stop while a few wagons changed teams again. Across the "ass bridge" over Flieden Creek, past Neuhof following the old military road, and then climbing through forests again. Finally the view into the valley opened up. The road led down, crossed the Fulda River near Bronnzell, and led into the city on the right side of the river.

Martin had ridden this way so many times that he knew almost every rock in the road bed. Past Fulda, he came up to Vacha—one more crossing that was a bone of contention, this one protected by a castle and this time disputed between the abbots and the landgraves of Hesse-Kassel. To get there from Fulda, a rider rode uphill and downhill to Hünfeld, with its walls, towers, establishment of secular canons, and a Gothic fortified church. Then up the Haune Valley to the top of the pass between Huebelsberg and Stallberg (extra teams required once more) and down to Rasdorf, where wagons traded the *Geleitsknechte* of their Fulda escort for a bunch of Hessians. Down hill to Geisa. Buttlar, and then up the valley of the Ulster. This was so steep that anyone could see the scrapes on the stony roadbed made by the skidding wheels of braking wagons and carriages. Then, following the little Suenna River, travellers crossed the Werra.

By the time he got to Vacha, he was really glad to see it. He stopped for a couple of nights. He didn't have any urgent deliveries this time. The same for Erfurt. Nobody had any deliveries for the new Grantville leg of the trip, so he turned around and headed back to *Mutti* and her complaints.

Round and Round

Fulda Barracks, late April 1633

Derek Utt, the military administrator for *Stift* Fulda, the abbey of Fulda and its subject territories, who had been installed by the government of the New United States, or NUS, when it assumed the administration of Catholic Franconia under the aegis of Gustavus Adolphus the previous fall, looked up from his consultation with Sergeant Helmuth Hartke. They were sitting on a picnic bench under a tree, just inside the gateway

to the Fulda Barracks. He was thinking *what on earth?*
The voice sounded like Nashville, Tennessee, but the
rider certainly was not a veteran of the Grand Old Opry.

> "I've got heartaches by the number
> "Troubles by the score,
> "Every day you love me less,
> "Each day I love you more."

"It's the courier," Hartke said. "He comes back and
forth through here every couple of weeks. He'll be
on his way back toward Frankfurt now."

He waved, shouting, "Anything for us?"

Martin Wackernagel turned his horse off the road.
"Not a thing." He grinned. "Your paymasters use the
official post office, but I can tell you that the payroll
arrived safely and has been deposited with your Herr
Stull in Fulda. I have newspapers from Grantville and
Erfurt for those willing to pay. If you will just give
me a few minutes to tether the nag and get him some
water, I would not say no to a beer."

Sergeant Hartke performed the introductions.

Wackernagel had learned the song "from an old
fiddler I met in Erfurt." Who had to be Benny Pierce,
Derek thought; there weren't any other old fiddlers from
Grantville wandering around central Thuringia as far
as he knew. Wackernagel had been happily spreading it
throughout the intervening towns and villages. Up-time,
Derek thought, any politically correct anthropologist
would have charged him with acutely negligent cultural
contamination, at a minimum. Where would *Grimm's
Fairy Tales* come from if, before someone like the
Grimm Brothers got around to collecting them in the

towns of the Kinzig Valley, they had been replaced by Hank Williams?

Frankfurt am Main

"How's business?" Martin asked.

Crispin came in from the work room, tossing a batch of pamphlets and placards onto the table next to the newspaper. "Wretched, wretched. One cat that gave birth to a two-headed kitten; two political satires in verse, both short; a new hymn; six advertising flyers, and a 'wanted' poster. How to make your own back-yard sundial. That's all the new orders that have come in since you left. The gossip is all about the new 'duplicating machines' that the Italian sold. Escher already has his running and Freytag is assembling the one he ordered.

"A lot of the guildsmen would like to see the 'duplicating machines' prohibited, of course." Crispin started to thumb through the packets that his brother-in-law had brought in. "But if you ask me, that's hopeless."

"Why?"

"They're simply too small. Even smaller than a normal press, and that can be loaded onto a wagon easily enough. What weighs us down as printers, if we need to move from one place to another, is transporting the lead type to set up a new shop—all the different fonts and different sizes; storage bins, everything. With these stencils, you can have the little machine anywhere and if a printer somewhere else makes the stencil and sends it to you, you don't need the type in your shop. Myself, if I could get hold of one, I'd develop a sideline in producing the stencils and selling them. It's a lot less weight when you ship one out than a bale of pamphlets or placards. Let the shop at the destination pay the freight for bringing in the paper and ink."

"They still need paper, don't they?" Martin asked.

Crispin gave him the same kind of look he would give a two-headed cat. "Of course, but paper is no problem. You can get paper anywhere. Just about every town in the Germanies has a paper mill. Think how much paper is just carried through the mail, for goodness sake. And used for newspapers."

Bonn, Archdiocese of Cologne

"Here are the stencils for your pamphlet and placard. I have drawn boxes where the woodcuts go, in the proper size. The woodcuts are separate; each one will have to be stamped into each copy separately. I couldn't get good enough resolution when I tried to include them in the stencils. That will take more time than all the remainder of the production put together. Each box that I have drawn is numbered. Each wood block is numbered. If your contact in Fulda messes up the production, that is his fault and not mine."

Alain van Beekx, formerly of Antwerp, forger of magnificently authentic documents and maker of extraordinarily filthy etchings, was now, at the request of Felix Gruyard, expanding into the production of stencils. It had taken him a couple of weeks to master the stencil technique in full, even with Vignelli's personal guidance, but he was now confident that his print shop could produce as many as anyone chose to order from him in a quite timely fashion.

Gruyard smiled.

"You are sure the machine will be there in time?" Gruyard asked.

"As well as one can every predict anything," Holmann said. He pulled out his copy of the most recent edition of Aitzinger's *Itinerarium Orbis Christiani*, which visualized the European road system for people who planned to travel. For the past half-century, nearly everyone had recognized the Cologne reporter's atlas as a very handy book, especially when it was paired with his week-by-week summaries of current events. In a lot of ways, these had been predecessors of the modern newspaper of the 1630s. From Aitzinger until the present day, Cologne had become a center for the publication of aid-books for travelers, which meant regular employment for a lot of full-time map makers. The most popular travel guides were those which laid out the routes followed by the imperial post riders and the couriers employed by the imperial cities and various territorial rulers. By taking these as far as possible, as close to one's actual goal as they ran, a traveler could be sure of a comparatively well-guarded route, even in the middle of all the disruptions of war.

Drawing his finger along one of the routes, Holmann indicated the path that the duplicating machine could be expected to travel from Tyrol to Fulda. "At the moment, there are no major obstacles to commerce. Through Switzerland as far as Basel; then down the Rhine as far as Mainz; then up the Imperial Road to Fulda." He shrugged. "If the machine is delayed, then the pamphlet will appear a couple weeks later than planned. Otherwise, fortune has been with us."

Gruyard nodded. "It was truly fortuitous that Hoheneck received the feelers extended by von Schlitz when he did. The connection with Menig at the paper mill is good. The one thing that I worried about, that might allow the authorities of the New United States in the *Stift* to trace the pamphlet to its origins, was the need for anyone who was to use the duplicating machine to purchase so much paper. How many people other than printers buy more than a quire at a time? But where is there naturally more paper than in a paper mill? They will tear apart every printing shop in Fulda searching for the plates or indications that the plates were there."

He smiled.

"So don't worry about your stencils." Holman waved his hand. "I have contracted with a private courier with a good reputation for their delivery. That will be more discreet than entrusting them to the Swedish-run postal system. His name is Martin Wackernagel."

Youthful Restlessness

Gelnhausen, late April 1633

"David Kronberg," Jachant Wohl said, "looks like a rabbit."

Her younger sister Feyel looked at her. "That's a horrible thing to say. You are probably his future wife, at least if our parents and his have anything to say about it."

"He does look like a rabbit, though." The third Wohl sister, Emelin, at ten, was young enough to announce that the emperor had no clothes on and still get away with it. "He would still look like a rabbit even if Jachant liked him."

"I've never seen a rabbit with black hair," Feyel pointed out. She was determined to play the part of a fair and impartial witness. She was even more determined to do this since her own marriage was already satisfactorily arranged and her betrothed husband did not resemble a rabbit in the least.

Emelin was not going to give up. "His nose is long. His cheeks twitch when he chews. He is short and round and has big ears."

"There aren't all that many people available for you to marry, Jachant," Feyel pointed out practically. "If the Kronbergs aren't rich, they are far from poor, and David will inherit from his uncles as well, since neither has children. *'Der dicke Meier'* has to have quite a bit of money. He is master builder for the whole Jewish ghetto in Frankfurt."

Jachant rested her chin on her hand. "Fat Meier looks like a rabbit, too. It runs in the family. I doubt that our parents would want me to marry a man who looks like a rabbit if his parents were poor. David Kronberg would give me children who look like rabbits."

"Papa and Mama are concerned about your well-being," Feyel said. "There is nothing wrong with David Kronberg."

"He wants to be a postal courier. Who ever heard of a Jewish postal courier?" Emelin asked.

"Everyone in Gelnhausen has heard of the idea, at least, since he said that he wants to be one. Don't

worry, Jachant. His parents will make him give it up."
Feyel patted her sister's shoulder.

"They can make him give up doing it. Can they make him give up wanting to do it?"

Feyel frowned. "Jews do travel around. Think of famous families, like the Nasis. Or the Abrabanels."

"Sephardim. They don't count." Jachant tossed her head.

"Even if David ben Abraham Kronberg doesn't become a mailman," Emelin said, "he'll still look like a rabbit."

Barracktown bei Fulda, late April 1633

Derek Utt was doing his best to sound wise and fatherly. This was something of a trick, since he certainly wasn't old enough to be Jeffrey Garand's father. Maybe he could try the older brother ploy instead. However, he was the senior NUS military man in Fulda as far as rank went, and . . .

Maybe he could get Gus Szymanski, the EMT, to have the fatherly chat.

Cowardice in the face of . . . he thought.

Maybe the direct approach would be best. Straight to the point.

"What in hell do you think you are doing boinking Sergeant Hartke's daughter?"

"Gertrud?" Jeffie looked at him.

"Does he have any others?"

"Not alive. Gertrud had a sister, but she died when she was a kid."

Derek winced, remembering the little girl he had

left up-time. Hannah had just started to toddle a few days before the Sunday afternoon he drove over to Grantville to go to the sport shop with his sister Lisa's husband Allan Dailey.

Jeffie hadn't stopped talking. "Well, about a month ago I was sitting on the table at the Hartkes' one evening. Sitting on the table, with my boots on the bench, spinning yarns, and Gertrud was sitting down on the bench. I looked down and I could sort of see into her cleavage, that white thing they all wear, she had it pretty low. And she was looking up. Her eyes were about the level of my knee and she kept on looking the length of my leg and on up to where my codpiece would be, that is if Americans wore the things and even most Germans don't any more, just the most old-fashioned old men, and the idea sort of occurred to me that she might not object, so the next chance I got, we wandered off and one thing led to another."

"If you get her pregnant," Derek said, "you are a married man. Trust me on this, Jeffie. She's not a whore and she's the daughter of one of the other sergeants in the regiment."

"Hartke hasn't said anything to me."

"Damn it, Jeffie, that's because he's *assuming* that if you get the girl pregnant, you'll marry her. It's the way it seems to work around here with respectable people, and what's more, if they have something like an age of consent, Gertrud can't be over it by much. I'm involved because in spite of the fact that you work with Hartke and have ever since he joined our forces after the fight at Badenburg, you haven't made much of a try at figuring out things like that—about how things work with the down-timers. And Hartke hasn't made much effort to figure out how they work with up-timers. But Dagmar damned well has and she gave me an alert on this. I can't afford to have you tick Hartke off. He's too important in keeping discipline among the down-time troops."

"Oh," Jeffie said. "Dagmar."

Sergeant Hartke was a Pomeranian. His wife—his second wife, actually—Dagmar was a Dane and had been the widow of a Dane when she married the sergeant. She regularly pointed out that when *she* got involved in all of this, the *Danes* were the glorious champions of the Protestant cause in this mess and the Swedes were nowhere in sight. Her first husband had been killed in the Danish defeat at Lutter am Barenburg in 1626.

In the five years between that and her marriage to Sergeant Hartke in 1631, Dagmar had survived five manless years in the train of various Protestant armies, fairly intact, by not missing a thing. She definitely had not missed the Garand-Gertrud connection. She had been very verbose about it, as Derek recalled.

"Errr," Jeffie said. "I know that Gertrud isn't a whore. She's living at home with her family. Actually, we haven't quite gotten to the point yet where I could get her pregnant. Almost. I'm working on it, so to speak, but there's not a lot of privacy going around. That first time we wandered outside, once we got there, I was wearing an overcoat and she was wearing a cape. We both had on hats and boots. I was wearing long johns; she had on six woolen petticoats. About all we managed to do was pull off our gloves and poke our fingers at some of each other's more interesting parts, so to speak, before we headed back in to the fireplace."

"Maybe," Derek said, "It will be a long winter." He could always hope.

"The ground is still pretty cold. There's still snow under the bushes. Not to mention that the leaves aren't fully out. When the weather gets a bit warmer and the bushes get bushier—then I'll get my hopes up. Other things are already up every time I see Gertrud."

Derek looked at him. Jeffie's grin was totally unrepentant. But . . .

"In that case," Derek said firmly, "I hereby order you to have a talk with Gus Szymanski tomorrow, if you haven't had one yet. Maybe he has some ideas about down-time techniques for delaying the probably inevitable."

Jeffie jumped up.

"I did not say 'dismissed.'"

"Sorry, Derek. I mean, sorry, Major Utt."

Derek sighed. Being military administrator in Fulda tended to be short on spit and polish. It was hard to impress a subordinate who somewhere deep down thought that you really were and really always would be just the little brother of one of his high school teachers.

Gelnhausen, May 1633

Riffa, daughter of Simon zur Sichel, looked out of the window. There was no especially beautiful scenery to keep her anchored there, but the view included David Kronberg, who was sitting on a bench and looking at the clouds.

She sighed. Some people said that David Kronberg was very odd. Most of the Jews in Gelnhausen said that David Kronberg was very odd. Riffa didn't think he was odd. Different, in an interesting sort of way, but not odd. If you had a husband who was a postal courier, he would come home bringing a lot of news.

Emelin Wohl, last week, said that he looked like a rabbit.

Riffa sighed. Objectively she had to agree that he looked sort of like a rabbit, but it was a really *cute* rabbit. The kind you wanted to take in your arms and cuddle, stroke its fur, feel its long silky ears. Snuggle it up to your bosom, where its little pink nose and whiskers could tickle your . . .

She pulled her thoughts back into order. Everyone knew that his parents and Jachant Wohl's parents were trying to make a match. Talk about having all the luck. Jachant would get to marry him, without even trying.

Not that there was the slightest chance that Riffa could ever marry him. There was no point in having impossible dreams. Her parents, Simon ben Itzig also called Simon zur Sichel and his wife, did not move in the same social circle as the Kronberg family. After all, Papa was just an itinerant peddler. It was the generosity of the Jewish community that allowed Mama and her to stay in Gelnhausen when he was traveling. They didn't really belong here. Or anywhere.

Often, she wondered if she would ever marry at all. Who would offer for her but some smelly, childless, old man who was hoping for better luck with a young, healthy, second wife?

❖   ❖   ❖

David was looking at the clouds with one eye, visualizing pictures as they floated across the sky. With the other one, he kept monitoring the little cottage marked by a sickle over its front door. If he was really lucky, Riffa might come out to go to the well, or run an errand for her mother, or something. If she did, he could watch her until she turned the corner. Maybe he could even watch her come back.

For years, he had thought that the Thurn and Taxis postal station was the most interesting thing in Gelnhausen. For the past few months, the cottage with the sickle had given it competition.

Someday, perhaps, he would do a great and daring deed. Something heroic. After that, Riffa zur Sichel would smile at him. Would smile down at him. She was about two inches taller than he was.

Preferably, that would happen before his parents married him off to Jachant Wohl, because if it did not, it would not be proper for him to smile back.

It occurred to Riffa that if she offered to do the marketing, the route would take her past the bench where David Kronberg was sitting. Maybe he would look at her.

"Mama," she said.

He looked at her. Not directly, of course, but she could feel him looking at her.

He would be the father of such adorable babies, like plump, fluffy little bunnies. She could feel even now how delightful it would be to hold them in her arms.

Just before she turned the corner toward the marketplace, she managed to wiggle a little as she walked along carrying her basket. She hoped that he was still looking, but she could scarcely turn around and check.

Fulda, May 1633

Jodocus Menig looked up from his work, irritated. Someone was pounding on the door and he was not expecting any customers. His paper mill was on a stream about a half-mile outside the Fulda city walls. Most people with whom he did business had no reason to come out here; he met them in town to take orders and such. He made his own arrangements with a teamster to haul the deliveries and he knew that he did not have any scheduled for today.

Wiping his hands on his apron, he ran to the front. It was the courier—Wackernagel was his name—with the large envelope he had been told to expect. Menig signed for it himself. His wife was dead. As he signed, he thought that he would have to do something about remarrying. It was nearly impossible for a man to carry on a business if he didn't have a wife.

He didn't want a Catholic wife, though, and most of the marriageable women here in and around the city of Fulda were Catholic.

Jodocus Menig came from Schlitz. He had moved his business down to Fulda when the up-timers took over, because the *Ritter*, Herr Karl von Schlitz, had offered to invest some money if he would make the move. Schlitz thought it would be a good idea to have a man in Fulda who could keep an eye out on developments for him, now that the up-timers had opened the city to Protestants again. The *Ritter* had considered Menig a good choice. Fulda didn't have a paper manufacturers guild, so all he had needed to do was lease the site and get the permits to erect the buildings.

He'd ask the *Ritter*'s steward. Bonifacius Bodamer would probably be able to think of some healthy, practical widow from Schlitz, a good housekeeper with not too many children from her first marriage. Still of child-bearing age.

More children wouldn't be a bad idea. When Kaethe had died, she had left him with just the one boy. You couldn't rely on just one child to care for you in your old age. Not the way that things were these days. However clever a child might be, he could get sick and die. Here today, gone tomorrow. That was the way of children, even when they seemed perfectly healthy.

Menig suddenly realized one horrible thing. Now that the stencils had arrived, he would have to figure out how to use the duplicating machine.

At least, his son Emrich had already put the machine together. Emrich was just barely fourteen. He was only starting to learn the art of making paper. But with these new devices that were appearing all over the place, all the time it seemed, he was better than his father.

Emrich had figured out how to put the machine together.

Maybe Emrich could figure out how to use it.

Jodocus certainly hoped Emrich could figure out how to use the stencils. He was expected to produce several hundred placards and pamphlets within the next two weeks.

He was not a printer. He had never planned to be a printer. He had never asked for a duplicating machine. He had never asked to be involved in his lord's politics.

"Put not your trust in princes." He should have known that when the *Ritter* offered to invest in expanding the business, he would be calling in favors.

✧   ✧   ✧

If the *Ritter* wanted pamphlets and placards, he would get them. Jodocus and Bonifacius agreed on this principle solemnly. They sat in the front *Stube* of the paper mill, drinking beer and discussing eligible widows. They solemnly assured one another that they were much too old dogs to be expected to learn new tricks, either of them.

"There has to be something that I just don't understand," Emrich Menig complained. "Every single time I run the tray through the rollers, to transfer the ink through the stencil to the paper, I get some ink coming through onto the top roller. Not a lot, but enough to make smears on the back of the next copy."

"You didn't complain when we were running off the placards." Liesel Bodamer, just two months older than Emrich, stopped cranking the rollers and came round to the other side of the duplicating machine.

"It didn't make any difference when we were doing the placards. They are just one-sided, to be tacked up to doors and posts and things. It doesn't matter if they have some ink smears on the back. But for the pamphlets, we're supposed to run the paper through on one side, let the ink dry, and then run it through on the other side. So if there are smears on the back of the first run, people won't be able to read the printing we put there during the second run."

"Let me look at the manual."

"If I have to release the top roller and clean it for every single sheet of paper we run, we'll never get these done on time."

"Give me the manual, Emrich!" Liesel swatted his arm. "Hand it over. Now."

"It doesn't say anything."

"Something has to be wrong with the instructions. They must have left something out."

Emrich stared at her, shocked to the core of his faith. "The manual for putting together the duplicating machine was exactly right."

"Maybe two different people wrote them. Maybe the printer just left a line out when he was setting type. There's all sorts of things that could go wrong. We just have to think."

"All right. I'll clean the top roller again while you're looking."

"While you're cleaning, think. If they really haven't told us how to fix this problem, you're going to have to figure out a way to fix it yourself."

"In this illustration, the picture of the duplicating machine doesn't match the text." Liesel handed the manual back to Emrich.

"Yeah." Emrich sat there for a while, staring at the duplicating machine.

"Are you expecting it to talk to you?"

"Sort of. Did we take everything out of the envelope that the stencils came in?"

"No. I've been taking them out one at a time, so we don't mix them up."

"Take a look, will you. Are there any extra sheets of the waxed paper, without any stencil holes in them?"

"No."

"I think we need a solid waxed sheet, on top of the paper we're printing, to protect the roller."

Liesel looked. "I don't know if that's what the picture was supposed to show, but I think it would work. It's not as if you have a paper shortage around here. Do you have any wax?"

"Some candle stubs, probably. Wherever *Vati* puts them to give back to the candlemaker when we buy more."

"Let's look in the kitchen."

Emrich didn't know his way around the kitchen very well. It took quite a while to find a flat baking pan with edges high enough to melt a layer of wax in it. They never did find one large enough to lay a whole piece of paper flat.

"We'll have to do it part at a time," Liesel said. "Where's your fire-starter? I need to melt the candle stubs."

Two hours later, they determined that putting the extra sheet of waxed paper on top of the tray did keep the roller clean.

They were also getting hungry.

Their fathers were getting drunk. More precisely, had already gotten there.

"Do you have anything to eat, here?" Liesel asked.

"Bread, but it's a little moldy. Sausage, kind of dried out. And Papa won't like it if we eat it up and don't leave any for him."

"Well, ratzen-fratzen-snatzen-matzen to *him*. Here." Liesel dug into her pocket. "I have a couple of *Heller*. Run over to Barracktown and ask Sergeant Hartke's wife if we can have some eggs. She has three laying hens as well as the pullets, I know, because she bought them from Bachmann's widow. We already started the fire to melt the candle wax. I'll cut up the sausage and soften it in boiling water while you're gone and try to scrape the mold off the bread and toast it over the fire. I can make an omelet with sausage and toast cubes in it."

"What do you suppose those children are doing?" Dagmar asked a few evenings later. "Emrich Menig has been over here every noon for the past four days asking to buy something to eat. Doesn't Menig feed him? And why is Liesel there?"

"Bodamer is there, too," Jeffie Garand answered. "I've seen him around. Menig must have a big order on hand. They're probably too busy to pay any attention to the kids."

He looked at Gertrud and winked.

"Perhaps we should go outside and take a stroll up in the direction of the paper mill, just to check that they are okay."

They got all the way up there, knocked on the door, and were admitted by Liesel, who said that everything was all right, thank you. She seemed to be telling the truth, so they went back at a leisurely pace that included a couple of detours.

"I think," Liesel said, "that it would be better to stamp the woodcuts into the squares before we fold the pages of the pamphlets and sew them together."

"Sew them together?"

"Just in and out with the needle and then knot the thread on the outside. It doesn't have to be fancy. That's what keeps pamphlets from falling apart."

"How do you know?"

"Lorenz Mangold, the councilman from Fulda, gave my Papa another pamphlet while he was in Fulda yesterday. He brought it back and was showing it to your Papa. Mangold got it from somewhere else. It's printed, I think, but he wants your Papa to make stencils and make more copies of it for him. It's sewed together like that. I can't think of any other way to keep the pages from falling apart. Mangold is coming out here tomorrow, Papa said."

"No," Emrich groaned. "No. Papa isn't going to make stencils. Papa isn't going to make pamphlets for Mangold. Liesel, we—you and me—are going to be cranking this duplicating machine until the day we die."

"Well, clean it up now. We can stop cranking until we finish stamping this batch. And pull the tray out. We'll have to use the ink pad in it for stamping the woodcuts, because they didn't think to send us a separate one."

"Emrich?" Liesel sounded a little doubtful. She was a country girl and quite familiar with the way that animals mated.

"Umm?"

"What the snake with the forked tongue is doing there, in the woodcut showing the woman Clara and the nun named Salome and the abbot. Is that possible?"

Emrich took stock of his limited knowledge of male anatomy, both human and serpentine. "I don't think so. I'm pretty sure not, even."

"That's what I thought. Is there any more of the sauerkraut left?"

Gelnhausen, June 1633

"It's not doing any good, Uncle Meier. Honestly. Thank you for coming, but it isn't helping."

"David," his father said, "it is not your place to be talking. The family is consulting about your future."

His uncle Salman ben Aron, called Samuel zur Krone, frowned a little and started to speak. His wife, Aunt Daertze—not just Aunt Daertze because she had married his uncle but because she was Daertze Zons, his mother's sister—put her hand on his arm to hush him.

"He has a right to some voice in his own future," Uncle Meier said.

"Not when the future he wants is so unimaginably and incomprehensibly wrong-headed." Samuel Wohl was sitting next to David's father. "The very idea that you would even consider letting him *apply* to become a postal courier is ridiculous."

Then Jachant Wohl was sitting there. Then her mother. Her mother and his mother, who was next, had their arms linked together.

They were all agreeing.

Jachant opened her mouth. "I refuse to even consider having a husband who would spend so much time as a vagrant."

"A postal courier is not a vagrant," David protested.

"David," his father said. "It is not your place to be talking."

"A postal courier is not a vagrant," someone else said. That was Zorline Neumark, his Uncle Meier's wife. "And they make reasonably good money. I know that Crispin's brother-in-law does."

The row of people on the other side of the table glared at her. Crispin, the grandson of the apostate. His grandfather had changed his name from Neumark to Neumann. How could Zorline admit that she still spoke with that branch of the family?

They all thought it. Hindle Kalman, Jachant's mother, said it.

Der dicke Meier defended his wife.

Jachant opened her mouth again. "You look like a rabbit, Meier ben Aron. And so does David Kronberg."

Her parents stared at her.

"It's true."

Everyone stared at her.

Except David, who took the chance to leave the room.

"He's leaving," Zorline Neumark told Hindle Kalman. Zivka, the wife of Simon zur Sichel, stood quietly in the back of the shop, listening. "David. Today. He says that he is going before he has an irretrievable fight with his parents. Meier suggested that he should come to Frankfurt with us, but he refuses to become another point of contention between brothers. He says that he is going to Fulda. So that is what your daughter Jachant and her runaway tongue have accomplished for us."

"To the up-timers?"

"He says that according to their 'constitution,' a religious test for holding public office is forbidden. He is going to apply to work as a postal courier there, somewhere in the New United States. Just walk in and apply, without even a letter of introduction."

Zivka had not missed the direction in which her daughter Riffa's eyes sometimes wandered. She went home.

"Oh," Riffa said. "I think that's the bravest and most daring thing that I ever heard of any man doing."

"I," Zivka said, "am going for water. After that, I

may visit the bath. I certainly will not be back for two hours at least; possibly three."

"Riffa," David said. "Why are you here? Outside of the walls?"

He had never been so close to her. He dreamed about her, but he had never approached her, because he knew that his parents would never agree that he could have her honorably, under the canopy. So he should not look. Even though he had looked, of course.

"I wanted to say something to you before you left."

"What do we have to say to each other?"

"I wanted you to know that I would be proud to be married to you. Even if Jachant Wohl will not. I just thought that I would like you to know that before you went away."

Now he looked up.

"Jachant Wohl won't take you, you know. Not if you leave. Her parents won't let you have her, either. Have you thought what you are doing? She's the best match in Gelnhausen. Pretty. Rich."

"You're prettier." The tone of David's voice carried full conviction.

Riffa had been about to say something else. Her mouth had been open. After a few seconds, she closed it, trying to remember what she had planned to say.

"Not richer. Is it true that you are going to the New United States?"

"To Fulda, yes. To talk to the up-timers there. I'm pretty sure that I can't get a job with the municipal couriers here in Gelnhausen. The messengers are all one another's relatives. They look out for each other. But I've spent enough time watching, all these years.

I know as much about what they do as anyone could who hasn't actually done it."

"All by yourself, someone said. Without even a letter of introduction."

"I'm not quite that foolhardy, no matter what some people think. Martin Wackernagel, the courier, gave me a recommendation to a Major Derek Utt. Wackernagel is acquainted with some of the people there."

"There's no Jewish community in Fulda."

"I know."

"How will you live, then?"

"Without one, I guess."

"Have you ever talked to my father?"

"No. Should I have?"

"He's a peddler, you know. That's why families like yours look down on him. After the Jews were expelled from Hanau in 1592, my grandfather went peddling. *Unvergleidet*, without a charter of protection from any Christian lord. My father did, too. When the duke let the Jews come back in 1603, my grandfather and father didn't come back. They kept peddling, from Denmark to Switzerland. Not far east, but sometimes west into Alsace. I was born on the road. There was no *mikvah* for my mother to cleanse herself in forty days. Not for over a year. I don't remember it well. I was eight when he obtained permission for my mother and me to stay in Gelnhausen when he is traveling. You could have asked him, some time when he was here. Asked him what it will be like for you now."

David looked at her. "Even if you don't remember it, you must have heard them talking. Would you live that way?"

"If I were with you," Riffa said. "If I could go to

Fulda with you . . . In the New United States, I have
heard, we do not need to be *vergleidet*. Or, we are
vergleidet by their 'constitution' itself, and not by
any prince."

David looked at her with some surprise.

"My father brings home newspapers."

"When I get a job there, as soon as I can, I will
come back for you. What will your parents do when
you go with me?"

Riffa shook her head. "I don't know. Come with
us, perhaps."

"That would be nice."

She smiled down at him. Then she went back home
to the cottage marked with the sickle and he went
to Fulda, invisible fireworks bursting within his head.

Ups and Downs

Schlitz, June 1633

Bonifacius Bodamer was standing outside his grist
mill, waiting for the mail.

It was Martin Wackernagel's opinion that Bodamer
was usually standing outside his mill waiting for something, while his men did the heavy work inside. Maybe
he had worked harder at an earlier stage of his life,
when he was a mill hand rather than a mill owner. In
any case, he also served as steward of the *Ritter*, Karl
von Schlitz, along this part of the route. To get from
Eisenach to Fulda, a person went through Schlitz. That
was just how the road ran.

This morning, Bodamer had other men with him.

Wackernagel perceived signs of rank. Just as a precaution, rather than simply handing the packet over to Bodamer, he pulled up his horse, dismounted, and bowed with what he hoped was the appropriate amount of respect for whomever they might be.

The two older men ignored him. The two younger men gave him a look which said that they were willing to ignore him now that he had made a reasonably appropriate obeisance, but would not have ignored him if he had failed to do so.

There were a lot of people like that around.

The two older, unidentified, men were chuckling to one another. Bodamer chuckled with them, obsequiously. He forgot to take the packet of mail that Wackernagel was still offering to him.

Liesel, Bodamer's daughter, came out of the mill and took the packet.

"May I water your horse?" she asked.

Wackernagel was still dismounted. "I would be grateful, ordinarily, but this monster is a bit frisky. I'm afraid that the millrace coming out of the pond is likely to spook him, so he will have to wait for a while."

"We have a barrel and leather bucket, right in the back of the building."

"Angel of mercy." He bowed to the girl with a flourish. "Show me where your barrel is, if you would be so kind, and I will lead him around."

"Who is with your father?" he asked once they were safely out of sight.

"Herr von Schlitz, our ruler, with his two sons."

That explained the arrogance.

"The other man, the one in green, is Lorenz Mangold. He is a city councilman in Fulda. He has been here several times, lately, talking to my father."

The chuckling that had been going on in front of the mill expanded into uproarious laughter.

"Something's funny."

"It's a pamphlet," Liesel said. "A satire. They are enjoying it a lot."

By the time they were done with the horse, the knight and his two sons were gone. Mangold was still standing there, waving some pieces of paper at Bodamer.

There was no reason for Wackernagel to go back and talk to them. The only words he heard were, "I wrote this one myself and I am very proud of it. I'll be happy to cover the costs, given how reasonable they are turning out to be."

Barracktown bei Fulda

At supper time, Martin turned in to the Hartke cottage. Dagmar the Dane always picked up anything he had for Barracktown when he came by. She always fed him, too.

A certain scurrilous pamphlet was the topic of the day.

"I tell you," Dagmar was saying. "According to my husband, Mr. Wesley Jenkins, the civilian administrator, was truly furious. He ordered all the placards torn down and sent soldiers to Neuenburg to bring the members of the Special Commission back to Fulda."

"Why so angry?"

"It showed one of his staff in a scandalous position with the abbot of Fulda. And named her."

"Ah," Wackernagel said. "Yes, I can see that. Was a military escort really warranted, though?"

"Maybe not. Even probably not. Most of the time, the roads here are fairly safe now. Although, just yesterday, Helmuth's daughter Gertrud went into Fulda itself and was accosted by the older son of *Ritter* von Schlitz."

Wackernagel frowned. He had seen that man just this morning, up at Bodamer's. "Were his father and brother with him?"

"In Fulda? I do not know. Not, certainly, at the time when he called Gertrud a slut and soldier's whore and pointed to the placards saying that the same fate waited for her. Other people in Fulda started pointing at her and calling her the 'up-timer's whore' too."

"Then?"

"Then Captain Wiegand came along with some of the Fulda militia and took her into the *Ratshaus*," Jeffie Garand said. He had his arm around Gertrud's shoulders. "She stayed there until the day was over and came back home with her father. According to Wiegand, von Schlitz was angry—tried to draw his sword on the captain. But the militia had other more urgent assignments, so they couldn't stop to deal with him the way he really deserved."

"Exactly what," Wackernagel asked, "was this placard about?"

Dagmar produced one. She had several. The soldiers had obeyed the orders to tear them down, which did not mean that they had destroyed such entertaining reading matter. And, in any case, they could be used to paper the walls of the cottages. The more layers of paper a woman pasted up on the wall, the fewer drafts would come through in the winter.

She had several copies of the pamphlet, too. She gave Martin a couple. He tucked them into his saddlebags.

They were about to start eating. Whether Sergeant Hartke was home yet or not, a meal could be kept warm only so long. A minor riot appeared to break out by the entrance to the compound. Jeffie jumped up and ran out; then came back with Hartke.

"I finally threw that sutler out," the older man was saying. "He's been trying for weeks to overcharge really drastically on the thread and notions for making the rest of the new uniforms and I've already warned him three times. Tell everyone tomorrow, Dagmar. He's not to be allowed back. Have some of the women take everything out of his cottage and throw it on the ground just outside the entrance. If he wants it, he can come and haul it away. If he doesn't bother, then it's free pickings."

The conversation meandered back to the scandalous pamphlet and stayed there all through the rest of the meal.

Wackernagel headed back down the road. There would still be a couple of hours of daylight and he didn't want to waste it.

Gertrud Hartke and Jeffie Garand wandered out of the compound, up in the direction of Menig's paper mill. They had discovered a rather nice stand of bushes there a couple of weeks before.

"Jeffie," Gertrud asked. "Can men really do all the things that those woodcuts in the pamphlet showed?"

"Not, um, precisely. No."

She didn't say anything.

"If you would really like to know what we *can* do, I'd be glad to demonstrate the whole procedure, so to speak. Think of it as a lesson in up-time scientific method. The hands-on experimental approach to finding out."

Gertrud thought about it. Up till now, she had really sort of been teasing Jeffie. He had made it so plain what he wanted from her, but at the same time he had been so unbelievably well-mannered about it, that she couldn't resist teasing a little. But . . . If all those people in Fulda already thought that she was a soldier's whore, why shouldn't she be one? Especially his?

"Okay," she said.

"Gertrud," Jeffie said. "You know what?"

She shook her head no. It was too dark to see, but he felt her hair move against his chin.

"Last winter, Derek—Major Utt, that is—said something. He said that if I got you pregnant, I was a married man."

"Oh."

"I'm not as forgetful as people sometimes think I am."

Gertrud snuggled in. She wouldn't have minded being a soldier's whore. Not really a lot, at least if Jeffie was the soldier. There were plenty of them in Barracktown. But a soldier's wife would be better. She wondered how long it would take for her to become a married woman.

Gelnhausen

Martin Wackernagel found it odd to pull into the post station in Gelnhausen and not see David Kronberg waiting. He finished his business and prepared to start out.

There was a young woman standing outside.

"You are Wackernagel?"

"Yes, that's me."

"Have you seen David Kronberg?"

"I passed him at Neuhof. He was heading for Fulda, just as he planned."

She smiled. "Do you know where he will be staying, in case my father might wish to find him?"

"I told him to stop at Barracktown. Sergeant Hartke just threw out one of the sutlers, so there's a cottage standing empty. I expect he can stay there a few days until he finds a job. If David's already gone when your father gets there, tell him to ask for Dagmar. That's the sergeant's wife. She'll know where he is."

Riffa went home and talked to her mother. A sutler thrown out. A cottage. Zivka went to bed thinking. Could she afford to wait for her husband to come home? A sutlery. A permanent business for an honest man. A home, perhaps.

Hanau

"Ask him in person," Meier zum Schwan had requested. "I've written a letter for you to take, explaining the details. But please deliver it in person and tell him how urgent it is for me."

So here he was, talking to a rabbi. Martin Wackernagel smiled to himself. At least he knew the history. Jews had settled in the county of Hanau long ago. About four hundred years ago, probably. They had been expelled not long ago, in 1592. Then Count Philipp Ludwig II came into power in 1603 and he changed it again. He invited Jews back to his capital city—only wealthy Jews, to be sure, but Jews. He let them build a synagogue; he issued a charter defining their legal status and protecting them. The community had grown steadily. From ten persons in 1603 to almost fifty families now.

Including the rabbi. *Der dicke Meier* wanted him to come to Gelnhausen to arbitrate the dispute within the Kronberg family.

"Isn't it a bit late?" Martin had asked.

"No. That's why David left when he did. Before it became too late; before someone said something that could not be retracted. Though Jachant Wohl came perilously close with her words about vagrants."

"Yes," Menahem ben Elnathan said. "Yes, I will go to Gelnhausen."

Wackernagel looked at the man. He wasn't young. He did not look particularly strong, either. "If it can wait for a week," he offered, "I will stop here on my next trip outbound and go with you to Gelnhausen. David Kronberg isn't there in any case. He has gone to Fulda."

"I would not refuse your offer," the rabbi answered.

"It will still be necessary to deal with all the others involved in the debacle."

"I brought your newspaper, too," Wackernagel said.

The rabbi picked it up and shook his head. "Useful, but so predictable. It's been the same pattern for years. Almost everything concerning the Ottoman Empire comes through Venice. Vienna sends news about Hungary, the Balkans, and the Turkish wars. Nearly all the articles with information about the Spanish possessions in southern Italy, Spain itself, Africa, Latin America, and the Philippines come through the imperial post office in Rome. If it pertains to England or France, it probably came through Antwerp although, possibly, now that the Swedes have a post office there, through Hamburg. Cologne gathers the news from the northern Netherlands and from the Germanies themselves, although that is now somewhat counterbalanced by the efforts of the postmaster in Frankfurt itself. A person has to read every story with an eye to who provided the information and how it is slanted."

He looked up hopefully. "Do you have unofficial gossip?"

Wackernagel offered a summary of the scurrilous pamphlet that had recently been circulated in Fulda.

"That is an unusually specific attack. Much of the material that has been sent to me recently is more generic in nature." Menahem ben Elnathan showed Wackernagel some examples of the anti-Semitic pamphlets that had been circulating in the CPE.

"Look," Wackernagel said. "Most of the pamphlets that you have bear no resemblance to the one in Fulda. But these two have a similar typeface and illustration style. I don't think that I have ever seen this typeface before."

"They are similar in another way," ben Elnathan observed. "Most of the pamphlets are general attacks. But you say that the two women mentioned in the Fulda exemplar are real." He picked up one of the other pamphlets. "As Rebecca Abrabanel, the wife of Michael Stearns, is quite real."

"I've never seen her," Wackernagel said, "Rebecca Abrabanel, that is. Or either of the Fulda women, but the up-timers in Fulda say that the face on the image of Clara Bachmeierin was a quite good likeness."

"Nor have I seen Rebecca Abrabanel. But something concerns me. The typology of Rebecca as the deceiver, deceiving Isaac into extending the blessing to Jacob rather than Esau, would not, I think, be the first thing that would spring into a Gentile's mind."

"If I could borrow that," Martin said, "I could show it to my brother-in-law. He's a printer; he might see something in it that we don't."

"You can borrow several. I'm not likely to run out."

Once More, with Feeling

Frankfurt am Main, June 1633

"What do you think of them, Crispin?" Martin asked. His brother-in-law looked down at the pamphlets.

"You want to know if I think they're nasty? Loathsome? Fetid?"

"I want to know if you recognize anything about

them. There's no printer's logo of any kind; not even an imaginary location and forged name of a printing house. No date of publication. I can tell that much for myself, but I'm not a specialist. You are."

"Let me look at them in the morning. In the daylight."

"I don't think they were printed."

"Crispin, they're lying on the table right in front of you. Of course they were printed."

"Umm, um. Look at this. It's printed. I printed it right here."

It was a neat pamphlet, full of illustrations, advising an expectant father how to build nursery furniture in his spare time. Self-improvement was the bread and butter of the small printer.

"Now, this one. Escher put it out last week. *How to Make Beer at Home.*"

Martin picked it up.

"And this one. It's from Freytag. *Sample Letters to Government Officials.* Both of these have the place and printer identified. They're trying to make money, after all. But just compare the pages."

Martin did not have much luck. Crispin patiently showed him the difference, point by point.

"I think these pamphlets you brought, both the Abrabanel one, which you say that according to ben Elnathan came from Magdeburg, and the one that showed up in Fulda, were produced on these new 'duplicating machines.'"

"That means?"

"I tell you, Martin, these new stencil systems will be running small printers out of business. If I don't manage to get hold of one of these 'duplicating machines' pretty soon, my own business is going to fold. It's not as if I make my money printing large editions of thick academic books. And Escher so far hasn't even let slip the name of the man he bought it from."

"Put an ad in the paper," Martin suggested.

"For what?" Merga asked. "Crispin isn't trying to sell something."

"Say you want to buy one. Escher and Freytag may not want to tell the rest of you where they bought them, but I'd say it's pretty likely that the maker would like to sell more."

The expression of Merga's face became quite predatory. "I'm going down to the post office right now." Which she did.

"While she's gone . . ." Crispin said.

Martin looked up. It wasn't like Crispin to sound so hesitant.

"This pamphlet that the Gelnhausen rabbi loaned to you . . . the one naming Rebecca Abrabanel . . ."

"Yes."

"I don't even like to suggest it. Jews get enough trouble in this world without my adding to it. But the way it is written. I can't help but wonder about the possibility of an apostate—a convert—writing it. First generation—one born and educated in Judaism. That pamphlet, and some of the others the rabbi collected. They rely quite a lot upon Talmudic tropes. If not an apostate, then perhaps a university-educated Hebraist."

"Either possibility is less desirable than the other."

"You might just mention them to the rabbi, though. Rabbis are trained to think their way through unpleasant possibilities. That's part of what they do."

❖   ❖   ❖

He couldn't leave without going upstairs and saying goodbye to his mother. Or he could, but he would regret it later.

"About settling down," she was saying.

"Look, *Mutti*," he said patiently. At least he made the effort to sound as if he were saying it patiently.

"It isn't just that I like being on the road, though I do like being on the road. I like it a lot. But working as a private messenger is a lot less subject to political vicissitudes than working for the imperial postal system used to be. Or, for that matter, than working for the Swedish postal system is now."

She looked skeptical.

"I wasn't dependent upon Johann van den Birghden's favor to get my job, which is just as well. I sort of doubt that van den Birghden would have hired the son of a man who worked for his main rival."

That was true enough—something that his mother couldn't argue with. Van den Birghden was not only the postmaster but also the newspaper publisher. It was the *Frankfurter Post-Avisen*. The only one, now. Martin's late father had worked as an itinerant salesman for Egenolph Emmel, a bookseller and van den Birghden's rival newspaperman. He had started the *Frankfurter Journal* in 1615.

Then van den Birghden had come to Frankfurt to run its newly established central post office for the Thurn und Taxis in Brussels. In 1617 he had founded the other paper. Emmel sued. In the course of the litigation, Birghden asserted that postmasters had a legal right to a monopoly on publishing newspapers.

"I've stayed out of the postmaster's way," Martin continued. "Van den Birghden is a busy man. Reminding him that my father ever worked for Emmel would not be a clever move. Even as a private courier, I have to work with the post offices, but it's not hard for me to avoid him. An ordinary person hardly ever has any reason to encounter the head of the postal system, especially not now that he is so busy establishing new routes. He's speeding up the field post system for the Swedish army. He's setting up alliances with the other postmasters working for the Swedes such as Wecheln in Leipzig and Stenglin in Augsburg. He's trying to speed up the links from Mainz to Hamburg and from there to Stockholm."

"Every one of those," his mother answered, "offers an opportunity for a man who is ready to settle down."

She looked at him.

"But," she said, "if you will not, perhaps you will not. Nonetheless, you could get married even if you continued to ride the Imperial Road. It is not likely, now, that Crispin and Merga will ever have children. I want to be a grandmother before I die."

He fled down the stairs. *Mutti's* new thought could be dangerous. Never, never before, had she separated the ideas of "getting married" and "settling down." Always before, one had gone with the other.

The Wheels of the Gods

Gelnhausen, July 1633

It wasn't pleasant, Zorline Neumark thought. The community had not just split since David Kronberg

left. It had shattered into a dozen pieces. It wasn't
clear that it could ever be put back together. The
only people who didn't seem to be involved, one way
or another, were Zivka zur Sichel and her daughter,
who had kept completely out of it.

Though they would probably be drawn in once
Zivka's husband Simon came back from his current
trip. Whenever he was in Gelnhausen, he made up
part of the *minyan*.

Now, though, the Wohls were not speaking to her
husband. Salman and Daertze were trying to keep
the peace between Meier and Abelin. Some of the
Zons' in-laws weren't speaking to any of them. The
parents of Feyel Wohl's betrothed were said to be
having second thoughts after Jachant's very unsuitable statements. Feyel and her betrothed, who really
did want to marry one another, now blamed Jachant.
Hindle was shrewish.

Zorline was very glad to see the arrival of Menahem ben Elnathan. In a way, she was glad to see him
riding with the Gentile courier. It sent a signal that
Samuel Wohl, *parnas* or not, would not have things
all his way. The president of a Jewish community was
not a dictator.

"He's back," Riffa reported to her mother. "The
courier. He brought the Hanauer rabbi, then went
to the post office again."

"Get your basket, then. I have hired the teamster
to come for the rest of it the day after we have left.
He has the key to the lock. The current rent we have
paid for the cottage with the sickle expires the day
after that. We will follow the rider to Fulda."

Barracktown bei Fulda

"Can you believe it?" David Kronberg asked earnestly. "It was a competition, but still . . . Only forty-two hours from Berlin to Hamburg. They say that the Brandenburg messengers are regularly covering Königsberg-Berlin in four days, now; Berlin-Cleves in six days when there aren't any armies in the way."

Three or four other post riders were gathered at the table, talking shop.

Not that David was a post rider, exactly, although he did have a job. He had happened to arrive in Fulda in the middle of a dispute between the NUS administration, the Swedes, and the city fathers over whether the city gates would be opened to allow passage of post riders in the night, since the main road led right through the city and the post office and change station with the remounts were inside the walls.

Since the city fathers would not budge from their stance that any proper set of gates remained closed from sunset to sunrise, the Swedes and the NUS moved the post office to Barracktown and surfaced a riding path around the city walls. David had ended up as a postal clerk, accepting, sorting, bagging, and routing the mail.

Since the up-timers had made this suggestion right after his first attempt to ride a horse *a diligence* for the whole length of a fifteen-mile *posta*, he seemed to be settling in happily enough. He still got to hang around a post office. That had been his real ambition.

Martin Wackernagel listened to the riders unhappily. None of the men sitting around the table seemed to have any doubts about the glories of riding short-distance *posta* lengths. None of them seemed to have any doubts about the wisdom of enforcing a government monopoly on mail handling.

Except Veit Huss. He was a teamster, not a post rider. Visions of stagecoaches danced in his head. Post chaises. Based on a novel, of all things, telling about life in England two hundred years in the future. A world in which the roads were so good that the mails were transported by coaches that also carried passengers.

"It will be decades before the roads permit anything like that," one of the riders said. "Especially in the Rhön region. Can you imagine trying to take one of those 'post chaises' at any speed from Hünfeld to Kassel by way of Hersfeld? Or from Fulda to Würzburg? Just along that old heights-road that follows the Doellbach upwards to Motten . . ." He started drawing a map with his finger in the moisture that the beer steins had dripped onto the table. "I've talked to some of the Frammersbach teamsters and they say . . ."

"Except, maybe, right around that Grantville place." Another man picked up his stein. "I've actually seen the roads they brought back in time. Even the down-time roads they are improving would carry coaches easily most of the year."

"My cousin Hans—" Huss began.

"Is a road contractor," the rider retorted. "He has visions that the New United States will pay him money to make the roads around Fulda look like the roads around Grantville. Fat chance."

"It wouldn't have to be all the roads. They could just start by improving the main mail routes to that standard . . . Some are already fairly good. Think about that comfortable stretch from the monastery of Thulba as far as Hammelburg on the Franconian Saale out at the edge of the Abbey's lands."

Martin's thoughts wandered.

Maybe, now that the king of Sweden and his new up-timer allies wanted more than just a field post system for the army, van den Birghden would become a consultant to many of the king of Sweden's allies. Maybe, the post office would need many more civilian carriers who would do for the CPE what the Thurn and Taxis did for the Holy Roman Empire.

Unless politics got in the way. There were advantages to being an independent courier. Sometimes, it was better not to work for the government. Martin had kept right on riding the Imperial Road in 1627 when the fortunes of war and pressures of politics had forced van den Birghden out as postmaster in Frankfurt.

Van den Birghden was a Protestant. Before the war started, it had been acceptable for a Protestant to hold an important job in the imperial system. Van den Birghden had enemies. The charge was that he had been spying for the Protestants—telling them what was in confidential letters that important imperial officials and commanders sent through the postal system. He had fought being fired, of course. It had taken them several months and several hearings to get rid of him. Ferdinand II replaced him with a Catholic, even though a lot of influential people from the archbishop-elector of Mainz to General Tilly himself had advised the emperor to keep him on.

Martin had kept on riding the Imperial Road when the king of Sweden's forces swept through in the fall of 1631 and reinstated van den Birghden.

While it was all going on, while the politicians fought over control of the postal system, Martin had kept riding. He might not be as fast, but his customers knew him and trusted him. Riding this route was a lot more than a living. Riding this route was his life.

"Across the top of that pass before you get to Speicherz . . ."

"Over another mountain in order to reach the Schondra . . ."

"Additional teams needed at Brückenau . . ."

"New bridge across the Sinn . . ."

The voices ran over and into one another.

"David," he said. "I hate to interrupt this thrilling conversation, but there's something you may want to know."

"My father has changed his mind?"

"Not exactly. Zivka zur Sichel and her daughter Riffa are at the Hartkes."

David Kronberg practically flew out of his seat.

Martin had deliberately built enough time into this run that he could stop and talk to Veit Huss and his cousin. Mail coaches would not be practical for a long time, Veit admitted, so what alternative was there to a mail monopoly? A regular freight wagon, such as Veit himself drove, was not suitable for the mails. It was simply too slow. The roads would not be ready for post chaises for a long time.

He kept thinking. The imperial cities had tried to hang onto their own messenger systems. It hadn't worked, because of the pressure that the grant of an imperial monopoly to Thurn and Taxis had placed on them.

Some of the territorial rulers still ran their own messenger services. Brandenburg, on the eastern edge of the CPE with interests far to the east in Prussia, outside the Holy Roman Empire, had its own good-sized office with over two dozen riders. Even inside the CPE, the electors of Brandenburg felt safer sending important correspondence between the branches of the Hohenzollerns in Berlin and those in Franconia by way of people whom they paid themselves. Not everyone was entirely sure that van den Birghden had been innocent of those charges of spying, after all.

But working for Brandenburg would take him off his beloved Imperial Road. If necessary, maybe things could be managed, but he would rather not.

Or maybe he could hire on with a freight line. The official postal system carried letters, sometimes whole sealed bags full of letters, but it didn't carry packages. If he located a long-haul line that carried from Frankfurt to Erfurt, he would move back and forth along the road more slowly, but at least he would move.

What would customers pay for the transport of light packages? Light enough that a man on horseback could carry several? Packages that did not really need a wagon and team, but were too bulky for a mail bag? Urgent packages?

Martin laughed, imagining a woodcut that depicted him on a horse with ten or a dozen lightweight packages tied to his back and his saddle, sticking out in all different directions. One hanging from his ear, perhaps. For a lot of horses, that would take some getting used to. A man would need the right kind of horse, steady and reliable.

What kind of customer would want a small or light package, too big for the mail bags but not heavy or bulky enough to require a freight wagon, taken somewhere fast? Who would want it enough to pay a tenth or twelfth of the cost of running the route and still leave the rider a decent profit?

Maybe there wouldn't be a new post office monopoly. The king of Sweden might not object to establishing one, but the Grantvillers were very enthusiastic about what they called "free enterprise."

Something to think about. Some way to keep riding the Imperial Road.

End of the Road?

Gelnhausen, August 1633

Simon zur Sichel came into Gelnhausen from a resupply stop in Frankfurt as he made his rounds. He found that Zivka and Riffa were gone and nobody in the community knew where.

When, they could guess, Zorline Neumark told him.

She and Meier zum Schwan were going back to Frankfurt. That was the general gossip. Meier had a business to run and there did not seem to be any sign that the feud in the Kronberg family would abate any time soon.

Samuel Wohl and Hindle Kalman had sent their daughter Jachant to cousins in Worms. The parents of Feyel's fiancé had made that a condition of continuing the betrothal.

When he found out that a teamster had emptied the cottage under the sign of the sickle out neatly and driven away with the goods, Simon started to feel much better.

No one in the community knew who the teamster had been.

He asked at the post office. "Veit Huss," the postmaster said. "He drives from Fulda to Frankfurt. He was on his way to Fulda when he drove out that day."

Simon zur Sichel decided to head for Fulda. If Zivka had gone there, she would have had a good reason.

"If you are going," the Hanauer rabbi said, "may I accompany you? I would like to observe the changes that the up-timers have made in Fulda for myself."

Barracktown bei Fulda, September 1633

The Barracktown Council agreed to accept Simon zur Sichel as one of the approved resident sutlers. He requested permission to throw out the front of the cottage by about ten feet to make the front room into a "general store." After some discussion of the concept, the council, chaired by Dagmar, agreed to the proposition.

Menahem ben Elnathan and Simon zur Sichel discussed the heavy responsibilities of matrimony with David Kronberg, who said that he would be quite ecstatic to assume them, thank you. At least, he qualified, if they involved Riffa zur Sichel.

Then he asked Simon what name he intended to carry now that his family was no longer living in the sickle cottage in Gelnhausen. This proved to be such a successful distraction that it spared him from further embarrassment for all the rest of the evening.

Zivka did the same for Riffa, who indicated a high degree of reciprocal enthusiasm.

David said that he did not think that his parents would agree. The rabbi said that if they were patient, he would see to it, so they all relaxed.

Martin Wackernagel and the rabbi continued their discussion of stencils and duplicating machines. Both of them talked to Sergeant Hartke and his wife Dagmar about pamphlets. Dagmar recalled the Menig-Bodamer connection. Wackernagel recalled the Bodamer-Schlitz-Mangold chuckling convention. Gertrud Hartke and Jeffie Garand recalled the odd-looking contraption that was on the stand at Menig's paper mill the evening they had walked up to check if Emrich and Liesel were okay. They hadn't thought about the room being full of stacks of paper at the time, Jeffie admitted, since a person really expected to see stacks of paper in a paper mill. Then someone remembered seeing Mangold at Menig's.

Jeffie said that he thought he had better tell Derek— Major Utt, that was.

Major Utt got them an appointment with the NUS administrator, Wesley Jenkins. Not "one of these days," but first thing on his calendar the very next morning, even though the whole day was scheduled for a big celebration of the up-timers' first down-time "airplane."

Fulda, September 1633

The NUS authorities arrested a lot of people, of course. First Jodocus Menig, who identified Karl von Schlitz as the person who paid for the import of the duplicating machine and stencils. They could not arrest him, of course, or his sons, since Schlitz, although in the CPE, was not in the NUS.

Captain Wiegand felt considerable relief that the miscreant had not been someone from Fulda. That lasted until Emrich Menig said that, by the way, they had just been getting ready to run off another set of stencils. He and Liesel Bodamer had made them, he reported proudly. They had followed the instructions in the manual and been entirely successful. These stencils had been brought to them by Lorenz Mangold.

Wiegand's apprehension lasted until someone read the manuscript, which proved to contain not anti-Semitic tracts but rather some of the worst heroic poetry ever written. Andrea Hill made some rather biting comments on the probable impact of "duplicating machines" on vanity publishing in the seventeenth century.

Wiegand's relief lasted until a search of Mangold's house, authorized before anybody got around to reading the manuscript found at Menig's, turned up several crates of pamphlets that were virulently anti-Semitic. And some more which advocated the resumption of witchcraft trials. Plus quite a few which were just weird. Nothing indecent, though. Mangold appeared to be downright prudish.

To the great disappointment of almost everybody else, Wes Jenkins refused to authorize the use of torture, even under these circumstances. Even though they pointed out that it was perfectly legal under the *Constitutio Criminalis Carolina*, which remained the law of the CPE because nobody had ever gotten around to repealing it. Wes said it wasn't legal under American law and that was that. And, moreover, it wasn't a capital offense anyway, as far as he knew, just to own the things.

All of which was terribly unsatisfactory.

Magdeburg, September 1633

"It's because we were thinking presses," Mike Stearns said. "Thinking inside the box. That's why we haven't been able to identify the bastards who are producing this filth. Even the Committees of Correspondence were thinking presses. Small presses; those are what they are distributing to their local organizations. That is what the Venice Committee of Correspondence is going to get. Improved small presses, but still presses using movable type. Because for copiers, we were thinking high-tech. We knew that the down-timers did have presses and that they did not have copiers."

He slapped his hand on the table, turning to Don Francisco Nasi. "How many of these duplicating machines are there now, Francisco? Inside the USE, spewing out this poison. Is there any way to make an estimate?"

Francisco Nasi shook his head. "I have people trying to find out how many Vignelli has shipped from Bozen. Some of the pamphlets are printed on presses, of course. We may still be able to trace those. But the duplicating machines are so simple that there is no way Vignelli can possibly maintain a monopoly on them. Any decent craftsman who sees one can copy it. Successfully, I must add."

"So these things, these libels, whether they are specifically anti-Semitic or not, will just continue to proliferate. Anywhere, essentially undetectable. Unless we open every large envelope in the postal system—which, I emphasize, we most certainly will not do—the stencils will travel for no more than the normal *porto*, anywhere west of a line running from Sweden's Baltic provinces to Hungary."

This time, Don Francisco nodded. "They do not even need to send the stencils. That is clear from the statements made by the young boy and girl in the Fulda case. They only need to send one copy of a pamphlet, or a manuscript. Anyone who has a duplicating machine can prepare a stencil. Some will be better than others, but then some printing presses turn out much better quality copy than others. It depends on the skill of the operator, the quality of the paper, the quality of the ink. For longer books, I expect, printing will continue to be the preferred method."

"Yeah, that was true up-time, too."

"So unless you wish to duplicate the *Porte*, examining everyone's mail for possibly dissenting literature . . ."

Mike shook his head. "No. No, of course not. We are not going to stop the mail and inspect every item. That would be against every principle of intellectual freedom, freedom of the press, that we are trying to introduce. It's just so . . ."

"Loathsome," Don Francisco suggested.

"'Loathsome' is a very inadequate word."

Hanau, November 1633

"It's a personal thank-you letter," Martin Wackernagel said. "From Prime Minister Stearns."

Menahem ben Elnathan took it. "I am honored."

"And one from Don Francisco Nasi."

"Perhaps I should be apprehensive."

"From all that I hear, they are sincerely grateful for

your contributions. Not to a solution of the problem of these scurrilous pamphlets, since perhaps there is none, but for assisting in defining it."

"No one among us did anything remarkable," the rabbi said. "But, then, most large events are the result of many small ones coming together."

"Exactly what do you intend to do to solve David and Riffa's problems? Perhaps I shouldn't ask, but I'm curious."

"It is well under way. There was no prospect that Abelin Kronberg and Bessle Zons would consent to young David's new job and proposed marriage. They have too much pride invested in preventing him from joining the post office and in arranging the Wohl marriage. I suggested that they should release their parental rights in regard to this son who has caused them so much trouble and heartache, so that he may be adopted as heir by his uncle Meier and Zorline Neumark. Once that is completed, then the new parents can—and will—consent to the marriage. I have correspondence for you to carry to Frankfurt today. If all goes well, you should be able to bring me the completed legal papers on your return trip."

Martin looked at the rabbi for a few minutes. Then, in the up-time manner, he saluted him.

Frankfurt am Main, November 1633

"Where did you get it?" Crispin asked suspiciously.

"The administrator in Fulda for the New United States said that he owed me a favor. So I said that he could do me one, since they had confiscated it as evidence. It's the duplicating machine that Menig had at his paper mill, producing those scandalous pamphlets. It's yours legally. I have receipts."

Crispin looked at it with distaste. "Do you have an exorcist to get the evil spirits out of it?"

"Not exactly. But you'll be paying for it for several years, so don't feel that you got something for nothing."

"How?"

"I brought Menig's son to apprentice with you. He's at my rooms. No fee."

"I thought he was the one who actually ran the machine."

"He is, but the up-timers think he is not old enough to be held, as the woman named Mrs. Hill put it, 'criminally responsible.' I offered you and Merga as an alternative, which Mr. Wesley Jenkins accepted. He is, from what I have observed so far, an incredibly ingenious boy who will occupy a great deal of your time."

Merga looked at her husband.

"All right," he said. "We'll take it. Him. Both of them. The machine and the boy."

"What about the girl?" Merga asked. "Bodamer's daughter. Liesel. What have they done to her?"

"Gone to her mother's people, for the time being, at least. Bodamer is one of Schlitz's subjects and the *Ritter*'s lawyers asserted jurisdiction on his behalf, even though he is under arrest himself. Mrs. Hill was very angry about it."

"Beyond that," Martin asked after a while, "how's business?"

"I'm developing a new line," Crispin said. "Merga's idea. We haven't heard from the merchant selling the duplicating machines, yet, but then he is certainly not in Frankfurt. These things take time. I am creating a new small newspaper to circulate locally and present advertisements for things that people want. There must be many people in Frankfurt who want some item, and other people who have it but no longer want it, but who do not know one another. With the duplicating machine, now, the cost of production for these 'want ads' will be reduced a lot . . ."

"Stop delaying, Martin," Merga said. "You have to go upstairs and say hello to *Mutti*."

When Wackernagel came back down the stairs, he moaned. "You've got to do something, Merga. You absolutely have to get her off this 'settle down and get married.' Find her an avocation. A 'hobby' as the up-timers say. Some other interest."

She looked up from the stand where she was watching Emrich Menig piece the duplicating machine together. "Getting you married and settled down is more than an avocation. It is her vocation, her calling."

"Merga, you have *got* to do something." Martin's desperation was clear from the tone of his voice. "I can't settle down. Not here, not anywhere."

"Why on earth not, Marty?"

"Because I *am* married. In Erfurt. Well, in a village right outside the city. And in Vacha. And in Steinau. With calling of the banns and everything. They were all such darling girls when I met them. I couldn't bear to disappoint them, so I told the local pastors that I was an orphan from Breslau. And if any one of them finds out . . . ever. Or the church! There are a lot of really good reasons that I love the Imperial Road."

"How *many* reasons?" Merga asked. She put as much "foreboding" into the tone of her voice as she could possibly squeeze through her vocal cords.

"Besides my girls? Eight, right now."

Merga gasped.

Her brother gave her the grin he had used—in his older sister's opinion, with an unreasonable degree of success—to get out from under impending disciplinary measures since he was three years old. "But Maria is expecting again."

Happy Wanderer

Frankfurt am Main, July 1634

"Settle down and marry. Or marry and settle down. Or marry and don't settle down—keep riding the *Reichsstrasse*, for all I care, though your wife may have different ideas. But marry."

Martin Wackernagel left Frankfurt am Main with his mother's admonitions ringing in his ears. This time with the variation that now that his sister Merga and her husband Crispin Neumann had taken in "that unmanageable boy"—otherwise known as Emrich Menig—if he didn't marry and settle down, everything would, in all probability, be inherited by a stranger.

"Emrich's not likely to be a stranger by the time we all die," which had been his first ploy, didn't go over very well.

Neither did, "Abraham named Eliezer of Damascus, a stranger, as his heir. And Eliezer would have been, if God hadn't intervened with a miracle for Sarah. If he wants Merga to have a miracle at her age, I presume that he's still perfectly capable of giving her one."

Nor even, "There's always Juditha." His younger sister, Juditha, almost fifteen years younger than Merga and ten years younger than himself, wasn't married yet. Nor did she come home regularly to let her mother complain about it. She had gone into service in the household of a Lutheran pastor at fourteen, followed her mistress to Strassburg when the pastor received a new call three years later, and wrote, perhaps, once every three months. If she was in the mood. Over which Mutti was greatly aggrieved, of course, moaning on and on about, "what is the point that she has saved a good dowry, above and beyond what your sainted father left for her and which I have invested so carefully and preserved from loss through the miseries of this entire war, if she shows no inclination to ask for it?"

Once he safely made his escape from the pursuing maternal voice, he followed his regular route—extended, now, beyond what it had been a few years before. From Frankfurt am Main by way of Gelnhausen, Steinau, Fulda, Vacha, Eisenach, Erfurt, yes. He still rode that part of the *Reichsstrasse*, the Imperial Road. But rarely, any more, the occasional further leg to Leipzig. Rather, from Erfurt, his regular path went through Arnstadt and Badenburg to Grantville.

Badenburg. Ah, Badenburg had many attractions. Prominent among them was a young woman named Helena Hamm. Not a girl. Wackernagel wasn't that interested in girls any more. He greatly preferred women.

He hadn't asked, but he had a fair amount of experience in observing women. He would place Helena at twenty-five or twenty-six years old.

Badenburg

"Three separate damnations, may all of them fall upon your head, you shrew." Willibald Fraas jerked his head up. "You have ruined this pour, coming in and startling Dietrich like that. Freytag in Arnstadt expects delivery of these steins within a week. Whose work is it pays for the costs of this household?"

"If you weren't so lazy, the steins would have been done last week. Last minute, everything at the last minute. You have no more sense of timeliness than a stewed prune." Agnes Bachmeierin slammed her fist down on the table where her husband and son were working.

"Don't think to browbeat me with your shoe, you grumpy old sow."

Helena Hamm watched the customer she had been serving leave the shop. Knowing that he had heard her stepfather and her mother. Knowing that one more story of the battles that occurred at the *Sign of the Platter* would go out into the gossip of Badenburg.

If her father had not died . . .

She shook her head impatiently.

Her father had been dead for a decade. Her mother, the formidable Agnes Bachmeierin, had fought the pewterers' guild with every devious legal device at her disposal in order to keep the family business for her sons. She hadn't managed to avoid remarriage to another master pewterer. That had been too much to hope for. However, Georg Friedrich Hamm (the Elder, deceased) had not been an ordinary pewterer. It was a specialty shop. He had supplied orders from all over central Thuringia. The marriage contract stipulated that Willibald Fraas would run the shop only until such time as her oldest surviving son by her first husband—whichever son that might turn out to be— qualified as a master and was ready to take it over.

Yes, her mother was clever. If Dietrich or Georg Friedrich the Younger should die or not wish to take over the shop, the daughters of her first marriage were the next in line. If neither of them had married a master pewterer, then Fraas had the first refusal right to *buy* the shop for any children he might have in his marriage to Agnes. Not inherit it. *Buy* it, at a fully and fairly assessed market price, to be split between the girls from the first marriage as their dowries. The marriage contract didn't even allow him that privilege for children of a possible second marriage, should Agnes have died without bearing him children. He would have had to compete with—bid against—any other pewterer who might be interested in the purchase.

But Agnes had borne him four. Three, two boys and a girl, were still alive.

There was no love lost between Willibald Fraas and his wife. There never had been.

Love? There wasn't even any mild friendship between Willibald Fraas and his wife. There wasn't even a truce or a cease-fire, such as that which seemed likely to occur in the Netherlands very soon now.

But . . . Helena was the oldest. She had been fifteen when her father died. She remembered perfectly well what things had been like between him and her mother. Exactly the way they were between her mother and stepfather. Agnes Bachmeierin was not an easy woman to live with. Especially not during those months when she suspected she was pregnant again but had not yet felt the baby's movement to confirm it. Particularly when she had no desire to be pregnant again, at all.

Months like this month. And, probably, next month.

"So, I suppose, whether you admit that she startled me or not, once more you will declare that my work isn't good enough." Her brother Dietrich Hamm, his voice as whiny as usual, had joined the fray in the back of the shop. "I can see it now. No matter what I achieve, it's never going to be good enough for a masterwork, is it? And you'll use your influence with the rest of the guild to bring the others around to your point of view. In spite of the fact that my father served as guildmaster."

"Boy, you have less brains than you do ear wax," Fraas exploded. "Your mind is like a rotten nut with no kernel."

Dietrich was completely convinced that his stepfather was trying to exclude him from achieving his mastership. Which, Helena had to admit, was not beyond the realm of possibility. The marriage contract, combined with their father's will, ensured that Dietrich would take over. According to their provisions, if Dietrich survived another three years, Willibald Fraas would be working for his stepson.

"Tickle-brained, clumsy, ill-nurtured—"

"If I am badly trained, then it was you who trained me badly."

If, of course, Dietrich had qualified as a master pewterer by then.

If not, Fraas could hang on for another ten years,

until her younger brother could qualify. Willibald was cranky, obnoxious, unpleasant, and capable of making the lives of everyone around him miserable. He was not just uninterested in the changes that Karl Schmidt was bringing to the guilds in Badenburg. He was hostile to every one of them.

Dietrich, encouraged by his mother and the Bachmeier uncle for whom he had been named, wanted to pursue every one of them.

But not with any real energy, much less hard work. Part of Helena had to admit that even if everything Dietrich claimed about their stepfather's intentions was entirely true, he was still basically a dissatisfied whiner and always would be.

He wasn't a very good pewterer, either. Even if Mama hadn't disturbed him, the odds were high that the pour would have had flaws.

Which Willibald knew.

Which to some extent justified Mama's complaints about his having left it too long. He should have allowed for the distinct possibility that, with Dietrich involved in the project, they would need to pour these elaborate handles again.

Martin Wackernagel paused at the door. The best description of the usual tone that he encountered when he stopped at the *Sign of the Platter* might be "constant sniping." Fraas provided him with a lot of commissions, but he had a nasty temper, which was most frequently directed at his wife; then at his three stepchildren; then at his own children. Not that he was a violent man—just a hostile one. Though his life as a place-holder for his stepsons couldn't be easy.

Helena was in the retail shop when he came in. She usually was. So he smiled at her. "Over in Grantville," he said, cocking his head in the direction of the back room, "they call it 'stress.'"

Helena was more than content to find a bit of respite from the hostilities by flirting with a good-looking courier whenever he dropped in with orders and letters. It wasn't as if anyone else was seriously courting her.

So, Helena thought. *Flirt I will.* Twenty-six going on twenty-seven and no serious suitor in sight. Wackernagel was a good-looking man and she was old enough to know what she was doing. She deserved a little harmless, inexpensive entertainment delivered right to her doorstep.

Grantville

Since the weather was warm, Wackernagel took advantage of an outdoor "Old Folk's Music" night at the Thuringen Gardens. A man could get away with buying just one beer at the outside tables, if he sat at the edge, by the fence. With his responsibilities, he didn't have a lot of spare change most of the time.

He leaned back, listening to the band. They'd been appearing occasionally for close to a year now. One of the women got up and made an introduction of something called, "Please help me. I'm falling in love with you." It seemed like a very long name for a song. One of the men ... Wackernagel thought a moment. His name was Jerry Simmons. Simmons started on the plea of a lover who was asking the object of his affections to reject him.

Wackernagel smiled into his beer. Now, that was unusual. He didn't think he'd ever heard a love song with that theme before. Mostly the lover was asking the girl to let him into her heart and her bed—not keep him out of it.

Simmons moved on to the second verse. The man was unhappily married but determined to remain faithful. Now, wouldn't that make the priests and ministers happy? Too bad none of them seemed be here tonight. This song could be turned into a whole sermon theme. But wait. At the end of the second verse, it looked like the guy might succumb to temptation. Wackernagel perked up. Maybe it was just as well that the upstanding Pastor Ludwig Kastenmayer was safely at home in the rectory next to St. Martin's in the Fields Lutheran Church, probably reading edifying bedtime stories to his numerous preachers' kids.

But no. The singer concludes that it would be a sin. The girl must close the door to temptation on him. *Damn, what an anticlimax.* Nice tune, though. He called, "Encore, encore." Which, one of the down-time mail carriers had told him, in the Thuringen Gardens, meant just what it said. Not, "sing something more." It meant, "sing it again, Sam."

Why, "Sam?" Not a single one of the acts he had heard in Grantville had a singer named "Sam." He would have to find out when he had a chance. Before he left tomorrow, he would stop at the public library and ask.

Jerry Simmons sang it again. Wackernagel listened, committing the tune to memory and writing the words on a piece of scratch paper. It would be an excellent song to sing to girls he wasn't really serious about.

He couldn't afford to get serious very many more

times. His income was stretched about as far as it would go, even with Maria's market garden for the Erfurt trade, what Rufina could bring in with her spinning and hostel for travelers, and the fact that Edeltraud had been able to continue on as a waitress when her father's inn was sold after his death.

He could sing it to Helena Hamm in Badenburg on his way home. It was a very pretty song.

Fulda

The gossip in the Fulda Barracks was better than that in Fulda itself. Things were pretty quiet, though, in spite of the Ram Rebellion going on in the other sections of Franconia. Dagmar, Sergeant Hartke's wife, said that the main concern of the soldiers was whether or not it would extend into Stift Fulda, since it was certainly lively enough down around Würzburg and Bamberg. And whether they will be allowed to go out and shoot some peasants if it did. Life had been dull.

Martin taught them his new song, admitting that he didn't know whether it was a "genuine Hank Williams" or not. The woman who introduced the singer hadn't said, and he'd forgotten to ask that when he stopped at the library to find out about "Sam."

As a kind of consolation prize, he treated Dagmar and the sergeant to a synopsis of the plot of *Casablanca*. One nice thing about regular visits to Grantville was that a man always came out with something to trade. Not goods—he was a courier, not a merchant. But ideas.

Badenburg, August 1634

By the time Martin got to Badenburg again, the kidnaping of Clara Bachmeierin in Stift Fulda was old news. Old, but crucial to the household in which Helena Hamm resided. Clara was her aunt, the sister of the inestimably belligerent Agnes. So he delivered all the information he had gathered.

"It's not that we don't care about the other people that the SoTF sent over there," Helena said, "but none of the rest of them are related to us. What do you really think?"

"They're doing their best." What else did he have to say?

From the back room, the apparently interminable family squabble flew on. This time, a new voice. A young one. Screaming, "But I don't *want* to apprentice as a pewterer. I don't *want* to spend my life molding tableware and figurines. I *want* to stay at the Latin school and then go to the university."

"Want, want, want. Why should it make any difference what you want, you little pipsqueak? Did anyone ask me what I wanted? Metals are important."

"The only metal I want to deal with is those new steel pen nibs that they're making in Jena, now. I want one for my stylus. Or . . ."

Helena sighed. "Jergfritz. My younger brother. Georg Friedrich Hamm, the Younger."

Wackernagel grinned. "Just as charming as your other brother, I perceive."

"Willibald has no patience with him. But Dietrich doesn't, either. Dietrich knows that if he should die, and all men are mortal, perhaps more so in the middle of this war than in a time of peace, then Fraas will have another ten years of controlling the shop before Jergfritz is old enough to take over. By that time, my stepfather will be close to sixty and a daily routine of pouring hot metal may have lost some of its appeal. So Dietrich is convinced that my stepfather's nefarious plot is to shut him out in favor of his younger brother."

They could still hear invisible dialogue going on.

"You want to be a pen-pusher instead of a respectable tradesman? Scribbling your life away instead of making something useful? It's high time for you to be articled."

"Or a key," Jergfritz yelled back. "I'd be willing to deal with a piece of metal if it was a key to my office in a fine government building."

Martin flirted a little longer and then proceeded along his route to Grantville. Where the news arrived that all was well in Fulda, the SoTF administrators having been retrieved.

Which, he hoped, might improve the general mood of the Fraas/Bachmeierin/Hamm household in Badenburg. But he doubted it.

On the Road Again

September 1634

In Grantville this time, he also discovered that the mayor, Henry Dreeson, was planning a "good will tour" of Buchenland, which would culminate in Frankfurt. And which would involve him.

That was genuinely new news. He stopped in Baden-burg, where he told Helena. He stopped in Bindersleben bei Erfurt, where he told Maria. He stopped in Vacha, where he told Rufina. He stopped in Fulda and at the Fulda Barracks, where he saw Sergeant Hartke, Dagmar, David Kronberg, other friends, and picked up messages to be delivered to the Hanauer rabbi and to Meier zum Schwan in Frankfurt. He stopped in Steinau, where he told Edeltraud.

Between Steinau and Frankfurt, he thought long and hard. Maria had been very excited. So had Rufina. And Edeltraud. Each one of them insisted that he must bring his honorable charge, the mayor of Grantville, to stay overnight with the family in Bindersleben. And in Vacha. And in Steinau.

His heart was sinking. He could feel it dropping. By now it was somewhere in the region of his bowels, likely to be expelled on his next visit to a latrine. He was experiencing a feeling that he identified as "terrible dread." There wasn't a Good Omen that he could discern anywhere. Whereas there were a lot of distinctly Bad Omens.

Maria. His first and, therefore, legal wife. They'd been married nearly ten years now. She was a true orphan—parents dead, no aunts and uncles. A hired girl in a dairy. Mutti would have been furious that he chose such a wife. But she'd been so cute, and she smelled intriguingly like cheese. Where he got the idea of telling the pastor in Bindersleben that he was an orphan from Breslau himself, he couldn't even recall any more.

He'd already been making good money on the road. With no one to spend it on but himself, he had quite a bit saved, which impressed the Bindersleben pastor. He bought the lease of a little cottage with a garden and set her up in her own little cheesemaking business. Fancy cheeses, soft cheeses, for the weekly Erfurt market. When the Swedish army came through in 1631, she'd had a setback, because the foragers confiscated every cow in the village of Bindersleben, but they left the people unharmed. Cows could be replaced. They rejoiced at the births of four children; mourned the death of one of them. Little Margaretha, their Gretel, in 1631, had not been old enough or strong enough to survive the famine time.

Maria was a darling girl.

But, then, so was Rufina. They married in Vacha. A month after Maria's first child was born. Maria had been a bit ill-tempered during that first pregnancy and Rufina was, so, um, available every time he traveled through Vacha. Which meant that even though she was a Catholic, from the Fulda side of the town, the priest had approved her marriage to a Lutheran orphan from Breslau in September. Late September. Followed by the birth of their first child in February. Early February.

It had worked out well, though. He was able to buy the lease on a little cottage with a garden, right on the outskirts of the town, a block from the *Reichsstrasse*. She provided rooms to travelers and also was a spinner. They had rejoiced at the births of three children; mourned the death of one of them.

Rufina was a darling girl, too.

With Edeltraud, things had been a little more complicated. But also, in a way, easier. Old Caspar Kress at the Blue Goose in Steinau had only the two daughters and didn't really want to give either of them up. But only one son-in-law could take over the inn.

Caspar had married off Anna, the younger girl, to Thomas Diebolt, the younger son of a prosperous Gelnhausen innkeeper, the year before. Thomas had moved in and would take over the inn. His father had bought out a half-share; that money went to the dowries for the two daughters—which meant, of course, that Diebolt got half of his expenditure returned to the family for investment right away. The other half of the inn would be divided between the daughters, with Thomas having the right to buy Edeltraud out when the time came.

So far, so good. But Caspar would still have lost his second daughter when she married and moved away. Which would have been a small tragedy. Edeltraud was an excellent cook and waitress. So he had seen possibilities in his older daughter's interest in a courier. A man who traveled the *Reichsstrasse* and would leave her at home. Even though Caspar was a Calvinist, he made things right with the minister when it turned out that the courier, an orphan from Breslau, was a Lutheran. Thomas and Anna were happy too, since she was content to continue working at the inn after her marriage and they wouldn't have to find the capital to buy out her quarter-share when old Caspar died.

They married in July of 1629. Late July. Little Caspar was born early the next January, but he was sickly from the start and soon died. Since then, though, Edeltraud had given him three healthy, lively sons. Since old Caspar's death, she continued to live and work at the inn, her children penned up in a little room behind the kitchen along with Anna's two. Her quarter-share of the profits, above and beyond what he could contribute, made a decent income, with no rent or food to pay for out of pocket.

Edeltraud was a darling girl.

But none of them knew about the others. Of course. He was not some kind of Turk, to have a harem. He was a respectable married man.

Three times, but these things happened. None of them could ever learn about the others. O Lord above, what a disaster that would be.

And he couldn't have told Mutti about either Rufina or Edeltraud, even if he had been single when he married them. They weren't Lutheran. And Rufina, in particular, expended a great deal of effort trying to convert him to her own faith. It was her least attractive characteristic. But tolerable, entirely tolerable, given that all the rest of her characteristics were most attractive. Especially her . . . His mind temporarily wandered off into the realms of remembrance.

Maria and Rufina and Edeltraud really, really, wanted to see a horseless carriage up close. They were extremely excited about it. And so did all the children. Well, not Maria's Otto and Edeltraud's Conrad, because they were too young. But all the rest of them.

There was no point in not telling them. The trip was going to be in the newspapers. The Grantvillers intended to get a lot of publicity out of Mayor Dreeson's tour. They would certainly find out that he was going to leave his horse in Grantville, ride to Frankfurt and back in an "ATV." With cushioned seats. And a driver. Who might even teach him to drive it.

So he probably wouldn't be able to get out of stopping to show them all the ATV and introduce them to the mayor. Strike the word "probably." There would be no way to get out of stopping at all three of his households.

He was the guide, Mayor Dreeson said. Because he knew the route.

What to do?

Publicity. Have the vehicle go slowly, with frequent stops at many villages. Mayor Dreeson had a bad hip. He was an old man, with the physical needs of old men. Stop at almost every village on the route. Get out. Have the drivers explain the vehicle to the children.

He could suggest it, at least.

Maybe he could arrange the schedule so the stops in Bindersleben and Vacha and Steinau were short ones. Midday. With everybody's attention on the vehicle. Not overnight, with a chance for conversation.

Please, O Lord, not overnight with a chance for conversation. Thank you, O Lord, that women in the Germanies do not share the idiotic up-time custom of adopting the family name of their husbands. Please, O Lord of Hosts, make the children so interested in the ATV that they do not call me Papa. Or, if they do, please make it happen at only one of the stops.

Grantville

On his next return from Frankfurt, Wackernagel stopped in Fulda to pick up paperwork from Wes Jenkins, for Ed Piazza, to set up Dreeson's trip to the Fulda area. Dreeson had agreed to go, contingent upon getting his wife Veronica and Mary Simpson successfully retrieved from Basel, so planning was in full spate. That wasn't the only thing Wackernagel carried on the trip, of course: a courier would go broke if he only took one commission at a time. But the paperwork was urgent, so his pleasant interlude spent chatting with Helena Hamm in Badenburg was brief. Unfortunately.

He also pitched his inspiration to Ed Piazza. "It's a political trip, I understand. You should have the driver to make stops in a lot of towns and villages. The mayor can get out, move around. He won't get so tired, that way. The cars will attract crowds of fascinated kids, whose parents will follow them. From here to Badenburg, not so much. It's close to Grantville, so the people are used to seeing cars and trucks. Not just driving on the road, but parked. Beyond Badenburg, though, even through Arnstadt, and up to Erfurt, people mostly see up-time vehicles going back and forth. Driving on the road. They've seen that plenty of times. They haven't, most of them, seen one stopped, where they could take a closer look, with a driver who was willing to explain how things worked."

Ed nodded.

Wackernagel clinched the deal. "You want to get votes for the Fourth of July Party all along the route, don't you? Not just over in Buchenland."

"I have the record here somewhere," Henry Dreeson said. "Somewhere in this pile." He started sorting through a batch of old 33 rpm LPs. "It was real popular, back in its day, and it was German, too, so maybe the down-timers would like it. Margie—that was my daughter, you know, Margie—sang it when she was in the Girl Scouts. And my granddaughter sang it in Girl Scouts, too. It's a kind of perennial. The kind they call a 'golden oldie.' Ah, here it is." He pulled a disk out of its cover. "It should suit you very well, Wackernagel. You're a 'happy wanderer' yourself, back and forth on your route all the time."

Wackernagel didn't like it as well as he liked Hank Williams.

On the other hand, it was Henry Dreeson's "Your Local Government in Action" tour through Buchenland: not his. If the mayor thought that this would be a good theme song, then maybe it would.

Then the singer came on with a verse in German. Oddly accented German, but definitely German. Cunz Kastenmayer, one of the numerous sons of Pastor Ludwig Kastenmayer, who had been recruited to serve as Dreeson's translator on the tour because of his linguistic talents, asked, "When was this sung, and where?"

The other half of the audience was a professional courier. "Where's this 'Rennsteig,'" Wackernagel asked.

"Right here in Thuringia," Cunz answered. "Or, rather, it runs down the ridges of the *Thüringerwald* and generally marks the border between Thuringia and Franconia. It goes right through Suhl, almost. It's been there as long as anyone can remember, back into the *media aeva* between classical times and the modern. A messenger route, about a hundred of your up-time miles long, Mayor Dreeson."

"Nowhere near as long as the Imperial Road, the *Reichsstrasse*," Wackernagel remarked with satisfaction.

"Needs a lot of repairs, too. The encyclopedia says that in the other history, it was Duke Ernst—Wettin's brother, the one who's regent in the Upper Palatinate now—who fixed it up, a few years from now in their future, as a fast way to move German troops into Austria in case of attacks by the Turks."

"Is it as old as the *Reichsstrasse*?" Wackernagel asked with some interest.

Cunz shook his head. "I don't know."

"Did either of you ever hear of Al Smith?" Dreeson asked.

Neither one had.

"Ran for President against Hoover in 1928. On the Democratic ticket. They called him the 'happy warrior.' Way back. Well, not as far back as Wordsworth. If you look in that book over there, Cunz, next to the bay window, you'll find the *Collected Works of William Wordsworth*. My grandfather died when I was just five years old, but he left that book to me in his will. The poem's in there, if you want to read it.

"Then later, in my day, that's what they called Hubert Humphrey, too. I listened to his speech on the radio—the one at the Democratic national convention in 1948. I was about fifteen, I guess. Old enough to pay attention. 'To those who say that this civil rights program is an infringement on states' rights, I say this, that the time has arrived in America for the Democratic Party to get out of the shadows of states' rights and walk forthrightly into the bright sunshine of human rights.'

"Hell, even Reagan used it. 'So, let us go forth with good cheer and stout hearts—happy warriors out to seize back a country and a world to freedom.' No point in tossing out a good slogan just because you didn't agree with the guy who said it. What else are we trying to do—the Fourth of July Party, I mean?"

Dreeson started the record playing again.

"I think we need a theme song for this tour we're taking over to Fulda and Frankfurt. *Happy Wanderer* should do it. It's close enough to 'happy warrior.' Even if it is about the wrong road."

Neither of them was in a position to argue. Not even when Mayor Dreeson decided that, in the absence of a sound system, the two of them would have the privilege of singing it at every single stop. Once Cunz had remodeled the German words a bit, to turn it into a political theme song.

"At least," Cunz said, "you can carry a tune. And I play the lute, which is a lot better than playing the bagpipes, for example, if he expects me to be singing, too."

October 1634

Wackernagel breathed a sigh of relief when the motorcade left Vacha, escorted by a portion of the soldiers from the Fulda Barracks Regiment. Utt's arrival had certainly been timely. In the short period Mayor Dreeson was at Rufina's house, it hadn't dawned on him that those fascinated kids belonged to his friend Wackernagel. Whereas the insistence of the military commander on increased security had moved the mayor to a different location without raising Rufina's suspicions. Which would certainly have risen up if her husband had suggested that they shouldn't provide hospitality for such an honored guest.

Scot free.

Except.

"You do realize," Cunz Kastenmayer said, "that you're

damned lucky they chose me to be the interpreter on this trip. Not my brother the junior minister. Not my brother the bureaucrat who has sworn an oath to uphold the laws. Just a law student."

Wackernagel started to answer when the bushes at the edge of the road parted and a girl jumped in front of the lead car.

Which wasn't that dangerous. Because of the condition of the road between Vacha and Fulda, along with having to accommodate the mounted escort, the ATVs weren't moving over five miles per hour.

A couple of the soldiers rode ahead.

The girl waved both hands in the air to show she was unarmed.

Wackernagel jumped out and yelled, "Liesel, what are you doing?"

"Running away," Liesel Bodamer answered cheerfully. "I hate my guardians. They're mean and make me learn to embroider. Papa might not have been much of a father in a lot of ways, but at least he didn't keep me inside the house all the time. So I'm going to Fulda. Mrs. Hill didn't want them to send me to my mother's relatives in Schlitz, to start with. So I'm going to her and I thought I'd hitch a ride."

"Tell her to hop in," Dreeson said. "We can sort it out in Fulda better then we can out here in the middle of the road."

Liesel hopped.

"How's Emrich?" was her first question.

The rest of her questions were so numerous that Kastenmayer had to give up on making any more comments until they got into Fulda itself and turned her over to Andrea Hill.

Just Outside of Steinau

"Martin?" Cunz Kastenmayer said.

"Yes?" They were mounting their horses, having given up their seats in Henry Dreeson's ATV to Sergeant Hartke's wife Dagmar and her stepdaughter Gertrud.

"There's a familiar-looking female coming down the road. On foot."

Wackernagel looked back and emitted a hearty "Hell and damnation." Followed by, "Utt!"

Derek Utt turned around. "You want to take her with us?"

"Over my dead body," Wackernagel said.

Utt detailed a couple of his soldiers to return Liesel Bodamer to Fulda and the custody of Andrea Hill.

The motorcade moved on.

Frankfurt am Main

"At least we don't have to do it all over again on the way back," Cunz said.

Wackernagel smiled. "Would it be appropriate for us to pause and give thanks for life's small blessings?"

"Have you given further thought to the blessing I pointed out to you a few weeks ago? In regard to your luck in not having the company of either of my older brothers?"

"The junior pastor and the city clerk?"

"Precisely. We'll be at the inn in Steinau within a couple of hours. The *Blue Goose*, where we stopped coming down to Frankfurt."

Wackernagel nodded.

"Will you be spending the night in the family quarters again?"

"Do you care?"

"Oddly enough, yes." Cunz paused. "Also about the women in Vacha and Bindersleben. And the children."

Wackernagel winced.

"As will Herr Dreeson's wife. Although the mayor does very well, he still has learned German recently. He fails to grasp many of the nuances of how people address one another. The redoubtable Veronica does not share this handicap."

"Edeltraud would be very disappointed if I seemed to treat her coldly in the presence of influential associates."

Cunz shrugged. "It's your choice. Possibly your grave."

Fulda

"Well, of course you'll come with us, Wes. You and Clara. With me. After what you went through with Gruyard and von Schlitz and their thugs, it's the least I can offer."

Wackernagel, listening, saw a light. "Well, then. You don't need a guide going back. The driver knows the road now, and you have Utt's soldiers as an escort. I'll just rent a horse in Fulda, pick up some commissions, and go back to riding my regular route, rather than accompanying the motorcade all the way back to Grantville."

Cunz Kastenmayer smothered a smile.

Especially when Mayor Dreeson's reply was a firm, "Oh, no, Wackernagel. I couldn't see my way to letting you do that, after all the help you've been. We'll leave the soldiers who were riding in the rear ATV to ride back to Grantville. You and Cunz come right along with us, in the other car." He paused. "But how are we going to split up the couples? Ronnie and I can take the back seat of the front car, but that means that Wes will have to be in one and Clara in the other. No, wait. Cunz can ride in front, in our car. You can be in front with the driver of the rear car, and Wes and Clara in back. Unless Wes and I have business to talk. Then he can ride with me and Ronnie back with Clara . . ." Henry limped away.

Badenburg

Although Henry remained happily oblivious to nuances and Wes equaled his inability to perceive them . . . Veronica and Clara did not. Not at Vacha. Not at Bindersleben.

Not in Badenburg. Where it became fairly clear that not only did the courier have three wives, but also a girlfriend. While waiting for a problem with the engine of the rear ATV to be repaired, which involved bringing a part from Grantville, they observed Wackernagel making a delivery to the Sign of the Platter.

And flirting.

With Clara's niece, Helena Hamm.

So what were they going to do about it?

"Did you know about this, young Kastenmayer?" was not a propitious opening sentence for any conversation.

Cunz felt like he was about ten years old again. In school. Caught.

"Ah. Well, not about your niece. We didn't stop long in Badenburg on the trip outward."

"I am going to stop this. What is it at they say in the movies that they show in Grantville. The westerns?"

He grasped the reference immediately. "Head them off at the pass."

"Yes. Precisely. Find Wackernagel and get him in here. I am going to tell Helena. At once. Also, he shall know that if he does not leave Helena alone, if he does not comply, I will tell the other women. He is not going to ruin my niece's life, the wretch. The miserable, irresponsible, abominable . . ." She searched her vocabulary. "Creep. That is what Andrea would say. Creep."

Veronica nodded.

"They made me so mad," Helena said. "It's not as if we were doing anything except laughing. Which I get little enough of. Self-righteous old . . . biddies."

Wackernagel shrugged. "You heard what they said."

"They can't do anything to me. Not really." Helena leaned her elbows on the counter. "It's not as if I had a fiancé who could break our betrothal in outrage. Or anything close to a fiancé. So, I suppose, it all depends on whether or not you want to risk it."

Wackernagel picked up his hat. "I'll plan on seeing you the next time I come through, then."

Grantville

"I don't know when he'll be back, Clara," Wes said. "Someone else brought the bag in from Fulda this week. The guy said that the people in Fulda, Utt and the others, have been picking up some information about Gruyard and what happened to the abbot. Schweinsberg, that is. I wouldn't trust the new man, Hoheneck, farther than I could shake a stick at him, as Granny used to say.

"Meier zum Schwan in Frankfurt picked up some information. Sent it to the Hanauer rabbi, who diverted Wackernagel off to make a direct trip to Magdeburg with stuff for Francisco Nasi."

"Well, good riddance." She paused. "Wesley?"

"Ummn."

"Now that you have been assigned to this 'uniform matrimonial legislation' project for the SoTF and maybe the whole USE? What is the law on this man? What does it say? All three of the towns are in the SoTF now, but when he married, they were in three different countries. All in the Holy Roman Empire, but three different jurisdictions. Bindersleben, then, was under Erfurt, but over Erfurt, that part, was the archbishop of Mainz. Steinau belonged to the counts of Hanau. Vacha to the abbey of Fulda. Who is . . . responsible?"

Wes sighed. "Clara, honey, have you seen any of those little statues around Grantville. The ones with the three monkeys. One with his hands over his ears, one with his hands over his eyes, one with his hands over his mouth?"

"Yes. Someone, I can't remember who right now, has one on his desk."

"There's a lot to be said for that motto."

"What motto?"

"The monkey statue motto. 'Hear no evil, see no evil, speak no evil.'"

✧   ✧   ✧

"I sort of hope you didn't arrive by way of Baden-burg," Wes said.

Wackernagel gave him one of those smiles. "By way of Jena, this time. I rode the railway from Halle. It was . . . interesting. I had heard of the surveying being done up north of Fulda, of course, through southern Hesse-Kassel. But until I experienced it for myself . . . I suppose it's something I will have to factor into my future plans."

"All right, then. My wife is a woman with strong opinions, you understand."

"I agree entirely."

"You know what they are, too." Having disposed of family obligations, Wes got back to government business. "Now, I have something that has to get to Derek Utt as fast as you can move it. The boy's taking every drop of advantage he can squeeze from the lemon during this interregnum over there, without a civilian administrator to ride herd on him. Since I left and before Mel Springer can get there to take over. He took it hard when Hoheneck let us know what had happened to Schweinsberg. Real hard."

Wackernagel took the packet.

Wes reached into his shirt pocket. "Take this to him, too. It's a letter from Mary Kat."

Wackernagel raised his eyebrows.

"His wife." Wes grinned. "They were married last February and haven't seen each other since the honeymoon. Which lasted three days. Remind him from me that if he doesn't take his long-overdue leave and come home for Christmas, he's going to have a really pissed lady lawyer on his tail."

Badenburg, November 1634

"Ah," Wackernagel said. "The fair Helena, whose face launched a thousand ships."

"This face," Helena said, "has never seen a boat bigger than a barge on the Ilm."

"Must you disillusion me? Such a skewering of my best efforts is positively discouraging."

She leaned forward, her elbows resting on the counter. She knew she shouldn't be doing this. Not for her sake, but for his. She had no doubt that Aunt Clara sincerely meant every threat she made.

On the other hand—he was by far the most entertaining man she had ever met. She was old enough to know what she was doing.

"If not a thousand ships," Wackernagel said, "then a hundred small barges, at the very least." He kissed her fingertips.

She giggled. And told herself that she could manage Aunt Clara. If it came to that.

December 1634

Etienne Baril, the Huguenot lawyer who worked for Andrea Hill in Fulda, still regarded Wes Jenkins as his real pipeline into the SoTF and, therefore, the USE governmental structure. The next time Wackernagel came through, he gave him a letter when the courier dropped in to ask how Liesel was doing.

"She's in school," Andrea said. "As long as the

roads are bad, I think she'll stay there. Liesel may be a little hard to handle, but she certainly isn't dumb."

Wes looked at the letter, took off his glasses to polish them, and said, "Can you hang around for a day or so and then go up to Magdeburg for me? I'd like Clara to do an analysis of this before I send it on to Nasi."

"If it doesn't go beyond a couple of days. I'll send a message with Wattenbach that I'm delayed and have him cover my usual stops. But Mutti expects me home for the holidays. She'll fret if I'm not there."

Wes had a little difficult juxtaposing the concepts of "Martin Wackernagel" and "fretting mother" in his mind.

It didn't work out too badly. He got the packets to Magdeburg, hit Bindersleben on Christmas Eve, Vacha a couple of days later (he and Rufina had given the children their presents earlier in the month, on the Feast of Saint Nicholas, as was the Catholic custom), Steinau for New Year's, and Frankfurt for Twelfth Night.

He'd had practice, of course. Although some years, he made the stops in the reverse order.

Bindersleben bei Erfurt, January 1635

Something was wrong. He knew it as soon as he tethered his horse and stepped into the tavern.

"Martin. Oh, Martin," the tavernkeeper's old mother said. "I'll call the pastor." She turned toward the kitchen. "Hanni, run, put on your cloak and run. Bring the pastor right away." Then she put her hand on his arm. "Don't go to your cottage, Martin. Wait for Pastor Asmus. Don't go to your cottage. There's no one there."

"It was so sudden," Pastor Asmus's wife said. "Just last week, and we had no way to reach you. We knew you would be on the *Reichsstrasse*, somewhere. She had just told us that she was expecting another child. Another blessing. Then, Tuesday evening, little Kaethe came running up to Midwife Knorrin's house, saying that her mother was lying on the floor, bleeding. We called a physician from Erfurt. He came riding out in the dark and the cold, but by morning she was gone. Oh, poor Maria. Not that she isn't in a better place. But the children? She has no relatives and you are an orphan. Plus you are scarcely here more than a day in each month."

Wackernagel rested his forehead on his fists, his elbows on his knees.

"Eight years old, Kaethe," Pastor Asmus said. "Six, two; Otto not yet a year. I remember when I married the two of you, thinking that if she had family to investigate your background, they would worry about just such a thing, with you on the road all the time."

Wackernagel raised his head. "If she had family to investigate my background, the children would be with that family now."

"The *Schultheiss* has taken them in, temporarily. But he and his wife have six of their own. It's not a permanent solution. But there's the cottage and garden. It's not as if they will be charity cases. You can afford to have them bound out to good families. The village council and church elders are already making inquiries for you."

Wackernagel shook his head. Thinking, thinking. No. He could not endure to have them bound out. Separated from each other. They slept in a single trundle bed at night, cuddled together like a litter of puppies in this cold winter weather.

But, since he had represented himself as an orphan for so long, he couldn't say that he had family in Frankfurt who would take them.

"Or," the pastor was saying, "if you want to keep the household together, to continue its existence more or less undisturbed, all of us will be happy to try to find you another nice wife. Within the next month. I think that is as long as you can really presume on the kindness of the *Schultheiss*, and it takes three weeks to read the banns."

The pastor's wife and the tavernkeeper's mother both nodded solemnly.

He shook his head.

"I need to see the children," he said. He looked out at the snow-covered ground. "I can't leave my horse standing there. It's so cold. Could you bury her?"

"Don't worry about the horse," Hanni said. "On my way back from the rectory, I took him to the stable and groomed him."

Pastor Asmus answered the other question. "Not yet. She is in the crypt. We loaned her one of the church's shrouds. Burial will have to wait for a thaw. So I waited until you came to preach the funeral sermon. Shall we do that tomorrow?"

Wackernagel stood up. "I guess we might as well. Thank you, Pastor Asmus. All of you. Thank you for everything."

Rufina would not be understanding. He sat in the church, listening to the words of the twenty-third psalm. And Maria would not have wanted her children brought up by a Catholic. Edeltraud might be understanding. Growing up in an inn tended to make a young woman a little more . . . comprehending of the ways of the world. But . . . Thomas and Anna were not likely to be, and it would be a burden on the two sisters, as well, to have four more small children to care for, in the middle of a busy hostel, in addition to their own six. Plus, they were Calvinists. Maria would not have wanted her children to be brought up by Calvinists.

"Our father, who art in heaven." The words of the prayer, recited by the congregation, passed over him. Almost the whole village had come to the service.

Maria had been a darling girl.

"We think it would be best," the *Schultheiss* said.

"No. It's not what I want for them. For me."

"What do you want to do, then, Martin?"

"Can I leave my horse in your stable, Hanni?" He turned to the tavernkeeper. "For a couple of weeks?"

"Of course."

"Then, I'll go into Erfurt tomorrow. See a lawyer about the cottage and garden—he'll come out to talk to the village council. You'll have approval of anyone who assumes the lease or buys it out, of course. Maria bought one of those new handcarts—the kind farm wives are using to take produce to market in the summer. For her cheeses. I've made friends, along the road. People who will take my children in, keep them together, long enough for me to deal with this. I'll pack them and their things in the cart, good and warm, with hot bricks and pans of coals, and take them down to Badenburg.

"I can't thank all of you enough, for everything you have done. But I just can't bear to bind them out.

"I'll bring the cart back. It's part of Maria's estate. The lawyer can put it into the inventory before I go.

Badenburg

It wasn't warm, not really. If if were April, it would be a chilly day. But it was warm for January. Helena stood on the steps, her apron wrapped around her hands, watching the early sunset of midwinter. There weren't any customers in the shop, she had caught up the bookkeeping, and right now she couldn't stand to listen to Willibald, Mama, and Dietrich in the back for one more minute.

She didn't notice the man with the handcart at first. Not until he stopped right in front of her. Even then . . . Martin did not look like himself.

"She died," he said. "Maria died. I've brought the children to you."

She picked them up, one at a time, and carried them indoors. After shooing Martin inside and telling him to get warm at the hearth.

The children were toasty. Not happy, and in the case of Otto in serious need of a clean diaper, but warm.

"It hasn't been bad, today," Martin said. "Except that my feet are wet. My boots are designed for riding, not walking."

"Well, then, take them off and put on dry socks. Surely you have some." Her voice was cross. "If you don't, I'll get a pair of Dietrich's."

She knew perfectly well that she was going to take these children in.

Just because Martin had brought them to her.

She also knew perfectly well how her mother would react. And Willibald. And Dietrich. And, for that matter, the rest of her siblings and half-siblings. Her aunts and uncles. Particularly Aunt Clara.

So much for any prospects of ever having a serious suitor. Much less a fiancé. Or a husband.

Old enough to enjoy a harmless flirtation with no repercussions. Like *hell* she was.

Maybe sometimes your mother and aunts really did know better.

She opened the door to the back of the shop. In the dying light, Willibald and Dietrich were clearing up the day's work. Mama, already heavy with this pregnancy, was perched on a high stool, tallying up the successful pours.

"Guess what?" she said.

Grantville, late January 1635

"Agnes just couldn't believe that Helena did it," Clara told Kortney Pence. Anything to take her mind off the prodding and poking of a prenatal exam. "Without so much as a by-your-leave to anyone else in the family."

"The man can afford to pay for their keep," Kortney said. "It's not as if she was taking in charity cases."

"But the extra work. And with Agnes pregnant again. What do you suppose happened to that poor woman?"

Kortney looked down. Clara, pregnant for the first time at thirty-nine, did pretty well in hiding her panic as her due date got closer.

Not so well that an experienced nurse-midwife couldn't detect it, though.

"Nothing that's going to happen to you," she said firmly. "I didn't get to examine her, but from what Wackernagel told Helena, I'd bet on an ectopic pregnancy." She pulled a chart of the human female reproductive system down from the top of the metal closet. "Here . . . you've seen this before. I've shown it to you. The ovaries, where you store the eggs. The womb, where the baby grows. And these—the fallopian tubes. If the fertilized egg gets stuck before it reaches the womb and the baby starts to grow in the tube, well, there's just no room. You get a rupture. Hemorrage. And, a lot of the time, death. Always, with down-time medicine. Sometimes, even up-time." She put away the chart. "But you're well beyond that. The baby's fine. Go home and harass your relatives."

The rumors about anti-Semitic demonstrations kept coming in. Wesley was involved, of course, through the SoTF Consular Service. Plus, there had been those pamphlets in Fulda. There were new pamphlets now.

Harangues in the towns around Grantville.

Questions from Stearns and Nasi in Magdeburg.

Wackernagel, every now and then, bringing things in from Frankfurt am Main.

Nobody could quite put a finger on it.

Not until the fourth of March, when everything erupted. When someone, nobody knew who, shot Henry Dreeson and Enoch Wiley. In front of Grantville's synagogue. During an attack on it. Which the police weren't there to handle because of a demonstration against the Leahy Medical Center. A demonstration that turned violent.

Hanau, March 5, 1635

"The rumors of a pogrom in Grantville," the Hanauer rabbi said.

"I rode down as soon as it came in on the radio," David Kronberg said. "We have a good receiver at the post office now. Better, actually, than the SoTF administration's own. Sometimes they come down and listen to ours."

"How many?" the president of the congregation asked.

David knew what they meant. How many new martyrs to commemorate.

"Um, none. No deaths. Some minor injuries. Everyone will recover. The attackers never actually managed to break into the synagogue. Which is good, considering how many were gathered there for Purim."

"We heard there were many dead in Grantville yesterday."

"Yes. The casualty count was pretty high. But none of ours. Nobody knows how it connects together yet. At the hospital, several of the Grantville *Polizei* and many more of the attackers. None of ours were there at all. In front of the synagogue, yes, there was an attack against it. The mayor and the Calvinist minister came to calm the crowd. Somebody—no one knows who, yet, shot them. Another up-timer who attacked the attackers, riding a hog, was killed with an axe. A piano, one of the great harpsichords they have, fell on the minister's wife and broke her leg."

A question.

"No. I have no idea why she was there with a piano. None at all. It was the Christian sabbath. They say that people came pouring out of the churches. But not to attack. To defend. All the rest of the dead were the attackers."

"A hog? In front of the synagogue?"

"Not a pig. A Harley."

David realized that didn't help.

He tried again. "A motorcycle."

Still no resonance in Hanau.

"A horseless carriage with only two wheels. Like the ATVs they showed during Mayor Dreeson's tour, cut in half. If anyone among you bothered to go look."

He sighed. He shouldn't have said that.

"They ride astride them, as if they were horses."

Another question.

"No, I have no idea at all why they call them hogs. But they are machines, not swine." Of that, at least, David was certain.

"If they never broke into the synagogue, how come some of ours were injured?"

"They were the Hebraic Defense League members who came to fight off the attackers."

A lot of questions, all at once.

"A better question," someone said, might be, "what is the proper commemoration of gentile martyrs killed while opposing an attack on a synagogue?"

The Hanauer rabbi sighed. "I expect that will occupy many a discussion for a long time to come."

"On Purim," someone else added. "Who is our Mordechai? Our Esther?"

"If you mean the Hebraic Defense League," David answered, "I think it has about fifty members. Most of them Sephardim. Which, if you ask me, ought to give us something to think about. But no Esther, as far as I know."

"Rebecca Abrabanel," someone else said. "Even if she was not present, she is the new Esther."

The Hanauer rabbi sighed. He did not care for visionaries.

Grantville, mid-March 1635

"Wes," Preston Richards said. "I've got some bad news for Clara, I'm afraid."

"What now?"

"Well, we've been tracing the men who were killed in the demonstration out at the hospital on the fourth. It's pretty slow. But we did manage to figure out that most of the guys that Bryant Holloway brought in came through his fire department training contacts. So the fire watch wardens from towns around have each sent someone down to take a look in the morgue."

"And? Is it doing any good?"

"Fourteen identifications so far. But that leads me to the bad news. One of the corpses belongs to a boy—young man—named Dietrich Hamm, from Badenburg. Pretty well known as a malcontent. Not about anything in particular, most of the time. Just always unhappy about life in general. The kind of kid who carries a grudge against fate. But he was Clara's nephew. So—we'll need the names of next of kin, if you can give them to us. We can take it from there. Arrange for him to be sent back to his family. She doesn't have to do anything, considering that she's pregnant. And that you've got problems of your own with Bryant and Lenore."

Badenburg, 27 March 1635

"It was a brawl, Helena," the neighbor said. "Willibald objected to some things that people were saying about Dietrich—what he was involved in, over in Grantville. Defending the family honor. I don't think anyone meant to kill him, but these things can get out of hand. Meinhard was swinging a bottle. Just to hit him with, but it broke against the corner of the bar when he brought it around. It was sharper than any knife, what was left in Meinhard's hand. A point of glass. Thick glass. It just kept coming around, that swing. It slashed his throat."

"Helena?" Jergfritz asked. "Helena, what are we going to do now?"

She didn't say anything.

His voice got shriller. "What?"

"Right now?" She looked around the shop. "It's closing time. I'd better bar the door and pull the shutters closed." "Right now, I'm going to fix supper. All of us have to eat. Mama, you, NaNa, our half-sister and brothers, Martin's children. Me. No matter what happens, we still have to eat. The watchmen will be here soon enough."

Badenburg, 30 March 1635

The baby was crying. The midwife handed it over to Helena to clean up. She took a look. Another girl. Warm rose water. Dim light. A gentle welcome to a difficult world for this last child of the late Agnes Bachmeierin, *verw*. Fraas, *verw*. Hamm.

Twice a widow. Ten times a mother in two marriages. Seven children alive to mourn her.

"Helena," her sister asked. Her name was Anna Clara, now nineteen years old, but everyone had called her NaNa since she was a baby. "What are we going to do now?"

She finished swaddling the baby and turned around. "Hire a wet nurse. We don't have any time to waste. Get down to the pastor's house and tell him we need one right now. Get a couple of references. Whatever else happens, she'll need to eat if she is to live."

NaNa walked across the room to look at the baby. "What are we going to call her?"

Helena looked over to where the midwife was starting to prepare her mother's body.

"Willibald wanted to name Mag for his mother, but Mama wouldn't. We'll call her Herburgis." She looked back at her sister. "On the way back from the pastor's, stop at the sexton's. We'll need his horse and wagon for Mutti's funeral."

Grantville, April 1635

"Clara, I tell you," her brother said. "That man is not only still stopping in Badenburg to see Helena every single time he passes through, but he was *married*. His wife died in January. She's been taking care of his children ever since. And now, with Willibald and Agnes both dead. And Dietrich, too. The shop isn't bringing in a cent. There's nothing to sell. Willibald concentrated on meeting special orders—he didn't have much stock on hand. We have to do something."

Clara eyed him consideringly.

What should she say?

Her first temptation was to ask "which wife," but she was prudent enough not to.

Maybe she had learned something from Wesley.

At eight months pregnant, she was not going to risk Wesley's precious baby by running up to Badenburg to handle this, either.

"I'll do something," she promised. "Something drastic. The very instant I have time. But with all the problems— Mayor Dreeson, Reverend Wiley. The person I would usually ask to assist me is Veronica, but she has her own difficulties. It was hard enough going up for the funerals."

He got up to leave.

"Wait," Clara said. "Just in case they don't have enough cash on hand to hire a really reliable wet nurse for the baby. I saved quite a lot, really, while I was in Fulda." She handed him a purse.

Badenburg, May 1635

"Don't keep standing up," Helena said. "It doesn't make sense for you to stand up. I have to keep walking. She cries unless I walk with her. All night, sometimes."

Martin didn't sit down, but he did lean against the wall. "It's the only thing that makes sense," he said. Coaxing. "Come to Frankfurt. Mother my children. They have become very attached to you."

"How can I leave my brothers and sisters?"

"How can you stay?" he asked practically. "Are you willing to marry a man chosen for you by the pewterer's guild?"

She looked at him. "You already have two wives."

He inclined his head. Slowly. "But I am free to marry."

"You are also the sexiest damned man I have ever met in my life."

He smiled.

"What about the people who know? Aunt Clara. Mrs. Dreeson. Young Kastenmayer?"

"You will be my legal wife. In Frankfurt. The one my mother and sisters know about."

Herburgis's wails gradually subsided to sleepy sniffles. Her head drooped onto Helena's shoulder. Carefully, very carefully, she put her in the cradle. "And that will pardon the existence of the others in their eyes?"

Martin sat down on the other end of the kitchen bench. "So far, your aunt has not carried out her threat to tell."

"So far, I haven't married you."

They looked at one another for a while.

"What you do in Steinau and Vacha will be your own business."

He looked at her sharply.

"We can see Pastor Schultheiss and have him start calling the banns before you leave this time. It takes three Sundays."

Badenburg, June 1635

"Actually, Cunz, it's really easier for me, don't you see, to marry Helena than it would be for me to explain the whole thing to either Rufina or Edeltraud?"

"I have no doubt at all." Cunz Kastenmayer smiled. "Have you tried explaining it to Steffan Schultheiss?"

"Helena thought it would be more prudent not to bring it up. She said that it might trouble his conscience." Martin looked at him anxiously. "You don't feel like you have to, do you?"

Cunz looked at him. "Why simpler?"

"They both think they are already married to me. When, actually, they aren't. Plus, I would have to choose between them—which marriage to legalize—which I could scarcely bear to do, because they are both such darling girls."

"Is Helena?"

"Is Helena what?"

"A darling girl?"

"She was, I thought. Last summer."

Clara Bachmeierin *verw.* Stade and *verh.* Jenkins traveled to Badenburg, her new daughter in her arms, to express the view that she was more than a little upset by this plan. Considering that the man had two other wives, which she told Helena months and months ago!

She arrived in the middle of a family battle.

"I'm *not* going to leave school and apprentice to a pewterer," Jergfritz proclaimed. If you try to make me, I'll just run away from home." He stopped a minute. "Like Liesel Bodamer did. Martin told me about that."

"You're the heir, now that Dietrich is dead."

"Let someone else inherit it." At thirteen, he was too young to focus on the economic realities, Clara thought.

But he wasn't.

"David Schreiner is going to marry Aunt Marliese next month."

Clara nodded. This was true. Maria Elisabetha and David had been betrothed since the previous autumn. She had told Wesley's family about it at Thanksgiving. She remembered that.

"He's the city clerk. He says that I can live with them while I finish Latin school. And he'll see to a university education for me. And find me a clerkship when I'm done, if I do well." Jergfritz looked up defiantly. "And if you let me stay with them, they'll take Hanswilli and Mag, too."

Those were Agnes's two oldest children by Willibald Fraas. Johann Willibald and Maria Agnes.

Now the boy had his arms crossed over his chest. "That will just leave Hansjerg and the baby for the rest of you to worry about. I think it's a good deal, myself. And I made it with them. Without help from any of you," he waved one arm, encompassing everyone else in the room, "grown-ups."

"But," Helena sputtered, "how did you figure all this out?"

"If the king of Sweden could fight battles when he wasn't any more than a year older than me, I figured that at the bare least I ought to be able to take care of myself." He reverted to looking like a sulky child. "I'll be damned if I'm going to spend my life in a pewter shop."

"I'm not about to marry Johann Drechsler just because he's a competent pewterer."

"But . . . what else can you possibly do, NaNa? He's willing . . ."

"Uncle . . . you didn't have to live with it." She turned her head. "But you did, Helena. You heard it every single day of your life, the way Mama and Willibald fussed at each other because he hated so much that it really wasn't his business. Do you think I want to live that again? What's so wonderful about this shop?"

"It's been in the family for generations untold. Our grandfather, our grandmother's father, and before him."

"I don't see you volunteering to marry Drechsler and take it over. You're marrying your courier and going off to live in Frankfurt."

"And if I did marry Drechsler, who's to say that Hanswilli or Hansjerg will want to be pewterers, any more than Jergfritz does? That's years away."

"What do you want, then?" Clara asked.

"Let's sell him the business on a mortgage. Drechsler can run it well enough to make a good living for himself. I think that with the changes in the guild rules that Karl Schmidt has pushed through, the Badenburg city council will let us do that. All of us will get some income. Not a lot, but some. Johann's sister Dorothea is already married to Jorgen Fraas, who's Willibald's nephew. Well, his father was Willibald's half-brother. So it's all in the family, sort of, even if he doesn't marry in."

Helena shook her head. "He isn't married. He'll still need a wife before he can take over as a master. The guilds won't change that rule. Someone needs to run the household and take care of the apprentices he brings in. Say that he does apprentice Hanswilli in a few years—would you want him living somewhere without a master's wife to look out for his welfare?"

"Well, let Johann find his own wife. It doesn't have to be me. Maria Anna Fraas would do fine. She's only three years older than I am, but she's Willibald's half-sister, even if she is twenty-five years younger than he was. She's our own cousin, too. Aunt Anna Catharina Bachmeierin's daughter, even if that aunt did die so young that I don't even remember her." NaNa grinned a little maliciously. "And I know she wants to get married. It's all she talks about. I expect she would marry a gelded ox if he agreed to put a ring on her finger."

"That says where you think you can get money. And how you think we should handle the shop." Clara looked at her niece again. "What do you want to do with the money once you have it?"

"I want to take my share and go to Grantville. Study to be an apothecary. I've talked to them, already—Raymond Little, the man's name is. And to Frau Garnet Szymanski at the Tech Center. I have to learn to be a nurse, first. Then I can apprentice at one of the 'pharmacy' businesses. It would take a long time, at least three or four years until I can start the apprenticeship, but I can do it."

She looked at the others, her expression an echo of Jergfritz's. "I know I can."

"Where will you live?"

NaNa relaxed. Just the question meant that Helena had surrendered.

"With us, this year." Aunt Clara answered the question for her. "Until there is room in Bamberg for the Bureau of Consular Affairs to be moved. After that . . . Lenore will be going to Bamberg even before we do, but I'm sure that Chandra—Wesley's other daughter—will be happy to have another adult in her house."

So much for complete independence, NaNa thought. But Chandra, whatever she was like, had to be a big improvement on Johann Drechsler as a prospective roommate.

✧   ✧   ✧

"My share of the mortgage money coming in from the shop . . ." Helena said. "You'll have a big household to support in Frankfurt."

"Not that big," Wackernagel said. "You and my four children."

"You're forgetting Hansjerg and Herburgis. Plus a wet nurse for Herburgis. For quite some time, yet. If you think that I'm going to raise my half-sister on pap . . ."

"Of course not." That answer came fast. Fast enough to suit his—betrothed.

"You can't let your other children starve, so whatever you've been contributing to those households will have to keep going to them. I trust that you do have whatever money you got from selling Maria's cottage and garden put safely away for her children?"

"Yes." Wackernagel nodded. "With the mayor and pastor of Bindersleben as trustees, along with a banker in Erfurt."

"Good enough. Now about my share of the money from the mortgage . . ." Helena looked at her future husband consideringly. "Your income should be going up. With my share of the income invested, you can start expanding your business to include additional riders and small packages. You mentioned that idea, once, when we were talking in the shop, last summer, when you first began flirting with me at the retail counter of the Sign of the Platter. However . . . before you get the use of my money, there's going to be a prenuptial contract. Ironclad, believe me."

She looked at Cunz Kastenmayer. "Draw one up. I know you can use the money. I'll have a licentiate look it over, but paying him for that will be cheaper than paying him to do it from scratch."

"Helena," Clara asked that evening. A little anxiously. "What are you going to do if his other two wives die? What if you end up having to take their children into your household, too?"

Helena winced. She would really rather not think about that prospect. But she was a realist, so she had thought about it. "Open a school," she said a little snippily.

Which should have ended that particular conversation, but Aunt Clara wasn't a woman to let well enough alone.

"What if he has . . . you know . . . more children? With them?"

Helena's mouth tightened. "I can't see that it's any worse than whoring around. Which men do, often enough, when they are away from home. Probably better, since he's not likely to catch syphilis from them and bring it home to me."

"But . . ."

"Leave it be, Aunt Clara," Helena said firmly. "He's a courier. I won't see significantly less of him than if those other women were not in the picture. And I will be, after all, the legal wife. Plus, unlike Maria, I know the truth. Unlike her, I will have leverage if Martin gets out of line. Not to mention that since I have family here in Badenburg and in Grantville, I'll have a good reason to travel with him occasionally to see my brothers and sisters. To see you. Check up on what he's doing when he's out on the Imperial Road. And with whom. I know what I'm getting."

She stood up. In the cradle, Herburgis was starting to fuss.

"I've told him that what he does in Vacha and Steinau is his business. I'll keep my word on that. But if he thinks that he's ever going to acquire another 'darling girl,' he'd better think again."

Grantville

"Cunz," Clara asked Pastor Kastenmayer's son. "How much danger is there that one of these days the pastors from Grantville and Badenburg, Bindersleben and Vacha and Steinau, might all get together—at a conference or something—and compare notes on Wackernagel and his multiple families? That all of it could come out?"

"Well . . . I'm speaking as a lawyer, now. Not to the morals of the matter."

"Yes."

"It's not very likely that their pastors would ever be at the same ministerial conference, since Rufina is Catholic and Edeltraud is Calvinist. Getting them together at one conference is more . . . ecumenical, I think the Grantvillers call it . . . than anything likely to happen in our lifetimes. If Maria's pastor ever got together with Steffan Schultheiss in Badenburg, there wouldn't be a problem. Maria was dead before he married your niece. That's okay—it's fine with the church if widowers remarry. Even rapidly, when they have children to take care of. Papa married Salome a lot sooner after my mother died than Martin is marrying Helena."

"Wesley?" Clara asked that evening.

"Mmm?" Her husband's head was bent over a pile of papers he had brought home from the office.

"You know that record keeping system that Jenny Maddox has in the Grantville Vital Statistics Office? The one with cards with holes punched around the edge, so you can pull out the ones you want with a wire rod?"

"Umhmm."

"Would something like that work for the whole SoTF. Or even the whole USE?"

Wes finally raised his head and focused his eyes on his wife. "I don't see why not, if you had a centralized office. People will still need the records locally, of course, so they shouldn't send in the only copy. But there's really no reason why they couldn't send in a duplicate. Or even two duplicates. One at the level of the provincial governments and one at the national level. It would take a lot of clerks to track it, of course. Increase the cost of printed forms a bit."

"Before the marriage takes place? Sort of like calling the banns, but with a . . . wider reach?"

"Sure, you could do it that way." Wes subsided back into his paperwork.

Clara settled the nursing Maria Eleonor a little more comfortably in her arms. A wolfish grin crossed her face. She took a silent vow to make it her personal project to see that the USE developed a system of centralized and cross-referenced marriage records.

Just as soon as possible.

Martin Wackernagel certainly had all the wives he needed.

Probably more than he needed, but there was nothing she could do about that without ruining her niece's future.

What did Kortney Pence say all the time? Yes. *Prevention, the best medicine.*

Frankfurt am Main

Wackernagel would have liked to return to Frankfurt by a different route. One that didn't involve Vacha and Steinau.

That, however, would have caused him to miss any number of scheduled pickups and deliveries. So he just made sure that they didn't stop in either of those towns.

This measure should have gotten him, and everyone else, to Frankfurt without incident.

Except that Andrea Hill buttonholed him in Fulda with the news that Liesel Bodamer was bound and determined to go to Frankfurt and find her friend Emrich Menig. Since the episode the previous October when she tried to follow Dagmar and Gertrud, but had been caught, she had tried four more times. Not in the middle of winter—the girl had enough sense not to want to freeze to death. But three times since early April.

"Menig's with your sister and her husband, isn't he?" Frau Hill asked.

Wackernagel had to admit that he was. Still alive. As amazing as that might be, considering the boy's inquisitive nature.

"Then take her along for a visit, please."

He shrugged. What was one more?

Mutti was happy. Her son Martin had brought home a wife. She was ecstatic. The wife was Lutheran. From an important guild family in Badenburg. Closely related to the wife of the former SoTF civilian administrator in Fulda. With a dowry and income from her late father's shop, to boot. How could he have done better?

Well, perhaps it would have been ideal if she wasn't encumbered by her half-brother and half-sister. Not to mention the four other children who were in her care. Nieces and nephews, presumably, since they called her "Auntie." Odd that they called Martin "Papa," but maybe they remembered their late mother better than they did their father. Helena said that she had died only six months ago. Poor little orphans.

"Martin," Merga asked. "Why on earth did you bring this girl along?"

"Frau Hill said that she kept running away. She wanted to get to Emrich."

"Do you expect Crispin and me to keep her?"

"If you can't make her go back to Frau Hill. Here's her address in Fulda. The two of you can work something out with the girl's guardians, can't you?" Wackernagel gave his sister his most engaging, impudent, mischievous, "have I been a bad little boy" smile.

A smile of proven value.

Merga drew a deep breath. "I am coming very close to choking you. On the general theory that you . . . you audacious and unrepentant scoundrel . . . have once more gotten away with your misdeeds. Not only free and clear, but with rewards."

She stood there, her hands resting on her ever more ample hips.

"I *would* choke you, if Mutti weren't so happy."

He smiled again.

Window of Opportunity

Section One: In the beginning . . .

The morning and evening of the first day
Mainz, March 1634

Eberhard was asleep. Rather, he had been asleep until the drumming started. "What in hell?"

Tata stood up on the bed and poked her head through the tiny third-story window of the Horn of Plenty. "Just some soldiers."

"They're not for me. I'm not late. The world may be full of sunshine, but it's my day off and I don't even have a hangover." He reached up for her wrist and pulled her back down.

She plopped onto his stocky body, wriggled, and told him to quit it right now because he might have the day off, but she didn't.

Reichard Donner's wife Justina also heard the drum. She looked out the front window of the main floor, more than a little warily. Her husband wasn't famous for his attention to submitting paperwork in multiple copies or keeping track of the details, so she thought that her wariness was fully justified. The Horn of Plenty had a record of too many times that its proprietor hadn't, quite, complied with those abundant city regulations designed to ensure good order and civic peace.

"What events do we have scheduled for the coming week?" Anything that will cause problems with the *Polizeiordnungen*?

"Nothing unusual," Reichard answered from behind the bar. "The two wedding parties are the largest functions. I have the written authorization from the city council for both of those. Well, it's almost approved. Everything will be ready by Thursday, certainly. Since both the groom and the bride's fathers for the Koster-Backe reception are local artisans, the families are bringing in a lot of the food and drink themselves, which is making a bit of trouble with the pastry shops and our regular sausage vendors. Fifty guests approved. Up to thirty guests permitted for the Biel-Braun wedding. I have the extra military paperwork for that, since Jost Biel is a soldier and so is the bride's father. It's . . ."

Reichard scrabbled around in his piles of paper. "Well, I did have it, right here, somewhere . . ."

Justina nodded. Marcus Pistor, Brahe's Hessian chaplain for the Calvinists in his garrison, would perform the Biel-Braun ceremony here at the inn, in the public room, since Mainz had no Calvinist church or chapel and they were all, in this family, good Calvinists from the Palatinate, subjects of the unfortunate Winter King's heir. *May Elector Karl Ludwig's soul be preserved from the influence of those Spanish Papists in the Netherlands who took him prisoner,* she thought. *Chaplain Pistor will have made sure that Reichard received the permissions. Now, if he hasn't misplaced them . . .*

Reichard, who hadn't even glanced up, was still talking while he sorted more paper into various piles. "Here it is. Right here, under the receipts. Everything's in order. Why? Is there a problem?"

"Lift up your head and listen. There are soldiers headed our way. That's what the noise is. Hear the noise?" She turned around, waving her hands at him. "There are four or so of them, Colonel von Zitzewitz's men from the uniforms, with a drummer. Also with a corporal and probably they're not just looking for a drink at this hour. What regulation have we offended now? Well, at least the children are at school, so I don't have to worry about having them mouth off and cause trouble. Except for Tata, of course; she's home. Anyway, four soldiers aren't enough to do too much damage, usually."

Kunigunde Treidelin, Justina's widowed sister and the tavern's main cook, came out of the kitchen, complaining as usual about a world in which a woman could live for half a century and still not be permitted by the authorities to finish out her waning days in peace and tranquility. "It's your fault entirely, Reichard, for getting involved with those Committee of Correspondence people and letting them meet here. The Swedes and the city council both keep a sharper eye on the Horn of Plenty than they would otherwise, just because of that. You know that as well as I do."

"I am the *chairman* of the Mainz CoC," Donner

pointed out rather mildly. "It would be rather ridiculous if I didn't let the group meet here. According to the theories of Althusius, since—"

"'The Mainz CoC'—as if that means anything. It's not as if you have anything like they do in Magdeburg, with toughs and enforcers. You get all the grief and what do you have to show for it? Nothing. It's not as if there's a CoC-raised regiment anywhere near Mainz. They're all up north with the emperor. We've got Swedish regulars, German mercenaries, and maybe a dozen soldiers scattered among them with even the slightest interest in politics. Hah!" Kunigunde turned her head. "Something's boiling over." She stomped back into the kitchen.

Tata, more formally known as their daughter Agathe, who had pulled on her clothes and come down instead of going back to bed, took her place at the window. "*Pffft*. That's Corporal Hertling. You know him. He's been here often enough. He's in Eberhard's company, so it shouldn't be a problem, whatever it is."

Walther Hertling motioned for his little troop to stop and rapped sharply on the door.

Tata waved her parents back, opened the door, glared at him, and asked, "Why are you bothering us?"

"Look, Tata, it isn't my fault."

Justina relaxed. Interventions by one's social superiors that were likely to lead to measures of harsh oppression were rarely accompanied by plaintive apologies or the use of nicknames.

"It may not be your fault, but you're here. With your goons."

"They aren't goons," Walther protested, looking as firm has he could. Which, considering that he was

barely twenty, was not particularly firm. He had gotten
his rank because his father had once upon a time been
Duke Eberhard's father's bootblack. "They're . . ." He
tried to think of some term more martial, impartial,
and less embarrassing to his captain than *babysitters*.
"They're, uh, the Captain Duke's personal *Leibkom-
panie*. Bodyguards, sort of."

Lorenz Bauer, Jacob Kolb, Ludwig Merckel, and
Christoph Heisel strove mightily to look as un-goonlike
as possible. Since all four were long-time mercenaries
in their thirties, with the scars to show for it, this
was not particularly easy. Still, if Corporal Hertling,
otherwise known as the immediate conduit to their
now-reliable paymaster, urged them to look harmless,
the least they could do was try.

"Eberhard says that he's off today."

"That's not the problem. At least, the problem isn't
about anything he's not done. It's about something
he's supposed to do next. It's, uh, about Hartmann
Simrock."

"Theobald's friend?"

"Yeah. Uh, Theobald Pistor took home a copy of
some of the speeches that Simrock has been giving
here at the CoC meetings."

"Ouch. Dumb, dumb, dumb, stupid. University
student or no university student, Theo has no sense
at all. I can't believe that he's Margarethe's brother."

"And, of course, he left them on the breakfast table
where they're quartered. At least, that's what Margarethe told Lieutenant Duke Friedrich. He left them
on the breakfast table where their father, Chaplain
Pistor, found them. And read them. Especially the one
about . . . well, you know. He is a military chaplain,

after all, so he took it to someone on Brahe's staff. And we've been ordered to investigate."

Reichard swept up his various piles of receipts and stuck them into a cubbyhole under the bar. "'We' being?"

"Uh, well, the captain's company. Him. Us. And his brothers."

Hertling wasn't worried about Donner, but he was a little intimidated by Frau Justina, so he turned around so he could talk directly to her. "Uh, that wasn't the brightest thing Simrock could have done, you know. Calling for the equivalent of a Ram Rebellion in Mainz and the Rhine Palatinate. Especially not criticizing General Brahe the way he did. Captain Duke Eberhard has the highest respect for the general's military talent and bravery. So it's just lucky that . . ." He stumbled, not quite sure how to phrase what was coming next in a manner that might be interpreted as mildly tactful.

Merckel was less concerned about tact. ". . . damned fucking lucky that the captain is actually fucking Tata here, or you'd all be in a deep pile of shit, you stupid assholes."

Justina winced. It wasn't that Reichard was unhappy about the attraction that led the young German officer on General Brahe's staff to regularly attend meetings of the Committee of Correspondence at the Horn of Plenty, in the company of his brothers and then spend the night, even though he had finally been allotted a much nicer room in the new unmarried officers' quarters. He was perfectly aware that Eberhard's interest did not lie entirely in the realm of radical political theory. Or even primarily in the realm of radical political theory.

No, Reichard was a practical man. His comment on

the arrangement had been that this was the greatest stroke of luck the Donner family had ever had and was ever likely to have.

Still, there was such a thing as tact. Maybe not where Merckel was concerned, though.

Besides, with increasing exposure, Eberhard was gradually becoming more interested in the political portion of his evenings. Still, though, the Horn of Plenty's primary attraction for him had a neat figure rather than a lot of economic figures. Feminine cooperation rather than the need to establish a purchasing cooperative was the crucial element that led to the extension of the captain's regular presence at the inn and the protection that resulted from that presence.

It was protection that they needed, in Justina's opinion, as long as Reichard kept flirting with those radical CoC ideas. She intended to take full advantage of it as long as there was a window of opportunity. Which meant, in effect, as long as Eberhard remained interested in their daughter. Which would be long enough, she hoped, to get the protection in some way institutionalized and make the continued existence of the Horn of Plenty and the Mainz CoC somewhat less precarious.

"Uh," Hertling said. "The captain will have something to say about it, I suppose, once he talks to the boy."

The subject of their discussion, having dressed somewhat less hastily than Tata, wandered into the taproom. Duke Eberhard of Württemberg yawned. "Which one of the boys is in trouble this time? About what?

Hertling duly saluted the square-faced, brown-haired, slightly long-nosed young man. Personally, he thought that his noble captain looked more like most people's idea of a sturdy peasant than a dashing cavalier, no more aristocratic than anyone else on the streets of Stuttgart or Mainz, including, for what it was worth, himself. That wasn't an opinion he was given to sharing with other people, though. *Der gute Walther* was prudent for his years.

"Neither of your brothers, sir. Simrock. If you could come down to General Brahe's headquarters with us . . ."

"I suppose that's not a request?"

Tata's eyes followed their departing backs. "So much for the idea of taking a boat down the river to Bingen with Friedrich and Margarethe and looking at Castle Ehrenfels today."

"Castles," her father said. "Castles, bah!"

Reichard Donner surveyed the room. The view was depressing. Mainz just wasn't a hotbed of revolutionary fervor. Perhaps he would have been better advised to move to Heidelberg. However, to be practical, there hadn't been an inn for him to take over in Heidelberg, whereas, in Mainz—owing to a fortuitous series of childless marriages and deaths from smallpox and plague, not to mention dysentery and measles, running through several imperial cities and tying all the way back to his long-ago godfather, one Reichard Wackernagel, belt-maker in Frankfurt am Main, husband of Justina's Aunt Maria—the Horn of Plenty had become available.

Even so. In addition to the two students, Pistor and Simrock, the attendees were not politically promising.

Pistor's sister Margarethe only came because her brother and her boyfriend did.

Philipp Schaumann, perpetual belt-maker's journeyman, aged about sixty-five, the hapless and hopeless perpetual suitor of his sister-in-law Kunigunde, came because Kunigunde lived here as well as because he was the younger brother of Justina and Kunigunde's late uncle's equally deceased wife. Also, he had been an acquaintance of Reichard's own late godfather back when they were both journeymen.

Sybilla Binder, about fifty and never married, was a friend of Kunigunde and the unhappy daughter of a belt-maker. She faced being thrown out of work when her father retired or died—one of which was certain to happen soon—and had no wish to spend her declining years spinning in the municipal hospital.

Ursula Widder, about fifty, Sybilla's friend, also never married, was the equally unhappy daughter of a tanner who had died and left her no option but to go into service. So she was now Kunigunde's general maid-of-all-work in the kitchen of the Horn of Plenty. It wasn't as if she had to put forth much effort to attend the CoC meetings.

Plus four soldiers and a corporal who were definitely not from a CoC-raised regiment and who attended because they were tasked by Gustavus Adolphus's commander in Mainz to see what they could do to prevent problems with . . .

. . . three very young dukes of Württemberg, one of whom was sitting with his arm around Tata's shoulder and twirling her reddish-tawny hair and fondling the various bits and pieces of her rotund body that he could conveniently reach.

The rest of his children were already in bed, which was some comfort.

"It's *not* an up-time idea," Simrock was insisting. "It's in Montaigne's *Essays* and they've been around for, oh, at least fifty years." For Simrock, not quite twenty himself, fifty years was ancient history. "How did he put it? 'No matter that we may mount on stilts, we still must walk on our own legs. And on the highest throne in the world, we still sit only on our own bottom.'"

Theobald shook his head. "I don't think that Montaigne thought it up all by himself. He probably swiped it from the Greeks or Romans."

A revolutionary's lot in Mainz was not a happy one. Maybe he could trade the Horn of Plenty for an inn in Magdeburg.

Bonn, Archdiocese of Cologne, March 1634

"We simply can't do what you want us to," Walter Deveroux said. "You're out of your fucking mind."

This wasn't the most prudent thing to say to the personal confessor of the archbishop-elector of Cologne, said archbishop-elector, Ferdinand of Bavaria, brother of Duke Maximilian, being at the moment the man who was paying them. Walter Butler sighed. It was true, though. The idea that they should take their dragoons on a *razzia* through Hesse, or if that route would not work, past Mainz and Frankfurt-am-Main, up the Kinzig valley to Fulda, was ridiculous. Absurd. A recipe for disaster.

Now the Capuchin was suggesting that just the colonels go in. Some of the Buchenland imperial knights were far from being happy at being placed under the administration of the up-timers. Upstarts, it was more accurate to say. They could provide a couple hundred men. Ferdinand's confessor got up. "You're the professionals. The archbishop wants to damage the prestige of the USE administration in Fulda. Figure something out and let me know what you decide."

"The Irish colonels, after consulting with Franz von Hatzfeldt, have accepted his suggestion in regard to kidnapping the abbot of Fulda," the Capuchin said. "It will be attention-getting, the sort of thing that will bring a lot of bad publicity down on the up-timers, but still not wasteful of manpower if Your Eminence should need for their regiments to take the field any time this coming summer. They believe they can coordinate it fairly easily with the imperial knights in Buchenland, and manage the matter with only local, on the ground, assistance. It should be a fast 'in and out.' They'll pick up as many of the up-time administrators as they can, take Felix Gruyard along to question them, but only bring the abbot out— maximum disruption for minimum cost."

Ferdinand of Bavaria frowned. "What about Wamboldt von Umstadt? Fulda is really under the jurisdiction of the archbishop-elector of Mainz. He may have something to say about this plan."

The Capuchin shook his head. "He is a refugee in Cologne. Under those circumstances, I feel sure that he will allow himself to be guided by your wisdom, Your Eminence."

Johann Adolf von Hoheneck cleared his throat. "I am not so sure of that. Archbishop Anselm Casimir is close to the Jesuits. Closer than he is to you

Capuchins. He's particularly close to Friedrich von Spee, who has been in Grantville. Even if he has taken refuge from the Swedes—even though he has been in Bonn since the winter of 1631—I'm afraid that his sympathies might not . . . Well. Additionally, as provost of St. Petersburg, on behalf of the Abbey of Fulda, I really must stipulate that whatever you do in the matter of the current abbot should not be construed as adversely affecting the rights, privileges, and responsibilities of the abbey itself."

"Your concern for your fellow Benedictines is admirable, I am sure," the Capuchin said. "It would be more so if you did not have hopes of becoming Schweinsberg's successor as abbot."

Ferdinand of Bavaria waved a hand. "Make it happen. But I want the questioning to be effective and efficient. It's all very well to say that since the Irish colonels speak English, they will be in a better position than any of my other subordinates to question the up-timers, but make sure that they take Felix Gruyard along."

"Father Taaffe and Father Carew are setting up for mass." Dislav stuck his head into the room. "Dislav" was the nickname of Ladislas Dusek, a servant who had been with Walter Butler's wife since her father assigned him as the footman to serve her nursery on the day she was born.

"Coming, coming." Butler stood up. "Thick-headed, impertinent Czech," he grumbled to Robert Geraldin. "I'd never let any other servant get away with being that rude. Once Dislav found out that I started as a common soldier, he got it in his head that I'm utterly unworthy of a noble Bohemian lady. He seems to think that I'm a wicked uncle and that he has to protect Anna Marie from me."

"You do have a temper," Deveroux pointed out. "And you did start out as a grunt, even if the commander of the Irish Legion was vaguely your relative. Besides, he thinks that you shouldn't have brought her with you on this drag all the way across southern and western Germany. Either one of her married sisters would have been happy to have her stay with them."

"How the hell am I supposed to get her pregnant if I'm in Bonn and she's in Vienna?"

"Touchy this morning, are we?"

"It's not that the news has been good all spring. God, but I loathe Swedes."

"Still feeling the pain after that little matter of Frankfurt-am-Oder? Lord, Butler, it's been three years."

"It was . . ."

"Yes, a trifle embarrassing to be taken prisoner. Look, it happens to all of us, just about, one time or another. In any case, we're all in this together, now. Since Wallenstein found out that all of us were involved in the plot to assassinate him—well, not just a plot, since we actually succeeded—in that other world, you have to admit that our career choices are limited. We're lucky to have been hired by the archbishop of Cologne." Deveroux stood up. "We're due at mass. MacDonald?"

"Leave him there," Geraldin said. "He's already drunk. Or still drunk. He was carousing with Borcke and Browne until all hours of the night. He's getting to be less than useless."

✦　　　✦　　　✦

"When I married you two years ago," Anna Marie von Dohna said, "I did not bargain for becoming a camp follower. How does Father Taaffe describe this place? 'Several wagons and a large number of dragoons.' This tent is not exactly a well-designed country house. I have precisely two servants and am paying them from what little gold I managed to bring with me. I did not bargain for this. When I agreed to marry you, you had every prospect of promotion and estates from Ferdinand II, two excellent ones, Hirschberg and Neuperstein."

"They were also in Bohemia," Walter Butler said sourly. "We ran into a little problem the year after that. Remember Wallenstein? Remember that he found out that I was a rather prominent participant in his assassination-that-did-not-happen-in-this-new-universe?"

"I was better off as Bartolomeus's widow than I am with you. I would at least still be at home."

"You didn't think so at the time. You were greedy; you made your bed; now lie in it."

If Butler could have slammed the door, he would have. Unfortunately, the tent did not provide a door he could slam.

The morning and the evening of the second day
Mainz, March 1634

"So that's the status of the Mainz Committee of Correspondence headquartered at the Horn of Plenty tavern. Chaplain Pistor is not happy with the way Captain Duke Eberhard handled his complaint about Simrock."

"What would he have preferred?"

"A hanging for treason would have suited his mood

nicely. Moving along to the next agenda item, we have yet another complaint from Georg Wulf von Wildenstein about the Americans—Thuringians—whatever one wants to call them—and their policies in Fulda." Johan Botvidsson shuffled the papers in front of him.

"The complaint concerns?" Nils Brahe asked. Gustavus Adolphus's chief administrator in Mainz was more than a little irritable.

"I believe the best description might be 'Catholic coddling,'" Botvidsson replied calmly.

"That's something von Wildenstein sees everywhere," Brahe retorted. "Everyone knows the man. When the king appointed him as chief administrator in Bamberg after Horn took the city in February 1632—that was months before he turned Franconia over to the Americans—almost the first thing that the man did was order the holding of Calvinist worship services in the Jesuit church. It was so egregious an offense against any kind of reasonable policy that even the *Lutheran* chaplains filed a formal protest. Why, me, O Lord, why me?"

"Johan had me read the letter too," Mans Ulfsparre commented. "At the moment, he seems particularly outraged because the Franconians, Fulda included, have voted to become an integral part of the NUS complex, which will now be calling itself the 'State of Thuringia-Franconia.' That makes it now the largest province in the USE, in addition to having provided Stearns as prime minister—not only the largest province, but one with a significantly large Catholic population, whereas the king came into this war as the champion of Protestantism."

"He should be happy to have Stearns as prime minister. The man is, officially at least, a Presbyterian. A Calvinist." Erik Stenbock, the other junior member of the inner circle, like Ulfsparre all of age twenty-two, grinned. "The highest-ranking Calvinist in the new imperial administration. Even higher than the landgraves of Hesse, Wilhelm and Hermann."

"Ordinary common sense has very little to do with the way that von Wildenstein reacts to things." Brahe's mood remained sour.

"Why?" Ulfsparre asked.

"I'm not sure," Botvidsson admitted. One of the causes of his outstanding success as a quartermaster-cum-aide-de-camp was his willingness to admit what he did not know. "More and more, I'm coming to think . . ." He paused and looked at Brahe. "We have too many Swedes on this inner council and not enough Germans. Swedes are fine for setting and carrying out military policy, but when it comes to understanding why these people do some of the things they do—and how—we need more information. Or, at least—" He paused and looked at the stacks of paper on the table. "Different information."

"The same's true for the people in Fulda," Ulfsparre said. "One of Wildenstein's points really is valid. What do we really know about how they plan to handle the Ram Rebellion? Almost nothing. Their president in Grantville is in regular contact with Magdeburg, sure. But what about here? Should we be setting up a closer liaison with them? So far, we've almost ignored them."

Stenbock grinned again. "Why not solve two problems at once? Send the three young, most unfortunately radicalized, Württemberg dukes up to Fulda to spend some time under the supervision of *their* military administrator. That will get them out of your hair for a couple of months, at least. Letting them cool their heels for a while after this last confrontation can't hurt. Perhaps you could send Pistor—the chaplain, not the student—with them, as a response to Wildenstein. Not that it will help, given that he's a rabid Counter-Remonstrant and was right in the middle of things in 1619 when the Dutch exiled the Arminians, but it will get him out of your hair for a couple of months, too, with luck. Assure Wildenstein that he'll be monitoring the situation very closely. We don't have to tell him that right now, the main situation that Pistor is interested in keeping an eye on is the one developing between his daughter and young Lieutenant Duke Friedrich. Do we?"

Brahe actually smiled. "Use the radio. Ask for an immediate response."

"What did this man Jenkins in Fulda say?" Brahe asked several meetings later.

Botvidsson picked up a sheet of paper. "It is possible that you are not the only administrator who has young men who are difficult to control on his staff."

"Yes?"

"Jenkins's military administrator, a man named Derek Utt, writes that he will be happy to send a couple of his people down to Mainz to, and I quote, 'meet-and-greet your youthful delinquents and judge as to whether Fulda is prepared to host them or not.'"

The morning and the evening of the third day

Their drummer rattled his sticks in a "make way, make way" rhythm.

"That's one more thing," Lieutenant Duke Friedrich

said. "Why do soldiers take drummers when they're just out on ordinary errands? I can see why they use the drums when a whole unit is marching through a town, to warn carters to move their teams and wagons, and vendors to pull their carts to the side. Otherwise, there wouldn't be room on the streets for six men abreast, row after row. But we're just walking. Why should the people of Mainz have to move apart for us on this particular morning?"

"If you're asking why we do it," Corporal Hertling said, "it's because all the other units do it. Do you really want to trip over—"

The rest of his answer came in the form of the body of a sturdy, middle-aged woman hurtling through the door of a shop, followed by a male voice screaming, "impudent bitch!"

". . . bodies," Hertling finished. He had intended "dogs and small children," but this seemed to preempt the rest of what he had planned to say.

"That one's not going to be moving out of our way any time soon," Friedrich said, "drum or no drum."

Ensign Duke Ulrich ran ahead of the others. "It's Sybilla," he said, leaning down. "One of the old ladies who come to the CoC meetings."

"Why?" Corporal Hertling started to ask.

He was interrupted by a scowling man who followed the body through the door. "Talk to me like that, will you? We're legally quartered in this district. We're legally quartered in this house. What matter is it to you that we've taken the good bedroom and the good bed? Aren't we in the service of His Majesty of Sweden? Aren't we protecting you Germans from the Catholics? Ah, forgot, didn't I. You are Catholic, off to a papist mass every Sunday. Why should I care if sleeping in an unheated attic is making your father's lungs worse? Why?"

"I know you," Hertling said. "Sybilla's complained about you before. You're Rohrbach."

Captain Duke Eberhard made a gesture that everyone present understood. Bauer, Kolb, Merckel, and Heisel moved.

"We'll need a surgeon," Ulrich said. "She's broken something."

"Her neck, it looks like," Merckel had seen worse, but this was bad enough. "Not much point in paying a surgeon for that."

"Arrest him," Eberhard said to Hertling.

"*Arrest* me!" Rohrbach made a quarter-turn and boxed Kolb's ears. "Why arrest me? She's the one who was talking rebellion. She's the one who was saying that she shouldn't have to put up with having soldiers in her house. She's the one who was talking about Boston and the constitution of the United States of America, and that in a just world, soldiers would not be quartered on the civilian population, eating their food and dirtying their sheets, making work. She's the one—"

"Arrest him," Eberhard said again. Kolb, still shaking his head, pinned Rohrbach's arms behind him.

"What unit does he belong to?"

"Von Glasenapp's, I think."

"Hell." Ulrich stood up. "Another of the Pomeranians, as if our own darling Colonel von Zitzewitz and von Manteufel weren't bad enough."

"He's a Mecklenburger," Friedrich said. "Rohrbach, that is."

"Pomeranian, Mecklenburger, what's the difference?"

"We'll take it up with Brahe's headquarters," Eberhard said. "The Swedes are responsible for the behavior of regiments stationed in the city, even if the commanding officers are mostly German."

"Should I stay here," Ulrich asked. "Should I call Herr Donner? Should I, umm . . ." He waved at Sybilla's body. "Do something? Call the watch? We can't just leave her here in the street."

"The whole thing was disgusting. It was like von Glasenapp didn't even think that Sybilla was . . . well, like he didn't think that her death was worthy of any respect." Lieutenant Duke Friedrich was not happy. "He's not even going to have Rohrbach flogged."

"That's probably because he didn't think that her death *was* worthy of respect," Ulrich said. "He wouldn't even agree that his regiment should contribute toward her funeral expenses. He'd have been more upset if he'd had to put down a good horse."

"Who *is* going to pay for her funeral? Old Binder sure can't. He's more than half dead himself, the way he coughs and rasps and rattles."

"Simrock's going to take up a collection."

Ulrich spat on the floor. "Glasenapp. *Von* Glasenapp. What right does that stupid Pomeranian have to call himself a noble? He's just a provincial easterner. His ancestors were probably Slavs. He doesn't act nobly. When Montaigne is writing about the quality of mercy, he suggests that to avoid civil conflict, the nobility must become like the peasantry and submit to a higher authority. He said that *roturier* soldiers, from the middle classes, were often braver and more honorable than those from the nobility."

"Montaigne wasn't a real noble, either," Eberhard pointed out. "Not even by French standards, much less German ones. Not *noblesse d'épée*. He was a country gentleman, well-mannered and well-educated, certainly, but his great-grandfather made a fortune in commerce and bought the estate and the title. His mother's family were still in trade. And the quartering system isn't all bad. If we hadn't been quartered at the Horn of Plenty when we first arrived in Mainz, I'd probably never have met Tata."

"I'm not so sure that's a good idea." Ensign Duke Ulrich eyed his beer.

"Why shouldn't I renounce my title?" Lieutenant Duke Friedrich slapped his little brother's arm. "Look at me, not at that stein. It's not as if anyone pays attention to it any more. Brahe certainly doesn't. Between Horn and Bernhard, not to mention the emperor's dispositions in regard to our supposed welfare, we can't even stick our noses into our supposed duchy. Also, for heaven's sake, I've joined the CoC. I'm a flaming young radical, right in there with Spartacus. I'm not supposed to be a duke any more. And I certainly don't want people to think that I sympathize with people like von Glasenapp."

"Among other things," Captain Duke Eberhard pointed out, "under our house laws, you're not of age yet, so you can't. Not legally."

"There must be somewhere that I can. Remember the newspaper articles about that reception in Magdeburg last fall, when Gustavus appointed Stearns as prime minister? All those young aristocrats came up to him and said they were renouncing their titles."

"It was in November. There was a whole list of them in the paper. I only noticed one single duke among them. Below that, not even a *Freiherr*. A couple of fifth or sixth sons of imperial knights was about as high as it went. Practically all of them were untitled, mediatized, rural von This or von That, just like your much-admired Spartacus. He's the third son of some untitled Saxon *Niederadel*. What did younger sons of the lower nobility have to lose? Effectively, nothing. What did they have to gain? They got to speak with the new prime minister, which was possibly worth something. Maybe they can carve a career in the new government's bureaucracy somewhere, or get a chance to run for the new House of Commons and represent the interests of their fathers and older brothers there. They probably figured that the now-Wilhelm-Wettin knew something they didn't, but I haven't seen many *Hochadel* following his example. They're waiting to see if the 'prime minister comes from the House of Commons only' idea lasts."

Friedrich's expression brightened. "There's an idea. You give me permission to renounce my title and I'll run for the House of Commons for you, one of these days."

The morning and the evening of the fourth day

"I could scarcely have humiliated von Glasenapp front of a group of junior officers," Brahe said. "He would lose all of his authority and he doesn't command very much respect as it is. Most of his men despise him."

"True. But . . ." Botvidsson shook his head.

"I humiliated him in front of his fellow colonels. Sufficiently, I believe, that there's not likely to be an equivalent occurrence among the soldiers under him in the future. Or among the soldiers under the others, for that matter."

"I'm afraid that's not going to be enough."

"It isn't, but it has to be. Sometimes one finds oneself in such a situation."

"I wasn't about to have Rohrbach flogged publicly," von Glasenapp muttered. "Not when those infernal Württembergers and Donner were howling that I had to."

"Might have been better if you had," von Zitzewitz said. "I have to deal with them—Captain Duke Eberhard and his brothers. They're on my staff. Probably as retribution for my sins."

"I had him flogged privately. Hard. Not that Brahe left me any option. Don't tell those boys, though. I'm not willing to give the impression that I'm a man who caves in to public pressure. If I see an article in the newspaper even hinting that I had Rohrbach flogged, I'll be looking for the leak until the day I die and the leaker will be sorry."

"Might be better if I did tell them. Quietly, of course."

"I mean it, Zitzewitz. Don't tell them. Let junior officers think that they can influence you and that's the end of military discipline. That goes double and triple for junior officers who have a higher rank in the nobility and their own ways of getting the ear of General Brahe."

❖   ❖   ❖

"What are you doing, Reichard?" Justina looked at the market order her husband had just drafted. "We won't need a lot of food for Sybilla's wake. She didn't have many friends. She was a whiny, unpleasant woman, even if she was a loyal daughter to old Hans and a CoC member."

Ursula Widder nodded. "She was only fourteen when her mother died. She took over keeping the house and assisting in the shop. Most of her parents' friends are dead. Her younger brothers and sisters are dead or gone. Married or not, she never had any children. Old Hans can't afford to hire mourners. There won't be many people."

Donner shook his head. "It will be a big funeral. Simrock and Theo are getting other students to come. Boys that age eat a lot."

"Reichard," Justina said direfully. "Reichard, what are you up to?"

"Recruiting, my darling treasure. Recruiting."

The newspaper came out early that morning, well before the funeral was due to begin.

Somehow, the lead story featured the brutal death of a native daughter of the city, an honorable and faithful daughter of the city, also the hard-working only caretaker of her aging, invalid father.

Yes, the brutal death of a native daughter of the city at the hands of an equally brutal soldier quartered upon its civilians. A brutal soldier from Mecklenburg, a province which was far distant from the Rhineland, not to mention full of brutal Lutheran heretics.

In passing, the reporter mentioned, just in case his reading public had forgotten, the Swedes were all

Lutheran heretics, too—Lutheran heretics who had confiscated the historical *Johanniskirche* to use as their own.

"Damn you, Simrock," Reichard Donner exploded.

"I said I'd get a story in the paper for you," Simrock protested. "A story that would get the people aroused. Mainzers by and large just don't get very aroused by Spartacus's theories. Sorry about that. My cousin wrote what he thought would work. My uncle was delighted to publish it. You want a crowd, you get a crowd."

"Simrock, you have no common sense at all. The last thing we need is a religious riot. The Committees of Correspondence advocate religious toleration, remember. Repeat after me, twenty times, *toleration*. Have you gotten that word into your head?"

Simrock shrugged. "My uncle's not exactly a fan of the CoC. Sometimes you have to take what you can get."

". . . sorry we weren't here when you arrived." Reichard Donner distributed another round of beers. "We were all at the funeral." He waved toward Kunigunde and Ursula, who were sobbing at a corner table as they made quick work of the contents of their mugs.

"The riot," Eberhard added.

"Paying our respects to the dead and debating Montaigne," Theo added.

"Dodging flying rocks." Justina glared at the boys. "Evading the city watch. Running for our lives."

"You've read Montaigne, of course," Simrock said to their guests from Fulda.

Jeffie Garand's response was, "Errr . . ."

Joel Matowski, somewhat more articulately, replied, "I don't believe that I have."

Joel actually didn't believe that he had even heard

of anyone named Montaigne, but didn't think that it would be tactful to say so right at the moment, since the author, whoever he might be, was clearly near and dear to the hearts of the Mainz CoC, who seemed to talk about him a lot more than they talked about Spartacus and the other people who were writing pamphlets for Gretchen Richter.

"But you're up-timers," Simrock protested. "You have all those books. Everyone's heard about your libraries. Florio's translation of Montaigne's *Essais* has been in print since 1603. That's thirty years. Longer than any of us have been alive."

He looked over at the senior Donners—parents, aunt, and the aunt's friends. "Longer than *most* of us have been alive. You must have read it."

Reichard Donner intercepted the glance. "Eat up, everybody. There's plenty of food left from the wake."

"The wake that didn't happen," Justina said. "The wake that didn't happen because *somebody . . .*" She glared at Simrock. ". . . *somebody* planted an article in the paper that caused a riot and the city council called out the watch and the soldiers to put it down and they wouldn't let anybody at all come to the Horn of Plenty afterwards."

Jeffie was still thinking about Montaigne. "I think the people who stuck with Mrs. Hawkins's French classes at high school until the fourth year read something by that guy. They read it in French, though."

"So you have read the *Essais*."

"Well, no, I didn't take French. I took Spanish. It was kind of complicated. My dad came from Baton Rouge and was Cajun and he and Mom were divorced, so she didn't want me to learn French."

Theo, sublime in not caring that he was no more familiar with the concepts "Baton Rouge" and "Cajun" than Jeffie Garand was familiar with the *Essais*, turned to his sister and whispered, "Montaigne also wrote, 'I prefer the company of peasants because they have not been educated sufficiently to reason incorrectly.' Maybe that's the variety of up-timer we've got here."

"Well," Simrock said, "it's still true whether you've read the book or not. Every person, no matter how high-born, is still what one of your up-time writers called a 'work in progress.' You're not finished until you're dead. As Montaigne wrote, 'How many valiant men we have seen to survive their own reputation!' In your world, Gustavus Adolphus seems to have acquired a remarkably bright and shiny reputation. It remains to be seen what he's going to end up with in this one."

Both Duke Eberhard and Corporal Hertling shifted a little uncomfortably and looked around. Aside from the two up-timers, though, only the regulars were in attendance. Reichard's recruiting scheme had proven to be a singular failure.

"Montaigne also says that ambition is not a vice of little people," Friedrich said. "Ambition isn't necessarily a bad thing. 'Since ambition may teach men valor, temperance, generosity, and justice . . .'"

Eberhard hoped that his brother was just trying to be helpful, rather than to fan the flames. He himself found political debates a little unsettling, even though his tutors had, obviously, trained him, as a future ruler, to take part in them. And, of course, Montaigne himself had written, "There is no conversation more boring than the one where everybody agrees."

Jeffie Garand leaned over and whispered to Joel,

"Remember that musical we did in high school about the English girl? The one where she sang about the two guys who talked all the time and finished up, 'I'm so sick of words?' I think these guys have got a words monopoly."

He picked up a stack of flyers that were lying on the table. "What are these?"

Corporal Hertling moved over to the up-timers and looked over Jeffie's shoulder.

"Cartoons by Crispijn van de Passe," Simrock said. "The older Crispijn, that is. He's famous. He's been working out of Utrecht for the past several years."

"He's also as old as the hills," Reichard griped. "He must be nearly seventy. Can't you kids ever talk about anyone modern?"

"I've heard of his daughter," Joel said. "Magdalena. She works for Markgraf and Smith Aviation, the ones who are building the Monster. She's Dutch, I think."

"Oh, yeah." Jeffie nodded. "I've heard about her, too. Never heard of her father, though." He frowned at the cluttered design and dark, heavily hatched background of the engraving. "Not exactly *Doonesbury*. Not even *L'il Abner*. I don't like it."

A declaration of Arminian principles at a conclave of Counter-Remonstrants could not have caused a more violent eruption of indignation. The up-timers learned far more than they had ever wanted to know about the scene that van de Passe had most recently depicted—the archbishop-elector of Mainz, the archbishop-elector's conflicts with Nils Brahe who was Gustavus Adolphus's military administrator, the archbishop-elector's attempts to mediate some kind of an ecumenical version of religious tolerance with a man named Georg Calixtus.

Theo, upon noting that neither Jeffie nor Joel had ever heard of Calixtus, was profoundly struck by the glaring gaps in their education. "He's a professor at Helmstedt, of course. For the last couple of years, he's been advocating religious discussion between representatives of the various confessions based on the Holy Scriptures and the proponents of Catholic doctrine. He seems to think that if people just went back to the early church, before Constantine, everything would work out and the world would be full of sweetness and light. He's even been to Jena, lobbying Gerhard and the other orthodox Lutheran theologians."

Chaplain Pistor would have been proud of the disgust dripping from his son's tongue.

"He's a Philippist," Simrock's voice was mild. "An extreme Philippist. The Flacians hate him."

"And Helmstedt is what and where?" The derisory tone of Jeffie's voice was designed to disguise the fact that he really didn't have the vaguest clue.

"I'm not so sure that Montaigne had the right of it about peasants," Theo whispered to Margarethe. "They just plain haven't been educated sufficiently at all."

Hertling looked over Joel's shoulder. "Who are the two guys so loaded down with olive branches that they're staggering under the weight?"

"Well, one of them's the count from Rudolstadt, over by Grantville." Jeffie grinned. "You can tell him because he's wearing a gimme cap with the bill turned backwards. I don't know the other one."

"Heinrich Friedrich von Hatzfeldt," Margarethe said. "He's the oldest brother of the prince-bishop of Würzburg. The Catholic bishop of Würzburg, in Franconia, where the people just voted to join the up-timers." Margarethe's voice was much calmer than her brother's had been. She was sitting in the taproom looking like a misplaced, very small, medieval Italian madonna, with dark brown eyes, straight dark brown hair, and a perfectly oval face.

Simrock interrupted. "Their mother's a von Sickingen. Their father worked here for the archbishop of Mainz most of his life in various kinds of administrative jobs. He's a canon at St. Alban's—you can look him up, if you want to, because he's right in town still. He didn't leave when the Swedes came in. Franz, the bishop, is in Bonn with the archbishop—this archbishop—and Ferdinand of Bavaria, that's the other archbishop, most of the time."

"They don't call this part of the Rhineland 'priests' alley' for nothing," Reichard Donner muttered.

Margarethe tossed her head. "This man, the bishop's brother, goes back and forth. People say he's trying to broker some agreement for Franz to go back to Würzberg and work along with the up-timers, sort of like the prince-abbot did in Fulda."

Walther Hertling grinned. "I don't suppose the archbishop—the Mainz archbishop, not the Bavarian in Cologne—would complain if the Swedes let him come back to Mainz, either."

Joel turned around and looked at Hertling. "Don't hold your breath. For the deals to get anywhere, they'd both have to do what the abbot did—drop the 'prince' part out of their titles."

"In that case," Duke Eberhard said, "I certainly won't hold mine."

The morning and the evening of the fifth day

"At least," Jeffie whispered, "the town's small enough that we can pretty much see it in one morning. Be grateful for small favors."

Simrock, assuming the duty of host since he was a local boy, had just explained as much as he knew—as much, that was, as his teachers at the Latin School in the city had known—about Mainz's "Roman stones," which turned out to be forty-seven still-standing columns from a long-gone nearly five-mile-long aqueduct, not to mention every other relic of antiquity he was aware of.

Jeffie proved to be only minimally enthusiastic about educational tourism. He kept whispering to Joel. "I could see some point if it was still carrying water, but a batch of rock pilings is a batch of rock pilings, no matter now old they are. I could have looked at pilings back home."

Reichard Donner, who had come along out of sheer curiosity, overheard him. "Yes. Too old, too old."

Ulrich hopped down from on top of one of the pilings, landing with a solid thunk. "Well, if this is too old, let's try the cathedral."

"It's Catholic," Theo said.

Ulrich swung himself into place next to Jeffie Garand, but looked at Theo. "You do 'glum' pretty well. 'Morose,' too. Fifty years from now, I'll be laughing at you because you're such a cantankerous old man."

The cathedral, which they had seen from a distance on their way into town, since it was far higher than any other landmark, proved on closer inspection to be, in Jeffie's whisper, "a great big pile of red brick with a lot of gingerbread." He looked at it critically. "It's not any prettier than St. Mary's in Grantville."

Joel snorted. "It's Romanesque. That's why St. Mary's looks the way it does. Mr. Piazza told us that back in CCD classes. St. Mary's is neo-Romanesque. American architects copied this stuff. St. Mary's is just smaller and the bricks are yellow instead of red."

"You need to look at the bronze doors," Simrock said. "They're old."

"As old as the rock piles under the aqueduct that's not there any more?" Jeffie grinned.

Simrock counted to twenty. "Not quite. About nine hundred years newer, but they're still old. They're about seven hundred years old."

"Too old," Reichard said. "What's remarkable is that they're still here, seeing that they're bronze. Over time, almost anything cast in bronze has gotten melted down in one war or another to make weapons. That's one of the perks that artillery companies have when they take a town. They get to confiscate the church bells to melt them into more cannon, so they can demolish more towns."

Simrock nodded. "It's really astonishing that the doors have survived."

"We should go inside and look at the stained glass," Joel said. "Colored windows with those Gothic pointy tops and curlicues worked into the glass are always *cultural*, as Ms. Mailey would say."

"As in, 'Don't you barbarians have any culture at all?'" Jeffie said to Ulrich. "I wish I hadn't grown too responsible to climb up on those pilings with you."

"Responsible?" Joel snorted. "You?"

"That's 'Sergeant Garand,' now, if you please."

"The windows are idolatrous," Theo protested. "Well, they are. Graven images."

Everyone else ignored him.

"Who is, or was, Ms. Mailey?" Simrock asked. To Eberhard, he whispered, "She may have had a point. I'm pretty sure she did."

The party inspected the stained glass windows. Joel cocked his head. "I think the ones in St. Mary's are prettier. Imported from Austria, you know. The coal barons really did our church up right."

"I thought there weren't any barons in America," Eberhard said.

They explained coal barons on their way to the party's next destination.

"The *Johanniskirche*," Simrock said. "St. John's. The Swedes have turned it into a Lutheran parish church for the city. The canons in the chapter at the cathedral are complaining, of course—not to mention the canons from what used to be the *Johanniskirche*. General Brahe told them that they should be happy that he took the smaller church and left the cathedral to the Catholics."

Theo inserted a mutter about the lack of a Calvinist parish church.

Reichard pointed with pride to the service being provided to the Calvinists of Mainz by the public room of the Horn of Plenty.

Simrock diverted them down another street overbuilt with half-timbered *Fachwerk* houses. "Now here, going through the *Kirschgarten*, and coming to the *Leichhofstrasse* . . ."

"You've got a 'Graveyard Street'?"

"Well, it does go to the cemetery." He shrugged. "And this is the hospital."

Jeffie cocked his head. "How on earth old is that?"

Simrock chewed his upper lip. "Four hundred years, I'd say. Give or take a few in either direction."

Jeffie cocked his head and whispered to Joel, "The accumulated germs would give Dr. Nichols nightmares, I bet."

"Where did Gutenberg invent the printing press?" Joel asked, masking that comment. On their way to that sacred spot, he asked again, "What's the big building site?"

Simrock shook his head. "They started on building a new electoral residence about six years ago, but it got interrupted by the war. Now it's just a muddy mess."

Jeffie shook his head. "The whole town doesn't look much like the pictures in the guidebook that was in Len Tanner's collection—the one Mary Kat saw."

Joel was getting tired. "Can it with acting like a brat, Jeffie. That's because all the stuff they built between now and then is missing. It's like Fulda, that way. Mainz hasn't gone Baroque yet."

"Where are Friedrich and Margarethe?"

"They said they had things to do."

Friedrich looked over his shoulder. "Shouldn't we be sneaking in at night, or something?"

Margarethe shook her head. "If it were night, Rohrbach would be here. He hasn't moved out of the room over the shop just because Sybilla is dead and old Binder has moved to the Horn of Plenty to cough the rest of his life away. If it were night, he would be right here, asleep. The whole point, Fritzi, is to come in the middle of the day while he is gone, carrying the key in my hand for everyone to see. Anyone who notices us will suppose that old man Binder sent us on a very proper and public errand." She looked at him, her dark eyes big and round. "That's something I learned when I was much younger. If you plan to disobey your father, it's tremendously important to look like such an idea would never cross your mind."

"Where did you get three dozen rotten eggs, anyway?" Friedrich was honestly curious. He had no idea how to go about procuring such an item.

"I have my methods."

"Where, my delightful little doe?"

"Don't call me that. I hate it. That's what Theo calls me."

"Where did you get the eggs?"

"It's *spring*, Fritzi."

"What does spring have to do with it?"

"Kunigunde's hens in the back courtyard of the Horn of Plenty have been setting, but she doesn't have a rooster and since she keeps them in coops no neighbor's rooster can get to them, so the eggs they lay are sterile. They're a nasty bunch of peckers." She held out her arm, demonstrating several small wounds. "She's left them alone, because they won't lay any more while they're broody, anyway. The eggs are nice and ripe."

She pulled the ticking back from the mattress very carefully. It wouldn't do to have feathers flying loose all over the room. Even a clod like Rohrbach might notice that. She situated the eggs among the feathers and replaced the ticking even more carefully.

"Hah."

"That's it?"

"No, of course not." She scowled at him. "Now we go up to the garret and pack up Sybilla's clothing. Everyone in the neighborhood will know that she would have wanted Kunigunde and Ursula to share it between them. We will carry it out. We will stop and talk to a few people in the street who will see us carrying it. We won't mention that we are carrying it, because they might wonder why we are talking about something so obvious, but we will answer if anyone asks how old man Binder is."

"We do? We will?"

"Of course we do. Don't they teach you anything practical in 'how to be a noble school'?"

The morning and the evening of the sixth day
Fulda, April 1634

"And the news from Mainz is?" Derek Utt contemplated his delegation.

"We spent quite a bit of time with them," Joel said.

Derek Utt raised one eyebrow. "Doing what?"

"Hanging out, sort of," Jeffie Garand said cheerfully. "Actually, they're a lot like us when we were their age, if our parents had been rich when we were born and sent us to fancy prep schools, that is. Not outstandingly smart or dumb. Not unusually ugly or handsome. Just regular guys. If they don't watch what they eat and keep up an exercise program, all three of them are going to be buying their clothes in the corner of the men's shop that has a sign hanging over it that says 'Portly Short' by the time they're thirty. By the time they're forty for sure."

"What we were doing was trying to find out what Wes wanted to know." Joel Matowski seriously tried to look helpful and conscientious. "Eberhard's nineteen. Friedrich's eighteen. Ulrich will be sixteen next month. The reason all three of them are on Nils Brahe's staff in Mainz is that they're supposed to be learning their trade in the army, so to speak. Eberhard thinks that Ulrich should still be under a tutor's guidance, but he wouldn't go to Strassburg with their sisters—he made a big fuss about it, apparently—so the older boys brought him along where they can keep an eye on him."

"Why Mainz, given all the problems in Swabia? And given that in theory they're dukes of a good chunk of the general geographical spot that's Swabia. Why not with Horn?"

"Well, if he sent them to Horn, it might make problems with the margraves of Baden. That's Swabia, too. Or remind the Württembergers that they do have their own dukes when other European countries aren't using their home turf as a battleground. I doubt that Gustav wants a self-determination movement on the Ram Rebellion model down in the southeast right about now."

Utt grimaced. "Damn, but I hate politics."

"They're all over the place," Joel said earnestly. "Politics, I mean. If it wasn't for the problems in the Netherlands, these kids would probably be with Frederik Hendrik. They can't very well be with Gustavus up north, given that they're first cousins to Christian IV of Denmark's sons—their moms were sisters. I gathered from Eberhard that it would be sort of touchy. Plus, on their mom's side, too, they're also some kind of cousins of George William over in Brandenburg, who's probably next on Gustav's tick-off list, once he deals with the Danes. So our illustrious emperor was sort of short on options about where to put them, I guess. Didn't want to offend them to the point that they would swing over to the other side. Didn't want to put them in the way of temptation, either. Actually, they haven't taken offense too bad. Eberhard's pretty realistic about the whole thing and the other two are following his lead."

"Is that the whole family?" Wes Jenkins asked.

"They've got three sisters hiding out from Horn and Bernhard in Strassburg." Jeffie grinned. "According to Eberhard, all three of them swear that they're going to grow up to be old maids. Antonia's older than the boys. According to their description, she was born to give Ms. Mailey a run for her money in the 'terrifying bluestocking' sweepstakes. For the time being, though, she's got the two little sisters on her hands, to finish bringing up in her image."

"So, if Brahe were to send them up here for a short course in Americanization—where are the potential pitfalls?"

"Eberhard doesn't racket around in whorehouses, if that's what you're asking," Joel said. "He's got one girl—Agathe Donner, they call her Tata—and he'll probably bring her along if he comes up to Fulda."

Derek swallowed. "Tata?"

"Yeah." Jeffie winked. "She's got quite a pair of tatas on her, really impressive, but that's not the reason for her nickname. It's just short for Agathe. One of her little brothers couldn't say her name right when he was learning to talk. I don't think it would be smart to tell them what it means in English."

"Really, Derek—ah, that is, sir," Joel said. "It's not

as if she'd be the only informal alliance out at Barracktown. Sure, he sleeps with her, but otherwise, he pretty much keeps it zipped up, which is pretty fair behavior for a nineteen-year-old kid who was brought up to think the world ought to be his oyster and then got slapped in the face by real life the year after his dad died. Some 'grand tour' his mom could afford by the time the uncles got their claws into what was left after she dealt with their dad's debts—their Junior Dukeships got to go to Strassburg, Basel, Mömpelgard, Lyon, and Geneva. Then they came straight back home. I suppose you could stretch a point and say that Lyon counts as France, but . . . they didn't make it to Italy or Austria or England."

"Who's the girl?"

Jeffie grinned. "Would you believe the daughter of the head of Mainz's Committee of Correspondence? Such as it is."

"Ah," Derek Utt moaned. "No."

"Her dad's perfectly happy about it. He's a lot happier than the father of Lieutenant Duke Friedrich's girlfriend."

"Who is?"

"The chaplain for the Calvinists in Brahe's regiments."

"The father's the chaplain, not the girlfriend," Jeffie said deadpan.

"He's from Hesse—from Kassel, really. His name's Marcus Pistor. A real extremist, in a Calvinist sort of way. The way Eberhard put it was, 'He studied under Gomar himself and is fanatically anti-Vorstian,' as if that was supposed to mean something to me. Well, hell, it definitely means something to him, so I guess we ought to look it up." Joel sighed.

"Her name's Margarethe and believe me, her dad has really pissed her off, not to mention *vice versa*." Jeffie grinned. "She looks like Bambi's mother, but don't believe all that sweetness and light for a minute. Margarethe looks harmless, but it's deceptively harmless. Theo even calls her *Rehgeißchen* when he wants to make her mad."

"'Little Doe,'" Joel nodded. "Like some made-up American Indian maiden in a movie."

"They don't like making it easy on themselves, do they?"

"Not really."

"Ensign Duke Ulrich doesn't have a steady girlfriend," Jeffie offered hopefully.

"He's only fifteen," Joel snorted.

Jeffie plowed on. "He's getting to that age, though. But I made it clear that if they do come up to Fulda, I have dibs on Gertrud Hartke."

"Does Gertrud agree to this condition?" Wes Jenkins asked.

"Oh, sure." Jeffie beamed confidently. "She absolutely adores me."

The morning and the evening of the seventh day Essen, May 1634

Louis de Geer stood at the window, looking out at the ever-expanding industrial base of his new republic. It wasn't pretty, but neither was his copper mining franchise in Sweden. The beauty of industrialization lay in the money that arrived in an entrepreneur's bank account.

"The rumors seem to be," his informant was saying, "that the archbishop of Cologne has hired three, maybe four, Irish generals—well, colonels, at least—with their mercenary regiments, out of Austria. Supposedly, he made the down-payment the end of April. People seem to expect that they'll arrive in Bonn by the middle of May."

"Which ones?"

"Butler, Geraldin, and Deveroux, Deveroux, something like that. Dennis MacDonald is supposed to be with them, but none of my men have actually seen him. They managed to get their cavalry across Swabia somehow. Maximilian let them cross Bavaria, of course, since his brother wanted them. As for their route the rest of the way, I hear that Nasi is peering suspiciously at Egon von Fürstenberg. He is not at all happy about the proposal that the emperor is floating to unify Swabia and set a Lutheran margrave of Baden on top of him as administrator. Probably with a Lutheran military commander, too, if Sweden leaves Horn with the USE after this year's campaigns."

"We could have lived happily and successfully without the arrival of those three—without all four of them, really. Oh, well." De Geer turned to his secretary. "Send a memo to Nils Brahe in Mainz."

Ignoring the interruption, de Geer's informant continued on. "Also, our men have lost track of Felix Gruyard."

"Any idea where he may have gone?" the secretary asked, steno book in hand.

"Wherever the charming Ferdinand of Bavaria, archbishop and elector of Cologne and faithful minion of his elder brother Maximilian, chooses to send him—with uniformly undesirable results, from our perspective."

"Such sarcasm. Your Calvinism is showing, Louis. Ferdinand's not the only ruler who employs a full-time torturer."

"He's the only one who employs Gruyard."

"There is that."

"It's not that I don't have faith in God's providence," Louis de Geer said. "It's just that there are days when I suspect that He's resting again."

Section Two: A good and spacious land . . .

Mainz, May 1634

Morning prayers could be hard on one's conscience, if one went about the process of self-examination honestly.

Nils Brahe was inclined toward honesty, as much in judging himself as in judging others. As Montaigne had written, quoting Cicero, "to judge a man, we must for a long time follow and mark his steps, to see whether constancy of purpose is firm and well-founded within him." *Cui vivendi via considerata atque provisa est.* Not to mention that the Bible also contained more than a few well-chosen words on the topic of hypocrisy. So.

Ahrensbök.

Envy was not an admirable characteristic. Indeed, it was a sin. The Catholics classified it as a mortal sin. Although Lutheran theology insisted that all sins were equal in the sight of God, perhaps it was particularly sinful to envy Lennart Torstensson, who had just brought Gustavus Adolphus such a great victory. Even if the king had been heard to say that "after Torstensson," one was the prospective best strategic talent in the Swedish army.

Oh, but the word "after" did grate.

Envy of one's older brother was not an admirable characteristic. In anybody, at any time. Being a younger brother was a dispensation of divine providence. It was particularly un-admirable when one discovered it in oneself. Still, Per's political career in Sweden was taking off like one of the airplanes at the USE's landing field in Mainz.

Whereas one was more or less stuck in Mainz.

Or was one?

Nils Brahe, still a few months away from turning thirty years old, looked up from his daily Bible readings and folded his hands behind his head, shifting his thoughts from the impersonal mode to the personal.

According to his own close friend Erik Hand, the king had approved Johan Banér's project against Ingolstadt. Which was exasperating.

In spite of that grating word "after," he drew some consolation from knowing the king trusted him enough that there was no equivalent of Hand watching over his activities.

His sister Ebba was already married to Banér's brother Axel.

His sister Kerstin was still unmarried. She was only about fifteen years younger than Erik who was, after all, the king's cousin, even if his mother was illegitimate. Fifteen years wasn't bad. Even with the crippled arm, Erik was a handsome man. Almost everyone agreed on that. Opinion was as close to unanimous as it ever got.

He missed his wife. He would write her and ask her to come to Mainz, bringing Kerstin along. They could stay for a while—preferably until such time as Anna Margareta was expecting another child. Then she could go home again. After all, *somebody* had to run the estates while he was himself off contributing to the king's imperial dreams.

Anna Margareta could bring the children. He missed his children, too.

"Are you sure?"

"As sure as I can possibly be," Botvidsson answered. "My information is absolutely reliable. Bernhard of Saxe-Weimar has withdrawn his cavalry units to the south. Ohm, Caldenbach, and Rosen—all three of them. They should be south of Strassburg by the day after tomorrow, which is, in my best opinion, about where they will halt and set up a screen. Which means that he's not contemplating a Turenne-style raid up the Main into the State of Thuringia-Franconia, which makes me happy. Nor is Bernhard moving any of his infantry north from the Franche Comté, so it doesn't look like he plans to meet up with the cavalry and strike east against Württemberg again, which probably is making Gustav Horn a happy man, or at least as happy as he ever gets."

Nils Brahe smiled at his council. "True. Now he'll be worrying about what else Bernhard has in mind as far as Swabia is concerned. Or where else. If I were in the Breisgau, I would be nervous. But come, gentlemen, we have no time to waste."

"What?"

"Since Bernhard has been so kind as to make straight what long was crooked and the rougher places plain . . ."

Every man at the table grasped the reference to the fortieth chapter of the book of the prophet Isaiah at once.

Botvidsson nodded. "A highway for our God into northern Alsace." His mouth quirked. "A highway to the oil fields at Pechelbronn, which should be of great value, given what has happened at Wietze."

Brahe nodded, his manner a little abstracted. "Of great value to us, or at least something we need to keep out of the hands of the French. Do we need to talk to the count of Hanau-Lichtenberg?"

"Already done. He's willing to agree to the same terms as the Brunswickers have done in regard to the exploitation at Wietze."

Brahe nodded again, this time with satisfaction. "Remind me. What's the place called now?"

"Merkwiller. Or Merckweiler, if you prefer the German spelling."

"Are we getting any support from Fulda?" Stenbock asked.

Botvidsson shook his head. "Jenkins only has the one regiment there. He'll try to send a few 'observers' with us, for at least part of the campaign. Major Utt himself and a couple of the other up-timers, for a month or so. They're already on their way. I don't think we can reasonably ask or expect any more from him. It's not as if he doesn't have problems of his own."

The only additional question anyone asked was, "When?"

"Tomorrow," Brahe answered. "I have plans in place, of course."

Which he did. Of course. Envy might be a sin, but honest ambition and a desire to serve one's king well were not.

And an unexpected window of opportunity had opened up. He had planned for the contingency.

The other men scrambled out of the room. The next twenty-four hours would be very busy. Brahe smiled as he watched them go.

Envy was a sin. But perhaps one could reverse the king's estimate of one's abilities in comparison to those demonstrated by Lennart Torstensson, in which case envy would no longer be an immediate problem, there being no cause for it.

In the von Sickingen lands, near the Rhine Palatinate, May 1634

Jeffie Garand squirmed into a somewhat more comfortable position on a rock that had never been designed as a stool. Leaning over, he whispered to Eberhard, "'Every dog has his day?' I can't believe that some down-timer said that."

"Montaigne did. General Brahe was just quoting him."

"Why do General Brahe and Major Utt sound like my high school history teacher?"

"They're trying to understand each other," Joel Matowski said. "Anyway, Major Utt's sister teaches English at the high school, so maybe he caught that teacherish attitude from her."

"Major Utt was a coach over in Fairmont before the Ring of Fire. He only got caught in the Ring because he was at the bait store with Allan Dailey that afternoon. Coaches shouldn't talk like Ms. Mailey."

"He'd graduated from college," Joel said. "I hadn't finished when the Ring hit, but it's true what they say—just going to college does something to you, in the way you think. Lots of coaches teach social studies to fill in their schedules. Mr. Samuels is the *head* of the social studies department now and he was the football coach before the Ring of Fire. Now hush."

Utt was looking at his toes, which were stretched out toward the campfire. "There was a shift in politics, at least in the English-speaking world, some time between the Glorious Revolution and the American Revolution."

At a question from Lieutenant Duke Friedrich, he stopped to briefly define each of those and give its dates in the Other Time Line.

"Where was I? There was a shift from politics as a blood sport to politics as a gentleman's game. Most European monarchs stopped beheading their opponents—omitting the way the Hanoverians handled the Scottish Jacobites."

Another pause for explanations and definitions.

"Why? Hell, I'm not sure why. Maybe because of the shift of the major source of wealth, power, and influence from land, which is essentially static, to commerce, which is far more flexible and less limited, far more elastic and less static."

"What's elastic?" Ensign Duke Ulrich asked. He was ignored.

"Maybe, partly, possibly, it was also because the shift meant that other types of connection among people became more important and influential than that of family and hereditary succession. I can't give you an answer. I'm not sure that a meeting of the entire American Historical Association could have given you an answer."

"That conversation didn't exactly come to a conclusion," Eberhard said as he rolled himself up into his blanket.

"I expect it was meant to make us ask questions," Friedrich answered. "That's the sneaky thing about tutors. They're always trying to make a person think. Sometimes my mind gets absolutely exhausted just thinking about all the things they want me to think about."

"All we did today was walk," Ulrich complained the next evening.

"That's good, Your Grace, sir," Merckel said. "That's obscenely good. This is your first time in the field. Up till now, you've just been learning drill and theory. When you're out on a campaign, a day when all you do is walk is a good day. A day you spend trying to unstick carts that are stuck in the mud is a worse day. A day that someone else starts shooting at you is the pits."

Ulrich shrugged and went back to unsaddling his horse.

Friedrich pulled a hand-drawn map out of the inner pocket of his leather doublet. "If my map is even close to right, we're making pretty good progress."

"That's because it's not raining, Your Grace, sir," Merckel said. "A couple of days of rain and we'll mire right down. The glop underfoot will suck horseshoes off. The farriers won't be able to get a decent fire going to heat up the metal because water will be dripping through their tent onto the forge. Just wait. You'll see. Before too long, you'll see."

"Thomas Jefferson, of course, considered the yeoman farmer to be the basis of a healthy political community in a republican form of government."

Brahe nodded. "One presumes that was based upon the Roman model of the Gracchi."

"Probably. He had a pretty good classical education. Better than Washington's, but probably not as good as either George Mason or George Wythe."

Turning his head around, he grinned at Garand, Matowski, and the three Württemberg dukes. "Which may just go to demonstrate that a really good classical education will not necessarily lead to a man's being elected as president of the United States. Washington and Jefferson are in every American history textbook ever printed, but Wythe and Mason only made it into the required fourth-grade course in state history in Virginia."

"I don't understand Jefferson's logic," Brahe said. "Remember Montaigne's critique of the Parians who were sent to reform the Milesians. The Parians visited the island, surveyed it, observed which farms and estates were best managed and governed. Then they appointed the owners of those to be the new magistrates and council of Miletus, on the hypothesis that men who took good care of their own property would take good care of public affairs. However, I personally judge that a man may manage his own lands well because he is essentially selfish, and have very little sense of the civic duty that would lead him to be equally concerned about others."

"Sounds to me like the Parians were subscribing to the view that whatever was good for General Motors was good for the nation," Utt said.

This statement required quite a bit of explanation.

"Anyway, good for Montaigne. I'm glad the fellow didn't fall for that idea. That wasn't the basis for Jefferson's opinion, either. It was more that as many citizens of a country as possible should be stakeholders in it."

The discussion went on until the fire went out.

"Where to next?" Merckel asked the next morning.

"Landstuhl," Corporal Hertling answered. "Captain Ulfsparre told me so."

"Where's Landstuhl?" Jeffie asked.

"A few miles west of Kaiserslautern. See." Lieutenant Duke Friedrich dug into his pocket and pulled out his map.

Ulrich hefted the saddle onto his horse. "What's at Landstuhl? Why is it worth our while to capture whatever it is? I hate to be a nuisance, but nobody ever seems to explain anything on this campaign."

"We aren't supposed to understand. We're just supposed to do what they tell us."

Joel Matowski shook his head. "*Ours not to reason why, Ours but to do or die* struck me as a really bad idea back when they made us read it in high school."

"The villages belong to a branch of the *Freiherren* von Sickingen," Eberhard said.

"Any relation to Franz von Sickingen?" Joel asked. "The famous one?"

"Famous?" Ensign Duke Ulrich stuck out his tongue.

"Do you have any idea what he did to our ancestor, the first Duke Ulrich, back in 1518?"

"It wasn't just him, brat," Friedrich said. "It was the whole Swabian League."

"He built a big fortress at Landstuhl, but it was destroyed by artillery. That wasn't much more than five years after he attacked our ancestor."

"Sounds like he lived in interesting times." Joel Matowski laughed.

"But the emperor restored his son, and the Sickingens built the fortress back," Friedrich said.

Hertling nodded.

"This is the Hohenburg sub-line of the Sickingens." That was the kind of information that any Swabian nobleman, Eberhard included, had received drilled into him by tutors from the time he could toddle. "Old Franz was a great leader of the imperial knights and a defender of the Reformation. This bunch, though, converted back to Catholicism in—hmm—I think it was 1627. About then. It was the year before our father died, wasn't it?" He looked at Friedrich.

"That sounds right. He was exploding about it at breakfast one morning. We were old enough to eat with our parents instead of in the nursery."

"They converted because they were offered a really advantageous marriage with the Kämmerer von Worms-Dalberg family on condition that they turned Catholic. Ever since then, they've been forcing a really assertive version of the Counter-Reformation in their lands."

"What Captain Ulfsparre said was that they might well decide to fort up and resist when they see General Brahe and the Lutherans coming."

"They're cousins of the von Hatzfeldts, too."

"Which ones? There are dozens of von Hatzfeldts."

"The important ones. The bishop of Würzburg, his brother the imperial general, and the canon who's still in Mainz looking out for their interests as best he can."

"Isn't that charming?"

"We're not going right at Landstuhl, today, though. This village we're headed for is some way to the south. A dinky little place called Krickenbach. They think we need to go there before Brahe can have a shot at Landstuhl. Something to do with the quarries and which of the villages are deserted and which aren't, but I'm not sure what. 'Need to know' and all that sort of thing, I suppose."

"Deserted?"

"Because of the war. The Ring of Fire may have calmed things down a lot in Thuringia and Franconia, but over here the mercenaries have just kept moving. For one thing, a lot of these little noble territories are, one way or the other, dependencies of the Elector Palatine, which means they've been right in the middle of the political mess from the start."

Hertling frowned at the map. "Once we secure that, then over to Linden, north to Queidersbach, through Bann . . . After that we'll hit Landstuhl and have to do something about Nannstein."

"I hate deserted villages." Merckel picked up his hat. "Too many sheds that ought to be empty but can hold really nasty surprises if the other side has thought to put them there. It's harder for them to do that when there are still people around to object."

"General Brahe's not going to try to besiege Nannstein, I hope," Sergeant Hartke said. "I hate sieges."

"No, I don't think so," Eberhard said. "This campaign is supposed to be moving fast. The Sickingens don't have much of a garrison there. The general will just surround it and cut it off. Once the we've taken the whole west bank of the Rhine down past Strassburg, they won't have many options left."

"Hey, Joel," Jeffie yelled. "Look at this. There's a place on this map called Frankenstein."

"That's not a defense point we have to worry about." Eberhard was quite serious. "It's not on our path and the walls were destroyed about seventy years ago. Nannstein's the one that might be a problem if it turns out to have more of a garrison than the general thinks it does."

He couldn't imagine why the two up-timers kept laughing.

Captain Duke Eberhard pulled up his horse. "As soon as we finish up here, Captain Ulfsparre said, we're to clear up and prepare to push south toward Pirmasens, then east to Weissenburg."

"I wish General Brahe hadn't taken most of the regiment west to Merkweiler," Friedrich said. "We're just one company."

Eberhard shook his head. "He's going to leave a good-sized garrison there to secure the Pechelbronn oil fields for the USE, since production is so far down at Wietze because of Turenne's raid. That's why he took Major Utt, Garand, and Matowski with him. He thinks the up-timers need to take a look at what's there so they can report to the technical people back in Magdeburg. It's so close to the borders of Lorraine that the French will be an ongoing problem if they keep mucking around in the politics of the Lorrainers. Then Brahe will secure Saarbrücken and head south himself. Since he'll be leaving the other regiments behind at Merkweiler, he wanted the rest of Colonel von Zitzewitz's men to be with him when he comes back toward us, just in case, even if all the information he has does indicate that Duke Bernhard has pulled back even farther, to the south of Colmar. Come on."

They came around a curve. Eberhard stopped again, the other men behind him.

"Captain, sir."

"Yes."

"I don't like the look of that village up ahead."

"Merckel, you haven't liked the look of any village we've seen these past three days."

"Are we sure we know where General Brahe's other regiments are?" Friedrich asked.

"The communications people are using the 'radio' sets. As of last night, when they strung up the antenna wire, if *they* really know where they are—which is by no means a sure thing in this uncertain world in which we live—then we know where they are. Manteufel is past Haguenau. Glasenapp is past Schlettstadt, nearly to Colmar. That's as far as we're going on this campaign. The general doesn't want to overextend his lines, Captain Ulfsparre said."

Hertling sighed. "So what you really mean, sir, is that we think we know where they thought they were yesterday. What's more, they say that they are doing well, which is as good as it's going to get." He looked down the valley at the village Merckel was worrying about.

"If Merckel doesn't like the look of it," Ulrich said,

"maybe we ought to investigate. He was right about that shed yesterday morning."

Heisel clambered up on a boulder for a better look. "The farmers aren't all gone. I saw someone move—or maybe I saw something move—and there's smoke, just a little, every now and then, coming from that yellow-painted house behind the brown one."

"Is it safe to assume that it's just a few farmers?" Friedrich asked.

"Hell, no," Hertling answered.

"Bauer, do you like the way that we didn't run into problems over at Nannstein? From what you've heard over the years, would it be typical of the von Sickingens just to close the gates and let us go past without offering any resistance?"

"No, sir."

"Just, 'no, sir'?"

"Not at all, sir. I don't like it one damn bit better than Merckel, sir. Kolb, what do you think?" The four goons closed up around their captain, who was also, in a real sense, still their responsibility.

"I think the rest of you should stay here, and that Captain Duke Eberhard should tell Lieutenant von Damnitz, Heisel, and me to take a half dozen men to skirt around along that brook and come up behind the yellow house."

"Where *is* von Damnitz?" Ulrich looked around.

Hertling waved. "Somewhere back behind us, complaining about all these hills. What did Jeffie Garand call it?"

"'Claustrophobia,'" Friedrich answered. "He can't help it, I guess. He's between Ulrich and me in age and this is the first time he's been out of Pomerania.

He's a nephew of von Glasenapp, I think. He's only been in Mainz for two months. It's really pretty flat there, too. He just doesn't see enough sky to suit him down here in the Palatinate and Alsace. He told me one evening that he's going nearly nuts, not being able to see where he's going around the curves on the roads with all the trees looming over him. And what's worse, he looked down on his right, off the drop. Sergeant Beyschlag is back there with him, trying to buck him up a little. He should be all right once he catches up. The road has veered away from the ravine. Somebody ought to send him back up north where things are flat. Let him be a military hero somewhere around Wismar."

"Flat land—lots of it, anyhow—sounds like it would be weird." Ulrich turned to Merckel. "Have you ever seen any land that was absolutely flat?"

"When we were up north. That was ten years or so ago, maybe more. It's like a river bottom that just goes on and on and on."

"Yeah, but those usually have some hills or cliffs on each side, not so far away that you can't see them."

Hertling shuddered. "I think it would drive *me* nuts up north there, with the land just going on and on and on, like he says, no end to it until you meet the sea."

Ulrich shuddered. "The sea would be worse, I think. Just the reports of the sea battles this spring are enough to strike terror into the heart of a paladin. That's even leaving out that ships sink. In a boat, even in a big river like the Rhine, you've at least got a sporting chance to make it to shore."

"If you can swim," Merckel said. "I can't."

"I don't think we'd better wait for von Damnitz. He'll catch up with us in a few minutes. Merckel and Kolb are right—we should take a look at what's back there. Hertling, I'll take you and Friedrich with me. You, Friedrich . . ." Eberhard looked around. ". . . Kolb and Heisel. Pick a couple of others."

Hertling turned his horse to take a survey of the available resources. Nearly half the men were farther back with von Damnitz and Beyschlag.

"Uh, Captain . . ."

"Yes, Kolb."

"If I were you—not being you, of course—I'd wait for von Damnitz to show."

"It's coming on towards dusk. We haven't passed any place we can reasonably camp tonight, and anyway, I really don't want to camp too close to that village without knowing who or what is in it. It could be some of von Sickingen's garrison from Nannstein. It could be other soldiers, but if so, they won't be on our side, because we pretty much know where our side is. It could just be locals who don't like soldiers. Either way, they've probably been in this neighborhood long enough to know a lot more about it than we do. Things like which paths are best for sneaking up on someone else in the dark."

Kolb nodded. "That's a point, but . . ."

Eberhard dismounted. "Come on, with me." After a little rearranging of weaponry to accommodate progress on foot rather than horseback, they headed up the banks of the brook.

"There's someone in there, all right. What now?" Heisel began to pile his equipment on a stump in the coppice behind the yellow house.

"I don't want them heading down the road toward Ulrich," Eberhard said. "It's our job—one of our jobs, anyway—to take care of him. Among other things. Kolb, go make a noise, maybe ten yards that way, loud enough that whoever is in that house is sure to hear it. Make some kind of a noise that a deer thrashing through the underbrush wouldn't make. I want to spook them. Heisel, right after that, throw the first stink bomb. Use your own judgment about the best target."

"How about I just throw a good-sized rock at the shed? Then when they come out to see what that was, I hit the shed with one stink bomb and the back door of the house with another one?"

"Sounds like a good plan." Eberhard certainly hoped that it was a good plan, since he didn't have another one.

Ten yards away, Kolb utilized one of his few civilian talents, acquired some years before when he was attached to a unit of Swiss mercenaries. He yodeled.

Heisel threw the rock. He hit the shed, too. Baseball had extended to Mainz by 1634 and he was a pitcher. He didn't hit the shed because he was a pitcher. He had become a pitcher because he could hit almost any target with anything he threw. He regarded throwing strikes or balls over something as big as home plate as a mildly entertaining hobby that endeared him to the other men in the regiment.

At that point, unfortunately . . .

Two dozen men from von Sickingen's garrison at Nannstein were in the yellow house. So far, so good. Unfortunately for "the plan," nobody ran out at random to check the yodel or the shed. Following a previously

practiced tactic, they left the house through the front
door and slid into the trees on either side of the road.

"Clusterfuck," Heisel said. He just loved the sound
of that up-time expression. "They're riflemen. *Jäger*. A
couple of them will be behind us before you can fart."

"What the hell did you expect? We're in the middle of a goddamned forest. It's bound to be full of
poachers. Where there are poachers, there are game
wardens." Kolb cleared his throat and spat a puddle
of phlegm on the ground.

"They're headed down toward where we left Ulrich."
Friedrich didn't bother to keep his voice down. "We've
got to get after them." He started to break ranks, only
to be hauled back roughly by Heisel.

"Slowly," Eberhard said. "We've got to get behind
them, but stay together and be careful." He turned
around and pointed. "You, and you. Hide behind the
shed and watch out for the ones Heisel thinks will
come up behind us. He's probably right."

Ulrich sat on his horse in the middle of the narrow mud road, waiting. He couldn't see what was
happening in the village, behind the houses. He even
hadn't really intended to be in the middle, on the
grass verge that was slightly elevated between the ruts
made by the passage of farm carts back and forth,
but his horse had a mind of its own. Given the least
inattention upon his rider's part, the gelding would
move off dust onto grass.

He had no idea where the first rifle shot came
from. He looked around. Merckel's horse was down.
Merckel had come off cleanly and was picking himself
up. A second shot came out of the trees, perhaps five

yards ahead of them, from the right. Ulrich opened his mouth to order the men down, but there were three more shots before he could say anything. One came directly from his left, he was pretty sure. One of the soldiers came off. His horse, grazed on the withers, ran straight down the road toward the village.

"They're all along, on both sides of us," one of the soldiers yelled.

Just then, von Damnitz and the men with him came up behind them on the road, riding too fast to stop before they had rounded the curve and come into sight of the riflemen. Von Damnitz was senior in rank to Ulrich. He was senior in rank to anyone else in the party on the road, so Ulrich turned to him for direction.

Instead of issuing orders, von Damnitz froze in place, yelling "Don't retreat." The men who were with him bunched up, making it impossible for Ulrich's small party to turn and head back down the narrow road, away from the village.

"Don't retreat" didn't last long. Von Damnitz went down. His horse, panicked, forced its way along the shoulder of the road and followed Merckel's horse toward the village.

Horses being horses, the rest of them, who were not trained cavalry mounts, since nobody had expected this little company to mount a cavalry action, concluded that since two horses were running away, they probably knew something that was bad for the herd. Ulrich managed to control his gelding, but six of the horses, with the men mounted on them, headed right into the line of fire.

Three of them made it through. The other three fell, blocking the road completely.

Beyschlag, Merckel, and Bauer tried to get the young duke out of the line of fire, but there wasn't really any single line of fire. The shots from the trees were coming at them from at various angles and from various directions up and down both sides of the road.

Ulrich yelled, "Since we can't go back, go forward. You'll have to jump." The group headed forward, in the direction of the village. His gelding jumped. Beyschlag's shied and plunged into the trees before it followed. Merckel, on foot, ran around the pile of dead horses, trying to catch up. Bauer went down; his horse followed Merckel and sideswiped him, knocking him into a tree.

Von Sickingen's *Jäger* kept up a steady rate of fire. It might not be as fast as it would have been if they were equipped with up-time weapons, but they had worked together for a long time—most of them for a decade, some for nearly two. In a situation like this, they could almost read each other's minds.

Eberhard's group stayed together and were careful. They did not expect to come to the edge of the village, start to move down toward the location of the gunfire, and suddenly be charged at by a half-dozen panicked horses. They dove toward the shoulders and trees, but not all of them fast enough. Friedrich got his head and shoulders out of the way, but a horseshoe, a sturdy iron horseshoe affixed to the hoof of the mixed breed part-draft horse that had been pressed into service to carry Bauer's weight, came down on his left foot.

A half-dozen men came out of the brown house.

Merckel, still running toward the village, howled, "Look out behind you." Eberhard, turning, was hit by another of the horses and knocked down.

One of the men coming out of the brown house yelled back at Merckel. "Don't shoot us. If you're fighting Sickingen's men, you're our friends."

Merckel's best guess, in the middle of the whole mess, was that either the von Sickingen family were not popular landlords or that the village was populated by poachers. Possibly both.

The village men, with their weapons, almost evaporated into the trees from which the firing was coming.

"My name is Didier Schultz," the farmer said an hour or so later. "This is my house, where we were hiding in the loft, waiting for enough of von Sickingen's *Jäger* to come into sight at once to make it worthwhile for us to shoot them. If we had just picked off one, they would have pinpointed our location right away. The women and children are up in the hills. The livestock, too. That's the best practice. When soldiers come your way, run away. We would have been gone, too, but we just weren't fast enough. It's so close to dark now that there's no point in giving them an all clear this evening. In the morning, I'll send my son Henri up to bring everyone down. For now, though, I offer my hospitality, such as it is."

"We took Duke Ulrich next door," Merckel said. "Where it's a little quieter. His brothers, too."

Schultz nodded. "That is the house of my brother-in-law, Heinz Hochban." He gestured toward another man. "My son Henri is named for him."

"We don't have one of the famous up-time trained medics," Beyshlag said. "We don't even have a down-time trained medic. We're just a company, not a regiment. The surgeon went with Colonel von Zitzewitz and General Brahe. Heisel has already set Duke Eberhard's arm and splinted it, but he's pretty sure he has a broken collar-bone, too. He isn't up to setting that. Is there anyone in the village who can do something for Duke Ulrich?"

"The priest might," Schultz said, "but he's up in the hills with the women and children. He's the papist priest whom the von Sickingens have forced on us. We were all good Lutherans here." He thought a moment. "You're fighting for the Swedes, aren't you?"

"Yes," Beyschlag agreed. "Under General Nils Brahe."

"Good Lutherans," Schultz affirmed, "just like the Swedes. But the papist isn't bad at doing things for the sick. I do have to give him credit for that, and at least he's an old man who doesn't fool with our women and girls. He knows tinctures that can break a fever or dry up wet lungs. Sometimes, at least. It's all the will of God, really."

"I have opium," Hochban said. "The apothecary in Landstuhl gave it to me back when my mother was dying of the crab and screaming all night so no one could sleep. There was some left, but he wouldn't buy it back. It's only three years old, so probably it's still good." He paused, looking hopefully at Beyschlag. "Cost a fortune, too, it did."

"Give it to him," Hertling said. "We'll pay."

"The horses are in the lot," Schultz said, starting with what was, in his view, the most important question. "The live bodies of your soldiers are in the church. The live bodies of von Sickingen's men are locked up in the new granary. The dead ones of both are in the crypt where they won't bother anyone in this heat until you can send a messenger to find your commander. Tomorrow morning, when everyone else comes back down, we'll harvest whatever is usable from the bodies of the dead horses. Then we'll push the rest into the ravine."

"What do we do now?" Beyshlag asked.

"Wait for Captain Duke Eberhard to wake up, I guess," Hertling said. "That horse knocked him cold as well as breaking his arm."

"We need to send a messenger to General Brahe."

"Nobody's going tonight," Schultz said. "It's getting dark."

"We don't know where he is," Merckel said. "The captain knew where he was yesterday evening. 'Somewhere between Landstuhl and Merkweiler' isn't very helpful as far as directions go."

"No," Beyschlag said. "We have to use the radio. We have to stay here and call the general for help."

"Do you know how to use it?" Merckel could be trusted to get to the heart of any issue, at least if there was a discouraging word to be found.

"No, but I know where it is. At least, I know where it should be, the 'tuna tin transmitter' and the antenna. They were in the captain's saddle bags." Beyschlag stood up.

"So if that horse wasn't one of the dead ones, you can get it. If the horse didn't fall on it and smash it, that is."

Hertling pushed his hair back from his forehead. "Merckel . . ."

Beyschlag shook his head. "Even if you don't know how to use it, Hertling, you must have seen the captain use it. You're always standing right behind his shoulder."

"I've seen him use it. That's not quite the same thing."

"Does Lieutenant Duke Friedrich know how to use it?"

"I think so, but I'm not sure."

"He's with his brothers. They may die. He won't want to leave them."

"He won't be leaving them right now," Hochban said, opening the door. "I gave him some of the opium too, for his foot."

"I'm pretty sure the antenna plugs into this hole," Hertling said. "Heisel, tie the other end of this wire to a rock and throw it over the highest thing you can find in the village."

"Did I enlist in the army to spend my days throwing rocks over chimneys?"

"You enlisted to do what you're told. I'll hold on to this end of the wire. If I plug it in first, it might take the tuna tin with it, and we'd end up with the transmitter halfway up the roof of a house."

"How do you send the clicks?"

"You send them with this switch here. One way you send and the other way you receive what other units send you, but I'm not sure which way is which."

"Try it both ways. It won't hurt the machine."

"You hope," Merckel said.

"The only ones I know are for 'SOS.' What good will it do to send that if nobody at the other end knows who is sending it or where we are?"

"Beyschlag, was there a book with this thing?"

Beyschlag stood up again.

Heisel opened the book to a display of the letters of the alphabet, each with a combination of dots and dashes underneath it. Hertling checked the S and the O against his memory. "Yes, that's it."

"What do we need to tell them?"

"We're here, in a mess."

"Duke Ulrich is going to die."

"We're somewhere between Landstuhl and Pirmasens. But . . ." Beyschlag looked at the map he has fished out of Duke Friedrich's doublet. ". . . we don't know exactly how far we are from either one." He looked up at Schultz. "Where are we? What's the name of this village?"

"Weselberg," Hochban said.

"Sure. It would have been way too much to hope that the name would be short. At least it has an S in it."

"Radio operators like very short messages," Heisel said.

"Jeffie Garand has a word he likes. SNAFU. Look up those letters, Beyschlag, and write them out for me. Does anyone have any paper?"

"Use the back page of the Morse code book. It's blank. More to the point, does anyone have a pencil?"

"Schultz, do you have a lantern or a lamp? It's getting dark."

Schultz dug out an ancient clay oil lamp. "Tell them that they have to go past the old mill at Obernheim, because we're closer to Pirmasens than that. Everyone knows where the mill is. The burned-out village was Harsberg."

"It's actually good that it's getting dark. They like to send the radio messages out right before dark or right after dark."

"Beyschlag, write out a whole message. I'll start with the SOS. Here goes."

"Do you think we sent it often enough?"

"How do I know?"

"I tried it ten times each way, with the switch up and the switch down."

"I don't actually know how fast these radio messages travel," Beyschlag said. "Faster than a horse can gallop, I'm sure. And the radio can travel at night, when a horse can't unless he knows the road. Like Heisel said, the radio likes to travel at night."

"So what do we do now?"

"Wait and hope that General Brahe sends somebody for us."

". . . for the soul of our late brother in Christ, Ulrich, who was born a duke of Württemberg and died in the flower of his youth as a baptized and confirmed child of his savior, giving full faith to the forgiving grace of his God and acceptance of His righteousness."

"He was unconscious when he died," Merckel muttered. "He wasn't doing any believing at all."

"Hush, Lutz, the pastor isn't done."

"Man born of woman is of few days and full of trouble. He springs up like a flower and withers away; like a fleeting shadow, he does not endure (Job 14:1–2).

"As for man, his days are as grass; as a flower of the field, so he flourisheth. For the wind passeth over it, and it is gone; and the place thereof shall know it no more (Psalm 103:15–16)."

General Brahe's chaplain looked up from his prayer book. "Take comfort, however, from the promise that is associated with these words."

"For all flesh is as grass, and all the glory
of man as the flower of grass. The grass
withereth, and the flower thereof falleth
away: but the word of the Lord endureth
for ever (1 Peter 1:24–25)."

Friedrich laid his crutches down next to the stool. "I
just wish," he said, "that the Lord could have seen fit
to let our brother flourish and endure a little longer."

"It was a good funeral sermon." Eberhard rearranged
his sling. "But, sometimes, other words seem more
appropriate. Montaigne quoted some older writer as
saying, 'It is no marvel that hazard has such power
over us, since we live by hazard.' We die by hazard,
as well, it seems."

"I like the other passage better."

"For, whatsoever some say, valor is all alike,
and not one thing in the street or town, and
another in the camp or field. A man should bear
an illness in his bed as courageously as he does
an injury in the field, and fear death no more
at home in his house than abroad in an assault."

"I hope he didn't have time to be afraid at all. I
hope that it all happened so fast that he didn't even
see what hit him."

Mainz, May 1634

"The campaign was a great success," Botvidsson reported
with satisfaction. "General Brahe was expecting a short,

victorious war and that's what he got. The king—the emperor, I mean—is delighted and has extended his congratulations on behalf of the USE. According to the best intelligence we have received, the Sickingen family is headed for Bonn to take refuge with the archbishop elector of Cologne."

"I'm sure," Erik Stenbock said, "that dear Ferdinand will be delighted to have even more guests battening on his hospitality."

Buchenland, June 1634

"Who is this 'McDonnell' in the cartoon in the Mainz newspaper?" Geraldin asked. He threw it across the breakfast table in the castle of Karl von Schlitz, imperial knight of Buchenland.

"It's Dennis," Deveroux answered. "Drunk as a skunk. Some damned reporter must have heard about what happened last month. The Swedes can't tell the difference between 'Denis McDonnell' and 'Dennis MacDonald.'"

Geraldin examined his fingernails. "Neither can most Irishmen. He spells it 'McDonnell' sometimes himself."

Deveroux snorted. "We have a perfect right to misspell our own names. I'm sure I've signed mine a half-dozen different ways. Foreigners should be more considerate." He pointed across the table. "It's a pretty good likeness, don't you think, Dennis? The drool? The spittle? The vomit? The—"

"Arrrgh!"

"We miscalculated, back in March," Butler groused. "If we'd had any idea that Nils Brahe was going to take his forces haring off into the southern Palatinate and northern Alsace, we could have done a proper raid into Fulda. We wouldn't have run into any serious opposition. That Fulda Barracks Regiment is nothing but a bad joke."

"Spilt milk." Deveroux looked at von Schlitz. "You are sure, really sure, that the up-timers and Schweinsberg are wandering around this territory, with only minimal guards, trying to make the peasants happy?"

Von Schlitz had to do quite a bit of persuasion before the Irishmen were willing to believe it.

Butler shook his head. "If Taaffe and Carew were here, they would be trying to persuade me that this behavior by the up-timers is a dispensation of divine providence. It's almost enough to make me believe them."

Felix Gruyard smirked.

Fulda, June 1634

"So then they sent Duke Ulrich's body home." Derek Utt leaned against the window in the conference room, looking at the other up-timers in Fulda. "At least, they sent it as far as Belfort in Mömpelgard. That will be Montbéliard on the wall map there—that's the way the French spelled it, up-time. The family has a chapel there. It was too warm for them to try to get it across the Rhine to Stuttgart. If they want to bury it in the capital of the duchy, long-term, I guess the procedure is to wait a couple of years. Eberhard's feeling horrible about the whole thing, like it was his fault."

"Damn," Joel Matowski said. "He was just a kid. The youngest of them, I mean. And since we headed off west just a couple of days before the guys were supposed to come up to Fulda, he never did get a look at the American way of life, such as it is out here in the boondocks. He really wanted to do that. I was sort of hoping I'd be able to get some leave and take them on a tour of Grantville."

"Yeah," Jeffie Garand answered. "Too bad. You'd have had an excuse to see Alice again, too. I'm sure you weren't thinking about that. Not at all. On the other hand . . ."

"What?"

"Gertrud adores me. But she's still a down-timer, and Ulrich of Württemberg was a duke, even if he was only fifteen and it seemed likely that he'd develop the family pot belly if he lived long enough. If they had shown up here in Barracktown, it would've been like having a rock star competition back up-time. I'd have been real happy to see his backside if you'd taken him off to get a taste of West Virginia in Thuringia."

Section Three: Choose some wise, understanding and respected men . . .

Mainz, June 1634

Nils Brahe rapped his genuine up-time souvenir gavel on the table. Since it was a gift from Thomas Price Riddle of Grantville via his granddaughter Mary Kat and then via Derek Utt, to celebrate the acquisition of the Province of the Upper Rhine by the USE, he followed the rapping with a stern, English "Order in the Court."

The rest of the council looked at him blankly.

"The immediate results of the Congress of Copenhagen that concern us today pertain to the Province of the Main and the new Province of the Upper Rhine. Some of the correspondence we've received refers to the latter as the Upper Rhenish Province, but it is the same entity. Basically, for us here in Mainz, there's not much change. The king—the emperor—is keeping the Province of the Main under direct imperial administration, from the Fulda border down to the Rhine. The only real difference is that Frankfurt-am-Main is getting new rights to self-administration. Or, more precisely, Frankfurt is getting back its old privileges as an imperial city and seats in the USE parliament, one each in the House of Lords and House of Commons. We also have some negotiations to complete concerning the status of the former possessions of the archdiocese of Mainz over around Erfurt that now lie in the State of Thuringia-Franconia, and—"

"We do have to be careful," Botvidsson said.

"About what?"

"Do we have any firm direction from Chancellor Oxenstierna about how to handle the traditional rights of the king's Protestant allies whom he has placed, willy-nilly, into the Province of the Main now that it's a new, permanent entity of the USE? It was one thing for him to set up a temporary military administration of occupied territories. It's a problem of a different dimension for it to become a permanent civil government. Especially, I would point out, since you are still an appointed administrator rather than a man selected or elected by the Estates of the new province. Which we still have to set up—the Estates, I mean. I suppose we need to call one of these 'constitutional conventions' and establish a governmental structure. One that doesn't infringe on the traditional rights of . . ."

Stenbock and Ulfsparre started to chant in unison, imitating Oxenstierna's voice at the Congress of Copenhagen, "Hesse-Darmstadt, Solms, Isenburg, Gelnhausen, Hanau, Usingen, and Rieneck."

"Not to mention," Ulfsparre continued in his normal voice, "the now ex-rulers of each of the above, who aren't going to be anything more than members of a provincial House of Lords, like the one over in the SoTF, with the former count of Isenburg having to share and share alike with the mayor of Gelnhausen. It won't go over very well, I predict."

Brahe frowned at him.

"Five hours," Eberhard said at the Horn of Plenty that evening. "We sat at that table for five whole damn hours."

Hartmann Simrock raised one eyebrow. "Was it information you need to know?"

"Eventually. Not necessarily right this minute. None of what Brahe covered today makes much difference to us, personally." He waved generally in the direction of his brother Friedrich, who was at a different table with Margarethe and Theobald.

"Does that leave some of it or even a little bit of it that makes a difference to you personally?"

"Coming out of the Congress of Copenhagen? Sure."

Eberhard reached back and pulled a newspaper off the bar counter. Simrock grabbed it by one corner and waved it around the tap room in the Horn of Plenty.

"This issue has a new cartoon about the Congress of Copenhagen. I think it's one of van de Passe's best. You can identify everyone important easily enough."

Hertling got up and came across the room, leaving Merckel and the others to their dice.

"It's probably by one of his sons," Theo said. "Simon and the younger Crispijn have both been working in Copenhagen the last few years."

Margarethe stuck out her tongue. "Don't be pompous."

"Here's Gustavus with Princess Kristina, here's King Christian with Prince Ulrik, there are Mike Stearns and Rebecca Abrabanel. Oxenstierna's the one with the piles of note cards about to fall over and bury him. Don Fernando in the Netherlands is peeking through one window and the Holy Roman Emperor through the other one. That's the archbishop-elector of Cologne and Duke Maximilian of Bavaria under the table with horns in their ears, eavesdropping." Simrock paused for breath.

"What are they doing?" Tata asked.

"Putting together the pieces of one of the up-timer 'jigsaw puzzles.' It's van de Passe's commentary on the way the emperor and Stearns threw together the new USE provinces. The crowned heads of Europe are playing with the local jurisdictions. But if you look closely, they're forcing the pieces into place, even if they don't fit quite right."

Eberhard nodded. "Like their maybe-it'll-happen-someday Province of Swabia. The pieces that the

Swedes and up-timers want to cram in don't really fit at all. Did any of the rest of you read what Oxenstierna said about their 'future Province of Swabia, once it is pacified'?"

Simrock nodded. "A big chunk of the map. All of southwest Germany on the right bank of the Rhine, really, except for whatever Duke Bernhard may manage to slice off in the Breisgau and Baden."

Eberhard raised an eyebrow. "Did you notice the new imperial administrator for Swabia?"

Reichard Donner snorted. "Georg Friedrich—the margrave of Baden-Durlach. He's an old man—past sixty. It's no wonder that van de Passe drew him with white hair and a beard that makes him look like the up-time Santa Claus. He's not exactly an honorary appointment. He'll show up in Augsburg and go through the motions, but everybody expects that for all practical purposes, he'll delegate most of the work. He'll have to."

Friedrich stuck out his mug for another beer. "His heir's busy running their government-in-exile in Basel. And Christoph, his second son, is one hundred percent a soldier who doesn't have the patience to do it—administration and diplomacy and stuff like that."

"Georg Friedrich has a competent son-in-law," Simrock protested. "Count Wilhelm Ludwig of Nassau-Saarbrücken. Picking him as backup would build another bridge over to Frederik Hendrick in the Netherlands, too, since the Dutch stadholders are from the Nassau family."

"I know. But damn. The single biggest chunk of land in the new proposed 'Province of Swabia' is Württemberg. We . . ." Eberhard waved at Friedrich again. "Not only weren't we there—it would have been hard for us to travel, that's true—we were not even invited. The Congress of Copenhagen didn't even acknowledge that we exist. They didn't even hold any kind of a memorial for Ulrich's death. Not so much as an eulogy. Sometimes I think that Gustavus Adolphus just stuck us down here in Mainz, forgot about us, and doesn't want to be reminded."

"There's not much you can do about it."

"But there is something *else* I can do." Eberhard stood up on the bench and waved his good arm for attention. The various conversations dwindled down.

"My friends and colleagues. I have an announcement to make."

Kunigunde Treidelin and Philipp Schaumann kept arguing over their card game.

Reichard Donner rapped on the table. "Attention."

"As you may have noticed, my brother Friedrich is in love with Margarethe Pistora."

There were various shouts, hoots, and squalls of, "We've noticed."

"The rest of you, except Theobald, of course, probably don't know that he's actually offered to marry Margarethe—spoken to her father and all that. Papa Pistor is not impressed—as far as he is concerned, being Lutheran is a negative that far outbalances being a duke."

Friedrich snorted. "Especially a duke with a squashed foot and no lands or income left."

Eberhard ignored him. "That's 'hardly any lands and not much income.' We're still getting some money from the bits and pieces of estates our ancestors picked up in Alsace, or we couldn't pay for our beer, much less the rent for our sisters' townhouse in Strassburg."

"Anyhow!" Friedrich had picked that up from Jeffie Garand and used it whenever he could. It was such a useful word for a teenager. Depending on the tone of voice, it was appropriate for any of a dozen different situations.

"What's left of what used to be the bureaucrats of the duchy of Württemberg are against it, of course. The prospect wasn't so much of a strain for them to swallow before Ulrich was killed, but now there's just one spare, aside from the uncles and cousins. Except . . ."

He paused for dramatic effect.

"There isn't any spare at all any more. I'm the head of the family. I have given Friedrich permission to renounce his title—that's done, by the way, with all the legal paperwork signed, sealed, and filed—and I say that Friedrich and Margarethe can go ahead and get married."

The Mainz Committee of Correspondence, what there was of it, since Ursula Widder had gone back to the kitchen to bank the fires for the night, mostly applauded. Reichard Donner muttered, "Then why don't you go ahead and give yourself permission to marry Tata, you randy little twerp," using a different descriptive adjective, but not loudly enough for anyone but Justina to hear.

Then he sighed. The new universe created by the Ring of Fire was not a world of dreams. What had the up-time book said? Some animals are more equal than others—that was it. Even in this new universe, the daughter of a university-educated clergyman was considerably more equal to a former duke than the daughter of a man who was not the world's most efficient innkeeper was to a still-a-duke. He looked back up. Eberhard was, with some difficulty and a hand from Tata, climbing down off the table.

"So now," Theobald was saying to Simrock, "it's just a matter of sorting out the Lutheran *versus* Calvinist thing, which is likely to take a while, given the honorable chaplain our father's prejudices."

Simrock was talking to Eberhard. "Very charitable of you. I don't suppose all this has anything to do with your conclusion that you're not very likely to ever get Württemberg back, so why not?"

Hartmann Simrock was even more of a cynic than Donner. A young cynic, but a cynic.

"Umm," Tata snuggled against Eberhard under the duvet in her bed on the third floor of the Horn of Plenty. "You're so nice and warm." It was June, true. This particular June night, though, was not rare, as the English playwright had described a warm, sunny, June day. It was just like most of the rest of them had been—chilly, with drizzle, and penetrating damp rising up off the river. "I like their Major Utt."

"Why?"

"Have you seen his hair?"

"What there is of it," Eberhard admitted. "He's going bald."

"But what there is of it is *red*. *Red* red. *Really* red. If I could go stand next to him, I would look blonde in comparison."

"I like your hair the way it is."

"It's not funny. All the way through school, the other children called me *Füchsin*."

"Foxy is good. I think you're really foxy."

Eberhard liked Agathe Donner because she told him the truth. She never swore that she adored him passionately. She never declared that he was a great lover, which he was fairly sure that he was not. She never claimed that he was handsome. If she had, he would have doubted her. Among other things, he had been standing near to Major Utt for a good part of the day. What standing next to the up-timer made *him* feel was "short and dumpy."

He'd spent quite a bit of his life listening to girls, high-born or low-born, say flattering things to him just because he had been born the oldest son of the duke of Württemberg. They lied. He knew he wasn't tall, dark, handsome, or romantic.

Warm, though? He was willing to accept as strictly factual that he was nice and warm. He snuggled against Tata in return.

Mainz, July 1634

"For another thing, although not directly as a consequence of the actions taken by the archbishop of Cologne in regard to Essen . . ." Brahe paused and took a deep breath before he continued. The various members of his inner council looked at one another. "I have received a formal request from the archbishop of Mainz that he be allowed to return from exile in Bonn to his see here in Mainz."

"He has persuaded the up-timer who is, since last month, the 'cardinal-protector of the United States of Europe,' to get the emperor to give him a *salva guardia.*" Botvidsson's mouth pursed with distaste at the thought of a "cardinal protector" in any political entity of which the king of Sweden was emperor.

Brahe, suppressing his developing personal opinion that any Vasa with a practical interest in some day maybe ruling Poland had better, as Derek Utt would say, "get over it" as far as Catholics, Calvinists, and miscellaneous sectarians were concerned, continued serenely. "Wamboldt von Umstadt expresses that he is willing to reach an accommodation with the Province of the Main similar to that which the authorities of the State of Thuringia-Franconia have reached with Abbot Johann Bernhard Schenk von Schweinsberg in Fulda. This will involve our sending a delegation to Fulda to gather more detailed information in regard to precisely what that accommodation involves before we commit ourselves to an agreement."

He turned a page over and handed his notes to Botvidsson. "Cover the rest of this, will you, Johan. I have another meeting scheduled."

"The archbishop also indicates that Franz von Hatzfeldt is, or will be, or may be—his phrasing is a bit vague, here—proffering a similar offer to the SoTF authorities in regard to the Diocese of Würzburg."

Botvidsson stuck up one finger. "The emperor has also requested that his administrators in Mainz take a particular interest in the status of the city of Wetzlar, since the Imperial Supreme Court has settled there rather than in Magdeburg."

Everyone realized that this was polite phrasing for, "make sure that the landgrave of Hesse-Kassel, however valuable an ally he may be, doesn't get his claws into it."

Botvidsson stuck up a second finger. "And since

the deaths of counts Wolfgang Wilhelm and Philipp Wilhelm of Pfalz-Neuburg in the Essen war, with regard to their status as dukes of Jülich-Berg-Cleves-Mark, the ongoing inheritance controversies with Brandenburg, and the new developments in regard to the Republic of Essen . . ."

Duke Eberhard of Württemberg, now seated at the council table in deference to both his own services in the Upper Rhine campaign and his youngest brother's death, asked, "That doesn't have anything directly to do with us here, does it?"

"Not directly. But . . . derivatively. The heir to Jülich and Berg is now an infant, whose mother, Katharina Charlotte of Zweibrücken . . ."

"That's part of the Palatinate family," Eberhard whispered to Ulfsparre. "The French call it Deux Ponts, like that one Württemberg exclave can be either Mömpelgard or Montebéliard, depending on who's talking."

"Damn," Ulfsparre whispered back. "I hate the Rhineland."

"If you hate the upper Rhine, just wait until you get transferred someplace that you have to learn about the lower Rhine."

Ulfsparre frowned. "I already hate Elsass. Alsace, the French call it. It's annoying of them, like calling Lüttich by Liège. The Frenchies even call this city Mayence. They call Aachen Aix-la-Chapelle. They call Köln Cologne."

"The Dutch call it Keulen," Eberhard interrupted. "I saw that in a letter."

"Damn. A man no sooner finishes learning one language than he has to pick up another."

Botvidsson ignored the whispers. ". . . is the half-sister of the wife of Count Palatine Christian of Birkenfeld-Bischweiler, who has just been appointed by the emperor as his administrator of the new Province of the Upper Rhine."

"Different mothers," Duke Eberhard whispered. "Christian's wife's mother was a sister of Duke Henri de Rohan, the French Huguenot leader. He's in exile. He was in Venice, but I think he's in Lausanne now—Rohan, I mean, not Count Christian."

"This half-French, half-German stuff drives me nuts," Ulfsparre whispered back. "You were still sedated when they brought you out, but Sergeant Beyshlag told me that the owner of that farmhouse where the men took your brother Ulrich after he was injured had a French baptismal name and a German family name. His brother-in-law had a German baptismal name and a French family name. I tell you, it's crazy."

Ulfsparre couldn't seem to let it go. "Crazy," he repeated to Erik Stenbock over their beer after the meeting. "The whole Rhineland. With all due respect to Gustavus, why does he even want to include these stupid little patchwork territories down here in the southwest in the USE?"

"Merckweiler-Pechelbronn," Stenbock suggested mildly. "Jeffie Garand taught me a song from a 'musical play' performed once in their high school. The diva sings, "Oil. *Oil!* OIL!" getting louder and louder and louder. Most of the play makes bad jokes about small European countries, though. His best guess was that 'Lichtenberg' was supposed to be a combination of a couple of real small duchies. He didn't know which ones."

Ulfsparre was not to be diverted from his main complaint. "Look at Duke Eberhard's little CoC whore. The Donners came to Mainz from somewhere in the Pfalz."

"That's 'Palatinate' to the up-timers, my friend."

"They spell her name 'Agathe' like the French, but they pronounce it 'Agata' as if it was German. She *is* German." He winked. "Oooh, what a build."

"I wouldn't let Eberhard hear you call her a whore," Stenbock warned. "Her father's a halfway respectable innkeeper. She's not just an 'available' and the duke is fond of her, I think."

"Not saying it in his hearing doesn't keep me from thinking it." Ulfsparre shook his head. "He could do a lot better. It's not as if he'll be able to escort her to any of the social events that General Brahe will host once his wife and sister join him. Almost any family of the Mainz patriciate would be happy and honored for one of their daughters to serve as the duke of Württemberg's favored companion for as long as he is stationed in the city."

Nils Brahe's other meeting featured wine rather than beer, and a sumptuous lunch that had stretched well into the afternoon.

The longer he lived in the Rhineland, the more he appreciated wine rather than beer.

Derek Utt leaned back. "What do you think of this business with Wamboldt von Umstadt and Calixtus, by the way? Is it anything we'll have to worry about up in Fulda, since we've already worked things out with Schweinsberg? Do I need to bring it up with Wes?"

Nils Brahe stretched his lanky legs out somewhat farther under the table. "As Duke Ernst explains it to me—we correspond extensively—you are all sectarians.

You have embraced 'universal sectarianism' as a way of life, the Catholics and Calvinists as wholeheartedly as the sectarians themselves, there not being enough Lutherans or adherents of the Church of England among you to make a significant difference. And, yes, I have heard that your wife's grandmother is a most fervent adherent of the Church of England."

"So's Mary Kat, actually." Derek Utt laughed. "Not quite as gung-ho as her grandma, who is busily restoring the abandoned Episcopalian church building and recruiting for a priest, but definitely pretty much committed. There were more of them up-time. More of them in the United States of America, I mean, not just in the whole world. Millions of them, Lutherans and Episcopalians. Several million of each. Maybe four, five, six million of each."

"In an overall population that was how large?"

"Umm. About two hundred eighty million, I think. They were just starting to take the new census the year of the Ring of Fire, but that's somewhere in the range of what they were predicting."

"Sects," Nils Brahe said firmly. "They were sects. Our best estimate of the population of the USE now is somewhere between twelve and fifteen million. It should be toward the larger end since the emperor's campaigns of last month in the northwest. Using a fifteen-million population base for the USE, proportionally, that would mean that we would have . . ." He paused for mental calculations. ". . . somewhere between two hundred thousand and a quarter million Lutherans in the USE, rather than, probably, eight to nine million. Up-time, Lutherans and Episcopalians were sects as much as your Methodists and your Baptists just as much as your

Mormons and your Pentecostals. Just as much as our Mennonites and Socinians. Muselius in Grantville sent Duke Ernst a fascinating book by an up-time German named Ernst Troeltsch, found in the library of the Baptist pastor named Green. It's being reprinted in Jena and Muselius managed to get an advance copy. I've ordered one myself. Troeltsch maintained . . ."

Derek cocked his head to one side. "Just exactly how has Duke Ernst come to define the concept of 'universal sectarianism'? It's not something I've ever heard of."

"I believe he formulated it himself, based on various comments by Troeltsch," Brahe admitted. "Also after multiple readings of the proceedings of the Rudolstadt Colloquy. It doesn't just involve your concepts of separation of church and state—though, as a good Swedish Lutheran myself, I have to say that's drastic enough. Rather, there is the ingrained cultural concept—cultural, not a matter of constitutional law—as the up-time Lutheran speaker Gary Lambert phrased it at one point in the discussions, that 'everybody has the right to go to hell in his own way.' Which seems to be the fundamental religious belief among you— that you bear no responsibility for the salvation of anyone beyond the bounds and borders of your own 'denomination.' Which defines you all as sectarians, from his perspective, and mine, and the emperor's, no matter how you think of yourselves."

"And we are talking about this because?"

Brahe refilled his wine glass. "It's terribly Mennonite, really—it's a quintessentially sectarian perspective. There is the question of what we are going to do about it. No one can doubt that it is arising in everyone's mind."

"Perhaps not everyone's," Derek said. "Only consider Sergeant Garand."

Brahe snorted. "In the mind of every aware politician, let us say then. No matter how influential Michael Stearns is at present, the fact remains—there are only about three thousand of you up-timers in the USE's new population of fifteen million or so, and your three thousand are divided into multiple sects. There are three or four million more people at the emperor's disposal if one adds in all of Scandinavia, which it is only reasonable to presume that we may do since Ahrensbök and the revived Union of Kalmar, all Lutheran, add weight to the several million in Germany. So. Given that Wettin, also, is Lutheran and may become prime minister after the upcoming election, what is to prevent the establishment of Lutheranism as a state church throughout the USE? Please do not say, 'Larry Mazzare.'"

Derek laughed and reached for the bottle. "Did someone say that? Stearns is willing to live with Gustav's insistence on some kind of a Lutheran state church in the USE, if it's nothing more than a bow in the direction of 'first among equals.' The sort of thing that the Church of England had turned into, up-time, or the Lutherans in Denmark. They're writing that into the constitution, knowing perfectly well that he handles it differently in Sweden and probably won't ever change the way he handles it in Sweden."

Brahe nodded. "As far as Sweden goes, and will continue to go for that matter, 'co-terminous church and society' might describe it quite well."

"It's not that anyone thinks that the Lutherans and the rest of them here in the USE are going to learn to 'love one another, right now.' You might say that religious intolerance falls into the category of an undoubted fact. It might be more reasonable for you to ask exactly what Stearns thinks is going to prevent that state church, once the constitution establishes it, from going ahead and persecuting the rest of the religions in the USE no matter what the written constitution says. Ask me what's likely to happen in a real world situation, so to speak. Did you read that book that Mary Kat sent?"

Brahe smiled. "What were the motives for persecution? Professor Roland H. Bainton, clearly a most learned man among the up-timers and a sectarian of the Quaker persuasion himself, gives three prerequisites: '(1) The persecutor must believe that he is right; (2) that the point in question is important; (3) that coercion will be effective.' Personally, I am inclined to think that the third point will turn out to be the USE's saving grace from the perspective of you up-timers. Not toleration as a matter of conviction, for most people, but rather as a matter of sheer practicality, as I have learned, sometimes rather painfully, during these last eighteen months of administering a Catholic archdiocese. Duke Ernst has made it quite clear, in his letters, that his analysis is taking him in that direction. Whether or not he can persuade his older brother is, or course, another question."

"I have to admit to some curiosity as to why we're discussing the problem right at the moment."

"That goes back to your first question of this conversation—about whether your people in Fulda need to be concerned about Wamboldt von Umstadt."

Utt nodded. "Starting point. When the Swedes took Mainz in 1632, the archbishop of Mainz, Anselm Casimir Wamboldt von Umstadt, chose exile in Cologne."

"In Bonn, to be more precise. Under the protection of the archbishop-elector of Cologne, Or, in other words, under the protection of Ferdinand, the younger brother of Duke Maximilian of Bavaria. He is now reconsidering. I have a letter. Preliminary. Exploratory. Tentative, so to speak. Considering the circumstances under which he might be allowed to return to Mainz."

"Ah, considering, perhaps, such circumstances as those under which we permitted Schweinsberg to come back to Fulda? You might want to talk to Wes Jenkins. He was more in on the discussions between Piazza and Schweinsberg than I was. To be honest, I wasn't in on them at all. The army doesn't make policy. It just carries it out."

"If you say so." Nils Brahe was far from fully convinced on that point.

Botvidsson appeared at the door, giving the kind of wave that meant "your next appointment is waiting." They both stood up.

"Thanks for everything," Utt said. "I'll be heading back to Fulda tomorrow. I'll see you again one of these days, I guess."

"Taking those boys with you," Brahe stipulated.

"Taking them with me, not to mention their entourage. That was an interesting idea of yours, appointing Duke Eberhard to investigate Grantville's arrangement with Schweinsberg. I could have just had Ed Piazza send you a copy of the agreement, you know."

"Oh, yes. I know. I most definitely know."

❖   ❖   ❖

"So the archbishop-elector of Mainz is really willing to drop the 'prince' part of his title in order to come back," Simrock announced. "At least, that's what the newspapers are reporting."

Eberhard knew perfectly well that it was true, since he had been at the council meeting at which General Brahe had discussed it, but he couldn't say that, since it hadn't been announced. "I guess," he said, "that I should have held my breath."

"I get confused every time I look at that picture of him," Joel Matowski grabbed the paper. "Wamboldt von Umstadt, I mean. See."

Reichard Donner looked across the bar at the Horn of Plenty. "Why?"

"I'm Catholic myself."

Theo Pistor opened his mouth; then closed it again after Eberhard and Tata both gave him a good glare.

Joel caught it though. "Didn't know that, did you? Thought I was human, maybe? What's your beef? Simrock's Catholic and you're friends with him. Jeffie doesn't belong to any church at all, if that makes you feel better."

From Theo's expression, it clearly didn't.

Jeffie yawned and looked at him. "I think the CoC still has quite a way to go with you, boy."

Joel made a "stuff it" motion at him and looked back at Reichard. "I guess I think of archbishops looking sort of like the pictures of John Paul II that were in our CCD classroom when Ed Piazza taught us. I don't think of them as looking like leprechauns."

"Leprechauns?"

"The little Irish critters. *Finian's Rainbow*. It's

the little pointy face, the little pointy goatee. The little pointy points on his moustache. Really—I have trouble getting my mind around an archbishop with a moustache at all. The little pointy points on his collar. Most of all, the big widow's peak point where his hair is receding."

"CCD? Who was John Paul II?"

Joel decided that Herr Donner was likely to have a very informative evening. He opened his mouth.

Joel had a very informative evening, too. He had never heard of the synergistic controversy.

"Well, I hadn't either," Theo said cheerfully, "considering that it hasn't happened yet. But Papa has been collecting everything he can afford to buy about what will be happening—would have been happening—you know what I mean—in the churches for the next twenty-five years or so. For as long as he's likely to live. He wants to do whatever he can to make sure that things he doesn't like don't happen. Won't happen here. Does that make sense?"

Jeffie nodded. "Call in the cavalry and head them off at the pass."

"There's not a lot he'll be able to do about Calixtus, probably, considering that he's teaching at a Lutheran university in Brunswick, while Papa's a Calvinist. But he'll see if he can get Landgrave Wilhelm of Hesse-Kassel to talk to the Brunswickers and see if they'll put pressure on the Helmstedt faculty to fire the man. If any of the dukes can be brought to see the dangers of this 'Pietism' movement that's going to develop . . . Calixtus is a natural target for the Flacians. Without a university base, he'll have a lot less prestige if he keeps going around spouting this stuff about ecumenism. Papa has written to his former teacher, Gomar, to see if he'll intervene with Fredrik Hendrik in the Netherlands."

"Gomar," Reichard muttered. "He's as old as the hills. He must be seventy if he's a day. Can't you deal with modern writers?"

"Donner, you're the one who keeps quoting Althusius at us. He's just as old." Jeffie grinned. "I looked him up. Wes spent some of Fulda's stingy budget on a set of reprint encyclopedias. Bet you weren't sure that I can read and write."

"More to the point," Theo said, "Gomar opposes toleration for Catholics. And for Jews. And for Protestants who don't follow Calvin. And for Calvinists who aren't supralapsarians."

"Papa's even right-wing for a Gomarist," Margarethe added, as cheerily as if she were saying that Chaplain Pistor liked ice cream.

"Papa sticks to his principles."

"Hey, Theo," Jeffie slapped him on the shoulder. "You're in the CoC. You're supposed to be in favor of religious tolerance. That sounds more like you agree with your father."

"Well, I do agree with Papa—at least about some things. I guess I can learn to tolerate toleration, if I have to, but that doesn't mean I'm going to compromise my own beliefs. I can put up with the fact that some people are obstinate in their errors, but I don't have to like it."

"Papa can't even put up with it," Margarethe said. "That's where he and Theo are different."

"The Flacians can't put up with it, either," Eberhard said, "when it comes to Lutherans. Württemberg has

enough problems right now without another knock-
down, drag out, theological battle over Calixtus and
his ideas."

"Write to Count Ludwig Guenther," Joel recommended. "Maybe he can give you some pointers." He
turned a page. "See the new cartoon?"

Sure enough, it was another van de Passe. This time,
the scene involved a three-branched hall of mirrors
showing endless past and potential future Lutheran
theological colloquies in one direction, endless past
and future Catholic councils in another, and endless
to infinite ecumenical conversations in the middle.
At the juncture stood Count Ludwig Guenther of
Schwarzburg-Rudolstadt, wearing the backwards baseball cap that had become his trademark in the various
illustrations, even though the dignified middle-aged
nobleman had only donned the item upon one brief
occasion in real life.

"He's a Mennonite, you know," Simrock said.

"Not Count Ludwig Guenther," Eberhard protested.

"No, not the count. Van de Passe is a Mennonite."

Jeffie perked up. "I thought they were all farmers
who wear funny, flat hats."

"That was up-time, in the United States and Canada,
after they'd been put through the wringer for another
three hundred fifty years or so. Hey, the University
of Mainz bought a reprint of the 1911 edition of
the *Encyclopedia Britannica*, too." Simrock thought
a minute. "Or maybe those were Amish. Anabaptist
sectarians, anyway. In the here and now, the Mennonites are mostly pretty urban and pretty uppity."

Tata clapped. "Uppity like 'uppity women'?"

"You got it. Uppity. Van de Passe has moved around a

lot. He left Antwerp when they expelled the Protestants. He left Aachen when they expelled the Protestants. He managed about twenty years in Cologne before they expelled the Protestants. He did engravings and his wife ran a book and print shop to help support the family."

Joel winced. "Expelled, expelled, expelled. That sounds like a liturgy. I apologize on behalf of my church."

"Why?" Theo wrinkled his forehead. "If the Calvinists had expelled him, I wouldn't apologize for it."

"I think you should," Margarethe said, "if they had. But as it happened, they didn't get a chance. The Catholics beat them to it."

Joel didn't feel exactly like leading a cheer for the Counter-Reformation. Thank God for the USE's newly hatched cardinal protector—once known as Father Mazzare.

Friedrich looked at the morning edition with delight. "It's the first time I've ever been in the newspaper," he exclaimed.

"Father saw it too," Margarethe said. "He went off to file a complaint with General Brahe."

Eberhard snatched it away. "The quality of the cartoon doesn't quite measure up to a van de Passe."

"Hey, a person has to be really influential, politically, to earn a van de Passe cartoon. How many people outside of our family will really care that I have renounced my title? Or that you let me?"

"More than you would dream," Theo predicted. "Papa had Georg Wulf von Wildenstein in tow. He intends to get the landgrave of Hesse-Kassel involved on the grounds that Margarethe is one of his subjects."

"How did the newspaper find out?" Justina asked. "That's a better question."

"I like it," Reichard said. "Good publicity for the Horn of Plenty. Good example in regard to the equality of all men. The image of Margarethe as leading Brillo on a leash is particularly good, given the current events in Franconia. But who drew the cartoon?"

Every head in the taproom turned toward Hartmann Simrock.

"If it will make you feel better, you may consider their transfer to the Fulda Barracks Regiment in the SoTF forces as a disciplinary measure," Brahe said. "It is my sincere belief that the newspapers will make less furor about the title renunciation and morganatic marriage if they appear to have taken place under the aegis of the up-timers."

Colonel von Zitzewitz had not enjoyed having the young dukes of Württemberg under his command, but losing them was a considerable blow to his prestige, so on balance he was not happy.

"Mainz will be more tranquil without their presence, right now. Fulda will do very well and Utt has agreed that he will take them." Since von Zitzewitz didn't know, Brahe saw no reason to mention that he had been trying to palm this particular simmering pot of trouble off on Fulda for three months.

Zitzewitz inclined his head.

"Just think," Botvidsson added. "There is some consolation. Their friends Simrock and Pistor have patriotically volunteered for the army also, as a gesture of solidarity with Friedrich the ex-duke, since neither of them has a title to renounce. You might have had two more radical CoC sympathizers among your junior officers."

The colonel began to perceive the benefits that would compensate for his losses. He inclined his head again and backed out of the room.

Botvidsson mentioned that he needed a draft memo for communicating the information about the transfer of the young dukes to the king. To the emperor, that was. They were, after all, dukes. Or, in one case, had been a duke just yesterday.

"Bury it," Brahe said. "Bury it somewhere between a list of statistics on how many improved latrines we have constructed and a report on how many of the draft horses have gone down with colic. In front of the latrine statistics, put a memo on the training of city gate guards. Behind the horse colic, attach a discussion of how we are handling the directive that we are to get rid of the train of camp followers when the army is moving. Do not include anything about the renunciation of titles, and I see no real reason to pester the king with Pistor's complaints about the marriage. The chaplain is a Calvinist, after all, and so is his daughter, so what concern is her marriage to Gustavus Adolphus?"

"I understand."

"Make sure the communications center is aware that this information in these reports is *not* urgent and that far from having a courier ride hard, much less utilizing the radio or any other innovative modern technology, definitely not going to the expense of railways or planes, this is the type of material that best travels by way of what Major Utt calls 'a slow boat to China.'"

Barracktown bei Fulda

On the theory that he did not customarily bring every new recruit to Wes Jenkins's attention, Derek Utt determined that the transfers were a strictly regimental matter. He buried the names of his four new recruits—well, nine new recruits, counting Corporal Hertling and the four goons, er, bodyguards, er, experienced soldiers—in a list of quite a number of other new recruits, which he sent off attached to a non-urgent report to Scott Blackwell in Würzburg, from which destination it might eventually make its way to someone in Grantville. The only special note he made for Blackwell next to their names was "CoC."

Mainz, July 1634

"Papa won't give me permission to marry, and I can't get married in Mainz without it." Margarethe pouted while she pitted cherries.

"Not to mention that Friedrich is in Fulda. That really makes it more difficult for you to get married." Tata picked up another onion and started to dice it for the noonday stew.

"So you understand." Margarethe's tears might have been real. Equally well, they might have been the result of standing next to the onion board.

"Papa and Mama don't understand how much I miss Eberhard either," Tata sniffed. "It was very unsympathetic and unfeeling of Major Utt to refuse to take us along. Especially Margarethe, since she's going to get married. We hope. Doesn't he have any sympathy for romance?"

Since the question was rhetorical, no one answered it, but Kunigunde Treidelin and Ursula Widder made sympathetic noises. Both of them had succumbed to a spurt of unusual sentimentalism after Eberhard's dramatic announcement of the forthcoming marriage in the Horn of Plenty taproom.

"So it's obvious that we need to go to Fulda. Isn't it, *Tante* Kuni?"

"Maybe I *could* help." Kunigunde looked at Ursula. "I have a little money hidden away."

"In case of a rainy day," Ursula said.

"Don't be silly. There are a lot of rainy days, even in summer." Kunigunde had a literal mind. "In case the armies come again and we have to flee."

"Do you have a wedding dress?" Ursula asked.

Margarethe shook her head. "I don't have any money of my own, ever. Papa used to give Theo money and he would share it with me, but since Papa's been so annoyed with Theo recently, he won't give him anything. He even refused to pay for his tuition at the university for another term. He was going to send him to some awful Calvinist *Hochshule*. That's really the main reason he volunteered for the army. He was broke."

"Somehow I didn't think it was patriotism," Ursula said.

"Who would?" Tata picked up another onion. "Simrock volunteered because his uncle at the newspaper, who's also his guardian, told him it would be better for him to get out of Mainz, since somebody investigating the riot at Sybilla's funeral has figured out that he planted the article."

"I was going to be married once," Ursula said. "We lived in the Palatinate, then. We had waited so long, because my fiancé had to support his mother. Then the elector agreed to become king of Bohemia and my fiancé went to Prague as a wagoner in their glorious procession. He didn't come back and didn't come back. He died there, at the first Battle of White Mountain. I was going to be married in a red dress."

Tata dropped her onion and hugged Ursula. It might have been the onion juice on her hands that made the older woman's eyes water. Ursula hugged her back and turned to Margarethe. "I'll buy you a brand new dress to be married in. It will be cherry red and you will look quite lovely."

The dress cost more than they expected, which is the way of gorgeous dresses, even though Kunigunde got a good bargain on the fabric and Ursula knew a seamstress who didn't overcharge and so far had avoided the notice of the tailors' guild.

"We don't have enough money left," Kunigunde complained. "Not enough for a safe trip. We need to be able to trust the driver you ride with and make sure that there are some respectable families traveling in the same group. Trustworthy carters don't come cheap."

They dug into the monthly kitchen budget for the inn. The patrons of the Horn of Plenty were going to get rather meager fare for the rest of July.

The girls looked more than pleased with themselves when a freight wagon deposited them and their possessions in front of the Fulda Barracks a week later.

Barracktown bei Fulda, July, 1634

"Ah." Dagmar Nilsdotter was in tears as she held her husband's hand. "What a beautiful wedding, Helmuth. What a lovely bride. My heart is strangely moved. Strangely warmed."

Sergeant Hartke was not quite so volubly impressed, but he did admit that both Lieutenant Friedrich Württemberger and Margarethe Pistora appeared to be rather delighted with both themselves and the situation. They had just taken advantage of the SoTF's liberal citizenship policy, unusually low age of majority, and practice of "universal sectarianism" by getting married in the Barracktown sutlery in a ceremony presided over by the mayor of Barracktown, otherwise known as Sergeant Helmuth Hartke, who for this purpose was a duly licensed civilian celebrant.

"Not bad, as ceremonies go," Simrock said. "And Venus herself ministers resolution and hardiness unto tender youth as yet subject to the discipline of the rod, and teaches the ruthless soldier the soft and tenderly effeminate heart of women . . ."

"Montaigne again, I presume?" Jeffie Garand leaned back against the wall, looking toward the entrance. On one side of the door, Merckel and Kolb, on the other side Heisel and Bauer, were watching the room attentively while trying their best to look like casual wedding guests.

Simrock nodded.

"You're quoting out of context," Theo warned. "He ended that sentence with 'in their mothers laps.' He wasn't talking about weddings."

Dagmar turned to Duke Eberhard. "Your brother looks so handsome in his uniform, Captain Your Grace."

He smiled. "I was just thinking that Friedrich actually looks rather like a large salmon fillet in that orange-ish uniform, not to mention that he clashes badly with Margarethe's cherry red dress, but I'm not in any position to complain, since I'm was wearing an orange-ish uniform myself. But he does look handsome, even if he is still on crutches."

"Is the foot very bad?" someone behind them asked.

"Once General Brahe's people caught up to us at Weselberg, the medic prevented gangrene." Hertling snagged a piece of thin, folded and rolled dough filled with some sweet fruit off a passing tray. "The foot itself—he will always have to wear a very tight, heavy boot to protect it. The bones are not right. General Brahe's regiment had a medic, not an up-time miracle-making surgeon. When he is an old man, he will be predicting the weather on the basis of how much his foot aches."

"This food is great." Jeffie looked around. "Who cooked it? Who arranged all this?"

Simrock patted a nearby reddish head. "Tata arranged it. She's been helping with wedding receptions since she was a toddler, whenever her family wasn't on the run and had an inn to settle down in. She just snapped her fingers and it happened."

"It was a bit more complicated than that. You're right though. Riffa's mother is a terrific cook."

"Once upon a time," Jeffie said. "Once upon a time, long ago, for my high school graduation, to be precise, Mom took me and Justin to Las Vegas."

"Where is Las Vegas? What is Las Vegas?"

"It is, was, will be a city in Nevada. I'm just thinking. I do that sometimes." Jeffie turned around and called, "Frau Hartke."

"My name is Dagmar Nilsdotter. Hartke is my husband."

"Well, then, Ms. Nilsdotter. Sorry, but that just doesn't sound very respectful to say to Gertrud's mom. How many of these do they have in Fulda, now? These civil weddings, I mean?"

"Oh, many. Two or three a week, perhaps, because people come from many miles away to have Helmuth marry them, because many villages do not have civil celebrants licensed yet. Any mayor may become one, but they have to apply and be approved. Most priests and pastors will not marry young people without the consent of their parents, even if it is legal."

"Thanks a lot." He followed Simrock's example in patting the top of Tata's head. "I really ought to talk to you and Riffa's mom sometime this week. You could make a mint if you set up a Vegas-style wedding chapel here."

Gertrud kicked his ankle.

Eberhard put his arm around Tata's waist. "Hands off, guys." He sighed. "I wish that Ulrich could have been here."

The four goons were moving to block the entrance.

Theo turned around, peering out the window. "We have more company."

"I should never have accepted Donner's offer." Marcus Pistor's voice shrilled into a register that an Italian *castrato* would have envied.

"What offer? It's not Donner who just married your daughter." Jeffie was enjoying himself.

"His offer to use the Horn of Plenty to hold services for the Calvinist civilians in Mainz." The shrill was now accompanied by tiny globules of spit. "If I had performed only my duties as a military chaplain, my son would never have been seduced by the doctrines of the Committee of Correspondence and my daughter would never have met this outrageous Swabian . . ."

He paused, at loss for a suitable epithet. "Who are *you*?"

"Sergeant Jeffrey Garand, at your service, Your Reverence. Or however a reverend is properly addressed. I'm a bit vague on churchly etiquette. You can call me Jeffie."

Pistor did not respond to this friendly overture.

Jeffie chatted on. "At home, 'Mr. Whoever-it-is' usually doesn't offend a preacher, no matter what church he's from. It wouldn't even have offended Father Mazzare, but I did know to use 'Father' when he came around."

"Mazzare," exploded from the man with Pistor.

"How may we introduce you, My Lord?" Sergeant Hartke, standing behind Jeffie, had read enough from the man's demeanor and clothing that he decided to ante the forms of address up a step, hoping that would be sufficient.

"Georg Wulf von Wildenstein, in the service of the landgrave of Hesse-Kassel."

Hartke bowed. "Presumably, you wish to meet with . . ." He raised his eyebrows.

"I demand to meet with Major Utt," Pistor shrieked.

"No, Jenkins," von Wildenstein contradicted him. "Jenkins is the administrator. We must meet with Jenkins."

"Either or both of them should know better than to permit the marriage of a minor daughter without the permission of her father to a suitor not of her faith who is an . . ." Pistor still couldn't produce the suitable epithet.

"Ex-duke," Jeffie said. "If Lieutenant Württemberger hadn't given up his title, he would outrank you both. His brother still does outrank you both. Maybe he even outranks a landgrave. I'm not sure of that, but I think so. Eberhard was best man, so someone's in charge here. Anyway, Margarethe was eighteen last month, so she's of age under SoTF law."

Stift Fulda, August 1634

"That went pretty smoothly," Geraldin said. "One abbot, all neatly trussed up and loaded on a small hay cart. It's pretty fair hay, too. The horses should appreciate it."

"What about the other one?" MacDonald asked.

"Leave him down there. Get back to where you were supposed to meet the others. I'm on my way to Bonn."

MacDonald shrugged and headed back to meet Butler and Deveroux. They'd need to fetch Gruyard away from von Schlitz's and head back to Bonn right now. Not only was every country road and cow path in Fulda suddenly crawling with people searching for them, but once Geraldin delivered Schweinsberg into the custody of Ferdinand of Bavaria, the archbishop would be wanting the services of his torturer. Right now. Not the day after tomorrow, much less next week.

Mainz, August 1634

"Theobald will not be twenty years old until December. The army of the State of Thuringia-Franconia should not have accepted his enlistment without my authorization."

"They shouldn't have, but they did." Von Wildenstein was getting tired of this.

"How can they permit a child to do something as significant as change his citizenship? Children are young. Children stand in need of parental guidance. Children . . ."

". . . become adults at the age of eighteen in the SoTF. Unless you can persuade the USE parliament to pass a law overriding that, or persuade the *Reichsgericht* in Wetzlar to rule that people cannot change their citizenship from one state in the USE to another . . ."

Von Wildenstein's voice trailed off. His face brightened. "But these decisions about citizenship and the age of majority were placed by the up-timers in their constitution before the establishment of the USE— before November 1633. Since then, they are no longer an independent principality within a federation, but merely one of the provinces of the USE, even if they choose to call themselves a 'state' instead. I have been informed that in the up-time, some of the 'states' of the United States of America actually chose to call themselves 'commonwealths.' I don't know why, but essentially it made no difference. Their relation to the national government was the same. Thus, can the SoTF even offer its own citizenship any more?"

"Brilliant, absolutely brilliant." Pistor jumped up. "Most of the time, I am simply exhausted by trying to keep up with how quickly everything is changing in our world. This time, though, perhaps the changes will prove to be beneficial. I shall consult a lawyer right away and file a petition in Wetzlar. If you can persuade the landgrave of Hesse to take an interest, perhaps the imperial supreme court will expedite the consideration of my case."

"Perhaps it will." Von Wildenstein stood up. "In practice, however, that will mean that the justices will issue a decision twenty-five years from now rather than fifty years from now. For the time being, I am afraid, I cannot perceive any immediate way to reverse your children's . . . unfortunate actions." He turned around. "Let me make a purely practical comment. It is absolutely certain that you will not be able to retrieve your daughter Margarethe's virginity by means of a legal remedy."

"No one among the Catholic theologians, Lutheran theologians, Calvinist theologians, or sectarians, much less the small number of secularists who are becoming more vocal with every passing day, seems to be very enthusiastic about Wamboldt von Umstadt's initiatives. Few of them appear to be favorably impressed by Calixtus's ideas, either, not even when Wamboldt von Umstadt endorses them."

Nils Brahe yawned. "Botvidsson, there are moments when you display a positive genius for understatement." He rubbed his eyes. "Perhaps I should see about getting spectacles. Francisco Nasi told me that his have proved very helpful. Do you have the list I asked for?"

"The one delineating possible complications if we permit the archbishop of Mainz to return?"

"No, Johan, the one about the levels of likelihood that the cow may someday jump over the moon. Yes, please, that one."

Botvidsson shuffled some papers. "One item that I have not included here is that the new *Residentz* he began constructing in 1628 is a messy site full of holes and mud. It is an attractive nuisance to children, who endanger themselves by playing in it. It is an attractive nuisance to apprentices, who go there after dark and engage in entertainments of which their masters disapprove. It . . ."

". . . needs to be either flattened and turned into a public park, or completed. In the event that it is completed, the archbishop will no longer have any need of such a large combination of living quarters for himself and his staff and administrative offices, since the Province of the Main has assumed many of those duties—defense, the court system, real estate record administration for all property other than that directly owned by the archdiocese. Do you suppose Wamboldt von Umstadt would be open to considering an arrangement by which we take over the derelict site and construct our own badly-needed government center there, while assigning him . . ." Brahe frowned. ". . . something else. Think about what 'something else' might possibly be, would you, Johan. That's a nice central location."

Botvidsson made a note. "Now, as to the list. First, there's the problem concerning the Jewish community in Worms. I can provide you with details of that."

"Please do. In a separate memo. Can you make it short?"

"Unfortunately, no. It's complicated."

"Life is complicated. Next point."

"All of the imperial cities that haven't been acknowledged as independent city-states by the USE, not just Nürnberg, are worried about their status after what happened at the Congress of Copenhagen. It's entirely possible that a coalition of the smaller imperial cities may make common cause with dispossessed ecclesiastical princes to lobby for some arrangement similar to the one that the imperial knights and independent monasteries had in the defunct *Reichstag*, by which they did not hold individual seats, but elected one of their number to represent them and cast a vote on their behalf. Nürnberg is large enough, of course, that if it joined the USE, it would almost certainly be acknowledged as a city-province like Augsburg and Ulm, but . . ."

"Noted," Brahe said. "Prepare me a separate memo on that, will you. Let's get to the rest of the points. I've been at this desk for . . ." He peered outside into the gathering twilight. "The days are getting shorter, but it's safe to say that I've put in a fourteen-hour day so far."

Botvidsson moved on to the next sheet of paper. "To return to the topic we were discussing earlier. To borrow a colorful phrase from Major Utt, it appears that Cardinal-Protector Mazzare has 'told him to get on the stick and do something ecumenical real soon now.' It appears, in fact, that Mazzare has talked to Prime Minister Stearns. If the archbishop wants an imperial *salva guardia* for his return to Mainz, he first has to agree to work, not only with Calixtus, but to send a representative—possibly several representatives—as 'observers,' at the next Lutheran theological colloquy."

"*Next* Lutheran theological colloquy? They were at it from January through May. Count Ludwig Guenther of Schwarzburg-Rudolstadt reported the results at the Congress of Copenhagen."

Botvidsson looked at his superior with some pity. "But, sir. Everybody pretty much believes that the king—the emperor—will move against Saxony and Brandenburg in the spring. Then it will all have to be done over again, factoring in the practical problem that the electoral family of Brandenburg is Calvinist and the heir is the nephew of Gustav's queen. The next Lutheran colloquy must face reality. Under the USE constitution, although it grants Lutheranism 'state church' status, it does so in such a way that the emperor must either formally abolish the 1555 Peace of Augsburg or somehow integrate the Calvinists and sects into it."

Brahe nodded. "Either way, Lutheranism will lose the privileged position it has held under it, ending up with—as our friend Major Utt might say, 'all of the flash and none of the cash.'"

"Correct," Botvidsson admitted. He smiled. "But, then, so will the Catholics, which is one reason, I'm sure, that Mazzare wants archiepiscopal representatives there to watch the Lutherans while it happens."

Barracktown bei Fulda, September 1634

By September, the Barracktown CoC meetings had moved from the Hartke cabin to the main room of the sutlery. This was partly because they had quite a few more members than they had two months earlier. This was partly because Gertrud did, after all, have several younger half-siblings. Dagmar thought they had a right to do their lessons and play their games in peace. It was partly because the meetings sometimes became rather raucous. Mostly, however, it was because Riffa's mother was such a good cook.

"What I think," Tata began.

"What *she* thinks," Jeffie echoed.

"What *they* think," Joel Matowski said, pointing at Friedrich, Tata, and Margarethe.

"Is pretty much what the Committees of Correspondence think, at least as far as the Fulda Barracks Regiment is concerned." Eberhard laughed.

"Well, it is," Tata said. "We're the organizers here, just like my father is in Mainz. We keep our ears to the ground, our eyes on the prize, our fingers busy corresponding with the leaders of the Ram Rebellion in Franconia, our posters of Brillo and Ewegenia posted, and any other description you can think of to indicate that we are true sons and daughters of Gretchen Richter."

"Have you ever seen Henry Dreeson's house?" Joel shook his head. "No, don't answer that literally. I know that you haven't. It was a rhetorical question, Tata. You have an unfortunately literal mind. Gretchen doesn't need any more sons and daughters. She has a quiver full already, to borrow biblical language."

"Ideological sons and daughters," Tata answered with dignity. "Disciples. Followers."

"Pains in the . . ."

Margarethe slapped Jeffie's ear. "Watch your language. You are in the presence of a respectable married lady."

"I am? Where is she? Ow! Gertrúd, she'd already swatted me. You didn't have to slap me, too."

"What I *started* to say was—"

"What she *started* to say was . . ."

"Jeffrey Garand, if you don't stop that, I swear that I will hang you."

"I apologize, teacher. I swear. Only pardon me this time and I promise to be good forevermore."

"It's not really a good idea to make promises that you can't keep," Eberhard commented.

"I might be good forevermore. Who knows?"

"Try, 'until Tuesday at noon.' It has a higher level of probability."

The door swung open.

"Hey," Jeffie said, "it's the mailman."

"With news, I'm sorry to say."

"Why?"

"It's just in from Mainz, by way of Frankfurt. Hoheneck, the *Probst* at the St. Petersburg estate of Fulda Abbey, arrived in Mainz. He says that Archbishop Ferdinand of Cologne had Schweinsberg tortured to death by a man named Gruyard. We took a casualty. There won't be another rescue. No legends like in your 'westerns.' The cavalry won't be riding out to bring him home."

For several minutes, the meeting lost whatever semblance of order it had ever possessed.

"Tata," Friedrich said. "What were you going to say before David came in?"

"We need a publicity campaign. We need to make everyone aware of the contribution of the common man—and woman, of course—and ordinary citizens of Buchenland to the rescue of the kidnapped administrators." She threw a kiss to Joel.

"We need newspaper articles." She pointed to

Theo. "We need cartoons." She pointed at Simrock. "Actually, we need better cartoons than you draw, but beggars can't be choosers and you do have a knack for making the faces easy to recognize."

"But everyone knows that the Fulda Barracks Regiment marched out bravely, singing its anthem, and rescued Wes and Clara. That's already been in all the papers."

"Anthem, schmanthem," Riffa zur Sichel said. "They spend a lot more time singing naughty lyrics set to the theme song from the 'Bridge over the River Kwai' in every language any man in the barracks has ever heard of than they do to singing their anthem."

"It's all very well to give credit to the regiment, and they did go marching out, but so did a lot of civilians. We need a campaign to give credit to the housewives, to the farm boys, to the . . ."

Eberhard laughed. "Although it may be covetousness that settles in the mind of a shop apprentice, brought up in idleness and ease, and gives him so much assurance that he does not hesitate to leave his home-bred life, forego his place of education," he paused and waved to Theo and Simrock, "and enter into a small boat, yielding himself to the mercy of the blustering waves, merciless winds, and wrathful Neptune, yet it is also true that ambition teaches discretion and wisdom."

"Montaigne again, I assume?" Jeffie said.

"Yes."

David Kronberg, Riffa's husband, otherwise known as the mailman although he was actually a post office clerk, shook his head. "What Eberhard was hinting, Tata, is that even though we're willing to admit that a lot of the searchers volunteered just because they wanted to help, still—there *was* a reward out. Your publicity campaign is going to have to work around that."

She glared at them both. "We'll manage."

Frankfurt am Main, October 1634

Derek Utt sat on his horse, watching, as Veronica—Gretchen's grandma, Henry Dreeson's wife, and terror of the known universe—disembarked onto the pier and greeted Henry, who was halfway through his goodwill tour of Buchenland County, SoTF, in preparation for the upcoming elections. While the crowd watched Veronica and Henry, he switched his eyes to the man dressed all in black in the back of the boat.

A couple of other passengers got off. Veronica, bless her miserly soul, had bought the cheapest possible ticket on a regular passenger barge—not, of course, that the barge captain didn't know who she was. He had made every effort to provide her with a comfortable trip up the Main.

According to one report, Duke Bernhard's man, Raudegen, who had accompanied the old terror on the Rhine portion of her journey back from Bavaria, had threatened, in the hearing of everyone on the Mainz pier, to break the fingers of all the barge's crewmen if they did one single thing that would cause him to receive one more complaint from Veronica Schusterin *verw.* Richter and *verh.* Dreeson.

The man in black slid out of the group, heading directly toward Utt, holding out a sheaf of paper. Credentials and more credentials, including a *salva guardia* from Nils Brahe in Mainz and another one from Wamboldt von Umstadt.

His credentials were much more impressive than his appearance. Personally signed safe conducts from Brahe and the archbishop of Mainz equaled "another VIP on hand."

Utt, who had to stay with Dreeson for the entire time he was scheduled to be in Frankfurt and then return to Fulda with Grantville's mayor safely in his charge, passed Johann Adolf von Hoheneck on to a junior officer with orders to take him up to Fulda with an escort. For the time being, Wes Jenkins could worry about him.

Barracktown bei Fulda, October 1634

"Every cartoonist in the country must be about to fall dead with exhaustion this month." David Kronberg threw a stack of newspapers on the sutlery sales counter. "Look at this. Dreeson and Veronica leading the march against the taverns in Frankfurt where the anti-Semitic agitators were congregating. Here's another one showing the treaty between Gustavus and the king in the Netherlands."

Simrock grabbed it. "Hey, this is a van de Passe. Here are Fernando and Maria Anna, Mike and Rebecca, Frederik Hendrik."

Margarethe giggled. "And here, on the next page, are all the prominent fat nobles, wealthy fat merchants, and their wealthy fat wives in the Spanish Netherlands, fighting over invitations to Maria Anna's wedding."

Jeffie took a look. "He's lightening up on all those dark lines he used to have in the background. Opening up his spaces." He handed the folded newspaper across to Pierre Biehr, the Barracktown schoolteacher, who shared it with Theo Pistor.

"There was an article in the Jena university paper a while back," Theo said, "The student paper that publishes technical stuff. Someone in Grantville took a camera and photographed a bunch of 'plates' she found in art books and encyclopedias. Some were English, by a man named Hogarth. Some were French. The article mentioned a man named Daumier. She—the photographer in Grantville was a woman—sent a package of them to van de Passe in Utrecht."

Simrock nodded. "Even though he's about seventy, now, he's not afraid of changing his style some. The lines here are different from what he was doing last spring. Let me run back to the barracks and get my cartoon folder." He dashed out.

"Tonight's CoC meeting is hereby cancelled," Tata announced. "I can tell already that everyone's going to be reading the papers instead of paying attention."

Fulda, October 1634

Johann Adolf von Hoheneck talked. Then he talked some more.

Wes Jenkins kept taking his glasses off and polishing them. Andrea Hill kept pushing her pencil into her hair, pulling it back out, and sticking it in somewhere else. Harlan Stull looked at the table as if his life depended on finding some kind of a bad spot in the beeswax polish. Roy Copenhaver looked at the ceiling. Fred Pence chewed thoughtfully on his thumbnail.

About an hour into Hoheneck's presentation, Derek Utt got up, walked over to the window, and leaned against the sill.

"So," Hoheneck concluded, "I told the priest who had been in the torture chamber, the one observing Gruyard at his work, to mark Schweinsberg's grave. I left for Mainz the same evening." He bowed.

Wes thanked him solemnly.

He withdrew.

"Whew," Andrea said. "I think that falls into the general category of 'getting all the gory details.'"

"The monks here at the abbey—the ones who stayed when the Swedes came in—aren't happy that the ones who ran away to Bonn have elected Hoheneck as the new abbot. Some of them are planning to appeal to . . ." Wes stopped. "Who do Benedictines appeal to? Do they have anything like the Jesuits' 'Father-General' who's been in the news lately?"

Harlan shrugged. "We can ask. I can't say the question had occurred to me. We've just been dealing with this one bunch of Benedictines here. None of them ever mentioned a higher-up to me."

"They've got something like regions—I think. But they don't have one guy at the top who can tell the individual abbeys what to do until you get up to the pope."

Henry Dreeson, on his way back to Grantville, was sitting in on the meeting. "That's their business. Might be interesting for us to know the answer, but it's their problem—internal. This guy is our problem—external. The point is, how do you plan to handle Hoheneck?"

Harlan frowned. "I can't say that I like it that he stuck with the brother of Evil Duke Max for so long.

Which side is he really on? In my opinion, he's being very cagy about where he was and what he was doing while the archbishop was arranging to have Schweinsberg and the others kidnapped."

Dreeson shifted in his chair. "How does he know so much about how Schweinsberg died? If he wasn't right there, involved in it himself, then he must have managed to have a really long talk with that priest before he 'immediately' left for Mainz."

"No telling." Wes Jenkins took off his glasses and polished them. "He has offered to continue his 'insider' ties with some of the archbishop of Cologne's men, for the time being. Essentially, he's offered to act as a double agent."

"I should put him in touch with Francisco Nasi," Utt said. "Nasi's not likely to be overly trusting, and he has more contacts than we do, in a lot of different places. Louis de Geer in Essen has been feeding quite a bit of information to Nils Brahe in Mainz, but that's one other thing that I suspect Nasi knows more about than we do.

Dreeson nodded.

"Actually," Derek continued, "Hoheneck has gone farther than just the offer to continue his 'insider' ties. He's volunteered to General Brahe that he's willing to return to Archbishop Ferdinand's headquarters and gather further damning evidence against Gruyard and cohorts, since he thinks he'd better make a trip to Bonn and Cologne anyway, to talk the rest of the monks from the abbey into coming back to Fulda."

Harlan Stull tipped his chair back. "I have to say that I'm surprised."

"He made that offer to Brahe in Mainz, before

he came up here to Fulda. It's not that he thinks up-timers are wonderful. I think we—right here in this room—are the first contact he's had with anyone who came back in the Ring of Fire. But he feels a most un-Christian need to obtain retribution for Schweinsberg's death, and it looks right now like Swedes and the USE and SoTF authorities are his only options."

"I radioed Magdeburg last night," Wes said. "I'd like to see the kidnappers get theirs. I'm grateful that Hoheneck has pinned names on the marauding Irishmen and told us something about this Gruyard fellow. In the long run, though, I agree with Brahe that the material that Hoheneck brought from Archbishop Anselm Casimir is more important for a peaceful long-run settlement among all the parties that have interests along the Rhine than doing something about Schweinsberg right now is. Since Fulda borders on the Province of the Main and that's on the Rhine, peace in the region is not something we can ignore. I'm going to send the man back to Mainz, no matter how many suspicions I may have at the back of my mind."

Roy Copenhaver said, "The newspaper editorials aren't happy that we haven't managed to catch the Irishmen. The radio commentators aren't either. Jen sent me transcripts of some of the VOA broadcasts."

Wes shook his head. "The general theme coming down from the central office, as far as Schweinsberg is concerned, is, 'we can't get them now, but just give us time and we'll get them eventually.'" He stood up. "I'm adjourning this meeting. There's a party tonight for Henry and Veronica. Clara and I will be heading off with them tomorrow morning for Grantville. We'll all benefit from a little nap this afternoon."

✧   ✧   ✧

"Couldn't you have put this meeting off until tomorrow?" Andrea Hill yawned. "Last night was about the best party we've ever thrown."

"No. I have a proposal. As I see it, we have a window of opportunity." Derek Utt stretched his lanky frame up to its full not quite six feet and leaned his head against the window frame. The thin morning sun lit the top of his head, making it look almost as if it were on fire. When he moved away, into the shade of the room, his curly rust-colored hair reappeared. "No matter what Wes said, I can't just half-ignore the fact that they abducted the abbot of Fulda right out from under our nose and tortured him to death. And kidnapped a bunch of our own staff and held them prisoner."

Harlan Stull crossed his arms over his barrel chest. "Wes would never have approved this crazy idea."

"That's why I didn't bring it up until after Wes and Clara left. When he first arrived, I sure never thought that I'd be saying this, but in a way I agree with what Wes said in that farewell meeting. I sort of miss Schweinsberg."

"Why can't it wait until after Mel Springer gets here?" Harlan asked. "You know I have to go back myself, to brief him. He's been the man on the 'Fulda desk' in Grantville ever since Stearns reached his agreement with Gustavus Adolphus. That's not the same thing as having been here, living through it, but he's been assigned to replace Wes. Wes has to plunge right into his new job in the consular service, so he won't have time to give us any advice. Besides . . ."

"Besides, you're UMWA like Mike Stearns. Wes

wasn't UMWA and Mel isn't UMWA, which really means that you're in charge of making sure that the civilian administrator in Fulda doesn't get all too bureaucratic and cautious and CYA."

Harlan jumped.

Derek lounged against the window frame again, grinning. "That's no skin off my nose. If we get it started before Mel arrives, it will be too late for him to reverse gears. We couldn't do it by ourselves, but with Brahe's help, and his men . . ."

"Why can't we do it by ourselves? Why involve him?"

"We're just too damned conspicuous, Harlan. Look around. Most up-timers stand out like sore thumbs in a crowd of down-timers, even when they're wearing down-time clothes and shoes, have their hair cut by a down-timer barber, and speak German. I'm not sure what it is. Body build, to some extent. Posture. Attitude. But we're just not inconspicuous. We glow like light bulbs. It's the same for the Swedes. Think what it would be like if Brahe showed up in Naples, for a comparison, or if young Wrangel had gone into Bavaria instead of Cavriani's son. Talk about easily identifiable. The only way we could chase them down is in a regular military operation. Gustavus isn't going to give us enough manpower for that. He has different priorities. If someone is going to go sneaking after the guys who took Schweinsburg and hope to succeed, then it isn't going to be us. For just one thing, we don't have the intelligence contacts inside Ferdinand of Bavaria's people."

"Does anyone?"

"Hoheneck does, if he's telling us the truth about being willing to cooperate, which I think he is. Not out of idealism, but because he thinks having abbots of Fulda, 'of which he now are one,' so to speak, tortured to death is a *really bad idea*. Especially when it's guys who are supposed to be on their own side who did the torturing. It seems to have made him rethink his position rather drastically."

"So you're really suggesting that we should just hand it over to Hoheneck and Brahe?"

"Nope. It will give the Fulda Barracks Regiment—at least the ones I select out and detail to be part of the project—something constructive to do this winter, looking for where the Irishmen have gotten to by now. The others will think of the search party—I guess we can go ahead and call it a *posse comitatus*—as representing the rest of them. They're still a bit upset because we didn't let them squelch the elements of the Ram Rebellion that made their way into Fulda's jurisdiction, so letting them in on something sneaky that has a prospect of glory at the other end will be all to the good. And there's quite a bit of public opinion back home in Grantville, I think, that we should have done more than we have so far, on the general grounds that Schweinsberg, however improbably, was one of us, now. I'm sure my commanding officer would agree."

Harlan Stull frowned. "Does Frank Jackson know about this?"

Derek Utt shook his head. "I doubt it. Nobody's told me to bring him in on it. He's not in my chain of command, any more. Not in anyone's chain of command, other than his own guys in Magdeburg. He's a staff officer for Torstensson now."

"Who *is* your commanding officer, then? Who am I supposed to talk to once I get to Grantville?"

"Beyond—above—Scott Blackwell in Würzburg? Scott's my boss. Mine and Cliff Priest's boss, as far as military things are concerned. Just as Steve Salatto is the boss for civilian stuff, as far as Wes is—was—and Vince Marcantonio is concerned. Actually, I'm pretty sure that Scott answers directly to Ed Piazza now."

"Ed's the president of the SoTF. He's not in the military at all, just sort of the same relationship as the governor of any state had to its National Guard up-time." Harlan frowned.

"Lane Grooms, the MP colonel, is sort of 'acting' head of the military as far as Grantville—well, the whole Ring of Fire, West Virginia County now—is concerned, because his training cadre is there and he was the highest-ranked guy left after Frank moved to Magdeburg with his people. But I've found out, and this is crucial, Grooms's authority doesn't extend to the whole SoTF. It's just for West Virginia County defense—the Ring of Fire and the annexations since then. So if something involves domestic policy, Scott takes it to Steve Salatto and then through Steve to George Chehab. It stops with Chehab if it's purely internal SoTF, unless it's really important. Then it goes up to Ed Piazza. Chehab also takes it to Ed if it's got international implications. Scott doesn't actually run into a lot of purely military decisions. They almost all have civilian ramifications or, really, are civilian matters that need some military input."

"Well, do you expect me to tell Lane Grooms about this while I'm in Grantville? Wait a minute. Who *am* I supposed to tell, anyway? Damn it, Derek. With all the ad-hoccing that's been going on . . ."

"Technically, I'm in the SoTF forces, but we don't

exactly have our own army and foreign policy any more. We're a state, not a country. Scott knows what I'm planning. For the USE, the closest general is Brahe in Mainz. We get along. He's just turned thirty; a couple of years younger than I am. Pretty flexible. Gustav thinks that after Torstensson, he's the best general he has. Which, I'm inclined to say, the way he conducted that swoop all the way over to the Rhine last spring after Bernhard pulled back, makes me think that the emperor is right."

Harlan nodded. "Like this harebrained project you're asking me to approve."

"More like, 'look the other way.' We'll do it—get it started, at least—while you're gone briefing Springer." Derek grinned. "I don't suppose I could talk you into not telling *anybody*?"

First Harlan said, "No." Then—"*We*?"

"I'm only going as far as Mainz, with Hoheneck. I'll take Sergeant Hartke and the men he's picked out, plus a couple of our own guys, and leave them there for a few weeks. I want someone to be in the city to take charge of the culprits when the posse brings them back, if it manages to catch them, which I hope it does. I'd rather not see them assassinated in some back alley. That's revenge, not justice. I want a trial, Harlan. I want to see them sitting there in the dock, with a lot of newspaper coverage."

"What will Mary Kat say? Will the daughter of our honorable chief justice be thrilled to have her husband out scampering through the hills and valleys looking for kidnappers?"

"I'm not planning on doing any scampering myself— not unless something really unexpected comes up. I'll talk to Brahe in Mainz and then come back to Fulda and spend Christmas in Grantville. Anyway, unless you tell her, she won't find out until after it's all over. 'Need to know' and all that."

There were times when Harlan sort of wondered about the relationship between Derek and Mary Kat. The truth of the matter was that if he were going to go out and get in peril, he'd warn Eden, whether he was supposed to or not.

"If you have to tell anybody in Grantville, tell Ed Piazza. But not unless he asks."

"Can he do that?" Andrea Hill asked. "Can he just decide to do that?"

"I really don't know. It's way above my pay grade," Jeffie Garand pointed out. "It's more to the point that he's going to do it anyway, it looks like."

"Who *is* Derek's boss, anyway?" Roy Copenhaver asked. "Aside from Wes, who's gone, and Mel Springer, who hasn't arrived, that is. They're his civilian superiors in any case. Who's his military commander?"

Joel Matowski rubbed his forehead. "Well, when we came out here, we were NUS military with Frank Jackson in overall military command, Mike Stearns as president, and some loose obligation to GA as Captain Gars."

"I'm with you."

"Then in the fall of 1633, it changed. There's a SoTF now instead of a NUS, and it's a state in the USE. Since last spring, Frank's gone off to be a colonel on Torstensson's staff. He's a kind of aide-de-camp and isn't really commanding anybody, any more. The Grantville guys who are with him up in Magdeburg are sure part of the USE military, but nobody has told us that we're under Torstensson. Not directly."

"My closest guess," Jeffie Garand said, "is that the Fulda Barracks Regiment didn't get transferred into the USE army. I think we're what they're calling SoTF forces, sort of a state militia."

"But it's not that simple." Joel frowned.

Harlan Stull waved a hand. "Nothing's ever simple. There are still the Swedes in Mainz, and the Swedes around Grantville. Most people don't seem to notice that the way Kagg set up the barracks, he popped his Swedes down right between the Ring of Fire and the Saxon border. At best, these guys are sort of hybrids between being the Swedish army and the USE army—they're not straight USE, even if most of the men in the regiments are Germans. Gustavus has three or four of his best Swedish commanders protecting us, really. They're protecting his interests, sure, but they're protecting us, too. That's above and beyond Torstensson and the regiments up north, not to mention Banér in the Upper Palatinate dealing with Duke Maximilian. He has Horn down in Swabia, running all round Baden and Württemberg, keeping Duke Bernhard pinned down and also dealing with Duke Maximilian."

"I hadn't really thought of it that way," Joel admitted. "So Gustavus, all this time, has had Kagg and the Yellow Regiment right outside Grantville, really making sure that while he was tied up in the north himself, John George of Saxony didn't get any silly ideas about invading Thuringia, while he took a batch of way less experienced CoC regiments to deal with the League of Ostend. I guess nobody can say that he hasn't carried out what he promised when he agreed to the 'Captain General' bit."

Jeffie looked at Andrea. "What Harlan says is right. But the real question you're asking, I think, is, what about us—the NUS Army guys who were already in Franconia and Fulda when they made the switchover? Mike's off being prime minister. I know that the military administrators have discussed it with each other—Scott Blackwell in Würzburg and Cliff Priest in Bamberg and Derek. As best they can figure, we're not subordinate to Kagg. At least, Kagg doesn't think so, and the way Anse Hatfield handled the mess in Suhl made that pretty clear."

Joel interrupted him. "Like I said, nobody's had time to formalize anything, but we *think* we're probably equivalent to a SoTF National Guard now—thinking in up-time terms—and we answer to Ed Piazza, who's the president. He'd be the governor if we were a state up-time, so . . . He's appointed Lane Grooms to command the SoTF forces formally, but Grooms is a nearly hundred percent administrative type and none of us ever knew him very well. He's sitting in Grantville, shuffling paper. Derek figures that he and Cliff Priest answer to Scott Blackwell. Scott can worry about Grooms. Who's above Grooms? Right now, just Ed Piazza, I guess. But like Harlan said, nothing's ever simple."

"Short form, though," Jeffie said. "If Scott doesn't veto it and Brahe goes along—yeah, I think Derek can just decide to do it. Somebody may yell at him afterwards if it doesn't work, but that would happen even if they approved everything first."

Mainz, October 1634

"You can see my point," Derek Utt said to Brahe. "You know more—a lot more—about what is going on along the Rhine than Lane Grooms does back home in Grantville or even Scott Blackwell in Würzburg, not to mention that Scott and Steve Salatto are still mopping up remnants of Franconian imperial knights who opposed the Ram Rebellion and negotiating with Ableidinger and his supporters to stabilize the position of the Ram party in Franconian government. Nobody doubts that Ableidinger will be elected to the USE parliament from Franconia in the next election . . ."

Derek stopped and thought. His list of practical reasons for talking to Brahe at this much length went on for a page and a half. Really though . . . given the flair, élan, and dash that Brahe brought to grabbing what was now the USE's new Province of the Upper Rhine the previous May, it just seemed to him that Nils would be more sympathetic to the project than either Grooms or Blackwell. Partly—well, he wanted Nils to work with him on this because they had come to like each other. Brahe was the best friend he had made among the down-timers.

"I feel like I have to do something. It's not just that all of us somehow feel that we let Schweinsberg down. We do, though. He had put his eggs in our basket and we didn't manage to keep them from spilling out. One of our allies died in a torture chamber at the behest of Maximilian of Bavaria's brother. I suspect it's one of the reasons that Wes Jenkins asked for his transfer back to Grantville. He feels like he

was responsible and he didn't measure up. None of
the other up-timers in Fulda is happy about it. The
soldiers in the Fulda Barracks regiment are extremely
unhappy about it, even if they did perform well in
locating all the rest of our people that the Irishmen
picked up and getting them back home—well, back to
Fulda. Plus, it's been a PR nightmare in the papers,
not so much here on the Rhine, but home in Grantville. It seems like every blowhard in town wants to
send out a posse."

His mind came back from its musing to hear Brahe
saying that he thought it was a good idea to try to
strike at the kidnappers, but . . . "Finding—simply
locating—Butler and the other Irishmen will only
be the start of it. In the nature of things, cavalry is
mobile."

"Oh, I know. Like Grandma used to say, 'First,
catch your hare.' Before that, though, we have to
catch sight of him."

Nils Brahe kissed his wife as soon as she stepped
off the gangplank of the barge, laughed at her wrinkled
nose, and said, "Docks don't smell any better in the
Germanies than they do in Finland, or in Sweden,
for that matter."

Anna Margareta Bielke kissed him back. "I've smelled
worse. At least it's chilly here in Mainz. The awful odor
is a lot more awful in mid-summer, I'm sure." She had
arrived at the very end of the decent traveling season.
She brought the children to see him. She brought his
sister Kerstin for . . . other reasons.

That evening, after supper and in bed—the only
place they had a modicum of privacy, at least once

they drew the hangings—she shook her head. One of the purposes of the trip was to find a husband for her sister-in-law, but she was not enthusiastic about Nils's idea of trying to match Kerstin with Hand.

"Erik Haakansson is in the Oberpfalz; so he is not a convenient option for a match. He is not here to be persuaded. I do not believe that we can get him to agree to it at a distance. Just like most of his brothers, he is a very elusive bachelor."

"It's getting to the point that we have to do something." Kerstin's frustrated older brother brushed his hair back from his forehead. "She's twenty-five, and it's not as if she has any desire to make a career as a scholar in some German *Damenstift*. She really expects us to find her a suitable husband and I've simply been too busy to worry about it. So have you."

"What about the oldest of the Württemberg dukes— Eberhard. You've had a chance to observe him. She's older, of course, but not by that much—only six years. She's really in prime breeding age. Moreover, a duke is a duke. At the rate the world is being turned upside down, who's to say that he won't end up in control again in a few years. Think of that encyclopedia article you sent me about what happened to the changes that the little Corsican, Bonaparte his name was, made all over the map of Europe, and how the Congress of Vienna reversed them."

"I'm not sure that she would be of equal birth under the Württemberg house laws."

Anna Margareta sniffed. "The German *Hochadel* has this insane passion for *Ebenbürtigkeit*. There's no doubt that Gustav would really have preferred to marry your cousin than the daughter of the Brandenburg elector.

But, no, his mother, German that she is, didn't think a Brahe was of equal birth."

"As far as Gustav's mother was concerned, only the daughter of a ruling prince of some kind was equal to any other ruling prince. That's the way the Germans do it. But it wouldn't hurt to take a look at the prospect of Eberhard. Don't set your heart on it, though. We ought to be looking at other possibilities this winter. Ulfsparre is only three years younger than Kerstin; the same is true for Stenbock. They're both younger sons, of course, and shouldn't really be thinking of marriage until their careers are better established . . ."

"You are a younger son and you were only twenty-four when we married."

Brahe paused in his meditations. "And at least they're Swedish."

The posse left from Mainz. Hartke, from the Fulda Barracks Regiment, led them. Brahe based this on the theory that he both knew the up-timers and their concerns, and had been fighting across the Germanies for so long that he had a vague idea, at least, about most of the past campaigns. Not, of course, that most soldiers had a clear idea about the campaigns in which they had participated. Frequently, from one winter quarters to another, from one battle to the next, a private soldier had only the slightest idea where he was and how, if he had heard the name of the place, it might be spelled.

Hartke, being a Pomeranian, picked Hertling to go with them, because the boy had a keen ear for the Swabian dialect and, since the spring campaign, could make a fair stab at understanding German from the southern Palatinate and northern Alsace. Hertling had objected, being of the opinion that his proper place was "with his young dukes," until Eberhard and Friedrich ordered him to do what Sergeant Hartke told him. He obeyed with reasonably good cheer until Hartke also picked Bauer and Heisel. Once upon a time, they admitted, probably about the time of the Danish battle nearly ten years before (a description interpreted by the officers to signify Lutter am Bärenberg, or some clash that took place near to it in time), they had known a soldier who served under Geraldin. Additionally, of course, they looked the part of veteran mercenary soldiers looking for a new place.

Hartke's view was that Hertling's ensuing fit of the sulks only added to his plausibility in the role of a boy who had run from a company whose captain he disliked. Hertling took a radio, Eberhard and Friedrich having trained him in its use and taught him Morse code after the debacle at Weselberg the previous spring. As Eberhard had said, they didn't have much else to do while their injuries healed.

Brahe's regiments provided eight men, four of them as young as Hertling; the other four hardened veterans. Of the four youngsters, three, all of them from the Magdeburg region, Caspar Zeyler, Andreas Wincke, and Peter Schild, were trained radio operators. The fourth, Jacob Stettin, was a medic. Brahe also provided the posse with three of his precious tuna tin radio transmitters—precious because he only had a dozen or so to cover the entire Province of the Main and his temporary garrisons—still temporary, of course—at Merckweiler.

Not a single officer went with the party. Officers— the problem was that they tended to act like officers.

Officers didn't usually turn up out of the blue near anybody's encampment asking for work. They relied on networks of relatives, godparents, and friends to obtain a new position when the prior one vanished under more or less normal circumstances such as the death of the colonel or disbandment by the employer. However, Sergeant Hartke was seconded by Sergeant Lubbert Nadermann from von Manteufel's regiment. According to Captain Hohenbach, who was a friend of Erik Stenbock's, he had acquitted himself very well in the fighting outside Hagenau and had a good head on his shoulders. His other main qualification was that he came from a village named Vettelhofen, near Bonn, and knew the area, at least on the right bank of the Rhine, fairly well. He additionally claimed to have cousins named Schurtz who lived—or at least had lived before the start of the war—across the Rhine, somewhat north of Bonn, at Dollendorf.

Brahe and Utt had debated at considerable length as to whether they should make a greater effort to locate someone from the region of Cologne itself to go along. Eventually, they decided that it was not worthwhile, if only because of the possibility that such a man in one of their regiments might have been planted by Ferdinand of Bavaria. Such suspiciousness might be interpreted as a lack of faith in the general goodness of mankind.—Brahe admitted as much. It might, however, as Utt pointed out, contribute to the longevity of the other members of the posse.

Late October, almost into November, was an iffy time for anyone to start traveling. The river was still clear of ice, so to expedite matters, Brahe told them to take a boat as far as Koblenz. If things looked quiet there, they should split into two parties and take separate boats as far as Honnef and walk into Bonn divided into three different parties, of uneven numbers, but each of them having a radio. There they were to ask around in taverns and rooming houses—*inconspicuously* ask around in taverns and rooming houses—until they found someone who had an least an idea where the Irish colonels had gone. At that point, reunited by the divine, or up-time, boon of radio communications, they should follow the tracks of the four colonels. Nobody had the slightest hope of finding the tracks of Gruyard himself, but the pragmatic association was that he had been with one of them when they arrived in Bonn.

"At a minimum," Brahe said, "the plan has the advantage of simplicity."

"Well," Utt agreed, "its simple until we get to the point when they leave Bonn. After that, I can think of multiple possible ways for it to go wrong."

"It could go wrong well before Bonn," Botvidsson commented. "For example, the boat could sink between here and Koblenz. They could contract pneumonia and lose all the radios when it sank."

Brahe nodded. "Thank you, Johan. I think. Tell Sven to bring us some wine if you would be so kind. He may also ask Lady Anna Margareta and Lady Kerstin to join us for the remainder of the evening." He turned to Utt. "My wife has expressed great interest in the notion that your wife is a lawyer. She feels that legal training would be of immense assistance to women whose destiny it is to administer large estates while their husbands are away 'playing soldier.'"

Barracktown bei Fulda, November 1634

Tata didn't really think that going with the posse would have been more fun than staying comfortably in Barracktown, but she had more sense than to express this opinion to Eberhard, Friedrich, Simrock, and Theo. Even though at some level they knew why they were not appropriate to the task of the posse, in a spectacular display of the theological principal that abstract knowledge of a principle is not the same thing as believing in it as an article of faith, all four of them had their noses somewhat out of joint.

Euskirchen, Archdiocese of Cologne, November 1634

The inhabitants of Euskirchen were not particularly happy, honored, delighted, or cheered by the decision of the archbishop of Cologne to reside in their town for the winter. "Miserable" and "depressed" would have been better terms to describe the prevailing mood. On good days, perhaps, at least as far as the city council was concerned, an observer could have used "resigned."

The city council would have been more resigned if he had not brought four regiments of Irish dragoons with him. These—the officers, rather, and the more privileged of the noncoms—were quartered in the town, as were the archbishop's administrative staff, personal servants, and assorted hangers-on, along with their staff, servants, and assorted hangers-on, if any. The remaining portion of the regiments were bivouacked outside the walls.

That wasn't equivalent to being besieged, of course. Quite. Peddlers with their wares, peasants with their produce and occasional pig or sheep for sale, and travelers moved in and out through the gates.

Unfortunately, so did the dragoons. Their ideas of what was entertaining did not necessarily agree with what the fathers and shopkeepers of Euskirchen considered to be an afternoon or evening's harmless amusement.

Even more unfortunately, the archbishop was suffering from financial reverses. More plainly, Ferdinand of Bavaria was flat broke. He was not able to pay his mercenaries (or his staff or his personal servants, but they tended to be less of a problem for the city watch).

Since he was not paying the dragoons, a distressing number of peasants with produce and livestock for sale never made it as far as the city gates. The items they were transporting were, as the current terminology went, "conscripted" before they got that far. Conscripted meant that the dragoons confiscated them—without pay, other than promissory notes. The dragoons interpreted the entire situation as equivalent to a license to forage without exerting themselves to go anywhere. They waited for the villagers to come to them.

The arrangement was satisfactory only from their perspective.

Occasionally, of course, the officers ventured out and made their men let food vendors into the town. This happened most frequently when the household cooks and landlords who provided food for the officers quartered upon them were running short of provisions. Otherwise? At other times? Well, after all, the men had to eat.

The unfortunate city councilman who dared to protest that the civilian population of Euskirchen also needed to eat was handled appropriately. They fed his tongue to the dogs.

That was a suitable punishment, of course, but not particularly visible. Public relations were always important, so they tacked his pickled ears to the front door of the city hall.

Walter Deveroux entertained himself by using the point of his dirk to drill a small hole in the arm of an expensive chair in the parlor of the house where Butler had taken rooms for the winter. "If you ask me, we need to talk to Johann Schweikhard von Sickingen. He's in town with the archbishop."

Butler looked toward the stairs leading to the upstairs rooms. "My wife"—he waved in that general direction—"ran into his wife at mass last Sunday. They had a long conversation, much to the annoyance of the priest."

Deveroux stayed on topic. "Sickingen's men—some of them at least—actually ran into a small company of Brahe's forces on his own lands, down by Nannstein. Some little village called Weselberg."

MacDonald looked up blearily. "Where's that?"

"Southern Palatinate region, generally. The Sickingen territories are intermixed with those of the Elector Palatine. What's important is that Brahe's men locked Sickingen's riflemen into a granary for several days. It was good and strong, but it had ventilation of course, being a granary, so they managed to watch what was going on."

"Wouldn't it make more sense to talk to those men rather than talk to von Sickingen?"

"Undoubtedly, if we knew where they were. Sickingen, probably, has some idea of where they are. The Swedes released them on parole."

"What's the point?" MacDonald slammed his stein down. "There are Hessians outside of Bonn, not Swedes from Mainz. If the archbishop sends us back to the Bonn region in the spring, we'll be fighting Wilhelm of Hesse-Kassel, not Nils Brahe. The king in the Netherlands is looking over our other shoulder. If the archbishop sends us west in the spring, that would put us fighting the Dutch and any Spanish troops he still has, not Nils Brahe. Why worry about Brahe now?"

Geraldin slammed down his fist, harder than Mac-Donald had slammed the stein. "Think, Dennis. Think. Brahe's men had radio. Brahe was over by Merckweiler when the fight went down. He got a medic and part of another company to that small detachment inside of two days. Sickingen's men watched them. The Swedes—well, they were Germans, but in Brahe's regiment—threw a wire over trees. I've heard that much. We need to find out what else they saw. With Gustavus's treaty with Don Fernando and the fact that Hesse-Kassel is an ally . . . Think. I get very nervous thinking about facing opponents who pretty well always know where all their units are. If you don't, you're even drunker than you look."

MacDonald looked up. "It's thinking about that kind of thing that makes me drink."

✧ ✧ ✧

"Ursula Kämmerer von Worms-Dalberg is one of the few noblewomen near my age in this godforsaken town, Walter. She is the wife of the *Freiherr* von Sickingen. I invited her for an afternoon visit. We used our host's parlor. You use it for your meetings with Deveroux and the others. Is that too much to ask, that I should have some female companionship? I sent Dislav with the invitation. I spent a little of my gold—which is my gold, I remind you, that I brought with me from Bohemia—to purchase a few refreshments."

"You spent enough on those 'few refreshments' to provide plain food for you, for me, and for your precious Dislav for the next month. Almonds. Coffee. Dates. Where in hell did you even find them?"

"Dislav has his ways. I believe he obtained them from the cook for one of the city councilmen. The household is in mourning, so will not be entertaining this winter. She was happy to get the money. The civilians here say that food is getting very expensive because so little is coming into the town through the camp."

"It's not just going to be expensive for the civilians, you little idiot. It's just going to be plain expensive. That goes for us. I may be able to skim off some of what the men procure in the camp, but by spring, there won't be much of that. There are nearly three thousand men out there, eating. That's as many people as normally live in godforsaken Euskirchen. Can't you get it through your silly head that even if the peasants sell just as much as they usually do, either everybody will end up eating half as much, or everybody will run out of food halfway through the winter."

"Surely," Anna Marie von Dohna said, "we can just buy it somewhere else."

Sergeant Helmuth Hartke perched on a bale of dried peat and shook his head. "We know where they are, sure. But we can't get hold of them. If the general and the colonel just wanted them killed, maybe we could risk it. It wouldn't be smart, if you ask me, but we could. Go into Euskirchen, hang around, use any window of opportunity that presents itself to cut a throat, garrote a neck, put a dagger into a spinal cord . . ." He sighed, thinking how many lovely chances for close-in mayhem the world offered a man in the course of a normal day.

"But." He shook his head again. "General Brahe and Major Utt want them alive. They were very specific about this. Precise. Clear. So damned fucking clear that I can't even pretend that I misunderstood their orders. They don't want them dead at all. No, that's not quite true. They want them dead, real bad. But they want to put them on trial first, with a lot of publicity. Then they want to hang them."

Sergeant Lubbert Nadermann shook his own head, just as dolefully. "Not very practical, if you ask me. I've never understood officers. Me, I say, if you want to be rid of someone, then go ahead and get rid of him."

"That's why they make policy and we don't." Hartke looked back at the rest of the posse. "Pay attention now. The real point is that if we went in and just picked them off, we could leave the bodies there. But Brahe and Utt want them alive. It's a very different thing to bring a live body, no matter how tied up and gagged, through a guarded city gate, and then out through the camp where the dragoons are. Somebody's bound to ask, 'What's that?' Now I know that there are classic ways to smuggle live bodies around. One night, I remember, years ago, some Scotsman was telling a great tale around the fire about an queen from ancient Egypt, or maybe it was an ancient gypsy queen, who was rolled up in a rug."

Heisel nodded. "I heard that story myself. She was being smuggled in, though, not out, so she had time to plan and make arrangements. In the real world, trust me, you can't ever count on finding the right size of rug handy, and when you're going after somebody, carrying a rug with you is a real encumbrance. Awkward. It takes a pretty big rug, not one you can just roll up under your arm."

The younger soldiers sat wide-eyed, soaking in these words of wisdom from their elders.

"I 'accidentally' ran into that paddy in Geraldin's regiment—the one I used to know. We had a couple of beers and congratulated each other on still being alive." Heisel did his best to pat himself on the back. "He's not done too well, though. Pegleg. He's learned to be a farrier. He's willing to take on a boy to learn the trade from him. Not village blacksmith—just horseshoeing and harness work having to do with the metal bits. That should place one of you."

Schild, one of the radio operators, stuck up his hand. "My dad's a blacksmith. Well, he was before he died. I was eleven, but I used to hang around the forge. I know what the words they use mean, at least."

Hartke nodded. "Heisel, introduce them tomorrow. But don't give the tuna tin transmitter to the blacksmith's apprentice. The paddy will be too interested in machinery. Anyone else?"

Bauer stuck up his hand. "I did good."

"How?"

"Colonel Butler's wife has this footman. He hates Butler—thinks that he's mean to his lady. The way this guy, Dislav is his name, thinks about the lady, it's like she was his daughter. If we can leave someone behind doing anything in Euskirchen, just as long as he can get to the tavern where this Dislav goes when he has time off, he'll be able to hear a lot."

Sergeant Nadermann shifted restlessly. "Nobody in the town is hiring strangers, though. Everyone's short of money, but the food is more of a problem. If they need someone, they hire a nephew or a godson or their friend's cousin's stepbrother's former student—someone from Euskirchen who'll be eating there anyway."

"The general gave us some money," Hartke said. "Is anyone game just to go into Euskirchen and hang around, paying his own way?"

"I can try giving the impression, no matter who asks me, that I'm working for some other of the archbishop's out-of-town hangers-on." Caspar Zeyler grinned. "My mother always said that she'd never known such a natural-born liar in her life."

An hour later, they had things sorted out. Hartke, as a matter of caution, did not leave the tuna tin transmitter with the natural-born liar, either. He gave it to one of his own men, a seasoned veteran from the Fulda Barracks regiment, with orders to report back to Mainz whenever either the colonels or the dragoons showed signs of moving. "You and Heisel stick together. Don't use it unless they do move, though. No point in taking risks. Somebody might see you throwing the antenna. As far as I'm concerned, no news is just no news. No point in telling General Brahe that nothing has happened."

"You know, Sarge, what's weird, here in Euskirchen, compared to Fulda and Mainz?" Heisel asked.

"What?"

"I haven't seen a single newspaper reporter the whole time we've been here. I've hardly seen a newspaper."

Hartke nodded. "The Bavarian authorities, and this archbishop fellow is about as authoritarian a Bavarian as they come, are famous for having strong opinions concerning freedom of the press. They don't think there should be any. Censorship is big business in Bavaria."

The veteran grimaced. "Nor freedom of opinion either, I guess, considering those ears on the city hall door. Of course, I've seen heads on city gates, and bodies that have been up on the gallows for a couple of years, and a man pulled in pieces by four horses tied to his arms and legs. Once, up in Pomerania, we needed some information, so we tied a man to a board, tilted it so his head was down, and pissed into his nose and mouth until he broke. Lots of interesting stuff. Just losing a couple of ears really isn't so bad." The honorable holder of the tuna tin trotted off in the direction of his winter assignment, whistling.

The rest of the posse went back to Mainz.

Mainz, November 1634

"General?"

Nils Brahe slipped off the stool on which he was perched, moved away from his slanted desk-surface, and stretched his arms above his head. "Yes, Johan."

"There are some men here. They are Jews from Worms. They are requesting that you give them permission to talk to Wamboldt von Umstadt now that he has returned to the archdiocese."

"Why do they need my permission?"

"It has to do with imperial rights and prerogatives, I believe. In fact, their main concern seems to be whether or not Gustavus Adolphus is going to assume whatever authority the Holy Roman Emperor used to wield in the imperial cities, in regard to protection of the Jewish population. They are also submitting a petition for tax remissions, both because of the pestilence in 1632 and because of the heavy exactions to which their community has been subjected since the—ah—the problems in 1615."

"Problems?" Brahe pushed his hair back from his forehead and raised his eyebrows.

"Ah, yes. Problems. You became familiar with the history of the Fettmilch revolt in Frankfurt and the current anti-Jewish agitation there during the Dreeson tour this fall?"

"Yes."

"Similar, very similar. In Worms, there was forced emigration because of a guild-led revolution against the city council, demolition of the synagogue, laying waste to the cemetery, destruction of the tombstones. Just the usual things. The Elector Palatine—Frederick, the Winter King—put down the uprising and the emperor ordered that the Jews be readmitted and their imperial privileges reinstated. Now they wish to know if Gustavus plans to continue the imperial order now that the city is in the USE. If not, they would like to talk to the archbishop, in hopes that he will discuss the matter, firmly, with the bishop. They believe that his influence in the matter would be helpful. There has been a certain resurgence of anti-Semitic unrest in the wake of all the changes. The leaders of the artisans' guilds seem to think that they can take advantage . . ."

"Who are these men?"

"One of them is named Salomon zur Trommel. The other, David Ballin, is traveling with him, but does not appear to be particularly happy about it. They are accompanied by another Jew, one from Frankfurt-am-Main, called Meier zum Schwan, who appears to have some connection to the up-timers in Fulda. They are here on behalf of two Worms Jews, a scholar named Eliyahu Baal Shem and prosperous merchant called Abraham Aberle Landau, who did not—or, perhaps, if I understood their accents—could not travel for this purpose. Ballin is some relation to Landau's wife."

"Tell them that, in case they haven't noticed, the USE constitution establishes freedom of religion. Then send them off to the archbishop with my full permission. They can tell him about all of their problems at length."

"Maybe having the archbishop back won't be all bad. All that practice in hearing confessions, you know. His extended-problem-listening skills should be pretty good."

He yawned.

"Come to think of it, Johan. If anything else comes along that you think I can safely palm off on the archbishop, let me know. 'The devil finds work for idle hands,' and all that. It will help keep him out of mischief."

Brahe returned to the pile of paperwork on his pedestal desk.

Fulda, December 1634

Melvin Springer had brought up-time office furniture to Fulda with him. He had brought a wagon-load of it. His office in what had once been the abbot's administration building now had a vinyl-covered swivel chair, a somewhat larger than standard size oblong desk with a very shiny varnished finish, a matched set of four chartreuse-green molded vinyl chairs for visitors, two steel filing cabinets, and a large framed portrait of Ronald Reagan on the wall.

He folded his hands across his chest. "If I had known about the 'posse' project in advance, Utt, I never would have sanctioned it."

Derek nodded solemnly. In the week since Melvin Springer's arrival in Fulda, he had heard this sort of thing a lot.

At the moment, he was standing near one of the windows of the conference room of the SoTF administrative headquarters, positioned in such a way that if he nodded in one direction, his head was in the sun and his hair was carrot-colored, but if he cocked his head in the other direction, it appeared more rusty in the shade. Andrea Hill had previously protested that this maneuver had a very distracting effect on anyone who had to watch it.

Not that he would deliberately do something to distract Springer, of course. Springer would probably be okay once he got settled in, he told himself firmly. Just because Springer wasn't Wes Jenkins . . .

He refrained from saying, "At least, now we know where the Irishmen are and Brahe has planted a couple of our men and a couple of his men as horse handlers in their camp. To me, that counts as 'ahead of the game.'" He pushed his attention back to Mel Springer.

"Prudence as a watchword . . . caution . . . all due deliberation . . . approval by the proper authorities . . . moderation . . . a temperate approach in the face of uncertainties . . ." Springer's lecture marched on.

"Is Hoheneck back from Mainz, yet?" Harlan Stull asked. "Or did we miscalculate when we let him leave?" The veterans of NUS/SoTF service in Fulda had fled to Andrea Hill's chaotic domain since Mel Springer's arrival. He was perched on one of the high three-legged stools that her clerks used when they were searching through land records.

"He's not back that I know of." Roy Copenhaver shook his head. "He hasn't run off to the Bavarians, though. The last I heard, Brahe had parked him with Wamboldt von Umstadt for temporary safekeeping."

"There's some good news." Andrea pulled a pencil out of her hair. "Neuhoff, another of the provosts for the abbey, showed up yesterday, with several wagons. He brought back the monks' archives—they took them along when they ran away, back when Gustavus came through here the first time. That makes me suspect that Hoheneck intends to settle in. Neuhoff also brought back whatever they haven't used up that was in the treasury that they took along when they absconded in 1631, but I hear there's not much left."

"When it comes to funding, something's better than nothing." Harlan slid off the stool. "That does make it seem more like Hoheneck isn't intending to scarper.

Back to the old salt mines, I guess. Mel Springer has been talking to Derek. Now he wants another briefing from me."

"This makes how many?" Roy asked.

Harlan just rolled his eyes.

"There's a man out in the cathedral place with an easel set up." Simrock was talking way, way too fast.

Joel Matowski yawned. "He must like brisk weather. Other than that, there's almost always some artist wandering around town making sketches."

"But this one is sketching almost exactly like van de Passe engraves, and he's not doing it slowly and carefully, as if he were trying to imitate van de Passe's style. He does it quickly, offhand, as if the style is natural to him." Simrock bounced up and down on his toes.

"Well, go back and try to make friends. Chat a little. Find out if he'll open up."

"He's not likely to chat very freely with a guy wearing an orange uniform. Artists, especially if they're political cartoonists, tend to have a sort of antsy feeling about soldiers."

"You may have a point there. I'll go farther than that. You probably have a point there. Where are the girls?"

"They went into the stationery shop with Eberhard and Friedrich."

"You go in, tell Eberhard and Friedrich to stay right where they are, you stay with them, and ask the girls to come out on their own and go look over the guy's shoulder at what he's drawing. It's not as if Tata and Margarethe are ever at a loss for words."

It took the girls about fifteen minutes to make friends.

Friendship led to an invitation. The artist said he would be delighted to attend a Committee of Correspondence meeting held in a "wedding chapel" attached to the Fulda Barracks Regiment sutlery. In fact, he expressed the opinion that he had never imagined the existence of such an arrangement. He asked if the owners would be willing to let him sketch it. Tata said that she couldn't speak for Riffa's parents, but imagined that they certainly would be agreeable.

A half hour after first contact, peace had broken out all over.

"Van de Passe, yes. Your guess was correct. I am flattered, very flattered, to know that you recognize my family's style. That is my name. Willem van de Passe. I have been working in England since 1621, but this autumn I decided that it might be prudent to leave. My father has lived a charmed life—a checkered life, but a charmed one, taking into consideration that he is alive and well at the age of seventy. Those who despise him also, for some reason, merely expel him rather than arrest him or execute him. This has led to numerous sudden decisions to move all his belongings, but his life has not really been a dangerous one. The king of England, by contrast, has been arresting almost anyone who comes to his notice recently. I stopped in Utrecht to see my father and am on my way to Grantville to see my sister Magdalena."

"Why did you come by way of Fulda?"

"It's pretty much on my path. I came up the Rhine to Mainz, did some sketching there and picked up some ideas, and ran into Paul Moreau, who had been working up here in Fulda for a while."

"Will you be staying in Grantville?"

"I don't know. My brothers Crispijn the younger and Simon have been in Denmark for several years. They both say that Copenhagen is a good place to work, so I won't make my mind up until after I've talked with Magdalena."

"Did you see the cartoon that Hartmann made of Friedrich and me while you were there? The Mainz newspaper published it. Of course, the publisher is his uncle, but it's still exciting that he got something in the paper."

"It's really nice of you to let me look at your portfolio," Simrock said. "A lot of these are great. Is this all?"

"There's only this one folder more. When I left Utrecht, I headed down to the southeast, following some rumors. The rumors were right. Ferdinand of Bavaria is headquartered in Euskirchen for the winter. I didn't dare sketch in public, so these drawings are from memory."

Tata and Eberhard poked their heads over Simrock's shoulder.

"Sit down," Margarethe said. "I'll bring them all around and show you where you are sitting. One at a time. The least we can do is behave in a decent and orderly manner when the man is kind enough to show us his drawings."

"Yes, my dear would-be schoolmistress," her brother said.

"I would have been, if I hadn't met Friedrich."

"I know. I've heard it often enough." Friedrich grinned. "It's probably proof that there's no point in making plans for you Calvinists. Predestination will get to you every time."

"Friedrich." Theo frowned. "Don't be so irreverent." He picked up one of van de Passe's drawings and frowned again. "Who's this?"

"Didn't I label it?" Van de Passe took it back. "Ah. The Countess von Dohna—Colonel Walter Butler's wife—in full spate of a temper tantrum in the Euskirchen marketplace. She had just come from early weekday mass. Some girl selling cabbages from a wheelbarrow crossed her path and impeded her progress." He scribbled something in a corner. "Just to make sure I don't forget, as time goes by. Maybe I'll be able to use her."

"Butler?" Simrock asked. "Walter Butler? The Irish colonel? The one who kidnapped the abbot and Wes and the others in August?"

"In August," van de Passe said, "I was on the water, being very seasick during an interminable crossing on a boat that would have been over-ambitious if it called itself a decrepit tub. There was no hope of getting out on a short crossing, like Dover-Calais. King Charles's guards have too strict a watch up. I ended up having to do Bristol-Dublin on the tub and then book a separate passage to Amsterdam. Current events were my very lowest priority."

"You have the wife," Eberhard said thoughtfully. "Do you have Colonel Butler?"

"Oh, sure. All of them." Van de Passe shuffled around in his leather case. "Small scale—I couldn't very well try walking out of Euskirchen carrying an easel." He tossed a page on the table. "Deveroux." Another page, "Dislav, the countess's footman."

"We really ought to take these to the major, for him to look at, if you're willing," Friedrich said. "Maybe we should get them into the papers. That way, people all over the country can be on the lookout for the kidnappers, not just the posse. It's already back, anyway, so I guess they didn't find any of them."

Another page, "Just a hard case I spotted out on the edge of the dragoon camp."

"Good Lord!" Jeffie Garand screeched. "That's my future father-in-law."

"Did I get the wrong impression of him?"

"Hell, no. I guess the posse found something, after all."

"I'm not sure that I'm authorized to approve expenditure for such a purpose." Mel Springer pursed his mouth. "It's not a budget category. I'm willing to include a memorandum to George Chehab in the next despatch bag going to Grantville, but unless he's willing to approve a variation—"

"These guys killed Schweinsberg," Harlan Stull exploded. "Well, not them directly, but they kidnapped him and handed him over to the actual murderers. The guy who drew them is an engraver. There's equipment here in town—not what he's used to, but basic, at least. He's willing to stay and turn the drawings into etchings, but he has to eat while he does it. And you're not willing to pay him a piddling amount to get 'Wanted' posters printed up? That's . . . Wes would have . . ."

Andrea Hill put a hand on Harlan's elbow and tugged. On the other side, Roy Copenhaver kicked his ankle.

✧   ✧   ✧

"I'm a what?" Willem van de Passe asked.

"You're a military contractor." Derek Utt nodded solemnly. "Count yourself lucky. I've arranged for you to have your own cabin out in Barracktown and meals on wheels delivered by Riffa's mom. The printer who had the engraving equipment in his back room, but no engraver, will have it carted out tomorrow."

"What are 'meals on wheels' and who is Riffa?"

After supper in the Hartkes' cabin was still the best time and place for general shooting of the breeze when there wasn't a full-scale CoC meeting.

"Why are we going to all this trouble for a Mennonite?" Theo Pistor asked. He had perched on the end of one of the picnic-style tables with his boots on the bench.

Sergeant Hartke frowned at the boots. "Put them down."

Theo moved. "Getting the administration to pay for publishing van de Passe's sketches, and all. They're heretics. Mennonites, I mean. He's a heretic."

"We're getting the caricatures, dimbulb. If he uses the equipment to engrave his other drawings after hours, as long as he pays for his own disposables, it's no skin off our noses." Jeffie leaned back. "Besides, I want a copy of the one of Hartke here to give to Gertrud's mother for Christmas. Three Kings. Whatever. Whenever. For the holidays."

"Where is Dagmar?"

"Over at the sutlery, plotting something with Mama," Riffa said.

Jeffie, his right thumb pointed at Theo, looked

at Hartmann Simrock. "For a CoC member, I don't think that Theo is making much ideological progress."

"Ah, his politics are radical enough to satisfy almost anybody." Riffa came over from the other side of the room. "It's just when it comes to religion that he's not making much progress."

"Probably the best word is 'incremental,'" Simrock added. "Pretty small increments, too."

"Stop talking about me like I wasn't in the room." Theo shook his head so hard that both of his cowlicks stood straight up.

Joel Matowski ran through the front door, a panicked expression on his face. "Guess what just came in on the radio."

"Okay, I'll guess. What?"

"We're not going to have our Major Utt any more."

Everyone else in the common room jumped up with shrieks of horror.

"Was there an accident? Is he dead?"

"Did someone kill him?"

"Oh, God, please tell me that they aren't going to transfer him. The Fulda Barracks Regiment has established such a reputation for the overall worst military etiquette in the USE that anyone they send in his place will be trying to 'shape the men up.'"

"Tsk, tsk." Joel shook his head. "Such leaping to conclusions. You should all be ashamed of yourselves."

Gertrud took a swat at him. "Damn it, what?"

He struck a dramatic pose. "They gave him a promotion. We're going to get Colonel Utt back next month."

Gertrud looked at Jeffie. "You put him up to this, Jeffrey Garand. Didn't you? You had already heard, but if you had come running in like that, none of us would have believed it, you joker, so you got him to do it."

Hartke made a gesture that threatened to take off the head of his fellow sergeant. "For this, I should forbid you to marry my daughter next month."

His hands wrapped protectively around his neck, Jeffie ran out the door. Gertrud, pretending to be swinging a frying pan, followed him.

Mainz, December 1634

"Here we are, back in dear old Mainz." Eberhard sighed. After counting the cost, Tata had proclaimed that it would be cheaper for all of them to make the trip from Fulda and back again on a freight wagon instead of renting horses and then having to pay for their stabling for two weeks. Freight wagons did not deliver their passengers door-to-door. They were walking, slipping on the filthy, slushy, cobblestones.

"It's just for Christmas," Tata said. "General Brahe asked Major Utt if you and Friedrich could come. That was quite a while ago, a couple of months. Remember, that was when you ordered your new suit." Tata frowned suddenly. "How much did you pay for that suit? Margarethe says that Friedrich is just going to wear his Fulda Barracks Regiment dress orange whenever he has to go to some official function or unavoidable party. That's much thriftier."

"I get tired of the uniform. There's something to be said for dressing to match your status."

"Have you paid for it?" Tata put her hands on her hips. "Who loses when the forces of oppression fail to pay the hard-working people who supply their needs? How can a shoemaker feed his children when the tooled art objects that he creates for the feet of arrogant aristocrats result only in invoices that aren't paid for months, or sometimes for years? How . . ."

"Horn of Plenty in view," Friedrich called. "And none too soon. By the way, Tata, he paid for the suit."

Reichard and Justina, Kunigunde and Ursula, Philipp, and three youngsters with reddish hair came pouring out the door, all yelling, "Tata! It's Tata!"

"Veit, Lambert, Hans." Agathe did her best to hug all three of her younger brothers at once, but they, Veit in particular, were getting too big for her to accomplish the task. "Mama, Papa, *Tante* Kuni . . ."

The others went on in to the taproom, leaving the delirious jumping around of the family reunion to occur in the middle of the street.

"Good grief," Friedrich said. "She's only been gone for six months. We haven't seen our sisters for more than three years."

"Unless the political situation calms down, we may not see them for three more." Eberhard frowned. "When is the last time you wrote?"

"I am a virtuous brother. I write them regularly at least once a month." Friedrich stuck his nose up in the air.

Margarethe pinched it.

"Well, I've written them at least once a month ever since I got married. Before that, *ja*, it had been a while."

"Quite a while," Margarethe said. "More than a while."

"Margarethe makes me write them, so even though they've never met her, they already love her. Margarethe ordered ginger-flavored *Kuchen* from Nürnberg for the little ones and sent some of the treats that Riffa's mom bakes for Antonia. They should have it all by now, and love her even more. I thought maybe she should send them toys."

"Fritzi." Margarethe yanked on his hair. "Think how long it has been since you have seen them. The 'little ones' are fifteen and fourteen. They are growing up. You don't even know how tall they are. You don't know what colors they like. The sweets were all I could do. How can you know so little about your own family?"

Theo looked at Friedrich. "This isn't about you. This is about us. She misses Papa terribly, no matter how irritable he always has been a lot of the time." He gave her a quick hug. "We'll try, Margarethe. I'll go see him first. Maybe he'll be willing to reconcile."

"I really don't think so," she said. "He'll just be angry that we are celebrating Christmas with Tata's family. He thinks it's a papist holiday because the early popes matched it up to some pagan celebration. The Bible doesn't say exactly what day of the year Jesus was born."

It was a very fine new suit, Eberhard, thought, even if he was admiring himself. The extraordinarily large mirror that General Brahe's wife had installed in the vestibule of a house that had once been occupied by one of the more prosperous cathedral canons was impressive. The canon was now residing, in appropriate ecclesiastical poverty, in a small room in a boarding house near the cathedral.

He made another half-turn, admiring the effect of his hat.

He had bought the hat here in Mainz. It just wasn't possible to pack a hat with plumes for a trip from Fulda without crushing one of them.

Well, maybe it was possible for a professional valet, but he didn't have one. He was doing his own packing these days. He was not capable of packing a hat with plumes in such a way that one of them did not get crushed.

The receiving line moved again, perhaps four feet. Brahe and his wife came into view.

He didn't take off the hat. As a duke, he outranked a Swedish nobleman. As an officer, Brahe was not in his direct chain of command. The hat stayed on.

Tata's father would not approve.

There was a place for "all men are created equal," but it wasn't at an official reception with the cream of Mainz's secular and ecclesiastical patriciate, not to mention miscellaneous diplomats and the like, in attendance.

He wasn't going to take off his hat for the archbishop, either. Say what you would, it simply wasn't right for a good Lutheran to doff his hat to a subordinate of the earthly manifestation of the anti-Christ, the specific example of the manifestation now alive being named Urban VIII.

He supposed that the papists had a right to go to hell in their own way, as long as they didn't interfere with other people. Lutherans especially. Subscribing to the principle of religious toleration did not mean that he had to take off his hat for Anselm Casimir Wamboldt von Umstadt who was, when one came right down to it, by birth of far lower rank than a duke of Württemberg.

He reached the receiving line.

✧   ✧   ✧

Eberhard glanced cautiously to his left. Brahe's wife was walking toward him, a predatory gleam in her eye. He moved slightly to the right, behind Ulfsparre. He took off his hat. Without the plumes he would be, he hoped, effectively invisible.

Ulfsparre moved to the farther to the right.

"Stay," Eberhard said. "Please, Mans."

"They're set on marrying off Brahe's sister. I've been in their sights for weeks. The least you can do is vent some of the pressure, as the new club of 'steamheads' here in Mainz would say. You're going back to Fulda in two weeks. Before you leave, let me take you and your friends to see the new steam engine down by the docks." Ulfsparre slid between two substantial matrons and vanished into a gaggle of other young officers.

Eberhard sighed.

Anna Margareta Bielke tentatively floated some conversational gambits about the Lutheran view of matrimony as one of God's greatest gifts to mankind, far higher than the papist preference for celibacy.

Eberhard could hardly object. It was hard to contradict the *Shorter Catechism.*

She mentioned that the value of a good wife was above rubies.

Eberhard replied practically that given the current economic condition of the duchy, from which he was, in any case, exiled, rubies were pretty much out of the question, as were pearls, sapphires, emeralds, and diamonds.

She gestured at one of the display paintings on the wall.

Eberhard agreed solemnly that the story of Tobias and Susanna, although contained in the Apocrypha, was one of the most touching Biblical narratives.

She spoke of this. She prodded with reference to that.

Eberhard parried.

There was one consolation. Since he came through the reception line, he had not seen Lady Kerstin. She had politely offered her hand. She had not glanced at him flirtatiously. Presumably, she had danced, but not with him. She had disappeared.

The evening seemed interminable.

Toward the end, however, he had the satisfaction of not taking off his hat to the archbishop of Mainz. And several people complimented him on his new suit. It was in the up-time style. The tailor in Fulda had done a splendid job of reproducing the one shown in a magazine photograph of a man named "Liberace."

"You could do worse than Lady Kerstin," Erik Stenbock said. "Mans could do worse. I could do a lot worse. She's not ugly; she's not stupid; she's not silly. Silly and stupid aren't the same thing. A girl—Lady Kerstin is a grown woman, really—can be stupid and sensible, or smart and silly. Plus, the Brahes haven't lost their estates. She'll come to her husband with a great honking big dowry."

"Think of it as a compliment," Ulfsparre said. "I heard that they're even thinking about Erik Haakansson Hand as a possibility. They're looking as high as a cousin of the king. His mother was illegitimate, of course, but the Vasa blood is there."

"You didn't seem very complimented yesterday

evening," Eberhard said. "You were ducking out of sight as fast as you could scamper."

"I'm here. Hand is not in the Upper Palatinate any more, I don't think, but he's somewhere other than here."

Stenbock laughed. "From what I heard, he'll be somewhere other than Mainz until they either marry Lady Kerstin off or take her back to Sweden."

"You're not holding off because of your little CoC . . ." Ulfsparre stopped. Stenbock had kicked him under the table. ". . . girl from the Horn of Plenty, are you?" he finished. "Depending on Lady Kerstin's attitude—or how much attitude you're willing to put up with—you could keep *die Donnerin* on as your mistress. Or just drop her, if that's what is required for you to enter into a suitable marriage. She's young enough to find someone else, not to mention her . . ."

Stenbock kicked him under the table again.

"The gossip is all over the city," Justina said. "They say that Brahe's wife wants to make a marriage between Eberhard and her sister-in-law."

"Ach." Ursula Widder put her handkerchief to her eyes. "Our poor, sweet Tata. Abandoned by her lover."

"At least," Reichard said, "the CoC is well enough established in Mainz by now that it can survive without his patronage."

Eberhard tossed his clothes on the stool and threw himself into the bed as fast as he could. There weren't any fireplaces on the third floor of the Horn of Plenty. The little bedroom felt almost like home. It didn't feel like "home" like the ducal palaces in Stuttgart or Mömpelgard, but he hadn't seen those for years. It felt a lot more like home than his cabin at Barracktown bei Fulda did.

"I'm not going to do it."

Tata was already under the duvet. "I'm not so sure that 'just say no' is the best idea right now." She rolled over. "It's not that I want you to marry her, but honestly, Brahe's in a position either to press your cause with Gustavus Adolphus or to just leave you dangling the way you've been the last couple of years. If you were his brother-in-law, it seems to me, he'd be a lot more likely to act as your advocate."

"So my little CoC lady would like to see me reinstated? Re-duked, if you would? Not that I've ever formally renounced my title the way Friedrich has."

"No!" Tata picked up her pillow and hit him with it. "If you get re-duked, you'll go back home. If you get married . . . I don't *want* to see you re-duked at all. But for you, it might be the best thing. For you and Friedrich and Margarethe and your sisters." She put the pillow back under her head. "She's pregnant, you know."

"Brahe's sister isn't pregnant. At least, not by me. Is that why they want to marry her off? Did some randy Swedish royal get under her skirts? Maybe they can marry her off to Gustav's bastard son. He's only about eighteen months younger than I am."

"Margarethe, you nitwit. Margarethe is pregnant. You're going to be an uncle."

"Okay, Brahe's sister isn't pregnant. You're not pregnant, either?"

Tata shook her head. "I'm too careful. It's okay for Margarethe. She and Friedrich are married. We aren't and we never will be."

"I wouldn't give you up if I married the Lady Kerstin."

"Yes, you would, if you get re-duked. You might not want to, but you would. I'd leave. I was never cut out to be any nobleman's official mistress. Not even yours. My mouth would get me in trouble all the time, and that would make trouble for you. I'm not cut out for court life.

"Mouth." Eberhard pulled her down. "Your mouth isn't trouble. Your mouth is pretty and pink and cute." He outlined it with one finger. "The rest of you is cute, too. Let's see, your ear is cute, your . . .

The next morning, the window was covered with frost crystals. Eberhard pulled the duvet under his chin, crunched up his pillow into a ball, and lay there for a while, just looking at them glitter in the sunshine.

I'm *not* going to do it, he thought. The gain is all contingent and not worth the gamble.

He stared at the bright, white window pane while Tata snored softly. There had to be some way to refuse the idea.

No, not refuse it. Just drag things out until it gets dropped, the way so many other things get dropped. Dilly-dally until Brahe forgets about it, the way Gustavus Adolphus forgot about us. It's Brahe's wife who's pushing it, anyway. String things out until she goes back to Sweden and the campaigning season opens.

He pushed his good arm under Tata's shoulder and tickled her ribs until she woke up.

Section Four: Here are the stages in the journey...

Barracktown bei Fulda, January 1635

"Package delivery," David Kronberg said cheerfully. He tossed a package onto the sutlery sales counter. "It came in just before closing time."

"What's that on the label?" Riffa asked.

"It says, 'Do not open until Three Kings.'"

"Three Kings?" She scrunched up her forehead. "What's that?"

"Presents day, presents day, presents day." Gertrud chanted as she pounced on it with enthusiasm. "Oh. It's not for me. It's for Jeffie and Joel. Maybe it's a lump of coal and some switches."

"Wrong shape."

"Who's it from?"

"A bookstore in Frankfurt."

"A bookstore wouldn't be sending them a present. Someone must have ordered it."

"Eberhard and Friedrich, I bet." Gertrud tossed it on the counter. "They'll be here later."

"Jeffie and Joel or Eberhard and Friedrich?"

"The first two. The others aren't back from Mainz, yet. If the river doesn't freeze hard and the roads aren't too bad, they should be here Thursday."

"What if the Main does freeze hard and the roads are awful?"

Gertrud grimaced. "Then Jeffie and I may have to

postpone our wedding if we want them to be there.
And we do."

"Postpone? How long?"

"A few days. Until they get here." Gertrud shrugged.
"It's no big deal—not as if we were planning on dozens
of guests. Jeffie's mom and brother are already here.
Justin finished his EMT course for the Military Medical
Department and hasn't been assigned yet. Callmemarsha
says she hasn't had a vacation since the Ring of Fire and
Stevenson's Groceries owes her one. They can both stay
for at least two more weeks, so we can be flexible. It's not
as if we're cutting it close. The baby isn't due 'til July."

Denver Caldwell, one of the other up-timers at Fulda
Barracks, looked up. "That's just 'Marsha,' Gertrud.
I know she runs it all together into 'Callmemarsha-
becauseI'mnotoldenoughtobeanyone'smother-in-law.'
Trust me, though. Her name is Marsha."

"We really appreciate the Montaigne translation,
Eberhard," Joel said. "But I've got to tell you the
truth. The only way I can make sense of Florio's 1603
English is to read it out loud. Take where he's talking
about the sumptuary laws, for example.

"The manner wherewith our Lawes assay
to moderate the foolish and vaine expences of
table-cheare and apparell seemeth contrarie to
its end. The best course were to beget in men
a contempt of gold and silkwearinge as of vaine
and non-profitable things, whereas we encrease
their credit and price: a most indirect course to
withdraw men from them. As, for example, to let

none but Princes eat dainties, or weare velvets and clothes of Tissew, and interdict the people to doe it, what is it but to give reputation unto those things, and to encrease their longing to use them?

"When I look at 'encrease' or 'Tissew,' they don't seem to make sense, but when I read them out loud, they turn into 'increase' and 'tissue.' I did get really messed up by *table-cheare*. I thought at first it meant 'table chairs,' until I figured out that it meant good cheer at the table. Food, in other words."

Eberhard looked around. "The incredible variety of clothes here would have provided Montaigne with about as much good cheer as he could use if he could have seen them."

"Sweats. Lots of sweats. No tee-shirts, but then it's January. Up-time 'Sunday best.' Down-time 'Sunday best' or whatever you call it." Joel paused. "Andrea Hill in one of her weird combinations of up-time and down-time. That—really remarkable suit you have on."

"I had it made especially for Mainz, but I decided I might as well get some use out of it. Once the campaigning season starts . . . 'How soone doe plaine chamoy-jerkins and greasie canvase doublets creepe into fashion and credit amongst our souldiers if they lie in the field?'"

Jeffie wandered over. "Quoting Montaigne again, Eberhard? Thanks for that book you sent us. It has more antique English in one place than I've seen since Ms. Higham made us do Shakespeare in drama back in high school. I was the last one to the library, so I had to check out the *Collected Works* instead of just the one play."

"What's Willem doing over there?"

"Van de Passe? I didn't know he was still in Fulda. I thought he was heading for Grantville."

"He'll leave when my mom goes back," Jeffie said. "He got involved in doing some stuff for Derek out here at the barracks. He's not a bad guy. He drew a wedding portrait of us and signed it. Maybe it'll be worth something, someday. I'd better go. Gertrud beckons." He wandered across the room.

Behind Joel and Eberhard, someone went, "Pssst."

Eberhard looked around.

Gertrud's next-younger brother Johann, eyes gleaming, whispered "*charivari*."

Tata came prancing across the room. "*Ja*. I talked to Frau Hill before we went to Mainz. I brought back everything we need. A good, old-fashioned, West Virginia-German Rhineland *shivaree-charivari*."

Johann nodded enthusiastically. "I already put the ice in their bed. If it melts a little before the end of the reception, that's even better. If it stays frozen hard, she'll just shake it out of the sheets. Tata's little brothers sent a whole box of noisemakers. Rattles. Clappers. Whistles. Some lovely things that make a howl when you whirl them around in a circle. Erdmann has already made sure that every kid in Barracktown has one. Oh, how our big sister is going to suffer."

Mainz, January 1635

"Magnificent plates," Brahe said. "I've never seen such high-quality engravings from anything other than an artist's studio." He spread the prints out approvingly. "Butler, Deveroux, Geraldin, MacDonald. Who's this?"

"Felix Gruyard. That's why the project took a couple of weeks longer than we planned. Van de Passe had no idea who he was, but Paul Moreau, that crippled artist working at the St. Severi church in Fulda, finally agreed to go through van de Passe's sketches and see if he recognized anyone. Moreau's skittish. Well, given some of the things he's been through in his life, I don't blame him for being skittish. Useful, though. He's been rattling around through various studios and printing shops for nearly twenty years, ever since he was apprenticed. He also has the advantage of being completely reliable in his loyalty to the SoTF. Or, at least, completely reliable in his loyalty to Andrea Hill. He seems to think that she walks on water. I'm not sure whether he has any abstract loyalty to the USE at all."

"How come he recognized Gruyard? I've never heard that the Lorrainer is a habitué of art galleries."

"His specialty is the reason Moreau is crippled. On Ferdinand of Bavaria's behest."

"Oh. How many of these sets can we get smuggled onto the left bank of the Rhine?"

"Depends on how many we can afford to pay the freight, load onto the Monster, and have flown into Luxembourg. Under the table, Fernando and Maria Anna have given Nasi *carte blanche* to use Luxembourg as a basis for smuggling them in from the eastern border of Ferdinand's lair. Send some to the Hessians and they'll get them into Bonn. Get them to our friends in the USE city-state of Cologne and I guarantee they will trickle out. Send some to Essen and they'll drift south. Van de Passe himself will send batches of them in through a kind of underground network of Mennonites."

"Aren't they pacifists of some kind?"

"Ah, Nils. I ask you. How can the distribution of sketches possibly be construed as an act of violence?"

Euskirchen, Archdiocese of Cologne, January 1635

Ferdinand of Bavaria, archbishop of Cologne, assumed his most arrogant expression. "Without Werth and Mercy, my brother has been very handicapped in sponsoring anything that requires mobility for nearly a year. This has made him irritable. Dragoons are not cavalry, precisely." The archbishop looked down his ample nose. "Still, dragoons are better than nothing. Maximilian refuses to send me money with which to pay you . . ."

Walter Butler nodded. Rumors of Duke Maximilian's refusal had been current for the past couple of weeks.

"He is, however, willing to hire you. I have consented . . ."

However grudgingly, Butler thought, *and only because you're scraping the very bottom of your strongbox. There's no way you'll be able to pay us for another quarter unless you can find additional revenues*. He looked down, gauging the archbishop's mood. "If . . ." he began.

"I will pay you for the last quarter, the one ending last month, when you leave," his employer answered. "You and the other Irishmen."

Butler closed his mouth.

He had intended to say, "If you value your skin, you will scrape together the money to pay us from somewhere for this quarter and for the next quarter.

If we leave, the king in the Netherlands will come, and by the end of March, you will find yourself as one more nationalized, mediatized, Spanish-style prelate, just as the archbishop of Liége had already found himself, with your left bank lands an integral part of those very Netherlands." He snorted. If the archbishop didn't want to listen to professional advice when he had a professional available—well, blast him to hell.

"We'll have to move out by late February," Deveroux said. "I loathe winter marches, but they can be done. At least, we'll be moving south rather than north. And if the old skinflint does actually pay us, we can buy provisions. Late winter and early spring are the worst times to forage."

"Moving to the south is no guarantee of better weather." Geraldin rubbed some frost crystals off the window pane.

"It improves the odds. If we prepare for a winter march and are blessed by an early spring, so much the better."

"Aside from the mud and the floods. We have to cross the Rhine somewhere if we're going to finally put an end to Horn's endless Fabian maneuvering. He's managed to keep Bernhard and Maximilian practically immobilized for nearly four years now, without ever hazarding a battle, playing a damned chess game across the map of southwest Germany. 'You move here and I'll move there.' Pray for winter until we're across and spring in Swabia. I do not want to cross the Rhine river bottoms in the mud. I do not want to ride through the Black Forest on icy roads."

❖   ❖   ❖

Anna Marie von Dohna huddled as close to the Dutch-style ceramic stove as she could get. The stove was the best thing about the miserable, skimpy, low-ceilinged rooms that her husband had stuck them in for the winter. It managed to make some heat from even scanty amounts of damp peat—the only fuel available—and she idled away long hours of boredom by making up stories about the people in the designs on the tiles. Burning peat smelled like, well, burning peat, of course . . .

Her husband walked in and broke the news.

"Leaving?" she screeched. She stood up, throwing off her cloak. "Leaving in six weeks? Leaving before the end of winter? I'm not leaving. I'm staying right here."

"I am leaving and you are coming. You don't have a choice. I know for a certainty that you have nearly used up your gold. Frittered your gold away. Wasted it on luxuries over the holidays. I've come home almost every day since Epiphany to find you curled next to a fire with a bonbon in hand. Soon it will be 'peat gone, sweets gone.' Poor countess, reduced to eating stringy goat meat like the rest of us poor peasants."

"You only want me to come because I'm not pregnant yet. If I were breeding, you would find a way to leave me here. That's the only reason you keep dragging me from here to there to somewhere else."

"Why the hell else would I have married you, if I didn't want a son from the deal? What's the point if I don't get a son?"

In winter quarters, at least, he had a door to slam.

Dislav came in, carrying a blanket he had warmed in front of the kitchen fire downstairs.

Anna Marie, over twenty-five and childless now in

two marriages, wrapped her cloak around the blanket to hold the heat in and went back to the stove.

That evening, Dislav spent an hour drinking with his new friend Lorenz Bauer. It wasn't much of a tavern. The floor boards were slick from recent spills or sometimes sticky from long-past spills. The tables were simply sticky. But the beer was cheap.

Bauer, the next day, made a short visit to the honorable holder of the tuna tin.

That evening, Nils Brahe's radio monitors in Mainz picked up the first message out of Euskirchen since Hartke had left the men behind nearly three months earlier.

Barracktown bei Fulda, February 1635

"Did the men say when they are returning?" Sergeant Hartke asked.

"Not a word. Hertling is very disappointed." Eberhard reached his bowl across the table. Tata filled it with another helping of stew.

Mainz, February 1635

"Are you going to order your men out of Euskirchen, now?" Hoheneck asked.

Brahe shook his head. "They're not listening to receive orders from us. They can't keep the antenna up and spend time listening for signals. They're only to send. It's up to them how long they stay."

"Micromanagement," Utt said. "It's something we're not doing."

Hoheneck eyed him. "Micromanagement. When are you letting me come back to Fulda?"

"When I decide it's prudent."

"Herr Springer has no opinion on the matter?"

Utt hesitated. "No decisive opinion. No 'immovable object' sort of opinion." He wasn't about to tell Hoheneck that Mel Springer didn't seem to be able to muster a decisive opinion as to whether he preferred his breakfast toast to be light or dark.

"So," Brahe said, "what did you think of the election results?"

"As a professional soldier, I do not have an opinion on the election results." Utt grinned. "Would you be interested in my wife's opinion of the election results? If so, she was pretty disgusted by the newspaper reports of the Crown Loyalist party's celebration in Magdeburg, given that . . ."

"What concerns me more," Brahe said, "is that we have had another eruption from Georg Wulf von Wildenstein."

"Fulda—Buchenland County—has heard from him, too. There's always his underlying Calvinist dislike of the continued toleration of Catholics, but now he's gotten wind of the LDS mission in Barracktown. Not that the administration has ever tried to hide that Monroe and Betty Wilson are there and what they're trying to do, you understand, but we haven't exactly gone out and yelled to the four winds about it—much less that a bunch of the early materials for the Barracktown school, before we had any money to buy textbooks, were sent over by the Grantville branch."

"What concerns me is that von Wildenstein may use his long-standing ties to Wilhelm of Hesse-Kassel to try to narrow the official USE policy of religious toleration." Brahe frowned. "He's not likely to focus on the Lutherans at first, given that the emperor is one and it's constitutionally the USE state church, but I can see his putting pressure on the government's handling of various minorities. That includes the Jews, by the way. Wamboldt von Umstadt is worried."

Euskirchen, Archdiocese of Cologne, February 1635

When Brahe's posse members met, they met in the evening around the still-warm forge of the farrier for whom Schild was working. Not many people in the encampment, dragoons or camp followers, still had decent fuel—many of them had no fuel—but almost everyone recognized, however reluctantly, that a good fire was necessary if the horses were to be kept well shod.

"I think that's about it," Heisel said. "We know that they're all leaving. Zeyler, here . . ." He pointed toward the natural-born liar. "Zeyler has managed to find out that they're taking this Gruyard that the major has his knickers tied in knots about with them."

"I'm good," Zeyler said. "I really am. I'm practically a fixture in the kitchen of the inn where MacDonald is staying. When we're done here, you can give me a letter of recommendation to the famous Francisco Nasi and I shall become a great spy. Not a famous one, since that would defeat the purpose, but great."

"If nothing else, you have the *chutzpah*," Heisel

grumbled. "If you get to work for Nasi, you can ask him what the word means. I picked it up from an old Jew in Höchstädt, down south on the Danube, in 1632, when Gustavus's army was taking Donauwörth back from Duke Maximilian." He looked at Bauer. "What do you say?"

"I say we don't all go back to our own young dukes, yet. I say that I stay here, keeping an eye on Ferdinand of Bavaria, and you go with the Irishmen."

Bauer looked at Zeyler.

"I can stay with you. There will still be news here, about the archbishop. If you need a message run, my legs are younger."

"Honorable Tuna Tin?"

Hartke's veteran folded his scarred hands, leaning his chin on them, his elbows on his knees. "Once upon a time, my name was Julius Brandt. I have had several army names since I joined up, but that is what my parents had written down in the baptismal record. I come from Brunswick."

Heisel inclined his head. "Julius, my friend."

"I will send the message, Christoph. Then, like you, I will follow in the train of the Irish colonels' regiments. Who knows what we may yet find out." Brandt's smile was feral. "And I will keep the Honorable Tuna Tin, except between us. Of my army names, it's probably the best."

Lorraine, March 1635

"Well, Julius, my friend?"

"I agree. This is something we should transmit—that the Irishmen are going south through Lorraine. Here, though, Christoph? Where am I to throw the wire? Not in the middle of the camp, certainly."

"No point in trying tonight."

"Nor tomorrow night, if this keeps up." Brandt was sitting cross-legged on top of an overturned feeding trough. Little trickles of water ran under the tent wall, under the trough, and out again.

"What hellish weather. Butler requisitions the best house in every damned village for his Bohemian countess. Nothing but the best. Featherbeds, even, sometimes. Still—whine, whine, whine, whine, whine."

Brandt looked around at the wagons. "There must be five times as many camp followers as there are dragoons in the regiments. At least, it seems so."

"The regiments are low. It was a hard winter in Euskirchen. Wet lungs. Hunger. Cold. Dysentery. Desertions. It didn't help that the ground was frozen hard much of the time, so we had to stack the dead, waiting for a thaw." Heisel started counting on his fingers. "Each of the colonels should, in theory, have eight hundred dragoons. Deveroux has done best. He has perhaps six hundred; Butler close to that. Geraldin possibly still has five hundred. If MacDonald has three hundred effectives, I would be surprised. Two thousand men. Maybe a little less."

Brandt smiled. "So sad. MacDonald is trying to hide the situation, even from his colleagues, by having boys from the stables and women in trousers ride some of his horses. I fear that Duke Maximilian will be gravely disappointed in what he is getting for his money."

"Where do I throw the wire? Not inside the camp with so many people around."

"We will have to creep outside of the sentry lines. I don't think we can do it tonight, yet. That freezing rain has stopped, but there are clouds and no moon. If you should lose hold of the wire when you throw it, we won't be able to find it again. I doubt very much that there is an equivalent length of good wire anywhere else in this camp. General Brahe will have to wait for better weather."

"Have you seen Gruyard? They want to know about Gruyard."

"He is traveling with the chaplains—Taaffe and Carew—in Butler's wife's wagon."

"Good, then we know where he is. We need to transmit that, too."

"When God permits, Julius, my friend. It is not for us to control the weather."

"Maybe tonight."

"Tonight, whether we lose the antenna or not. Dislav heard one of the colonels say that tomorrow we turn toward the east. They plan for Deveroux to break away. He will take his own men and Geraldin's. They hope that he can do to Merckweiler what Turenne did to Wietze and then quickly rejoin Butler."

"Don't forget to tell them about Gruyard."

"At least, since I'm attached to Geraldin's horses, I'll be able to follow along on the raid. But you will have the tuna tin, so what good will it do for me to be there?"

"Such things happen. Fate. Destiny. It is all part of the divine plan."

Heisel's face suddenly brightened. "The regiments that General Brahe left at Merckweiler last year have tuna tins. They should have two or three spare tuna tins, perhaps. Extras, in case of failure of working parts. Perhaps I can run away from Geraldin, ahead of the dragoons, go into Merckweiler, tell them who I am, tell them what I know, and get a tuna tin of my own as a reward. I love those words, 'down-time built with up-time parts.' They are like poetry."

Brandt smirked. "Your idea just goes to show that even divine plans can be improved on. I wouldn't count on getting the tuna tin, though."

"Ah, no. As Jeffie the up-timer says, 'The only reward you get for a job well done is another job.'"

"Now that's scarcely an inspiring thought."

"Have you gotten the antenna up? We have to finish this job, first."

Barracktown bei Fulda, March 4, 1635

"It just came in on the Post Office receiver," David Kronberg said. All we got was in Morse, but VOA is providing live coverage. Maybe Mel Springer's new setup in downtown Fulda is doing better. Our crystal set is nothing but static."

"Damn, but I'm sorry to hear that about Henry Dreeson," Jeffie Garand said. "I liked old Henry. I didn't even mind playing 'High Hopes' for him on that march we did against the anti-Semites down in Frankfurt. Do you suppose they're the ones who did him in?"

Joel Matowski stood up. "Enoch Wiley was an okay guy, too. Well, for a Presbyterian. If there's such a thing as a hardshell Presbyterian, he was one. We'd better get ourselves down to the barracks, just in case the regiment is called out for something."

The door of the sutlery banged open.

"Close the door," Riffa said. "It's sleeting sideways."

"Move out," Sergeant Hartke said. "Orders from Colonel Utt. All men to the barracks. We have a message via military radio from Mainz. Starting with even numbers, every other unit marches to join General Brahe at first daylight. Odd numbers stay here in the garrison. You know which unit you are." Under his breath, he added, "I hope."

"In this weather?" Margarethe asked.

Friedrich kissed her. "Sorry, sweetheart. In this weather, if that's what it takes."

Mainz, March 1635

"Margarethe," Theo said. "You're being unreasonable. You can't go, *Rehgeißchen*. You're pregnant."

"I've seen pregnant women in the camps."

"That's because they don't have anywhere else to be," her husband answered. "You are not supposed to even be in Mainz. You were not supposed to follow us. Did you see Dagmar Nilsdotter tramping out into this muck with a four-month-old baby? No. She stayed in her cabin at Barracktown like a *mature, sensible* army wife. Did Gertrud come with Jeffie? No, she stayed with her mother like a *young, sensible, pregnant* army wife. Which is what you are, except that you are not being sensible. What do I have to do? Tear out my hair?" Friedrich grabbed a handful and tugged on it.

Margarethe sobbed. "But Fritzi, even Papa is going with the army."

"He's the military chaplain for Brahe's Calvinist

soldiers, my sweet sister." Theo slammed his fist on the table. "Of course he is going."

"But you," Friedrich said, "are not. I can't help it that you came this far, but no farther. You are going to wait right here at the Horn of Plenty until we come back."

"So, Nils, now you are a bachelor again, too." Derek Utt twirled his wine glass in his fingers. He didn't really want a drink right now. The night before you moved out always seemed to be the longest one in the year.

Brahe nodded. "Anna Margareta and the children left Wednesday. They are going up through Frankfurt and Fulda, then to Erfurt. From Erfurt to Magdeburg, and then as far north as the trains are still running, she, Elsa, and little Axel Petter will have the privilege of a railway ride. There was no reason for her to stay longer, once it was certain that I will be in the field during the summer. We will have another child in the autumn and there are projects to be accomplished on the estates in Finland. Money does not make itself."

"Mary Kat is expecting a baby, too. In August. Our first."

They congratulated one another on their husbandly prowess.

Utt thought a minute. "And your sister?"

Brahe gave him a wry smile. "It appears that while Erik Stenbock was last on my wife's list of prospective suitable husbands for her, Kerstin rated him as first. Confronted with the likelihood of being transported back to the northland, she took direct action in the form of simply telling me that she was going to marry him. She is twenty-five, of age by the strictest of standards, and I can only predict that once the mail arrives, my aunt, old Gustav Stenbock's widow, will be deliriously happy with her second son for snagging such an improbably prosperous bride. So there was no prospect of opposition there. My aunt still has three more children to marry off and, after all, Erik's sister Kristina is already married to my older brother Per, so . . . It's all in the family. It's not as if he's unsuitable. He just doesn't have much money, so he's seriously in need of a successful career—more than I can offer him here in Mainz. I gave them my blessing and arranged a promotion for him. They're off to work for Prince Frederik of Denmark in the Province of Westphalia, smug on her part and content on his."

"I'll send them my congratulations."

"I'm sure they'll be happy to accept."

Utt tipped his wine glass at a different angle, watching the candle flames dance through the liquid. "I hope you're satisfied with how I've been handling the Fulda Barracks Regiment's training. I realize it's pretty unconventional, no matter whether the standards are down-time or up-time."

"How does it differ from up-time?"

"Well, over in Grantville, they've really done their best to keep the model of 'bring the recruits in, gather them in one spot, put them through a routine called "basic training" a bunch at a time, and then assign them to units.' That's how I was trained, myself. It's just lucky that I stayed in the WVNG and kept my manuals. That's what Lane Grooms is doing now, even for the boys who are—if we are lucky—destined to be permanent reserves. He's thinking about defense against Saxony, of course, in a worst-case scenario."

Brahe nodded.

"Over here in Fulda, though . . . First of all, since our original contingent arrived in 1632, I haven't gotten a single new recruit sent out from Grantville, down-timer or up-timer. It's almost the same with the up-time civilian administrators, for that matter. The administration, first NUS and now SoTF, just plopped us down on what for them was the edge of known civilization and left us here. Except for the exchange of Springer for Jenkins, there hasn't been any new blood. Technically, I think, the proper word is 'marginalized.'"

Brahe nodded again. "'Edge' . . . 'margin' . . . Etymologically speaking, that is quite appropriate."

"So even though we've been doing very well, medically speaking—the people at Barracktown are happily surprised at how many of them are still alive—I've still had vacancies to fill. I recruit locally, one man at a time or a few men at a time, and there's just no way I can afford to send them over to Grantville so Lane Grooms can put them through his basic training routines. Just the travel expense . . ." His voice trailed off. "So we train them ourselves. First it was just me and the other up-timers waving the pamphlets around. Now I have quite a few down-timers who can train others using the up-time manuals, but it's still closer to what Washington was doing during the Revolution than what happened during later American wars."

Brahe shrugged. "My regiments do it pretty much the same way. Drill, maneuvers."

Utt grinned. "Those things. On a lot of those things, we let Hartke and the other down-timers train us up-timers. I figured that until the whole regiment was equipped with modern guns, they probably knew more about how to handle the available weapons than I did. Two-way OJT—on the job training for the actual campaigning. Among other things, I've had all the infantry guys also taught to ride and got them horses, so they can double as dragoons at a pinch. It's not cavalry, but I have more mobility than I would have otherwise. That's a big consideration when your manpower is so limited. There's no point of dreaming of mechanization over here when the big campaigns will be on the eastern front."

Brahe nodded, this time thoughtfully.

"Then also . . . Well, other things started when we hired this boy named Pierre Biehr. He was a would-be university student who ran out of tuition. We hired him to teach school for the Barracktown kids, but then he started working with the regiment on music training. That went pretty well. I started to think about organizing other kinds of indoor training in the winter, during bad weather. Why let them laze around in the barracks just because it's sleeting out? And why does everyone who trains soldiers have to be one? Turns out young Pierre has two older brothers and two older married sisters, everybody looking for a job. The oldest sister's husband was an unemployed drawing-master in Frankfurt-am-Main. I brought him up for one winter. Now almost every man who was already in the regiment that winter can not only read a map decently—he can also draw a reasonably good one. Not like a surveyor would, but by counting his steps to estimate 'how far' and recording what his eyes see. Sure, topo and trigonometry and GPS would be better, ideally, but they fall into the category of the push for the perfect driving out the 'adequate for the immediate purpose' and leaving you with the 'nothing at all.' I could come up with a poster: 'Fulda Barracks: the home of it'll do for now.'"

He looked at Brahe. "Are we going to get any sleep tonight?"

"We should probably try." Brahe tossed his wine into a vase of dried flowers and corked the bottle.

"Margarethe is locked in," Tata said. "Friedrich hugged her and kissed her. Then he went with Sergeant Hartke, down to sleep at Colonel Utt's quarters in case he needs them during the night. *Tante* Kunigunde is sleeping in the room with her and Papa locked the door. Mama will see to it that she stays here. If she is completely unreasonable, Mama will take her back to Fulda by force and turn her over to Dagmar. That will settle the issue."

"It should." Eberhard laughed. "If it doesn't, Dagmar can always call on our dear but indomitable sister Antonia in Strassburg for reinforcements. Kiss me goodnight, sweetheart. This could be our last featherbed for quite some time."

"Our last featherbed, but not our last bed." She snuggled down under the duvet. "I'm coming with you."

Eberhard yawned. "I know."

Sarreguemines, Lorraine, March 1635

"Thank God that we're finally indoors for a change." Deveroux looked around the comfortable inn in Sarreguemines. "How much farther?

Butler spread his best, now rather tattered and water-stained, map on their unwilling hostess's dining room hutch. "We've come probably close to three-fourths of the way to Merckweiler. There should be about fifty miles to go. It's fairly easy riding as far as Bitche, not too bad to Niederbronn, but from there on east . . ."

"Merckweiler has a lot more defenses than Wietze did." Geraldin twirled his dagger. He had become attached to it. In that other world, without the Ring of Fire, he would have used it to stab Wallenstein. "I'd feel a lot more comfortable if we had better information."

"Of course they do." Butler scowled with disgust. "The USE was complacent at Wietze. Over here, they aren't worrying about us, specifically, in regard to the Pechelbronn oil fields, but they're damned well worrying about Bernhard. Worrying about the French. Worrying about whether Duke Charles of Lorraine will do something stupid. Worrying and doing something about it."

Geraldin stuck the point of the dagger into the table. "Brahe left two regiments behind when he took the Province of the Upper Rhine last year. They've had time to build some decent fortifications."

"They shouldn't have any up-time weapons, though. I haven't even caught rumors of up-time supplies coming across the Palatinate to them."

"Where and how would we hear rumors? No one can understand a word that the local people say. What a godforsaken dialect." Dennis MacDonald helped himself liberally to their hostess's wine. "Not even our guide can understand the peasants."

"Two regiments are what Brahe left. How many men will still be in the garrison after winter quarters? I haven't heard that they've sent any reinforcements across, either." Geraldin pulled the dagger out again. "If he's lost as many men as we have . . ."

"The regiments were at full strength when he left them. Infantry, and they spent the winter indoors, so . . ." Deveroux started to doodle calculations on the paper in front of him. "If we distribute our available men this way . . ."

Anna Marie von Dohna looked up from her embroidery. "Before we left Euskirchen, the mayor's wife said something to von Sickingen's wife Ursula who passed it on to me. The mayor still gets the newspapers from Cologne smuggled in."

Butler looked at her with annoyance. "We're not interested in the society columns."

She shrugged and went back to what she had been doing. She had made the gesture. For once, she had tried to be a sturdy prop, as the book of Proverbs said that a wife should be to her husband. Ferdinand of Bavaria's obsession with censorship did not strike her as intelligent. Maybe he even censored himself. In any case, he had not told her husband. If Walter and the others really did not *want* to know that the count of Hanau-Lichtenberg was scheduled to make a ceremonial inspection of the new industries associated with his Pechelbronn oil fields, and that it seemed likely that he might arrive there accompanied by a significant escort before Deveroux could reach Merckweiler, who was she to insist?

"The crucial thing, if this is going to work, is that after the raid, we have to arrive at Germersheim at the same time. Nearly the same time, anyway—not a week apart, much less two weeks." Butler grabbed the paper on which Deveroux was scribbling. "Then across and toward Bruchsal. Damn, but I wish Bernhard's cavalry wasn't sitting there south of Strassburg going 'Nyah, nyah, nyah.' It would be so damned much easier to go south in the Rhine bottoms on the left bank."

"Germersheim? That was taken by the imperials in 1622. The last I heard, there weren't a dozen families left, huddling in half-rebuilt sheds and shacks. Have they built Bruchsal back? In 1622, it was destroyed completely."

"No. That's why I want to cross into Swabia there, if we can. No major, entrenched opposition on either side of the river. This part of the Palatinate was thoroughly scoured and the USE hasn't had it long enough to rebuild much. We'll be going through wasted landscapes—no forage. No hay. Some new grass, maybe, in fields that get sun, but mixed with weeds and a lot of underbrush. No peasants who have been hoarding food through the winter. That's why losing the baggage train—such as it is—would be a disaster."

"Why not Speyer?"

"The garrison's too strong. Could Brahe possibly have grabbed the left bank for the USE at a more inconvenient time? Coming west last year wasn't half this bad."

"If we don't get across at Germersheim, then we *will* have to go south looking for a ford. Probably as far as Hagenbach."

"I sure wish we could cross on a bridge. Wouldn't that be nice?"

"If wishes were horses, then beggars would ride.

There's no such thing as an undefended Rhine bridge. There's hardly any such thing as a Rhine bridge at all—the channels are too unreliable. There's no such thing as an undefended Rhine ferry. There's probably no such thing as a decent undefended Rhine ford, especially not in the spring when the water is rising and the channels are realigning themselves. You never can predict where a new channel is going to cut through."

"Stop complaining."

"Look, Deveroux. You and Geraldin are taking more than half of our fighting strength. Dennis and I will have the whole supply train and support personnel to move with us. If we get stranded at the Rhine crossing, we'll be sitting ducks for any USE garrison forces that peek out of Speyer or Landau long enough to spot us. Coordination, that's the key. If, in that other world, Ferdinand coming from Austria and Fernando coming from Italy managed it over far greater distances to triumph at Nördlingen, then in this world, over far shorter distances, we can pull off a coordinated operation, too."

MacDonald lifted his head. "If you say 'coordination' one more time, I'm going to puke."

"You look like you're going to puke anyway."

"We'd better write this out," Heisel said.

"Use as few words as possible." Brandt shook the little transmitter. "I think the 'battery' they put in this 'tuna tin' is dying. How can something that is not alive die?"

"They just mean that it stops working." Heisel printed carefully:

```
Irish dragoons east to
Merckweiler.
Intend kill oil Pechelbronn.
Deveroux. Geraldin. Horses.
Five days food saddlebags.
Small arms only.
Then Germersheim.
```

He frowned. "That's as short as I can make it."

"Do we need another line? Gruyard is going with them, along with Taaffe and Carew, the other chaplains. They're expecting to take enough casualties out of this project that their men will be needing confession and last rites. The general and Utt are greatly concerned with Gruyard."

Heisel shook his head. "Better save the battery."

Province of the Upper Rhine, March 1635

"For a girl who has never followed an army before, you've done great, Tata." Eberhard patted her bottom appreciatively.

"Ooooh, not there. I feel like there's nothing left between my skin and the bones I use for sitting. If I have to ride in that wagon much longer, even with a cushion between me and the board, the skin will be gone, too."

He peeked over her shoulder. "There's still a reasonable amount of you left."

"That's very reassuring. It wasn't so bad until we got to Kaiserslautern, but when the general heard that we were too late to prevent the raid on Pechelbronn, the pace he's kept up ever since has been insane. *Wahn-sinnig*. Why is he going so fast? Didn't the reports say that there was some damage, but the garrison and the count of Hanau-Lichtenberg's bodyguard are 'mopping things up'?"

"They're mopping locally, collecting the wounded and taking them prisoner, interrogating, and the like. Most of the garrison at Merckweiler isn't mounted, though. Those are infantry regiments. Brahe hadn't taught them to ride and mounted them, the way Colonel Utt has done for us at Fulda Barracks. Hanau-Lichtenberg's men were on pretty horses suitable for going on a leisurely trip with parties at the other end, not for extended hard riding. Deveroux is on the run, trying to rejoin Butler, wherever he may be. Our guy with the radio—assuming that he's still alive—is with Deveroux, so all we know about Butler is that he's probably somewhere between southeastern Lorraine and Germersheim."

"Which means that we are going somewhere fast?"

"Southeast, toward the Rhine, all the while praying that someone shows up with better intelligence."

"Lieutenant Friedrich Württemberger, Fulda Barracks Regiment mounted scouts, reporting back."

Passwords and other formalities accomplished, which took a while, Friedrich finally made it to his brother and Colonel Utt. The condensed version of his information was that there were a hell of a lot of people cluttering up the road ahead of them, about seven miles farther on.

"Wagons stuck in the mud on the road. Wagons that pulled out onto the verge to try to pass those—stuck in the mud. Wagons that pulled out into the abandoned fields to try to pass those—stuck in the mud even worse, some of them up to the beds. Horses unhitched and being held by small children, occasionally getting spooked by all the noise and mess. Horses that didn't get unhitched in time, also stuck in the mud, some of them squealing, which is no help for the people trying to hold the unhitched horses."

Brahe winced.

"I went around—as close as I could get and still keep out of sight. I'd say that the whole mess is nearly three miles long and close to a half-mile wide."

Jeffie Garand laughed. "A genuine down-time traffic jam, in other words."

"What about the dragoons?" Sergeant Hartke asked.

"The dragoons are up ahead of the mess, heading southeast as a rapid pace. That's mainly what churned up the road to the point that the first wagons got stuck, I think. In my opinion, sir, there is no place for our forces to go around the baggage train and overtake the dragoons. Just me—one man and one horse—I got off and led him part of the time. There's no hard surface out there. Just old, uncultivated stubble fields that this spring weather has turned to muck."

Bruchsal, Diocese of Speyer, proposed Province of Swabia, March 1635

The combined Swedish/SoTF camp was finally settling down for the evening. As soon as he escaped what appeared to be the perpetual staff meeting in Brahe's tent, Derek Utt started the final paragraph of his long-neglected letter to Mary Kat. "So we 'captured' Butler's camp followers." He dipped his metal-nibbed pen into the inkwell once more.

> What we really did was leave a small unit of soldiers, just to keep order, and several medics behind with Butler's camp followers. There's sickness among them. Pestilence. According to them, they didn't have it when they left Euskirchen, but picked it up while passing through Lorraine. One of the down-time medics believes that it's plague. He was very loud-mouthed about thinking that it's plague. If he was wrong, it was bad for him to panic people like that. If he was right, it's worse. We left almost all our chloram behind with them. We radioed. Fulda is sending plague fighters. Pray for us all.

In Brahe's tent, the meeting was still, to some extent, going on, in spite of the official adjournment. Brahe, still, occasionally wanted a "Swedes only" consultation.

"This time last year," Botvidsson pointed out, "Horn wouldn't have dared to come far enough north to meet us in Württemberg. He was much too preoccupied with Bernhard. Now . . . With any luck, Bernhard has granted us the luxury of doing a pincers movement on the Irishmen. Seems peculiar to have him on our side, though. Not exactly on our side, but . . ."

"If I have a choice," Brahe said, "a choice of having Bernhard the grand duke of the county of Burgundy or whatever grandiose title he may be giving himself by now as my ally, even sort-of, and Bernhard once duke of Saxe-Weimar as my enemy, I will not dither. I will take him as my ally any day, on any terms."

"Presumably, the king has reached the same conclusion."

"The enemy of my enemy . . ."

Nürtingen, Duchy of Württemberg, March 1635

The palace, which had been used as a retirement home for dowager duchesses, probably had not been in the best of condition even before the war. Now, twenty years after the last permanent resident died, it was in a wretched state. The most recent widow had been left with small children, so had stayed in Stuttgart before the war drove her away. Now she was dead and her daughters lived in Strassburg.

Moritz Klott, aide-de-camp, secretary, and, as he had learned from the up-timers, gofer, thought that General Horn should make the best of it. At least they had a roof over their heads, even if it did leak. However . . .

"I knew it," Gustav Horn ranted. "For as long as I have been assigned to this theater of operations, which is now nearly three years, Konrad Widerhold, with all the remains of the Württemberg forces he could gather, has been operating as an integral part of my army. Now, although we have not met up with Brahe and Utt yet, just because he knows that they are bringing the young dukes of Württemberg down into Swabia, what do I have?"

"I don't know, General." The liaison Bernhard had sent to work with Horn, an uncouth Lower Austrian who called himself Raudegen and had been promoted to colonel by Bernhard simply on the grounds of his ruthless efficiency, shook his head.

"That was a rhetorical question." Horn waved a piece of paper. "I have a petition from Widerhold to be permitted to place himself under Duke Eberhard's command."

He beckoned to Klott. "Take a letter. To Nils Brahe, administrator, general, et cetera. You know the titles and forms of address. Dear Nils:

> Read this damned petition from Widerhold (attached). Do you really want a captain in the forces of the State of Thuringia-Franconia to have what amounts to a full regiment and part of a second under his direct command, Nils? Is that what you want? For that matter, is it what Colonel Utt wants—to have one of his captains in charge of a force larger than his own? What were you thinking to bring those boys back into Swabia?

"Continue with the 'yours sincerely' and all that at the end." He waved the secretary out and looked back at Raudegen. "What's next?"

"There is plague to the southeast, coming up from Marseilles, moving toward this region. The grand duke is instituting all possible preventive measures. The three Paduan physicians . . ."

Raudegen's voice went on, floating past Horn's ears. "Instituting strict quarantine at the borders . . . the up-time nurse . . . small capacity for manufacture of chloramphenicol will probably not prove to be sufficient . . . universities of Basel and Strassburg . . . all possible resources . . ."

Horn rested his forehead on his hands. "May God preserve us all."

Bretten, Baden, April 1635

"Damn," Deveroux said. "We have to get south. We have Brahe on our tail. South and east. Every scout I send out says that Horn is blocking us. Pforzheim is blocked. Leonberg is blocked. He's turned the whole Stuttgart area into a garrison. The damned Swede seems to have thrown every man in his regiments into the screen. What's he trying to do?"

"Herd us north," Geraldin said pragmatically. "Keep us from passing across into Bavaria. Push us north, right into the Franconian border, if he can. Then let the USE troops take us."

Butler slammed his fist on the table. "Let's try to swing around to his north, by way of Bietigheim and Backnang. Maybe we can get on a southeast track from there."

Maulbronn, Duchy of Württemberg

"Nice monastery," Jeffie Garand said. "I thought that Protestants had given those up."

"The first Duke Ulrich secularized it when he turned Lutheran—took it away from the Cistercians," Friedrich said. "He kept the name 'monastery' for it, but it's been a boys' school ever since. Well, that is, it was up until the wars came. I was surprised to find anyone here at all. God knows, there's hardly anyone in Mühlacker. Before the war started, it had over a thousand people."

Johan Botvidsson appeared on their horizon, a letter in hand. "Do you know this man?"

Eberhard took the letter. "Konrad Widerhold? From Ziegenhain, up in Hesse? Of course I know him. I've known him since I was a child. He came into Württemberg military service in 1622, after Margrave Georg Friedrich of Baden lost that disastrous battle at Wimpfen to the imperials. Our father respected him immensely. When it comes to siege craft, nobody in this part of the Germanies is his equal."

"I know him, too," Sergeant Hartke said unexpectedly. "At least, Dagmar knows his wife."

Everybody in the room turned around.

"Widerhold is married to Anna Armgard. Her father used to be the commandant of Helgoland. It's a pretty small island. Dagmar's father was—still is, for that matter—the schoolteacher there. He—Dagmar's dad, his name is Niels Pedersen Menius—is something of an antiquarian, too, which is why he gave Dagmar and her sisters such peculiar names."

"Back to the topic," Derek Utt said.

"Anna, Wiederhold's wife, and Dagmar are the same age. They went to school together—all the years they went to school."

Utt smirked at Brahe. "Shall we tell Horn?"

"Only if we want to watch his hair turn white before he goes entirely bald."

Nils Brahe and Derek Utt were sharing a copy of the latest Frankfurt paper. The latest to reach them, at any rate.

"To be honest," Brahe said, I'm more relieved than anything else. The king may not be overjoyed by this latest joint behind-our-backs maneuver of Bernhard and the king in the Netherlands, but it turns Lorraine into a shield, albeit a very thin and narrow one, between the USE and France."

"By which you mean that if Turenne raids again, at least he'll have to go through somebody else's army first."

"Basically. Also, Fernando has conveniently swallowed up a very large number of Catholics. If those territories had been folded into the Province of Westphalia, they would have seriously changed the complexion of the region that Frederik of Denmark is administering. I can't quite see Wettin and Wilhelm of Hesse-Kassel, or, for that matter, Gustavus, wanting to add another province with a predominantly Catholic population to the USE. Either way, it would have turned into a huge bone of contention in parliament, right in the middle of the campaigning in the east."

"Which way next?" Derek Utt asked.

"Horn's block succeeded." Brahe gave one of his first genuine smiles in days. "So far, at least. How I love radios. His scouts say that the Irishmen are headed due east. If they keep going east, they'll hit Backnang, but the terrain isn't easy. Horn is moving his regiments east, south of Stuttgart, generally toward Schwäbisch-Gmünd. His cavalry's moving ahead. If they get there fast enough, before Butler gets past, the infantry are following in a forced march. Once they are there to hold the southern screen, the cavalry will start a screen to the north. He'll have a line between the dragoons and Bavaria."

"Well, then. Onward and upward, I suppose."

"General," Ulfsparre said. "General Brahe, sir, it's

Duke Friedrich. Er, that is, it's Lieutenant Württemberger. He's back from our latest scout. What he saw doesn't match with what we were getting from General Horn."

Mainz, April 1635

Springtime at the Horn of Plenty meant spring cleaning at the Horn of Plenty. Kunigunde and Ursula, with a fleet of temporarily hired maids, were turning the inn upside down and inside out. Bedding fluttered from the window sills. Sweeps shook soot down from the chimneys.

There was one resident for whom spring had no charms. "I wish I could have gone with Fritzi," Margarethe wailed. "I should have gone with Fritzi."

"Look at the cartoon, Margarethe," Justina said. "It's lovely. Another van de Passe, with the archbishop of Cologne cowering in a tent somewhere out in the dreary countryside."

"I don't want to look at cartoons. I just want Friedrich to come home."

Kunigunde and Ursula each handed her a handkerchief.

"If this weren't our own taproom," Reichard Donner said, "I would go out for a beer. Your wailing may drive me to it yet. Girl, if you don't stop sniveling, you are going to damage the child you are carrying. It will be born with the marks of teardrops running down its cheeks, not to mention snot dripping out of its nose."

❖   ❖   ❖

"At least the plague doesn't seem to have advanced east beyond Lorraine. Thus far. Except for the little pocket that our people stopped at the Rhine." Reichard Donner looked out at the meeting of the Mainz Committee of Correspondence. It could not be considered one of the larger or more effective CoC groups in the USE, but it no longer fit into the taproom at the Horn of Plenty. They had to rent space at the Freedom Arches. The holder of the Mainz franchise was of the opinion that business was business.

"Unless, of course, some of the dragoons had already contracted it and carried it into Swabia when the Irishmen managed to cross ahead of Brahe and Utt."

"You are a pessimist, Philipp Schaumann," Kunigunde said.

"It has stood me in good stead throughout my life."

"Does that mean," Margarethe asked, "that if Friedrich and Papa and Theo do capture the Irishmen, they might get the plague?"

Ursula handed her a handkerchief.

Justina sighed. "Pregnancy takes some girls this way. They weep from beginning to end."

"If I had to choose between that and morning sickness," Kunigunde observed, "I think I'd rather cry."

At the podium, Reichard was saying, "In regard to our campaign against the anti-Semitic agitators in response to the dastardly assassinations of Mayor Henry Dreeson of Grantville and the Reverend Enoch Wiley . . ."

"No," Wamboldt von Umstadt said to Johann Adolf von Hoheneck. "No, I do not approve of riots, or of mobs taking the law into their own hands. When it comes to my obligations in connection with protection of the Jewish population in the archdiocese of Mainz, however . . . Suffice it to say that I believe that the actions of the Committees of Correspondence have greatly lightened my burden for the next few years. That isn't to say, of course, that the organization won't be taking other positions and actions in the future that will make other aspects of my burden heavier."

Hoheneck pantomimed weighing items on the scales of *justitia.*

"A pagan goddess, if there ever was one," the archbishop said. "It's amazing how thoroughly we have managed to incorporate her into our supposedly Christian ideas about life."

Kornwestheim, Duchy of Württemberg, May 1635

"I have to give Butler credit," Brahe said. "I'd have thought it over ten times, and then ten times more, before bringing even mounted dragoons that close to Stuttgart, given how heavily Horn has it garrisoned."

"We're just lucky that our scouts caught them turning south. Horn's infantry—most of it—has stopped at Göppingen. He reports that he is prepared to turn them. The cavalry is going on north, in case the Irishmen head east again.

Waiblingen, Duchy of Württemberg, May 1635

"He's drunk," Dennis MacDonald's batman said, his face impassive.

"Since when hasn't he been drunk?" Geraldin turned around.

"He was possibly sober for about two hours, late Sunday morning. Father Taaffe conducted a field mass, with homily, that went on for ages and the colonel didn't remember to bring a flask."

The batman's answer was completely deadpan.

"So he's drunk. Old news."

"This time, he's drunk and riding a horse. He's gone outside the camp. When the sentry tried to stop him, the colonel cut him with his riding whip."

"Damn and blast. Send someone after him."

"Butler and Deveroux are riding ahead. They want to get into Schorndorf before the city council realizes we are coming. You're the only person here of the same rank as Colonel MacDonald. If you just send people after him . . ."

The batman didn't say it, for which Geraldin was grateful.

If Dennis was drunk enough to fight and sober enough to remember, he would have every member of the party sent to retrieve him up on charges of insubordination. Striking a superior officer. Who knew what. Floggings would ensue. Floggings at a minimum.

He sighed. "Order my horse saddled. Tell Shea to order his company mounted. I'll go after him."

"There's some guy cantering down the middle of the road down there around the bend, singing," Theo Pistor reported.

"So the local farmers are happy," Simrock said.

"He on a really expensive horse and he's not singing in German."

"Let's go see." Simrock shook his horse into a trot.

"Come back here, you two idiots." Lieutenant Friedrich Württemberger admitted to himself that he had just issued an order that was not in the official book.

Either they didn't hear him, or . . .

Chaplain Pistor suddenly showed up next to him. "What do those two young idiots think they are doing?"

For the first time since they met, Friedrich and his father-in-law were in harmony. Unfortunately, that was not enough to make Theo and Simrock rein in their mounts.

Pistor rode after them, screaming fatherly admonitions.

Friedrich looked at Hartke. "Move out. Catch up with them."

By the time they came around the bend, Theo and Simrock had stopped the singing man. Theo had hold of the horse's head.

A group of mounted dragoons appeared from around the next bend.

From that point, it was hack and slash, with a counterpoint of pistol shots.

"We won," Hartke pointed out a couple of hours later. "It wasn't exactly a by-the-book fracas, but we won. Sometimes these spontaneous skirmishes are the nastiest. In a set battle, the plan may not survive contact with the enemy, but at least you start with some kind of a plan. Sometimes you even have, 'if X, then Y, but if Q, then P and run like hell out.'"

"All logic would have indicated that the dragoons should have been moving in the other direction out of Waiblingen. East, not west." Simrock frowned.

"Human nature interfered with logic," Theo said. "The singing colonel was as drunk as a skunk."

"If Captain Duke Eberhard loses another brother," Hertling said. "If he does . . ."

"We were supposed to be watching out for them," Merckel said. "Two of us aren't even here. You left Bauer up at Euskirchen. I guess Heisel is still in the Irishmen's camp."

"We won," Brahe said. "Lieutenant Württemberger's small detachment delivered two of the four Irish colonels to you, too. I understand that to mean that you are halfway to your goal."

"You are perfectly correct," Derek Utt said. "We won."

"Who is on the next cot?" Chaplain Pistor asked. "Who is on the other side of you?"

Theo didn't have to twist around on his stool in the lazarette tent. He knew. "It's Friedrich."

Pistor didn't reply.

"Forgive them, Papa. Margarethe is expecting your first grandchild. 'Children's children are a crown to the aged.' Let me write and say that you forgive her, before it is too late. Remember, 'The Lord, the Lord, the compassionate and gracious God, slow to anger, abounding in love and faithfulness, maintaining love to thousands, and forgiving wickedness, rebellion, and sin.'"

Pistor snorted. "I am not so close to dead yet that you can get away with quoting scripture at me selectively. I taught you better than that, I hope, whether you learned the lesson or not. The next line from your first quotation is, 'And parents are the pride of their children.' Of your other one, the remainder of the verse reads, 'Yet he does not leave the guilty unpunished; he punishes the children and their children for the sin of the fathers to the third and fourth generation.' Nor should you try to bludgeon my tired mind with the parable of the wastrel son. The point of that is that the son repented. He realized he would be better off as the lowliest of his father's hired men. Can you tell me that Margarethe has repented this rebellious marriage? Can you assure me that she realizes she would be better off as a scullery maid in my kitchen than as the wife of that . . . ?"

He found no word adequate to describe his opinion of Friedrich Württemberger.

"Give her peace of heart, Papa. Please. 'Blessed are the peacemakers, for they will be called children of God.' and 'First go and be reconciled to your brother; then come and offer your gift.'"

Pistor shook his head. "No, the Word of God is not soft. Jesus said, 'All men will hate you because of me, but he who stands firm to the end will be saved.' Matthew reads also, 'I did not come to bring peace, but a sword . . . a man's enemies will be the members of his own household . . . anyone who loves his son or daughter more than me is not worthy of me . . .'"

"Papa . . ."

"'For where your treasure is, there your heart will be also.' Do not plague me further, Theo. The daughter I love chose a worldly treasure and until she repents, she has stored up for herself 'treasures on earth, where moth and rust destroy, and where thieves break in and steal.'"

"Forgive them before it is too late, Papa. Too late for Friedrich. Too late for you. Before you cry with the teacher in Ecclesiastes, 'In vain, in vain. Everything is utterly in vain.'"

Chaplain Pistor turned his head to the other side of the cot.

Derek Utt was tired of staff meetings. Still . . . he was holding one. Another one. "Brahe has to get back to Mainz to deal with the anti-Semitic movement in the Rhineland. Mostly it's been fairly orderly, but in places, it is getting out of hand."

Joel Matowski stood at as close to attention as he ever managed to get.

"You're going back to Fulda, Joel. You're in charge of the detachment returning MacDonald and Geraldin for trial. Kidnaping. Complicity to murder in connection with Schweinsberg's death. Have Hartke tell off twenty five men to go with you. He knows what I want, so he won't assign anyone who would get the idea of 'doing us a favor' by cutting their throats some dark night."

"Envy may be a sin, so color me green. I wish we had gotten that duty," Simrock said in disgust the next morning. "We don't get to take them back and see them hang. We get to sort through all the debris they abandoned in their tents."

"Yes, oh, whee." Theo picked up an oblong box that looked like a portable camp desk and unlatched it, unfolding the various parts. "This looks promising . . . what the hell?"

Simrock shook his head. "It's not a desk. It's a field

altar, with a little chalice and a tiny bottle of wine and some hosts—everything a priest needs to say mass."

"Here's a book in the drawer underneath. It's by some guy named 'Carve' who says that he's Butler's chaplain, right on the front page," Jeffie said. "Maybe he's a friend of Gruyard and they go around carving up people together."

"His name isn't 'Carve,'" Theo said with disgust. You're looking at capital letters, in Latin. There isn't any letter "U" the way there is in German—or in English, for that matter. The name's 'Carue' on the title page. In English, it ought to be "Carew,' I suppose, but if you printed that in Germany, almost everyone would want to say, 'Carev.' Stick with 'Carue.' Let me look."

Jeffie tossed it to him.

"This isn't a printed book. It's just a manuscript. He's just drawn the front to look as much like an engraved title page as he can. I guess he plans to publish it and wants the printer to have some idea of how he would like it to look, with family crests and stuff."

"What's it about?"

Simrock started paging through it. "God damn it, Jeffie. Run. Stop Matowski and the other the guys who are leaving with the Irishmen, right now."

Jeffie ran.

"Theo, get Colonel Utt."

"See," Simrock said to Derek Utt. "He's labeled it a 'book of travels.' *Reisebüchlein*, that is. Just the front page of it has the Latin-shaped letters. The rest of it's in German. My dictionary says that *Reisebüchlein* means a 'guide for travelers,' but . . ."

"It's a journal of the travels he's already done,"

Theo said. We read parts of it while Jeffie was chasing after you. It has notes on everywhere he's been, and where he's been is with Walter Butler as he ravaged his way across Europe these last ten years or so. He's been back to Ireland to visit his family a couple of times, but the rest of it, he's been with the Irish regiments—either with Butler or, if he wasn't in the field, with Deveroux."

"He's written down everywhere *they* have been," Simrock added. "And everything they've done. Talk about evidence . . ."

Jeffie shook his head. "He wasn't in Fulda with them when they kidnapped Schweinsberg, though. They left him behind with MacDonald."

Derek Utt looked at him sharply.

"Yeah, so we peeked."

"But he does say when they caught up with their regiments again, chasing after Archbishop Ferdinand after he retreated from Bonn."

"Simrock, take it to Joel," Utt said. "I'm sure the prosecutors will be happy to have it. Just let me write him a memo. Donner, you and Garand go with Sergeant Hartke to re-interview the rest of our prisoners. We're looking for someone named Thomas Carue, who may or may not be owning up to his name right now. Whatever he knows, we need to know it. Hartke, find me someone reliable in the middle of this mess. I need to send a memo on this over to General Brahe."

"You can ignore all the young prisoners, Sergeant Hartke," Simrock said on his way out the door, adding "sir" at the last minute, "unless you just want them to point him out to you if you can't find him any other way. This Carue has to be somewhere in his forties. The book says he's been a priest for a long time now. If you have anyone with you who can sort out different Irish accents, take him with you." Again, he tagged on, "sir," barely in time.

"Why?"

"The introduction says that he's from Tipperary." Simrock disappeared out the door.

"He's lucky that Brahe put him in the Fulda Barracks Regiment," Hartke commented. "In any other unit, he'd have been flogged to death by now. But he's really sort of useful, in his own way. Not as a soldier, exactly, but in his own way."

Utt smiled his agreement. Not that the Fulda Barracks Regiment had ever been, precisely, famous for its strict attention to military protocol. He was pretty sure that not even the most wildly radical CoC regiment could be worse at that.

"There's something I did notice," Hartke said. "Gruyard wasn't with the bunch we routed. That means he has to be with the batch that made it into Schorndorf."

"Both of them are dead," Theo said. "Papa and Friedrich. During the night."

"It wasn't unexpected." Eberhard stared at his boots. "Did he forgive them?"

"No," Theo said. "But he will."

Tata raised her eyebrows. "How can a dead man forgive?"

"'Like a fluttering sparrow or a darting swallow an undeserved curse does not come to rest.' That is part of the wisdom of Solomon. I am not going to leave Margarethe to live under an undeserved curse."

Theo straightened his shoulders. "She's going to get a letter from me, saying that they died in the same hospital tent, on neighboring cots. Which is perfectly true. The letter will also say that I exercised my persuasive powers to the utmost to bring Papa to a change of heart. That is also true. If she concludes that I succeeded . . . I'm not going to feel the slightest obligation to correct her assumption and I certainly hope . . ." He looked directly at Simrock, "that no one else ever will, either."

"Stuttgart," Eberhard said. "It isn't far from here to Stuttgart. Friedrich can be buried with our parents."

Tata put her head on his shoulder.

"I don't have the money to send Papa's body back to Hesse," Theo said. "He'll have to be buried here, like the other casualties, in unconsecrated ground."

Eberhard made a negative gesture. "Send him to Stuttgart with Friedrich. Bury him with our family. It's a Lutheran church and he's a Calvinist minister, but we own the crypt and for all practical purposes, we appoint the pastor. Pistor may turn over and over in the grave I give him, but it will probably make Margarethe feel better, so I decree that it will happen. Occasionally, there are advantages to simply being the boss."

"Eberhard," Tata said.

"What?"

"They shouldn't radio this to Mainz. They shouldn't radio this or put in a newspaper. Margarethe shouldn't find out that way. At the very least, they should let Theo send her a letter first."

He sighed. "It doesn't work that way. Whoever gets the news first will plaster it all over."

"Up-time," Joel said, "the army notified the next of kin. I've seen pictures, from the second world war. Two soldiers, walking up to a house, to tell the wife or mother."

"That was then. Now . . ." Eberhard looked out at the camp. "For half our men, probably, we don't even know who they really are, or where they come from."

"We know for Friedrich," Tata said stubbornly. "We know for Chaplain Pistor. Make them let me use the radio. I'll send a message to Papa. Someone in the CoC can tell her—not just some headline or broadcast. I'll make sure to say that Theo is alive and will be writing to her right away."

Section Five: See, I have given you this land.

Schorndorf, Württemberg, May 1635

"That was an outright catastrophe," Butler proclaimed. "We've lost nearly half the effectives we had when we left Euskirchen, two colonels, and a half-dozen other officers, before we have even reached Bavaria. Duke Maximilian is not going to be a happy man."

"And when Maximilian is unhappy, *everybody* is unhappy." Deveroux looked up. "Where did that phrase come from? It's been making the rounds for months."

"I greatly fear," Anna Marie von Dohna said, "that it originates from a comedy routine that is performed on the Voice of America."

Deveroux subsided.

"Where did you hear the Voice of America, O charming spouse of mine?"

"Dislav told me."

"At least we made it into Schorndorf."

"Barely."

"Once more," Brandt said. "The tuna tin is very weak, but I want to try just once more."

"Where am I going to throw the antenna, here inside a town?" Heisel asked.

"We are in the garrets, on the top floor of the castle. If you can lean out the window, after dark, and swing the wire with the rock on the end out a little and then up, over the roof tiles . . ."

"I don't think it's a good idea. What can be so important? Brahe has to know that the Irishmen are in here. He's right outside the walls. With a lot of new friends."

"One more time, with where the various units are quartered and how much ammunition they have. Our commanders do not know about the gunpowder in the city armory. Once more, only."

"I guess we might as well try it. This opening isn't very big, though."

Heisel tossed out the rock tied to the end of the wire and started to swing it, aiming for enough momentum to get it over the roof. Ten feet or so below the window, the wire caught on a spike that someone, at an unknown date, for a long-forgotten reason, had pounded partway into the mortar about six inches above the window on the floor below. The rock jerked back, breaking the window.

The window happened to belong to the room

assigned to Father Taaffe, who called a guard. That guard called some more guards, one of whom had a clever idea. He went outdoors and looked up while father Taaffe signaled from the window. Then he counted from the end of the building and identified the window above the priest's chamber. He identified the ones on either side of it, too, just to be on the safe side.

"Go," Brandt said. "My quarters are in this room. Yours are not. Go."

Heisel, a sensible man, went.

A group of guards caught Brandt, and hauled him in front of Butler, who turned him over to Gruyard for questioning. After some time, under extreme stress, he revealed Heisel's name.

Heisel's reaction to his own arrest was, "Well, tough shit."

Butler concluded that much of the "bad luck" that plagued him throughout this entire campaign had really been caused by these men and their tuna tin. He demanded information on when they were embedded with him, by whom, why, and what they were doing all along.

Gruyard went contentedly back to work.

Butler was truly astonished to hear that all this trouble and fuss was being made about the death of Schweinsberg and the raid into Fulda the autumn before.

"Talk about ancient history," he complained to Deveroux.

"Keep at them," he said to Gruyard.

The answers the two men reluctantly provided during the next session directed the interviewers toward Countess Anna Marie von Dohna's favored servant Dislav.

There was considerable discussion among those present in the torture chamber about whether or not Colonel Butler would really want to know this.

The conclusion was that even though he might not want to, he really needed to.

This was followed by considerably more discussion on the general topic of belling the cat.

Eventually they bucked it up the chain of command to Deveroux.

Butler was furious.

Butler's wife was even more furious when the guards came to arrest Dislav and transport him to the torture chamber.

Two of Deveroux's more mechanically inclined aides stared at the tuna tin.

"I am not an engineer, nor did I ever wish to be one," Turlough O'Brien said.

Ned Callaghan shook it. "The man whom Gruyard is questioning told the truth about one thing, at least. The object is dead."

"It certainly seems to be. It should be safe to open it, I guess."

An hour later, they stared at numerous small, oddly shaped, pieces of . . . unidentifiable stuff.

"Perhaps we shouldn't have taken it apart after all," Callaghan said. "Or, at least, maybe we should have taken notes and drawn a picture of how it looked when we first opened it."

"Maybe we should try to put it back together."

"Let's at least put it all back in the tin. After all,

Colonel Butler doesn't have any idea what it looked like inside before we removed the lid."

Neither of them connected the tuna tin with the rock on a wire that had broken Father Taffe's window. Irish dragoon regiments in the service of Bavarian dukes were not exactly hotbeds of cutting edge technology.

Then it occurred to O'Brien to take the tuna tin to Geraldin's farrier, who was known to have a mechanical turn of mind. "Maybe he can figure it out," he said.

The farrier was in the middle of shoeing a horse, so they left it with his apprentice. Peter Schild realized right away that something really bad must have happened to Heisel and Brandt.

"I don't have the slightest idea what it is," he said. "You'll have to wait until Master Nugent can look at it." His bewilderment seemed very sincere. Caspar Zeyler might be a natural-born liar, but Schild was no slouch. What's more, he had been practicing the skill for months, now.

"Does this strike you as sort of, 'meanwhile, back at the ranch'?" Jeffie asked Hertling. "Just camping here and staring at a set of walls after we've been chasing all over the map?"

"We can only hope the ones you call 'the high mucky-mucks' are plotting something good. Something outstanding or excellent, even. I thought you enjoyed talking to your friends who came with you in the Ring of Fire."

"Old home week, high school reunion, and a bean-fest, all in one. I haven't seen some of these Grantville guys who are with Horn for two or three years. Yeah, it's been nice to catch up. The local news columns in the Grantville paper tell me who's getting hatched, matched, and dispatched, but they don't usually say who was hitting on whose wife at someone else's wedding. Not unless it ends up in the 'Arrests' column."

"Those walls are fairly new, aren't they?" Jeffie asked.

Eberhard nodded. "They were built by the first Duke Ulrich close to a century ago, when people were just beginning to use the new designs. The old curtain walls were already irregular in shape. He rebuilt and added the bastions at the angles."

"What's the circumference?"

"About a mile. The ditching complicates things, of course. In some places, it's a good forty yards wide."

"Even so, once we get Horn's artillery up here," Hertling said, "we can make a fine mess." He was perched on a rock up on the Ottilienberg that overlooked the city.

"*Ja.* It's going to take a great deal of heaving and hauling, though. Damn," Hartke said, leaning over. "Look at the town. Something's on fire."

"Sure is," Hertling agreed. "Not good. Not on a windy day like this. Do you suppose anyone inside the walls has noticed?"

"If they had, they'd be running around like ants."

"They're starting to."

"By the bowels of Christ!"

"For shame, Gutzler. For shame to blaspheme so. If anyone hears you, the magistrate will fine you a stiff one." Barbara Mahlin shook her fist over her cart of well-picked-over second-hand clothing.

"My hat. Look at it blow. It's only for work—not

worth much more than those rags you sell. Some damned Irishman took my good one right off my head last market day, though, so now it's the only one I have. I want it back." Gutzler went dashing down the side of the square.

"Sure looks stupid, doesn't he, bouncing along like that with his pot belly flopping?" Johann Leylins guffawed. Then, "Great God Almighty! What was that? It looked like Gutzler's been swallowed by a ball of hellfire blowing out of the cook shop doorway."

Inside the cook shop, a fourteen-year-old apprentice, his hair singed off, picked himself up from against the back wall and looked in horror at the torch that, less than a minute before, had been his master. For less than half a half minute, he froze in place, remembering. The gust of wind, causing a blow-back down the chimney, scattering coals and sparks at old Master Steiss, who had just been putting the poker to the green wood. He'd jumped back and tripped. He'd tripped over . . . that cauldron of hot lard where they had just finished cooking funnel cakes, and the lard had gone flooding into the fireplace.

If nothing else, the apprentice was agile on his feet. He dived over the closed bottom half of the double door, out into the alley, landed with a somersault, stood up, and screamed "Fire!" at the top of his lungs.

"Who's that yelling?" Hans Frinck called from next door.

"That no-good young Michael Haug who works in the cook shop."

"Somebody should teach that boy not to cry 'wolf.'"

"He's . . ." Frinck's wife Agnes poked her head out the door. "Fire!" she shrieked. "Fire on a windy day. Fire!"

Frinck ran for his buckets.

Young Haug was running down the street calling "Fire watch! Fire watch!"

Melchior Schiffer had the fire watch functioning in ten minutes. They drilled for this. Bregenzer at the well pump, with Leylins's younger son trading off with him. A chain of women to pass the filled buckets. He counted. Here came Greiners, dashing toward him from the square, calling that Minder would have to take Gutzler's place, because Gutzler was dead. Reisch. Kapffer. Ensslin. They went to work in a practiced rhythm.

"Schiffer." The apprentice was jumping up and down. "Schiffer!"

"Get out of our way, boy."

"Schiffer, I have to go back in."

"Nobody goes back into a burning building. Get out of our way. We have to wet down the ones on each side. More, in this wind."

"But, Schiffer—"

He found himself flat on his back in the street.

"What I was going to say, if you'd have let me," Michael Haug said, "was that Master Steiss had an open barrel of flour in there. From the funnel cakes."

Ensslin was picking himself up. Reisch never would again.

Hess and Hirschman rounded the corner and slid to a stop.

Barbara Mahlin ran, abandoning her cart of old clothes in the middle of the square.

"Wet the farther buildings," Schiffer yelled. "Haug, you're nimble. Get up on Kunkel's roof and look for sparks. Hirschmann, you go up too. We'll throw you the bucket rope and you can pulley up some water."

They all worked together, just as they were supposed to, but just then the wind whipped around, first from due south and then for a few minutes from due west, before settling back to its original direction. Frinck's pewter shop caught, but luckily Haug and Hirschmann made it down the ladder before Kunkel's did. Then the potter's shop next beyond it. Schiffer stepped back as he watched the flames jump the alley. Kugler's, Burckhardt's, Weisser's, Reitter's, Palm's, Aichmann's. The saddlery. The cook shop just had to be in the southwest quadrant. The wind was blowing the fires toward all the rest of the town.

"Give it up," he called. "Give it up. Evacuate."

Jakob Breidner, the night watchman, came running. "They won't let us out. The gate guards. The cursed Irishmen. They say there's a siege on. They won't open the gates to let the women and children out."

"Get a couple of barrels of gunpowder, light fuses, and roll them to the damned gates. They'll open them then, I bet. Then . . ."

"Then get the rest of the gunpowder out through the gates," Breidner screamed. "As soon as you get a gate open, roll the barrels of gunpowder out, upwind, through the south gate. We've enough in store to do more damage to ourselves than the Swedes can possibly manage with no more than the few guns that Horn brought."

Schiffer was thinking. What was flammable? Wood, of course—the timber in the *Fachwerk* houses. Flour, as they had just had cause to observe. Wheat, oats, hay, linen, bedding, clothing, paper . . . and there went the apothecary's shop.

And, of course, it couldn't be helped that a lot of

people were trying to rescue possessions from their own houses that were in the path of the flames rather than contributing to stopping the fire overall. That always happened.

Neuhauser and Besserer. Members of the city council at last. Where were the four Bürgermeisters? Given how firmly the town's patricians excluded its ordinary people from a role in its government, the least they could do was belly up to the bar themselves when they were needed.

"We've been up at the castle, talking to the Irish officers," Besserer panted. Volz is still there. They don't understand about the wind at this season. Steinbock says . . ."

Schiffer never heard what Steinbock, the appointed ducal administrator of the city and district of Schorndorf, said. A muffled roar told him that one of the townsmen had managed to get a barrel of gunpowder up against the south gate before the fuse died.

"Open it," he screamed. "Open it with your bodies. If the guards shoot, die for your city. The rest of you, if someone falls, you keep going. Die a hero instead of just dying in the fire. That's what we'll all do if they keep us packed in here like chickens roasting on a spit. Go!"

The fire wasn't crackling any more. It was starting to roar.

The master of the Latin school had his boys organized, their arms full of books, and was herding them towards the south gate.

Here came Volz, down from the castle with two of the Irish officers.

He heard the ominous sound of a stone cracking

from the heat and added to his list of things that would burn. Plaster, whitewash, lime mortar.

"The church roof has caught," someone called. "We need to try to save the vestments, the altar cloth. The chalice and patens."

"There's no way we can save the building. Just the height of it makes it impossible. We simply can't get up there." Schiffer turned around. "What are the Irishmen doing?"

"Opening the gates—finally opening the gates— and trying to get their horses out. They won't let us Schorndorf people near them, except for the south gate that we blew. One of them shot Barbara Mahlin when she tried to push her way through with their horses."

"Their horses," someone said. "And our money. All the 'contributions' we have paid to keep them from plundering through the town. Controlled robbery instead of uncontrolled robbery, systematic instead of random. The officers are taking out the money chests."

"Go to the jail," Besserer called. "Let the prisoners loose—the ones the Irish locked up. Maybe they'll be grateful enough to help us fight the fire, but even if they aren't, we can't just let them broil there if the wind turns."

"It was good of them to bring the keys, but I'm not certain that I can walk." Julius Brandt tried to stand, but stumbled. "Leave me here and find Gruyard. He was in the jail when the fire broke out. You must take him to your Colonel Utt."

"No, Julius, my friend. Come. Walk. I will not leave

you to the fire. I will support you." Heisel pulled one of Brandt's arms over his shoulders.

"You must forgive me. I betrayed you. I gave them your name."

"There is nothing to forgive. Anyone would have done the same. I gave them Dislav's name. I find that it is far easier to make proclamations about being stoic under torture when you are not being tortured right at that moment. I have seen unpleasant things before. Even experienced them. In his own way, though, Gruyard is an artist." Heisel turned his head. "What is happening down the hall?"

"The man with the keys let some other prisoners out. He was offering clemency if they would come fight the fire."

"Scarcely feasible for us, I fear. I am not in shape to fight a field mouse."

"If we can only get to the Swedish lines . . ."

"The horses," Timothy Nugent screamed. "The horses. I can't hold them."

"I'll take a couple," Caspar said. He grabbed for the reins.

"Not that way."

"I'll come after you as soon as I can. I need to help a couple of old friends."

Zeyler headed for the jail.

The noise at the other end of the hall got louder. Letting Brandt down on the floor, Heisel limped toward the source of the disturbance."

"Dislav? What?"

"Maybe you promised to bring this human slime

to the up-timers for a fair trial as they see it," Dislav said. "I did not. See the pretty thumbscrews? I thought this was a quite original way to use them."

Heisel gagged.

Dislav shook his head. "The colonel beat my dear young lady when he found out that I was your friend. That was neither fair nor just."

"Uh. Dislav. Maybe we should get out of here. Shorndorf is burning."

The Czech shook his head. "The wind's blowing the other way. The castle will be all right, and the countess is in her quarters upstairs. I can't leave without her. Besides, I'm busy right now."

Schiffer had found a bullhorn. "The Swedes are coming in, some of them, at least. They're helping fight the fire. Look for orange uniforms and work with them. Otherwise, the Swedes still outside are picking off the Irish, one by one, as they come out with their mounts."

"What was that last noise we heard?"

"The church roof. The heat weakened the beams so much that it plunged right down into the sanctuary."

"This is going to have to be the last load."

The old man nodded his head. "But, wait. I still don't have the portable baptistry." He headed toward the sacristy.

"*Aus! Jetzt!* The roof is about to fall."

"I am the pastor of this parish, the *Dekan* of the parish of Schorndorf. Who are you to say 'Out! Now!' to me or order me around?"

The stocky young man in the orange uniform

grabbed the *Dekan* by the waist and threw him down the church steps, followed by a clatter of miscellaneous silver plated vessels on the stone steps.

"By my authority as a called servant of God . . ."

The roof fell.

"We'll never get out," Heisel said. "Look what's happening. Our men outside figure that anyone on a horse is an Irishman trying to escape. But Julius can't walk—the wounds on his legs just keep bleeding and his legs shake so. Maybe Gruyard got in a hurry and cut more muscle than he intended to. I don't think I can walk, either, even though Gruyard didn't slice me up quite so badly. At least, I didn't think so right after he finished the last session. I thought he was holding back, saving something for the next time."

"Leave it to me," Zeyler answered. "I'll think of something. Maybe some of Brahe's men who have come inside the walls will recognize us."

"It's getting dark." Merckel wiped the sweat from his forehead.

"We'll be watching the fire all night."

"Why doesn't it ever rain when you could use it? All that mud over by Germersheim, and now this dry wind. It's enough to make a man believe in hell."

"What it reminds me of," Jeffie Garand said, "is that Jerry Lee Lewis song. 'Great Balls of Fire.'" He went back to scooping earth on smouldering embers.

"Merckel," someone called. "Ludwig Merckel. Over here."

"Heisel," he said. "God be praised."

❖   ❖   ❖

"So far, the walls have contained the fire, Colonel Utt. I wouldn't count on it for tomorrow, though. It could still jump them if the wind really picks up." Moritz Klott, one of Horn's aides-de-camp eyed the embers of Schorndorf with a wary expression. "We know that your men are exhausted, but better keep them on alert."

"What's left? Anything more than I can see from here, that is?" Utt asked. They were standing at the south gate.

"Outside of the walls, there's a little suburb to the north—maybe three hundred people live there and it has a couple of inns." Klott checked his stack of paperwork. "We're using that for emergency housing for the survivors. The cemetery is outside the walls and has a little chapel. We'll hold the funerals there. Butler had given orders to have all that leveled so his men would have a clear view from the walls, but they hadn't gotten it done yet. We're lucky, in a way, that we were so close behind them. If they'd had a couple of weeks to dig in . . ."

"There are a lot of 'ifs.' If they had artillery, if, if, if. We have to deal with what is." Derek shook his head, looking at the young officers who were awaiting further instructions.

"Overall, though," Simrock said, "that was quite a roundup. Butler and Deveroux are in custody."

"Do we have Gruyard?" Derek was far from forgetting Schweinsberg's death and the popular reaction to it in Fulda and Grantville.

"We have what we are told is his body," Klott said. "Or the remnants of it. Searchers found it in the prison. It will be turned over to you."

"What else do I need to know?"

"Butler's wife is demanding to be allowed to leave. She rode out the fire on the far side of the castle and has her own staff, including a big, tough footman who seems to have been badly injured. Rather than accompany her husband to Fulda and stand by him during the trial, she wants to go back to Bohemia."

"Using what for money?"

"Some of Butler's accumulated loot, probably." Klott looked at Utt. "Have you dealt with her?"

"Not personally, no."

"General Horn has. She was demanding to be assigned one of the houses in the little suburb for her own personal use on the grounds that her chambers in the castle are all sooty. He's reached the conclusion that whatever she makes off with, it will be money well spent just to get rid of her."

"There sure isn't much of it left," Merckel said. "Great buildings turned into heaps of stones, into dust and ashes."

"The back part of the church. What's it called? Where the priests pray." Kolb sucked on his pipe. "That's still standing."

"The chancel. That back part is called a chancel. The front part is called a nave."

"Where'd you ever learn all that stuff, Lutz?"

Merckel looked away. "My father was a pastor. Back in Saxe-Weimar."

Kolb drew on his pipe again. "There are two complete houses standing. Count 'em. Two, both over against the wall, on the side the wind was coming from. Quite a few partials on the west side of town. Maybe some of them can be shored up."

"We're using the standing ones for infirmaries. After dark last night, we ran into a little old man in a black robe, standing by one of them and hugging a batch of old records. He is—was—the clerk at the Holy Spirit Hospital. That's all he managed to save—he said the whole civil archives, with people's wills and such, went up in smoke."

"Captain Duke Eberhard got the marriage and baptism records out of the church. That's what he was doing when . . ." Kolb looked down at his feet.

"And the castle. It's still there. Ugly clunker, with those big round towers at each end. If nobody had ever built a castle here to start with . . ."

Kolb shook his head. "In this location, right on the east border of the duchy? Nah. If it hadn't been our dukes, it would have been somebody else. It's a place that just begs for someone to plunk a fort down in it."

"It was a pretty enough town. Do you suppose they'll ever be able to build it all back?"

"Our duke!" the *Dekan* exclaimed in horror. "The young man who was so severely injured in saving me is truly our duke?"

"You got it in one, man," Jeffie Garand answered. "Eberhard saved your stinking hide." Then he switched to German. "The medics say they won't be able to save him. If he hadn't breathed in so much smoke that his lungs are bad, he might have a chance to get over the trauma of a double above-the-knee amputation. If his legs hadn't been crushed by that beam, he might have survived the smoke inhalation. He'd have had serious long-term lung damage, but he would have lived. As things stand, though . . ." Jeffie gave the *Dekan* a hard look. "If I were you, I'd go back, sort through all the things you swore absolutely had to be gotten out of your church building, and hope you have your funeral book."

The *Dekan* rose.

"Even better, if I were you," Jeffie added, "I'd make myself scarce before Hertling, Merckel, Kolb, and Heisel find you. Not to mention Colonel Utt. I wouldn't describe anyone in the Fulda Barracks regiment as being real happy right now."

A tent outside Schorndorf

"It's odd," Eberhard rasped. "Even after von Sickingen's men killed Ulrich, even after the Irishmen killed Friedrich, I didn't really expect to die. Not yet. Not now. Not so soon."

Tata nodded.

"Do you have my Montaigne? Where were we in the reading?"

"In the middle of the essay about cannibals."

He nodded.

Tata smiled. "Ah, yes. 'Valor is stability, not of legs and arms, but of the courage and the soul; it does not lie in the quality of our horse or our weapons, but in our own. He that falls obstinate in his courage—'" Her voice trailed away. She looked down toward the far end of the cot. "'*Si succiderit, de genu pugnat.*'—I learned that much Seneca from you in this last year. Sometimes, I think you love Seneca even more than you do Montaigne. Maybe even more than the Bible, though you shouldn't."

"'If his legs fail him, he fights on his knees.' That

presumes, of course, that he has knees left. I feel weirdly calm about this whole thing, not that I ever expected to be a philosopher. Maybe I'm not entirely in this universe the theologians think the Ring of Fire created. Maybe some essential part of me was left behind, with that other Eberhard, in the universe where we were born. Maybe we're only echoes of what we would have been."

He tried to push himself up against the pillows, wincing when Tata put her hands under his armpits to help him.

"No, don't give me any more of the opium. I need to have my mind clear enough that nobody can deny that I know what I'm doing. What are those next lines?

". . . he who, for any danger of imminent death, abates nothing of his assurance; who, dying, yet darts at his enemy a fierce and disdainful look, is overcome not by us, but by fortune; he is killed, not conquered; the most valiant are sometimes the most unfortunate. There are defeats more triumphant than victories."

"It wasn't a defeat, though," Tata said. "Not even a triumphant defeat like that of Leonidas and the Spartans. We won."

"At the expense of the destruction of one of my towns and most of its people. What's left of the people? Less than a hundred men, I'd guess. More women and children, but it's still in the hundreds rather than the thousands. How are they going to live? What kind of a *Landesvater* have I been to my children to bring this fate down on them?"

"Victory is victory. At least, since the Irishmen had quartered themselves here, they didn't destroy everything in the fields. The people who still live will eat next winter."

Eberhard shook his head.

Tata stood up and shook her fist at him. "It would have been a lot worse to let four cavalry regiments owing their allegiance to Maximilian have free range to raid through Swabia with the USE people chasing after them. That would have been right back to the bad old days, before the Ring of Fire came. That's what kind of a father you have been to your country. That's what Papa used to say to me when I was a naughty child and he whipped me—that it would be worse for me in the long run if he didn't use the rod when I needed it."

"All right. It's a victory. I won't be enjoying it, though. Has that damned clerk finished writing up the clean copies?"

"Almost."

"I wish I'd been able to see Friedrich and Margarethe's baby."

"Your sister will take care of them. She has gone from Strassburg to Mainz since Friedrich was killed. Papa radioed to us. She took your little sisters with her. From what I've heard of Antonia, anybody who tries to keep her from taking care of them will be very, very sorry."

"General Horn will make the emperor understand, won't he? Everything that was personally Friedrich's is to go to Margarethe and the baby, no matter what our uncles try to grab?"

"He was here when you dictated the will. He'll be back to witness when you sign it. Colonel Utt is here, and Duke Bernhard's man, the colonel they call Raudegen."

"Given under Our hand and seal at Schorndorf in Our duchy of Württemberg this twenty-eighth day of May in the year of our Lord 1635." Widerhold finished his reading.

Horn looked at Utt.

"You are certain that this is your will and testament?" Horn asked.

"Yes." Eberhard grinned. "All five copies."

"You are fully aware of the complications that may ensue—no, that certainly will ensue?"

"As our friend Colonel Utt here would be likely to say," Duke Eberhard grinned again. Every time, it looked more like a skull smiling. ". . . quoting his lawyerly wife, 'to the best of my knowledge and belief,' I am aware. Am I the omniscient deity to say that I am fully aware? Just let me sign."

"Your personal properties to be divided in four shares, one each to your sisters and one to Agathe Donner, here present, as life incomes. Absolutely to any heirs of their bodies, should they have such; in default of heirs of their bodies, to your brother Friedrich's child; in case such child should die without heirs of his or her body . . ."

"Yes, yes, yes. The quill, please."

"The duchy itself . . ."

Since Horn's clerk was still delaying, Tata dipped the quill and passed it to him. She turned to the quartermaster and other witnesses. "You heard him. All of you heard him."

Eberhard signed.

Widerhold's voice went on:

"The duchy of Württemberg itself, independent and separate from any arbitrary provisions that were made at the Congress of Copenhagen in June of the year of our Lord one thousand six hundred and thirty-four, in regard to the establishment of a Province of Swabia as one of the component political divisions of the United States of Europe under the governance of Gustavus II Adolphus, king of Sweden and emperor of said United States of Europe, said provisions having been made without regard to or consultation with the will of the people of said duchy—"

Eberhard interrupted him. "I leave the duchy with all its parts and dependencies, rights and responsibilities to its people. My people. I leave to the people of the duchy, now its citizens rather than its subjects, the right to govern themselves and not be disposed of, willy-nilly, by emperors or prime ministers or diplomatic congresses. With a lot of legal language to ensure that I've done everything I can to make it happen. And copies not just to the official representatives of Gustavus Adolphus, but also . . ."

Tata handed one of the signed copies to Derek Utt and another to Widerhold. "All hail Johannes Althusius and the sovereignty of the people."

In the silence of the room, Utt laughed.

Tata joined in the laughter.

At last, so did Eberhard. "The king of Sweden can make what he wants of it. I wish him joy. I wish the prime minister of the United States of Europe joy.

I wish my greedy uncles joy. I wish Margrave Georg Friedrich of Baden, supposed imperial administrator of a united Province of Swabia joy, and advise him to worry about Augsburg and the Bavarians, Tyrol and the Breisgau, with particular attention to Egon von Fürstenberg, instead of Württemberg." His voice weakened, grating. "Hell, Tata, I even wish your father joy. Hail to Reichard Donner, to the Horn of Plenty, and the hapless, hopeless, helpless Mainz Committee of Correspondence. *Ave atque vale.*"

The others went back to the things they had to do. Agathe stayed.

"Lift me, Tata. I'm sliding down."

She put her hands under his armpits again and pushed up.

"There's no window in here."

"I can open the tent flap."

"Do. Go stand in the sunshine."

She stood there a few minutes, looking out at the movement and listening to the noise of an army in camp.

"Joy, Tata. I wish you joy."

She waited a few minutes more before she called the chaplain.

Afterword by Eric Flint

I've been asked repeatedly, over the past few years, to provide fans of the 1632 series with a recommended order in which to read the various books in the series. And . . .

I've always tried to evade the issue. Partly, out of a stubborn (and perhaps infantile) resistance to cursed rules and regulations and such. Mostly, though, simply out of laziness. Damnation, it's *hard* to figure out a neat and precise sequence for this series. In fact, it's downright impossible.

That is so by design, not by accident. One of the things I'm trying to do with the 1632 series, to a degree never even attempted by any other alternate history series (including my own, such as the Belisarius series and the Sam Houston series), is to portray as far as possible the chaos and complexity of real history.

Fictional narrative has its own imperatives, and two of them produce a view of history which is radically false.

The first is that, willy-nilly, a fictional narrative

will tend to give support to the so-called Great Man Theory of history. If you're not familiar with this particular piece of intellectual drivel, it's the thesis that most historical development is caused by the ideas and/or actions of a small number of "great men." Personally, I think it's a toss-up whether the notion is more inane than it is offensive—indeed, ultimately immoral—or the reverse. But regardless of what I think in the abstract, when I sit down as an author to write an historically-based novel, it's very difficult not to slide in that direction. That's simply because, by its very nature, fictional narrative focuses on one or at most a handful of major characters. Because their actions are at the center of the *story*, the reader is inevitably given the impression that their actions are at the center of . . .

Well, if it's a novel like the ones I usually write, full of political and military fire and thunder . . .

Damn near everything. All the more so when I'm working with characters like Mike Stearns (or Belisarius or Sam Houston, in other series) who *are* legitimately central to historical developments.

The second problem is that a fictional narrative will inevitably make everything seem very neat and logical and orderly. Again, that's willy-nilly—because in the nature of things a story requires a *plot*, a plot is defined by a story arch, and arches are very orderly things.

But the real architecture of history is completely different. It's wildly complex, intricate to the point of being baroque in the details, and often downright contradictory.

What I've tried to do with the 1632 series, insofar

as possible, is to at least undermine those tendencies. And I've done so in a couple of ways.

First, I encourage—indeed, organize—other authors to participate in creating the 1632 universe. I do, of course, retain overall control of the material, but I exercise that control as lightly as possible. Occasionally, I will squelch a proposal by another author to write a story that establishes X, Y or Z, because for one reason or another that would create major problems for me in material I'm planning to work on later. But I'm far more likely to approve a proposal and publish such a story, even if it requires me to do some fancy footwork down the road.

Why? Because the continual and constant introduction of such unexpected developments keeps the series loose, so to speak. To put it another way, I try to use the imaginations of other authors as a substitute for the inevitable surprises that historical developments spring on all members of the human race.

The second method I use is to consciously and deliberately—some might even say, with malice aforethought—plan an over-arching framework for the series that does *not* follow any clear and definite sequence, in terms of the order in which the volumes should be read.

Whenever someone asks me "what's the right order?" for reading the 1632 series, I'm always tempted to respond: "I have no idea. What's the right order for studying the Thirty Years War? If you find it, apply that same method to the 1632 series."

However, that would be a bit churlish—and when it comes down to it, authors depend upon the goodwill of their readers. So, as best I can, here goes.

The first book in the series, obviously, is *1632*. That is the foundation novel for the entire series and the only one whose place in the sequence is definitely fixed.

Thereafter, you should read either the anthology titled *Ring of Fire* or the novel *1633*, which I co-authored with David Weber. It really doesn't matter that much which of these two volumes you read first, so long as you read them both before proceeding onward. That said, if I'm pinned against the wall and threatened with bodily harm, I'd recommend that you read *Ring of Fire* before you read *1633*.

That's because *1633* has a sequel which is so closely tied to it that the two volumes almost constitute one single huge novel. So, I suppose you'd do well to read them back to back.

That sequel is *1634: The Baltic War*, which I also co-authored with David Weber. Together with *1632* and *1633*, *1634: The Baltic War* constitutes what can be considered the "main line" or even the spinal cord of the entire series. Why? First, because it's in these three novels that I depict the major political and military developments which have a tremendous impact on the entire complex of stories. Secondly, because these "main line" volumes focus on certain key characters in the series—Mike Stearns and Rebecca Abrabanel, first and foremost, as well as Gretchen Richter and Jeff Higgins.

The next book which will appear in this main line sequence will be my solo novel, *1635: The Eastern Front*. No definite date has been set as yet for the publication of that volume, but it will almost certainly appear sometime in the last months of 2010.

Once you've read *1632*, *Ring of Fire*, *1633* and *1634: The Baltic War*, you will have a firm grasp of the basic framework of the series. From there, you can go in one of two directions: either read *1634: The Ram Rebellion* or *1634: The Galileo Affair*.

There are advantages and disadvantages either way. *1634: The Ram Rebellion* is an oddball volume, which has some of the characteristics of an anthology and some of the characteristics of a novel. It's perhaps a more challenging book to read than the Galileo volume, but it also has the virtue of being more closely tied to the main line books. *Ram Rebellion* is the first of several volumes which basically run parallel with the main line volumes but on what you might call a lower level of narrative. A more positive way of putting that is that these volumes depict the changes produced by the major developments in the main line novels, as those changes are seen by people who are much closer to the ground than the statesmen and generals who figure so prominently in books like *1632*, *1633*, and *1634: The Baltic War*.

Of course, the distinction is only approximate. There are plenty of characters in the main line novels— Thorsten Engler springs immediately to mind—who are every bit as "close to the ground" as any of the characters in *1634: The Ram Rebellion*.

Whichever book you read first, I do recommend that you read both of them before you move on to *1634: The Bavarian Crisis*. In a way, that's too bad, because *Bavarian Crisis* is something of a direct sequel to *1634: The Baltic War*. The problem with going immediately from *Baltic War* to *Bavarian Crisis*, however, is that there is a major political development portrayed at length and in great detail in *1634: The Galileo Affair* which antedates the events portrayed in the Bavarian story.

Still, you could read any one of those three volumes—to remind you, these are *1634: The Ram Rebellion, 1634: The Galileo Affair* and *1634: The Bavarian Crisis*—in any order you choose. Just keep in mind that if you read the Bavarian book before the other two you will be getting at least one major development out of chronological sequence.

After those three books are read . . .

Again, it's something of a toss-up between three more volumes: the second *Ring of Fire* anthology and the two novels, *1635: The Cannon Law* and *1635: The Dreeson Incident*. On balance, though, I'd recommend reading them in this order because you'll get more in the way of a chronological sequence:

> *Ring of Fire II*
> *1635: The Cannon Law*
> *1635: The Dreeson Incident*

The time frame involved here is by no means rigidly sequential, and there are plenty of complexities involved. To name just one, my story in the second *Ring of Fire* anthology, the short novel *The Austro-Hungarian Connection*, is simultaneously a sequel to Virginia's story in the same anthology, several stories in various issues of the *Gazette*—as well as my short novel in the first *Ring of Fire* anthology, *The Wallenstein Gambit*.

What can I say? It's a messy world—as is the real one. Still and all, I think the reading order recommended above is certainly as good as any and probably the best.

We come now to the current volume, which you

hold in your hand: Virginia DeMarce's *1635: The Tangled Web*. This collection of inter-related stories runs parallel to many of the episodes in *1635: The Dreeson Incident* and lays some of the basis for the stories which will be appearing in the next anthology, *1635: The Wars on the Rhine*.

That leaves the various issues of the *Gazette,* which are *really* hard to fit into any precise sequence. The truth is, you can read them pretty much any time you choose.

It would be well-nigh impossible for me to provide any usable framework for the twenty-six electronic issues of the magazine, so I will restrict myself simply to the five volumes of the *Gazette* which have appeared in paper editions. With the caveat that there is plenty of latitude, I'd suggest reading them as follows:

Read *Gazette I* after you've read *1632* and alongside *Ring of Fire*. Read *Gazettes II* and *III* alongside *1633* and *1634: The Baltic War*, whenever you're in the mood for short fiction. Do the same for *Gazette IV,* alongside the next three books in the sequence, *1634: The Ram Rebellion, 1634: The Galileo Affair* and *1634: The Bavarian Crisis*. Then read *Gazette V* after you've read *Ring of Fire II,* since my story in *Gazette V* is something of a direct sequel to my story in the *Ring of Fire* volume. You can read *Gazette V* alongside *1635: The Cannon Law* and *1635: The Dreeson Incident* whenever you're in the mood for short fiction.

And . . . that's it, as of now. There are a lot more volumes coming. In addition to the next two volumes, which will be *1635: The Eastern Front* and *1635: The Wars on the Rhine,* the following are also due to appear at some point:

In terms of solo novels, I will be writing two direct sequels to *Eastern Front* along with a novel sub-titled *The Anaconda Project.* That novel is something of a sequel to my short novel *The Wallenstein Gambit* in the first *Ring of Fire* anthology and will run parallel with and intersect with *The Eastern Front* and its sequels.

Andrew Dennis and I will be writing at least two and probably three volumes which serve as direct sequels to *1635: The Cannon Law* and continue the Italian-French-Spanish line of the series which we began in *1634: The Galileo Affair.* Before we get to those, however, we will be writing a sequel to the escape from the Tower of London episode in *The Baltic War.* That book will center on the British Isles and has as its main characters Julie and Alex Mackay. (With a number of other important ones, such as Darryl McCarthy, Victoria Short, Oliver Cromwell and Gayle Mason.)

What Dave Weber and I will do is develop a specifically naval side to the series, which will focus at least initially on Admiral Simpson and Eddie Cantrell. The first of those books is tentatively titled *1636: Admiral Simpson in the West Indies.* A later one will deal with the Ottoman Empire.

A number of other volumes are also planned:

With Mercedes Lackey, a comic novel (sub-titled *Stoned Souls*) that continues the adventures of Tom Stone and others.

With Virginia DeMarce, a novel which centers on the Rhineland and serves as a sequel both to this volume and *The Wars on the Rhine* anthology. The current working sub-title for that volume is *The Grand Duke of Burgundy*, but that will probably change by the time the book comes out in print.

With David Carrico, a mystery novel sub-titled *Symphony for the Devil.*

With Gorg Huff and Paula Goodlett, a romantic comedy sub-titled *The Viennese Waltz* which will run parallel to one of my sequels to *The Baltic War* and serves also as a sequel to a number of the stories they've written about the Barbie Consortium in various issues of the *Gazette.*

(If you're wondering why I'm only providing sub-titles, it's because I still don't know exactly which year they'll fall under. Either 1635 or 1636, depending on this and that and the other.)

Finally, with Mike Spehar, a volume set in Bohemia that will intersect with various novels of my own.

And there it stands. For the moment.

For those of you who dote on lists, here it is. But do keep in mind, when you examine this neatly ordered sequence, that the map is not the territory.

> *1632*
> *Ring of Fire*
> *1633*
> *1634: The Baltic War*

(Somewhere along the way, after you've finished *1632*, read the stories and articles in the first three paper edition volumes of the *Gazette*.)

1634: The Ram Rebellion
1634: The Galileo Affair
1634: The Bavarian Crisis

(Somewhere along the way, read the stories and articles in the fourth paper edition volume of the *Gazette*.)

Ring of Fire II
1635: The Cannon Law
1635: The Dreeson Incident
1635: The Tangled Web

(Somewhere along the way, read the stories in *Gazette V*.)

The following is an excerpt from:

RING OF FIRE III

EDITED BY
ERIC FLINT

Available from Baen Books
July 2011
hardcover

Birds of a Feather

Charles E. Gannon

Owen Roe O'Neill started at the burst of gunfire, not
because—as a veteran of the Lowlands Campaigns—
he was unaccustomed to the sounds of combat, but
because such sounds were now out of place near
Brussels in 1635. Old habit had him reaching toward
his sabre, but the pickets at the gate leading into the
combined field camps of the *tercios* Tyrconnell and
Preston seemed utterly unconcerned by the reports.
As O'Neill let his hand slip away from the hilt, his
executive officer, Felix O'Brian, jutted a chin forward:
never at ease atop a horse, O'Brian didn't dare take
either of his hands from the reins to point. "So what
would all that be, then?"

Ahead and to the right, a score of the men of *tercio*
Tyrconnell were skulking about in the trenchworks
surrounding the commander's blockhouse. So far as
Owen could make out, they seemed to be engaged
in some perverse, savage game of hide-and-seek with
an almost equal number of troopers from *tercio* Preston. As he approached, the soldiers of the Tyrconnell
regiment repeatedly bobbed and weaved around a

sequence of corners, usually in pairs. One stayed low, training a handgun or musketoon on the next bend in the trenchworks while the other dodged forward. If one of Preston's men popped his head around that far corner, the man with the gun fired, immediately reaching back for another weapon. If the approach was unopposed, the advancing trooper finished his short charge by sliding up to the corner and—without even checking first—lobbing a grenade around it.

Of course, these "dummy" grenades simply made a kind of ragged belching sound as they emitted puffs of thin grey smoke: rather anticlimactic. But the training and the tactics were startlingly new. And quite insane.

"This is what comes of O'Donnell's visit to the up-timers," Owen grumbled to O'Brian. "Thank God he's given over his command."

"It's only *rumored* that he's resigned his command," amended O'Brian carefully.

"Well, yes," Owen consented. "Too much to hope for until we see the truth of it, eh?" But as soon as he'd uttered the saucy gibe, Owen regretted it: Hugh O'Donnell, Earl of Tyrconnell, was hardly a poor commander. Quite the contrary. And humble enough, for all his many admitted talents. Maybe that's what made him so damned annoying—

"Seems we've picked up an escort," observed O'Brian, glancing behind.

Sure enough, close to a dozen monks—Franciscans, judging from the hooded brown habits—had swung in behind their guards, who remained tightly clustered around the *tercio* banners of Tyrone and O'Neill. One of the monks was pushing a handcart through the May mud, prompting Owen to wonder: *had someone died* en camp? Or maybe the brown robes had come to seek used clothes for the poor? If the latter, then the monks were in for a rude surprise: the Irish *tercios* were no longer a good source of that kind of easy charity. They were in dire want of it themselves, these days.

As he approached the *tercios'* staff tents, Owen noticed that, in addition to the pennants of the staff officers, a small banner of the Earl of Tyrconnell's own colors were flying. As he gave the day's camp countersign to the interior perimeter guards, he pondered the fluttering outline of the O'Donnell coat of arms. Strange: did this mean that Hugh was actually here—?

A lean fellow, sabre at his side, came bolting down the horse-track from the much larger commander's tent, perched atop a small rise. The approaching trooper was an ensign: probably Nugent, O'Neill conjectured, or maybe the younger of the Plunkett brothers. No matter, though: they were all cut from the same cloth and class. New families, all half-Sassenach; all lip-service Catholics. Some allies, those.

But Nugent or Plunkett or whoever it was had stopped, staring at the banners carried by O'Neill's oncoming entourage. Then he turned about and sprinted back up toward the commander's tent without even making a sign of greeting.

"Seems we've got their attention," muttered O'Neill through a controlled smile.

"See what you've done now?" O'Brian's voice was tinged with careful remonstrance. "They seen the Earl of Tyrone's colors. They'll think John is wid' us! They'll think—"

"Let 'em think. They do so much of it as it is, a little more can't hurt. Aye, and let 'em worry a bit, too."

"But—"

"But nothing. Here's the Great Man himself."

Thomas Preston had emerged from the commander's tent. He was an older man, one of the oldest of the Irish Wild Geese that had flocked to Flanders after the disaster at Kinsale, thirty-four years before. And Irish soldiery been flying to Flanders ever since: leaving behind increasing oppression and poverty, they had swelled the ranks of their four *tercios* now in the Lowlands. Mustering at slightly more than twelve thousand men, many of the newer recruits had been born here, grown here, learned the trade of the soldier here. And all knew that the recent consolidation of the Netherlands, and the consequent divisiveness amongst their Hapsburg employers, made their own future the most uncertain of all.

Preston did not look approving—or happy. After a few sharp phrases, he sent the runner back down the hill; he waited, arms akimbo, a dark scowl following the young ensign's return to O'Neill's honor-guard.

"Colonel O'Neill," the ensign panted before he'd come to a full stop, "Colonel Preston would have the commander's password from you."

O'Neill looked over the thin fellow's head—he was not much more than a *gossoon*, really—and stared at Preston. "Oh, he would, would he?"

"Yes, sir." A second group of pickets had come to flank the youngster. "Apologies, but Colonel Preston is most insistent. New security protocols, sir."

"Is that right? And those are his fine ideas, are they?"

"No, sir; they are Hugh O'Donn—I mean, the Earl of Tyrconnell's, sir."

Ah, but of course. The ever-innovative Earl of

Tyrconnell's legacy lived on in the camp he had abandoned almost a month ago, in the first week of April. O'Neill's gaze flicked briefly to the small O'Donnell coat of arms fluttering just behind him. Or, maybe he had *not* abandoned it, after all . . .

O'Neill urged his mount forward. "The commander's day-sign is 'Boru.'"

"Very good, sir, you may—"

But Owen Roe O'Neill had already passed, his entourage—including two officers from John O'Neill's Tyrone *tercio*—following closely behind. The monks, however, were detained by the guards at the staff tents.

O'Neill said nothing, gave no sign of recognition as he approached the commander's tent, with Preston's pennant snapping fitfully before it. Preston was equally undemonstrative. O'Neill stayed atop his mount, looked down at the older man and thought, *Sassenach bastard*, but said, with a shallow nod "Colonel."

Preston was not even that gracious. "Where is the Earl of Tyrone?"

"I expect he's enjoying a nap about now."

Preston's mustache seemed to prickle like a live creature. "Yet you fly his colors."

"I received your instructions to come without the earl. I have done so. But he is symbolically here with us in spirit—very *insulted* spirit—Colonel Preston."

"Damn it, O'Neill: the whole point of excluding him was so that you *wouldn't* be carrying his colors."

Owen, bristling reflexively at the profanity, found his anger suddenly defused by puzzlement: "You were worried about his—his colors?"

"Yes, blast it. And why did you bring those bloody Franciscans with you?"

O'Neill looked back down the low rise: most of the monks had moved past the first checkpoint, were drawing close to the second, where the commander's day-sign was to be given. Two lagged behind with the handcart, near the staff tents. "I assure you," muttered O'Neill," they're not my Franciscans. I'd not bring—"

The flap of Preston's tent ripped open. O'Neill gaped: Hugh Albert O'Donnell, in cuirass, was staring up at him, blue eyes bright and angry. "The Franciscans who came in with you—do you know them? Personally?"

"No, but—"

Hugh wasn't looking at him anymore. His strong neck corded as he shouted: "First platoon, down the hill! Guards: take hold of those monks. Immediately!"

Owen Roe O'Neill was, by all accounts and opinions—including his own—excellent at adapting to rapid changes on the battlefield. But this was not a battlefield, or rather, had not been one but a slim second ago. And that change—from common space to combat space—was not one he easily processed.

Stunned, he saw the nearest monks pull wheel locks from beneath their robes and discharge them into the second set of pickets at murderously close range. Further down the slope, one monk pushed the handcart into Tyrconnell's staff tent while his partner drew a pistol on the guards there.

In the same moment, the grimy soldiers who had been skulking to and fro in the trenches came boiling out, not bothering to dress ranks. But stranger still, they seemed in perfectly good order, operating not as a mass, but in groups of about five men each. This chaotic swarm of small, coherent teams streamed downhill, several tossing aside practice guns and pulling real ones, others drawing sabres and short swords. O'Neill's own guards retracted, clustered tight around him, weapons drawn, as the leading infiltrators drew grenades and shortswords from beneath their robes and closed in—

Just as the first teams from the trenches caught the assassins in the flank with a ragged chorus of pistol fire. Snaphaunces and wheel locks barked while a strange, thick revolver—a "pepperbox?"—cracked steadily, firing five times. When the fusillade was over, only one of the monks was still on his feet; a few on the ground moved feebly. A second wave of soldiers—sword-armed—closed the last few yards and finished the bloody execution. An alert trooper kicked the one lit grenade down the slope and away from the cart-track, where it detonated harmlessly.

Down at the staff tents, the monk who had drawn a pistol had evidently not done so any faster than one of the guards. The two weapons discharged simultaneously and the two men went down—just as the monk who'd trundled the hand cart into the staff tent came sprinting back out. The other guard who'd been slower on the draw went racing after him—and went airborne as the tent exploded in a deafening ball of flame.

By the time O'Neill had his horse back under control, the whole exchange was over. Almost twenty bodies lay scattered along the cart track, small fires guttered where the staff tents had been, and men of the Preston *tercio* were carrying two of their own wounded off to where the Tyrconnell regiment's young surgeon could tend to them. With his ears still ringing from the explosions, and his veins still humming with the sudden rush of the humor the up-timers called "adrenaline," Owen could only feel one thing: that he was glad to be alive.

Then he turned and saw Hugh O'Donnell's eyes—and wondered if his sense of relief was, perhaps, premature.

"Why did you bring John O'Neill's colors, Owen?" O'Donnell's voice and eyes were calm now. But most of the others in the commander's tent—those belonging to the staff officers who would have been blown to bits if they hadn't already been summoned here—remained far more agitated.

Owen relied on the tactic that had always served him well: when your adversary has you on the run, that's when you turn and hit back—-hard. "Maybe you should be asking yourself that question, Hugh O'Donnell. A Sassenach"—he glared at Preston, who glared right back—"tells the earl of Tyrone not to come to a council of the colonels? Well, let me tell you, even if John O'Neill is not 'permitted' to sit and talk with the regal likes of Preston—or you—I *will* come bearing his standard, and with it, the reminder of his authority—and that of his clan."

O'Donnell looked away, closed his eyes. "Owen, it wasn't Preston who excluded John. It was me. And I did it to protect him."

"Protect John? From what?"

O'Donnell cocked his head in the direction of the killing ground that led down to the gate. "From that . . . or worse. It was folly for us to have too many tempting targets in one place."

O'Neill paused. Then, voice level: "What do you mean?"

"I mean, if John *had* come, the last two royal heirs of Ireland would have been in the same place, at the same time. And with politics in the Lowland being what they are, signaling such a gathering was tantamount to inviting an attack. As we just saw."

O'Neill frowned. "But we've got peace—for now—so who'd want the two of you dead? And how would they—whoever they are—even know you're in the Lowlands at all, Hugh? The last any of us heard, you were off in Grantville."

O'Donnell nodded. "Reasonable questions, Owen. Will you listen to the answers, *before* you tell me how wrong I am?"

Owen nodded. "Of course; *that* I can do." And he grinned. O'Donnell returned the smile—and there were audible sighs of relief in the tent as the tension ebbed. "So let's have it, Hugh: who is trying to kill you and John? The English? Again?"

O'Donnell leaned back, hands folded firmly on the field table before him. "It could be them. But you also have your pick of new possible culprits. Local Catholics who feel Fernando has been too lenient with the Calvinists. Ministers in Madrid who want to topple Fernando as King in the Netherlands. Maybe Philip himself. In short, anyone who wants to give the Spanish crown a reasonable pretext for 'restoring order' in the Netherlands."

Owen shook his head. "I'm lost. How does attacking us achieve that?"

"We're a wild card, Owen—all of us Wild Geese. Four *tercios*, almost all full strength at three thousand men each. What happens to the Lowlands if we disband—or rebel?"

"Chaos. Prince Frederick might try to take charge, but he hasn't the troops. The locals will try to oust the Spanish. Fernando, a Hapsburg of Spain, and his wife, a Hapsburg of Austria, will soon be surrounded and in peril for their lives."

"And what happens? Who comes in, if we disband or just stay in barracks?"

"France might try to take advantage. Or maybe the Swede."

"Exactly—and would Philip want either?"

"Christ, no!" And then Owen saw it. "So, with us no longer ready to be an independent spine for Fernando's army, the local Spanish *tercios* call for help, and Philip has no choice but to intervene. Decisively."

O'Donnell nodded. "There are many possible variations on the theme, but that's the basic dirge. Half the court in Madrid is already calling for a 'stern approach' to Fernando's recent actions: after all, he did take the title 'King in the Netherlands' without Philip's permission. And since then, Philip has let his brother fend for himself...and we've all felt the results of that."

"What do you mean?"

"I mean, what has happened to your salaries over the last few months?"

Grumbles arose from every quarter of the tent.

O'Donnell spoke over them. "That's not Fernando's doing: he's not the one holding the purse strings. That would be Olivares, either working independently, or at Philip's behest. The Lowlands have long been a drain on the Spanish; over time, they've invested far more in this patch of ground than they've ever earned back. So, while Philip may not yet consider his brother a traitor, why should he pay for his *tercios*? Particularly those which aren't Spanish?"

"So we Irish are like a redheaded stepchild between spatting parents."

"Something very like it, yes." Hugh looked around the tent. "Which means that, any day now, your allegiances may be questioned. And whatever you might answer, you can be sure of this: one or another of your employers will be very unhappy with your answer."

"You mean, as unhappy as they were when you turned in your commission and titles?"

O'Donnell's voice was quiet. "You've heard then?"

O'Neill shook his head. "Not officially, no: your officers have been keeping it quiet. But when your *tercios* came over here into bivouac with Preston's, talk started—particularly when your men started getting orders from the Sassena—from Colonel Preston. And there were some as claimed that before you left, you'd folded up your tabard and sash of the Order of Alcantara and sent them back to Madrid."

"That I did."

Owen kept his voice carefully neutral: "So are you wanting us to follow your example?"

O'Donnell waved a negating hand. "I'd ask no man to follow my path. And there's no need for you to declare your allegiance until you're asked."

"Then why didn't you wait to do so, yourself?"

"Owen, when I was made a Knight-Captain of the Order of Alcantara, a Gentleman of His Majesty's Chamber, and a member of his Council of War, I took my oaths before, and to, the king himself. In his very person, in Spain. I had my benefits and titles directly from his hand, and was, at his personal instruction, naturalized as a Spanish citizen. Honor demands, then, that if I know in my heart I can no longer be Philip's loyal servant, I must relinquish all those privileges and garnishments at once. I can't bide my time, waiting to be cornered into admitting that my allegiances have changed—even as I continue to enjoy the king's coin and favor. Given the state of affairs here, honor may be all I have left—so it was both right and prudent that I keep it untarnished."

"Fairly spoken," Preston said. Owen found himself nodding; the earl of Tyrone's officers were doing the same.

—end excerpt—

from *Ring of Fire III*
available in hardcover,
July 2011, from Baen Books